OUR LADY
OF DARKNESS

THE SISTER FIDELMA MYSTERIES BY PETER TREMAYNE

*forthcoming

OUR LADY
OF DARKNESS

A Novel of Ancient Ireland

Peter Tremayne

St. Martin's Minotaur ♏ New York

www.minotaurbooks.com

ISBN 0-312-27295-2

First published in Great Britain by Headline Book Publishing
A division of Hodder Headline

First St. Martin's Minotaur Edition: September 2002

10 9 8 7 6 5 4 3 2 1

For Michael Thomas, literary agent, mentor and friend,
who steered me through the first thirty years
of professional authorship.

Darkness brings our fears to light rather than banishes them.

Lucius Annaeus Seneca
('The Younger' *c*. 4BC–AD 65)

HISTORICAL NOTE

The Sister Fidelma mysteries are set mainly in Ireland during the mid-seventh century AD.

Sister Fidelma is not simply a religieuse, a former member of the community of St Brigid of Kildare. She is also a qualified *dálaigh*, or advocate of the ancient law courts of Ireland. As this background will not be familiar to many readers, my Historical Note is designed to provide a few essential points of reference to make the stories more readily appreciated.

The Ireland of Fidelma's day consisted of five main provincial kingdoms; indeed, the modern Irish word for a province is still *cúige*, literally 'a fifth'. Four provincial kings – of Ulaidh (Ulster), of Connacht, of Muman (Munster) and of Laigin (Leinster) – gave their qualified allegiance to the *Ard Rí* or High King, who ruled from Tara, in the 'royal' fifth province of Midhe (Meath), which means the 'middle province'. Even among the provincial kingdoms, there was a decentralisation of power to petty-kingdoms and clan territories.

In this story one will find references to the conflict between Muman and Laigin over the borderland sub-kingdom of Osraige (Ossory), over which both claimed lordship. The details of that conflict are to be found in the Fidelma mystery *Suffer Little Children*.

The law of primogeniture, the inheritance by the eldest son or daughter, was an alien concept in Ireland. Kingship, from the lowliest clan chieftain to the High King, was only partially hereditary and mainly electoral. Each ruler had to prove himself or herself worthy of office and was elected by the *derbhfine* of their family – a minimum of three generations from a common ancestor gathered in conclave. If a ruler did not pursue the commonwealth of the people, they were impeached and removed from office. Therefore the monarchical system of ancient Ireland had more in common with a modern-day republic than with the feudal monarchies which had developed in medieval Europe.

Ireland, in the seventh century AD, was governed by a system of

vii

sophisticated laws called the Laws of the *Fénechus*, or land-tillers, which became more popularly known as the Brehon Laws, deriving from the word *breitheamh* – a judge. Tradition has it that these laws were first gathered in 714BC by the order of the High King, Ollamh Fódhla. Over a thousand years later, in AD438, the High King, Laoghaire, appointed a commission of nine learned people to study, revise, and commit the laws to the new writing in Latin characters. One of those serving on the commission was Patrick, eventually to become patron saint of Ireland. After three years, the commission produced a written text of the laws which is the first known codification.

The first complete surviving texts of the ancient laws of Ireland are preserved in an eleventh-century manuscript book in the Royal Irish Academy, Dublin. It was not until the seventeenth century that the English colonial administration in Ireland finally suppressed the use of the Brehon Law system. To even possess a copy of the law books was punishable, often by death or transportation.

The law system was not static, and every three years at the Féis Temhrach (Festival of Tara) the lawyers and administrators gathered to consider and revise the laws in the light of changing society and its needs.

Under these laws, women occupied a unique place. The Irish laws gave more rights and protection to women than any other Western law code at that time or until recent times. Women could, and did, aspire to all offices and professions as the co-equal with men. They could be political leaders, command their people in battle as warriors, be physicians, local magistrates, poets, artisans, lawyers and judges. We know the names of many female judges of Fidelma's period – Bríg Briugaid, Áine Ingine Iugaire and Darí among others. Darí, for example, was not only a judge but the author of a noted law text written in the sixth century AD.

Women were protected by law against sexual harassment, against discrimination, against rape. They had the right of divorce on equal terms from their husbands, with equitable separation laws, and could demand part of their husband's property as a divorce settlement; they had the right of inheritance of personal property and the right of sickness benefits when ill or hospitalised. (Ancient Ireland had Europe's oldest recorded system of hospitals.) Seen from today's perspective, the Brehon Laws helped to maintain an almost ideal environment for women.

This background, and its strong contrast with Ireland's neighbours, should be understood in order to appreciate Fidelma's role in these stories.

Fidelma was born at Cashel, capital of the kingdom of Muman (Munster) in south-west Ireland, in AD636. She was the youngest daughter of Fáilbe Fland, the King, who died the year after her birth. Fidelma was raised under the guidance of a distant cousin, Abbot Laisran of Durrow. When she reached the 'Age of Choice' (fourteen years), considered the time of maturity for women, she went to study at the bardic school of the Brehon Morann of Tara, as did many other young Irish girls. Eight years of study resulted in Fidelma obtaining the degree of *anruth*, only one degree below the highest offered at either bardic or ecclesiastical universities in ancient Ireland. The highest degree was *ollamh*, which is still the modern Irish word for a professor. Fidelma's studies were in law, both in the criminal code of the *Senchus Mór* and the civil code of the *Leabhar Acaill*. Thereby, she became a *dálaigh* or advocate of the courts.

Her main role could be compared to a modern Scottish sheriff-substitute, whose job is to gather and assess the evidence, independent of the police, to see if there is a case to be answered. The modern French *juge d'instruction* holds a similar role. However, sometimes Fidelma is faced with the task of prosecuting in the courts or, as in this story, defending, even rendering judgments in minor cases when a Brehon was not available.

In those days, most of the professional or intellectual classes were members of the new Christian religious houses, just as, in previous centuries, all members of the professions and intellectuals had been Druids. Fidelma became a member of the religious community of Kildare founded in the late fifth century AD by St Brigid. But by the time the action in this story takes place, Fidelma has left Kildare in disillusionment. The reason why may be found in the title story of the Fidelma short story collection *Hemlock at Vespers*.

While the seventh century AD was considered part of the European 'Dark Ages', for Ireland it was a period of 'Golden Enlightenment'. Students from every corner of Europe flocked to Irish universities to receive their education, including the sons of many of the Anglo-Saxon kings. At the great ecclesiastical university of Durrow, at this time, it is recorded that no fewer than eighteen different nations were represented among the students. At the same time, Irish male and female missionaries were setting out to reconvert a pagan Europe to

Christianity, establishing churches, monasteries, and centres of learning throughout Europe as far east as Kiev, in the Ukraine; as far north as the Faroes, and as far south as Taranto in southern Italy. Ireland was a byword for literacy and learning.

However, the Celtic Church of Ireland was in constant dispute with Rome on matters of liturgy and ritual. Rome had begun to reform itself in the fourth century, changing its dating of Easter and aspects of its liturgy. The Celtic Church and the Eastern Orthodox Church refused to follow Rome, but the Celtic Church was gradually absorbed by Rome between the ninth and eleventh centuries while the Eastern Orthodox Church has continued to remain independent of Rome. The Celtic Church of Ireland, during Fidelma's time, was much concerned with this conflict so that it is impossible to write of Church matters without referring to the philosophical warfare between them.

One thing that was shared by both the Celtic Church and Rome in the seventh century was that the concept of celibacy was not universal. While there were always ascetics in the Churches who sublimated physical love in a dedication to the deity, it was not until the Council of Nicea in AD325 that clerical marriages were condemned but not banned in the Western Church. The concept of celibacy arose in Rome mainly from the customs practised by the pagan priestesses of Vesta and the priests of Diana.

By the fifth century, Rome had forbidden its clerics from the rank of abbot and bishop to sleep with their wives and, shortly after, even to marry at all. The general clergy were discouraged from marrying by Rome but not forbidden to do so. Indeed, it was not until the reforming papacy of Leo IX (AD1049–1054) that a serious attempt was made to force the Western clergy to accept universal celibacy. The Celtic Church took centuries to give up its anti-celibacy attitudes and fall into line with Rome, while in the Eastern Orthodox Church, priests below the rank of abbot and bishop have retained their right to marry until this day.

An awareness of these facts concerning the liberal attitudes towards sexual relationships in the Celtic Church is essential towards understanding the background to the Fidelma stories.

The condemnation of the 'sin of the flesh' remained alien to the Celtic Church for a long time after Rome's attitude became a dogma. In Fidelma's world, both sexes inhabited abbeys and monastic foundations, which were known as *conhospitae*, or double houses, where men and women lived raising their children in Christ's service. Fidelma's own house of St Brigid of Kildare was one such community of both sexes during her time. When Brigid established her community of Kildare (Cill-Dara = the church of the oaks), she invited a bishop named Conláed to join her. Her first biography, completed fifty years after her death in AD650 during Fidelma's lifetime, was written by a monk of Kildare named Cogitosus, who makes it clear that it continued to be a mixed community in his day.

It should also be pointed out that, demonstrating their co-equal role with men, women were priests of the Celtic Church in this period. Brigid herself was ordained a bishop by Patrick's nephew, Mel, and her case was not unique. Rome actually wrote a protest, in the sixth century, at the Celtic practice of allowing women to celebrate the divine sacrifice of Mass.

Unlike the Roman Church, the Irish Church did not have a system of 'confessors' where 'sins' had to be confessed to clerics who then had the authority to absolve those sins in Christ's name. Instead, people chose a 'soul friend' (*anam chara*), out of clerics or laity, with whom they discussed matters of emotional and spiritual well-being.

To help readers locate themselves in Fidelma's part of Ireland in the seventh century, where its geo-political divisions will be mainly unfamiliar, I have provided a sketch map and, to help them more readily identify personal names, a list of principal characters is also given.

I have generally refused to use anachronistic place names for obvious reasons although I have bowed to a few modern usages e.g. Tara, rather than *Teamhair*; and Cashel, rather than *Caiseal Muman*; and Armagh in place of *Ard Macha*. However, I have cleaved to the name of Muman rather than the prolepsis form 'Munster' formed when the Norse *stadr* (place) was added to the Irish name Muman in the ninth century AD and eventually anglicised. Similarly, I have maintained the original name Laigin, rather than the anglicised form of Leinster based on the Norse form *Laighin-stadr*. I have, for easier reading, shortened Fearna Mhór (the great place of the alder trees), the principal city of the Laigin kings at this time, to Fearna as it is now anglicised as Ferns, Co. Wexford.

This story also deals with the conflict between the native Brehon Law and the introduction into Ireland at this time of an alternative law system by those clergy who were pro-Roman reformers; a system called the Penitentials. These Penitentials were initially the rules designed for the religious communities, mainly inspired by Graeco-Roman Christian cultural concepts, by which they were expected to conduct their lives. However, they often were extended over those communities living within the shadow of the great abbeys, depending on the personalities of the abbots and abbesses.

The Penitentials often developed a harsh system of rules and punishments, enforcing physical punishment on transgressors, a system of vengeance rather than the system of compensation and rehabilitation which formed the basis of Brehon Law. In many areas of Ireland, as the Roman form of Christianity took its hold among the religious and urban centres, the Penitentials began to displace the Brehon precepts. Executions, mutilations and floggings as forms of punishment were to be found in late medieval Ireland as they were in the rest of Europe. Yet this was not so in Fidelma's time and such ideas outraged the advocates of the Brehon system as readers may now discover.

Principal Characters

Sister Fidelma, of Cashel, a *dálaigh* or advocate of the law courts of seventh-century Ireland

Brother Eadulf, of Seaxmund's Ham, a Saxon monk from the land of the South Folk

Dego, a warrior of Cashel

Enda, a warrior of Cashel

Aidan, a warrior of Cashel

Morca, a Laigin innkeeper

Abbess Fainder, abbess of Fearna

Abbot Noé, *anam chara* ('soul friend') of King Fianamail

Brother Cett, a monk of Fearna

Brother Ibar, a monk of Fearna

Bishop Forbassach, Brehon of Laigin

Mel, captain of the guard at Fearna

Fianamail, King of Laigin

Lassar, owner of the Inn of the Yellow Mountain, sister of Mel

Sister Étromma, *rechtaire* or stewardess of the abbey of Fearna

Gormgilla, a victim

Fial, her friend

Brother Miach, physician of the abbey of Fearna

Gabrán, captain of a river boat and trader

Coba, a *bó-aire* or magistrate, chieftain of Cam Eolaing

Deog, widow of Daig who was captain of the watch at Fearna

Dau, a warrior at Cam Eolaing

Dalbach, a blind recluse

Muirecht, a young girl

Conna, a young girl

Brother Martan of the Church of Brigid

Barrán, Chief Brehon of the Five Kingdoms

OUR LADY
OF DARKNESS

Chapter One

The horses cantered along the dusk-shrouded mountain road. There were four of them, snorting and blowing as their riders urged them forward. The travellers consisted of three men and a woman. The men wore the garments and weaponry of warriors but the woman was distinguished from her companions not only by her sex but by the fact that she was clad in the robes of a religieuse. While the evening gloom cloaked their individual features, it was clear from the state of their mounts and the fatigued attitude with which they rode them that the four had journeyed many a kilometre that day.

'Are you sure that this is the right road?' called the woman, casting an anxious glance around at the entangling woods through which they were rapidly descending. The track across the mountain dipped steeper into the valley. Below them, just discernible in the fading light, was a broad glen with a sizable river snaking through it.

The young, dust-covered warrior who rode at her side spoke out.

'I have ridden many times as a courier from Cashel to Fearna, lady, and I know this route well. A kilometre or so ahead we will come to a place where another river flows from the west to join the river you see below us. There, by the joining of the rivers, is Morca's inn where we may spend the night.'

'But every hour counts, Dego,' replied the woman. 'Can't we press on to Fearna tonight?'

The warrior hesitated before replying, doubtless wondering how to make himself firm but phrasing his words with respect.

'Lady, I promised your brother, the King, that I and my companions would keep you safe on this journey. I would not advise travelling in this countryside at night. There are many dangers in this area for the likes of us. If we stay at the inn and make an early start in the morning, we will be at the castle of the King of Laigin well before noon tomorrow. And we will arrive refreshed after a night's rest, rather than tired and weary from riding through the night.'

The tall religieuse was silent and the warrior called Dego took her silence as an acceptance of his advice.

Dego was a member of the warrior guard of Colgú, King of Muman; it had been the King himself who had summoned him with an order to escort his sister, Fidelma of Cashel, to Fearna, the capital of the Kingdom of Laigin, whose lands bordered Colgú's kingdom. There had been little reason to ask why Fidelma was making this journey, for the news had been freely bruited about the great palace of Cashel.

Fidelma had arrived home from a pilgrim voyage to the Tomb of St James, her journey hastened by the news that Brother Eadulf, the Saxon emissary to Cashel from Archbishop Theodore of Canterbury, had been accused of murder. The details were as yet unclear but, so the gossip had it, Brother Eadulf had been returning to Canterbury, which lay in the land of the Saxons to the east when, passing through the kingdom of Laigin, he had been captured and accused of killing someone. There were no other details.

What was well known among the people of Cashel was that, during the past year, Brother Eadulf not only had become a friend of King Colgú but a close companion of his sister, Fidelma. The talk had it that Fidelma had determined to journey to Laigin in order to take up the defence of her friend, for she was not merely a religieuse but a *dálaigh*, an advocate, of the law courts of the five kingdoms.

Gossip or not, Dego knew that Fidelma had landed from the pilgrim ship at Ardmore, ridden hard for Cashel and spent barely an hour or so with her brother, before setting off for Fearna, Laigin's capital, where Eadulf was being held. In fact, Dego and his companions were hard pressed to keep up with the grim-faced Fidelma who seemed to be able to ride better than any of them.

Dego was nervous as he glanced at her now. There was a glint in her blue-green eyes which boded ill for anyone who would contradict her will. He was certain that his recommendation was the best course of action, but he was also anxious that Fidelma understood his reasons for suggesting it. He knew well enough that she was anxious to reach the Laigin capital as soon as possible.

'There is enmity between Cashel and Fearna, lady,' he ventured, after some thought. 'There is still war along the border of Osraige. Should we fall in with wandering bands of Laigin warriors, they might not respect the protection of your office.'

Fidelma's stern features softened momentarily.

'I am aware of the situation, Dego. You are wise in your advice.'

She said no more. Dego opened his mouth to speak again but another glance at her made him realise that to say anything else would merely be superfluous and might annoy her.

After all, there was none better qualified than Fidelma to know the position of the dispute between Cashel and Fearna. She had clashed with the excitable young King Fianamail of Laigin before. Fianamail was certainly no friend of Cashel and, in particular, he now nursed a grudge against Fidelma.

Young Dego, knowing this, admired his lady's courage for riding immediately to the aid of her Saxon friend, straight into the enemy's lands. Only the fact that she was a *dálaigh* of the courts allowed her to move so freely, without let or hindrance. No person in the five kingdoms would dare lay hands on her for they would face a terrible retribution; the loss of their honour price, to be outcast forever from society, without the law to protect them. No lawful person would knowingly lay hands on a *dálaigh* of the courts, especially one such as Fidelma who had been honoured by the High King, Sechnassach, himself. The mantle of a *dálaigh* of the courts was a greater protection than being either sister to the King of Muman or, indeed, being a religieuse of the Faith of Christ.

However, it was not those who subscribed to the law that Dego was worried about. He knew the minds of King Fianamail and his advisers could be dark and deep. It would be so easy to have Fidelma killed and swear it was done by a wandering band of outlaws. That was why Colgú had sought out his three best warriors and asked them to accompany his sister to Laigin. He did not order them to go for they would be in as much danger as she was, although he did present each with a wand of office indicating that they acted as his emissaries under the protection of the laws of an embassy. It was the maximum that was in his power to give them as legal protection.

Dego, and his companions, Enda and Aidan, riding behind with eyes constantly alert for danger, had no hesitation in accepting the charge laid on them, in spite of their misgivings about the trustworthiness of the King of Laigin. Where Fidelma went, they would willingly follow, for the people of Cashel reserved a special place of affection for the tall, red-haired young sister of their King.

'The inn is just ahead,' called Enda from behind.

Dego screwed up his eyes to penetrate the gloom.

He could see a lantern swinging from its pole, the traditional method by which innkeepers announced the presence of their establishments – to literally light the way for weary travellers. Dego halted his horse before the group of buildings. A couple of stable boys ran forward from the shadows to take their mounts and hold them while the riders undid their saddlebags and moved towards the tavern doors.

A broad-shouldered, elderly man opened the doors, letting a shaft of light fall across them as they approached the wooden steps on which he stood.

'Warriors from Muman!' The man frowned, as his eyes wandered over them, taking in their manner of clothing and weapons. The tone of his voice was not welcoming. 'We do not often see your kind in this land these days. Do you come in peace?'

Dego halted on the step below him and scowled. 'We come seeking your hospitality, Morca. Do you refuse to grant it?'

The ponderous innkeeper stared at him for a moment, trying to recognise him in the shadowy light.

'You know my name, warrior. How so?'

'I have often stayed here before. We are an embassy from the King of Cashel to the King of Laigin. I say again, do you refuse us hospitality?'

The innkeeper shrugged indifferently.

'It is not my place to refuse, especially if the company is so eminent as emissaries from the King of Cashel to my own King. If you seek the hospitality of this inn then you shall have it. Your silver is doubtless as good as any other's.'

He turned ungraciously, without a further word, and went back into the main room of the inn.

This large room had a fire burning in the hearth at one end. There were several tables at which people sat in various stages of eating and drinking. There was an old man at one end who was strumming a *cruit*, a small U-shaped harp. No one seemed to be paying any attention to his aimless wandering over the strings. Some of those present were obviously locals who had come to be sociable and drink with their neighbours while others were travellers enjoying an early evening meal. The whisper of 'warriors of Muman' had spread rapidly through the room and the assembly fell silent as they entered. Even the harpist hesitated and his fingers became still.

Dego glanced nervously around, hand resting lightly on the hilt of his sword.

'Do you see what I mean, lady?' he whispered to Fidelma. 'There is antagonism here and we must be wary.'

Fidelma gave him a swift smile of reassurance and led the way to an unoccupied table, setting down her saddle bag before seating herself. Dego, Enda and Aidan followed her example, yet the eyes of the warriors were not still. The score or so of other people remained quiet, watching them surreptitiously. The innkeeper had removed himself to the far side of the room, deliberately ignoring his new guests.

'Innkeeper!' Fidelma's voice cut sharply across the room.

Reluctantly, the burly man came across to them in the icy silence.

'You seem unwilling to perform your duties under the law.'

The man called Morca was obviously not expecting her belligerent comment. He recovered from his surprise and glowered at her.

'What does a religieuse know of the laws of innkeepers?' he sneered.

Fidelma returned his taunt with an even voice. 'I am a *dálaigh*, qualified to the level of *anruth*. Does that answer your question?'

The atmosphere seemed to grow even colder.

Dego's hand brushed against the hilt of his sword again; his muscles tensed.

Fidelma held the innkeeper's eyes in her own fiery green orbs like a snake ensnaring a rabbit. The man seemed transfixed. Her voice remained soft and mesmeric.

'You are obliged to provide us with your services and to do it with good grace. If you do not, you will be deemed guilty of *etech*; that is refusal to fulfil the obligation placed on you by law. You would then have to pay to each and every one of us the sum of our honour price. If it is deemed that you acted in knowledge and malice towards us, then you could also lose the *díre* of this inn; it could be destroyed and no compensation need be given you. Do I make the law clear to you, innkeeper?'

The man stood staring at her as if trying to summon his lost voice. Finally, he dropped his eyes from her fiery gaze, shuffled his feet and nodded.

'I meant no disrespect. The times . . . the times are difficult.'

'Times may be difficult but the law is the law and you must obey it,' she replied. 'Now, my companions and I want beds for the night and we also want a meal – immediately.'

The man bobbed his head once again, his stance changed to one of anxiety to be of service.

'It shall be provided at once, Sister. At once.'

He turned, calling for his wife and, as he did so, it seemed to be a signal for the silence to cease and the noise of conversation began again. The plaintive notes of the harp recommenced.

Dego sat back, relaxing with a wan smile.

'The Laigin certainly have no liking for us, lady.'

Fidelma sighed softly. 'They are, unfortunately, led, thinking they must obey the prejudices of their young King. However, the law must stand above all.'

The innkeeper's wife came forward with a smile that seemed slightly artificial. She brought them bowls of stew from a cauldron that had been simmering over the fire. Mead and bread were also provided.

For a while, the four visitors concentrated on their meal, having ridden hard that day and not having paused for a midday repast. It was only after they had eaten their fill and were relaxing with their earthenware mugs of mead that Fidelma began to take more notice of her immediate surroundings and of the other guests in the inn.

The other travellers consisted of a couple of religieux in brown homespun and a small group of merchants. In addition to these were the locals, mostly farmers, and there was a blacksmith enjoying a drink and a chat. Seated at the next table were two farmers engaged in conversation. It was some time before Fidelma realised that their conversation was not the usual farmers' discourse. She frowned, turning herself slightly to listen more attentively.

'It is right to make an example of the man. The Saxon stranger merits all he gets,' one of them was saying.

'The Saxons have always been a plague to this land, raiding and plundering our ships and coastal settlements,' the other agreed. 'Pirates they are and we have been too lenient with them for long enough. A war against the Saxons would bring better profits to Fianamail than a war with Muman.'

One of the farmers suddenly saw that he had caught Fidelma's attention. He became embarrassed, coughed and stood up.

'Well, I must be to my bed. I am ploughing the lower field tomorrow.' He turned and strode from the inn, bidding the innkeeper and his wife a good night.

Fidelma swung round on his companion. He was a younger man and she realised from his garb that he was a shepherd. Oblivious to the reason for his companion's hurried departure, he was finishing his mead.

Fidelma greeted him with a friendly nod.

'I overheard you speaking of Saxons,' she began brightly. 'Are you having problems with Saxon raiders in this land?'

The shepherd looked nervous at being addressed by a religieuse.

'The coastal ports of the South-East have suffered many raids by Saxon pirates, Sister,' he conceded gruffly. 'I have heard that three trading vessels, one from Gaul, were attacked and sunk off Cahore Point, after being robbed, only a week ago.'

'Did I understand from your conversation with your friend that one such pirate has been caught?'

The man frowned, as if to recollect the conversation, and then shook his head. 'Not a pirate exactly. The talk is of a Saxon who murdered a religieuse.'

Fidelma leaned backwards trying not to show the shock on her features. The murder of a religieuse! Surely this was not her Eadulf whom the man was talking about? It was nine days since the news had caught up with her at the coastal port in Iberia. That meant that the crime with which Eadulf had been charged was at least three weeks old. The one thing that concerned Fidelma was that events might have moved rapidly on and she would arrive too late to defend him, even though her brother had sent a message to Fianamail requesting a delay in the proceedings. However, the idea that Eadulf could possibly be involved in the murder of a religieuse was beyond belief.

'How could he have done such a terrible thing! Do you know the name by which this Saxon was called?'

'That I do not, Sister. Nor do I wish to. He be just a murdering Saxon dog, that's all I know or care.'

Fidelma looked at the man reprovingly. 'How do you know that he is a murdering dog, as you put it, unless you know the details? *Sapiens nihil affirmat quod non probat.*'

The shepherd was bewildered. She apologised at once for her arrogance in quoting Latin at him.

' "A wise man states as true nothing that he does not prove". Surely you would do better to await the pronouncement of the judge?'

'Why, the facts are already known. Not even the religious are attempting to defend him. It is said that the Saxon was a religieux and being one of their own, they might well be expected to attempt to conceal his depravity. He deserves his punishment.'

Fidelma stared at the man, irritated by his attitude.

'That is not justice,' she breathed. 'A man must be tried before he is condemned and punished. One cannot punish a person before they are judged by the Brehons.'

'But the man has already been tried, Sister. Tried and condemned.'

'Already tried?' Fidelma could not hide her shock.

'The word from Fearna is that he has been tried and found guilty. The King's Brehon is already satisfied as to his guilt.'

'The King's Brehon? His Chief Judge? Do you mean Bishop Forbassach?' Fidelma was struggling to keep calm.

'That is the man. Do you know of him?'

'That I do.'

Fidelma reflected bitterly. Bishop Forbassach was an old adversary of hers. She might have known that he would be involved.

'If the Saxon is guilty, is there talk about his punishment? What would be the honour price? What compensation is demanded from the Saxon?'

Under the law, anyone judged guilty of the crime of homicide, as with all other crimes, had to pay compensation. It was called the *eric* fine. Each person in the community had an honour price according to their rank and station. The perpetrator had to pay the compensation to the victim or, in the case of homicide, to the relatives of the victim. In addition there were the court costs. Sometimes, depending on the seriousness of the crime, the culprit lost all their civil rights and had to work within the community to rehabilitate themselves. If they did not, they could be reduced to the rank of little more than itinerant workers, scarcely better than a slave. They were called *daer-fudir*. However, the law wisely said that 'every dead man kills his liabilities'. Children of the culprits were placed back into society at the same honour price which their father or their mother had enjoyed prior to being found guilty of the crime.

The shepherd was staring at Fidelma as if the question surprised him.

'There is no *eric* fine asked for,' he said finally.

Fidelma did not understand and said so.

'Then what punishment is being talked of?'

The shepherd put down his empty mug and stood up, preparing to leave, wiping the back of his mouth on his sleeve.

'The King has declared that the judgment should be made under the new Christian Penitentials, this new system of laws they say comes from Rome. The Saxon has been sentenced to death. I think he has already been hanged.'

Chapter Two

The slow procession of religious emerged from the brass-studded oak doors of the chapel and into the cold, grey light of the central courtyard of the abbey. It was a large courtyard, flagged in dark granite stone, yet on all four sides there towered the cheerless stone walls of the abbey buildings, giving the illusion that the central space was smaller than it actually was.

The line of cowled monks, preceded by a single Brother of the community bearing an ornate metal cross, moved slowly, sedately, heads bowed, hands hidden in the folds of their robes, chanting a psalm in Latin. Behind them, at a short distance, came a similar number of cowled nuns, also with heads bowed and joining in the chant though accompanying the male voices on a higher note and harmonising with the air so as to make a descant. The effect was an eerie echoing in the confined space.

They moved to take positions on either side of the courtyard, standing facing a wooden platform on which stood a strange construction of three upright poles supporting a triangle of beams. A single rope hung from one of the beams, knotted into a noose. Just below the noose, a three-legged stool had been placed. Next to this grim apparatus, feet splayed apart, stood a tall man. He was stripped to the waist, his heavy, muscular arms folded across a broad, hairy chest. He stared without emotion at the religious procession; unmoved and unashamed of the task he was to perform on that macabre platform.

From the chapel doors came two more religious, a man and a woman, moving with easy strides towards the platform. The woman's lean form gave the impression of height which, close up, proved illusory, for she was only of medium stature, although her dark, slightly arrogant features gave her a commanding presence. Her habit and ornate crucifix, which was suspended from a chain around her neck, proclaimed her a religieuse of rank. By her side was a short man, with grim and grey visage. He, too, was dressed in a manner which proclaimed him to be of rank within the Faith.

They halted between the two rows of religious, just in front of the platform. The chanting died away at the imperceptible lift of the woman's hand.

One of the Sisters came hurrying forward and halted before her, inclining her head in respect.

'Are we ready to proceed, Sister?' asked the richly dressed religieuse.

'Everything is arranged, Mother Abbess.'

'Then let us proceed with God's grace.'

The Sister glanced towards an open door on the far side of the courtyard and raised a hand.

Almost at once it was opened and two stocky men, religieux by their robes, came forward dragging a young man between them. He was also wearing a religious habit, but this was torn and stained. His face was white and his lips trembled in fear. Sobs racked his frame as he was dragged across the flagstones of the courtyard towards the waiting group. The trio came to a halt before the abbess and her companion.

There was a silence for a moment which only the young man's distressed sobbing disturbed.

'Well, Brother Ibar,' the woman's voice was harsh and unforgiving, 'will you now confess your guilt since you stand on the threshold of your journey into the Otherworld?'

The young man began to make sounds, but they did not mean anything. He was too frightened to issue anything more articulate.

The abbess's male companion leaned forward.

'Confess, Brother Ibar.' His voice was sibilant and persuasive. 'Confess and avoid the pain of suffering in purgatory. Go to your God with the guilt removed from your soul and He will welcome you with joy.'

At last some recognisable words began to issue from the young man's throat.

'Father Abbot . . . Mother Abbess . . . I am innocent. As God is my witness, *I am innocent*.'

The woman's expression deepened into lines of disapproval.

'Do you know the words of Deuteronomy? Listen to them, Brother Ibar: ". . . after careful examination by the judges, if he be proved to be a false witness giving false evidence . . . you shall show no mercy; life for life, eye for eye, tooth for tooth, hand for hand, foot for foot". That is the word of the law of the Faith. Abhor your sins even now, Brother. Go to God cleansed of your sins.'

'I have not sinned, Mother Abbess,' cried the young man desperately. 'I cannot recant what I have not done.'

'Then know the inevitable outcome of your folly, for it is written: "I could see the dead, great and small, standing before the throne; and the books were opened. Then another book was opened, the roll of the living. From what was written in these books, the dead were judged upon the record of their deeds. The sea gave up its dead, and Death and Hades gave up the dead in their keeping; they were judged, each man on the record of his deeds. Then Death and Hades were flung into the lake of fire. This lake of fire is the second death; and into it were flung any whose names were not to be found in the roll of the living".'

She paused for breath and glanced at her male companion as if seeking approval. The man bowed his head and remained stony-faced.

'Let God's will be done, then,' he said without emotion.

The woman nodded to the two brawny monks who held the young man.

'So be it,' she intoned.

They spun their captive round to face the platform, pushing him forward in spite of his resistance; he would have fallen onto the structure had they not been holding him up. Even before he had fully recovered his balance they had twisted his arms behind his back and one of them had expertly secured them with a short length of rope.

'I am not guilty! Not guilty!' the young man was crying as he tried vainly to struggle with them. 'Ask about the manacles! The manacles! Ask!'

The burly man awaiting them on the platform, now moved forward and lifted the captive up as if he had been no more than a child. He placed him on the stool and pulled the noose around his neck, stifling his cries, while one of the escorts secured a rope around his feet.

Then the two escorts backed off the platform, leaving the executioner standing next to the young man, now precariously balanced on the stool, his neck in the noose.

The religious started their Latin chant again, their voices taking on a swifter, harsher note and, catching the grim eye of the executioner, the abbess nodded swiftly.

The muscular man simply kicked the stool from under the feet of the young man who gave one last, strangled cry before the noose tightened irrevocably. Then he swung to and fro, his legs kicking as he was slowly throttled to death by the rope.

13

Above the courtyard, staring down at the proceedings through a small iron grilled window, Brother Eadulf of Seaxmund's Ham shuddered, genuflected and muttered a swift prayer for the soul of the dead. He turned away from the window back into the gloomy cell.

Seated on the only stool in the cell, watching him with dark eyes sparkling with a frightening anticipation, was a thin-faced, cadaverous-looking man. He wore the robes of a religious and an ornate gold crucifix around his neck.

'So now, Saxon,' the man's voice was brittle and hectoring, 'perhaps you will give some thought to your own future.'

Brother Eadulf allowed a grim smile to mould his features in spite of what he had witnessed below.

'I did not think my future needed much thought. I believe that it is a very finite one so far as this world is concerned.'

The seated man's lips twisted in a sneer at the other's attempted humour.

'All the more reason to pay it some heed, Saxon. How we fulfil our last hours in this world impinges on our eternity in the Otherworld.'

Eadulf took a seat on the wooden cot. 'I will not quarrel with your knowledge of law, Bishop Forbassach, yet I am truly perplexed,' he said lightly. 'I have studied some years in this country but never once did I see an execution. Surely, your laws, the *Senchus Mór*, state that no one should be executed for any crime in the five kingdoms of Éireann if the *eric* fine or compensation is paid. What was the purpose of killing that young man down there?'

Bishop Forbassach, Chief Judge to King Fianamail of Laigin, therefore a Brehon as well as a bishop of the kingdom, pursed his lips in a cynical smile.

'Times change, Saxon. Times change. Our young King has decreed that Christian laws and punishments – what we called the Penitentials – must supersede the old ways of this land. What is good for the Faith throughout all other lands using Christ's laws must also be good enough for us.'

'Yet you are a Brehon, a judge, sworn to uphold the laws of the five kingdoms. How can you accept that Fianamail has the legal authority to change your ancient laws? That can only be done every three years at the great Festival of Tara by agreement with all the kings, Brehons, lawyers and laymen.'

'You seem to know a lot for a stranger in our land, Saxon. I will tell you. We are of the Faith before all other considerations. I swore not only to uphold the law but also to uphold the Faith. We should all accept the divine laws of the Church and reject the darkness of our pagan ways. But this is beside the point. I did not come to argue law with you, Saxon. You have been found guilty and have been sentenced. All that is now required of you is your admission of guilt so that you may make your peace with God.'

Eadulf folded his arms with a shake of his head.

'So that is why I was made to witness the execution of that poor young man? Well, Bishop Forbassach, I have already made my peace with God. You seek an admission of guilt from me merely to absolve yourself of your own guilt in giving a false judgment. I am innocent and will declare it as that poor young man did. May God greet young Brother Ibar kindly in the Otherworld.'

Bishop Forbassach rose to his feet. The smile had not left his thin features but it was more strained and more false than before. Eadulf sensed a simmering violence in the man, born of his frustration.

'Brother Ibar was foolish to cling to his plea of innocence as, indeed, are you.' He moved across to the cell window and stared down into the courtyard below for a moment or so. The body of the young man still swung from the gibbet, twitching now and again to display the gruesome fact that death was a long time claiming the unfortunate victim. Everyone apart from the patient executioner had disappeared.

'Interesting . . . that last cry of his,' Eadulf reflected aloud. '*Has* anyone asked about the manacles?'

Bishop Forbassach did not reply. After a moment or two he turned and walked to the door. He hesitated a moment, hand on the latch, then turned to regard Eadulf with cold, angry eyes.

'You have until noon tomorrow to make up your mind whether you will die with a lie on your lips, Saxon, or having cleansed your soul of your guilt over this foul crime.'

'It seems,' Brother Eadulf replied softly, as Forbassach banged on the door to attract the attention of the guard, 'that you are very anxious for me to admit to something of which I am innocent. I wonder why?'

For a moment Bishop Forbassach's mask slipped and, if looks could kill, Eadulf knew that he would have been dead at that moment.

'After midday tomorrow, Saxon, you will not have the luxury of being able to wonder.' The cell door opened and Bishop Forbassach left. Eadulf rose and moved rapidly to the door as it swung shut behind him and called loudly through the small grille: 'Then I shall have until noon tomorrow to meditate on your motivations. Maybe that will give me time enough to discover what dark evil is stirring here, Forbassach! What about the manacles?'

There was no answer. Eadulf listened for a moment to the receding sound of leather slapping on the granite flags of the corridor, the noise of the slamming of a distant door and the rasping of iron bolts.

Eadulf stood back. Alone again, he felt black despair descend on him. For all his attempts to hide his feelings from Forbassach, he could not hide them from himself. He walked over to the window and stared down at the gibbet below. The body of Brother Ibar swung slightly from the rope now. There was no longer any twitching in the limbs. Life had departed. Eadulf tried to force a prayer from his lips but no sounds would come. His mouth was dry, his tongue swollen. Tomorrow at midday he would be swinging down there on that gibbet. There was nothing to prevent it.

Fearna, the great place of the alder trees, was the principal settlement of the Uí Cheinnselaigh, the royal dynasty of the kingdom of Laigin. The town stood on the side of a hill at a point where two valleys, through which large rivers flowed, connected with each other like the two arms of a great 'Y' and formed a single broad valley where the same rivers now flowed as one southwards and then eastwards towards the sea.

Fidelma and her companions, having spent the night at Morca's inn, had taken the ford across the broad River Slaney, then the road which ran between the Slaney and the River Bann, on whose hills the capital of the Laigin kings stood. Their arrival among the sprawl of timber and stone buildings went unnoticed and unremarked as many travellers, merchants and traders, as well as emissaries from other kingdoms, came and went regularly. Strangers were so frequent in the township as to excite no comment.

Fearna was dominated by its two complex buildings. On a small promontory of the hill rose the fortress which was the stronghold of the Laigin kings. It was large but unspectacular, the type of circular citadel which arose in many parts of the five kingdoms of Éireann. Curiously, it was the Abbey of Máedóc that most dominated the countryside; a grey, granite complex, it towered close by the banks of the River Bann. Indeed, it had its own little quay at which boats from the settlements along the river moored to trade goods. Fearna had grown to importance as a centre of the river trade.

One might be forgiven, on a first visit to Fearna, for believing that it was the abbey which was the citadel of the Laigin kings. Although scarcely fifty years old, it already looked as if it had stood for centuries, for there was a strange atmosphere of gloom and decay about it. It looked more like a fortress than an abbey. The impression one had was of chill foreboding.

When King Brandubh had decided to build the abbey for his Christian mentor and his followers, the old King decreed that it was to be the most imposing building in his kingdom. Yet instead of a place of worship and joy, which should have been the purpose of such a building, it rose overwhelming and aggressive, like an sinister sore in the countryside.

It was scarcely fifty years ago that the Laigin kings had been converted to the Faith of Christ when Brandubh had accepted baptism from the Blessed Aidan, a man of Breifne, who had settled at Fearna. The Laigin people had called Aidan by the name of Máedóc, a pet form of his name which meant 'little fire'. The Blessed Máedóc had died forty years before; it was known that the brethren of the abbey jealously guarded his relics there.

Fidelma examined the building critically as they rode to the centre of the township: it was so unlike the habitations of the religious communities that she knew. She felt rather guilty at her thoughts for she knew the Blessed Máedóc was loved and respected throughout the land. Yet she remained firm in her belief that religion should be a matter of joy and not of oppression.

Dego pointed the way to Fianamail's fortress for he had been at Fearna before. The young warrior confidently led the way up the hill towards the fortress and, at the gates, halted to demand that the bemused guard summon his commander. Almost at once a soldier came forward, frowning as he recognised Dego and his companions as men in the service of the King of Cashel. As he hesitated, undecided what to do, Fidelma edged her horse forward.

'Find your steward,' she advised. 'Tell the *rechtaire* that it is Fidelma of Cashel who requires an audience with Fianamail.'

The guard commander, recognising the rank of the young religieuse who demanded entrance, was startled. Then he gave a stiff little bow before turning abruptly to send one of his men off to find the *rechtaire*, the steward, of the King's household. He politely enquired whether Fidelma and her companions would care to alight from their horses and enter the shelter of the guardroom. At a sharp snap of his fingers, stable boys came running out to take charge of the horses while Fidelma and her companions entered a room with a crackling fire. Their reception had not been overly enthusiastic but everything was done with the minimum amount of courtesy needed to obey the laws of hospitality.

It was only a few moments before the steward of the King's household came hurrying in.

'Fidelma of Cashel?' He was an elderly man with carefully brushed silver hair and his appearance and clothing spoke of someone who was fastidious in personal dress as he was punctilious in court protocol. He wore a silver chain of office. 'I am told that you the require an audience with the King?'

'That is so,' replied Fidelma. 'It is a matter of some urgency.'

The man's face remained grave. 'I am sure that it can be arranged. Perhaps you and . . .' his eyes flickered to where Dego, Aidan and Enda stood, 'and your escort would like to wash and relax while I make the arrangements?'

'I would prefer the audience to be immediate,' Fidelma replied, causing the steward to blink rapidly, which indicated his surprise. 'We have rested on our journey and that journey was necessitated by a matter of exigency, of life and death. I do not use the words without precision.'

The man hesitated. 'It is unusual . . .' he began.

'The matter is unusual,' interrupted Fidelma firmly.

'You are sister to the King of Muman, lady. Also you are a religieuse, and your reputation as a *dálaigh* is not unknown in Fearna. May I venture to ask in which of these capacities you come hither? The King is always ready to welcome visitors from neighbouring lands, especially the sister of Colgú of Cashel . . .'

Fidelma cut him short with a swift cutting gesture of her hand. She did not require flattery to camouflage his question.

'It is not as the sister of the King of Muman that I am here but as a *dálaigh* of the courts, bearing the rank of *anruth*.' Fidelma's voice was cold and assertive.

The steward raised his arm in an odd gesture which seemed to imply acquiescence.

'Then, if you will be so good as to wait, I will attend to see the King's pleasure.'

Fidelma was kept waiting twenty minutes before the steward returned. The captain of the guard, who had been detailed to wait with them, became increasingly embarrassed and stood shuffling his feet as time passed. Fidelma, although annoyed, felt sorry for him. When, after a while, the man cleared his throat and began to apologise, she smiled and told him it was not his fault.

When the steward finally reappeared he, too, looked awkward at the time it had taken to relay the request to the King and return with his answer.

'Fianamail has expressed himself willing to see you,' the old man said, dropping his gaze before her impatient glare. 'Will you follow me?' He hesitated and looked towards Dego. 'Your companions must await you here, of course.'

'Of course,' snapped Fidelma. She caught Dego's eye: she did not have to say anything. The young warrior inclined his head at her unspoken instruction.

'We will await your safe return, lady,' he called softly. He allowed the slightest inflection to linger on the word 'safe'.

Fidelma followed the elderly steward across the flagged courtyard and into the main fortress buildings. The palace seemed curiously empty compared with the crowds who usually thronged the castle of her brother. Isolated guards stood here and there. A few men and women, obviously servants, scurried to and fro on their appointed tasks, but there was no chatter, no laughter nor children playing. Of course, Fianamail was young and not yet married, but it was strange to see such a palace lacking in vitality and the warmth of family life and activity.

Fianamail was awaiting her in a small reception room, seated before a blazing log fire. He was not yet twenty years of age; a youth with foxy hair and with an attitude to match it. His eyes were close-set, giving him a cunning, almost furtive expression. He had succeeded his cousin, Faelán, as King of Laigin, when Faelán had died from the Yellow Plague just over a year ago. He was fiery, ambitious and, as Fidelma had judged him at their one and only meeting, nearly a year ago, easily misled by his advisers due to his own arrogance. Foolishly, Fianamail had condoned a plot to wrest control of the sub-kingdom of Osraige from Cashel and annex it to Laigin. Fidelma had revealed this plot during a hearing before the High King himself at the abbey of Ros Ailithir. The result was that the High King's Chief Brehon, Barrán, judged that the sub-kingdom, on the borderlands between the Muman kingdom and Laigin, would forever be subject to Cashel. The judgment had enraged Fianamail at the time. Now he let bands of Laigin warriors raid and pillage the borderlands while denying responsibility or knowledge. Fianamail was young and ambitious and determined to make a reputation for himself.

He did not rise when Fidelma entered the room, as courtesy would have dictated, but merely gestured with a limp hand to a seat on the opposite side of the large hearth.

'I remember you well, Fidelma of Cashel,' he greeted her. There was no smile or warmth on his thin, calculating features.

'And I you,' replied Fidelma with equal coldness.

'May I offer you refreshment?' The young man made a languid gesture to a nearby table on which wine and mead were placed.

Fidelma shook her head quickly. 'The matter I wish to discuss is pressing.'

'Pressing?' Fianamail raised his eyebrows interrogatively. 'What matter would that be?'

'The matter of Brother Eadulf of Seaxmund's Ham. Have you not received messages from my brother expressing the concerns of Cashel and asking—'

Fianamail sat up abruptly. His brows came together.

'Eadulf? The Saxon? I had a message but did not understand it. Why is Cashel interested in the Saxon?'

'Brother Eadulf of Seaxmund's Ham is an emissary between my brother and Theodore of Canterbury,' she confirmed. 'I have come here to defend him against that of which he has been accused.'

Fianamail's lips parted slightly; it seemed a gleeful expression.

'I delayed the trial as long as I could in regard for your brother, the King. Time passed, alas.'

Fidelma felt a growing chill. 'We heard a rumour on the road that he had already been tried. Surely, after my brother's intervention, the trial could have been delayed until I arrived?'

'Even a King cannot delay a trial indefinitely. The rumour you heard is true: he has already been tried and found guilty. It is all over now. He has no need of your defence.'

Chapter Three

Fidelma's face was white, mirroring the terrible anguish which she felt. It was almost as if the blood had suddenly drained from her body.

'All over? Do you mean that . . .?' She swallowed, hardly able to articulate the question that was uppermost in her mind.

'The Saxon will be executed at noon tomorrow,' Fianamail said indifferently.

A feeling of relief surged over Fidelma. 'Then he is not dead yet?' The words came out as a shuddering sigh. She closed her eyes with momentary solace.

The young King seemed oblivious to her emotions and kicked at a log which had fallen from the fire.

'He is as good as dead. The matter is now closed. You have had a long journey for nothing.'

Fidelma bent forward from her seat and stared towards Fianamail.

'I do not consider that the matter is closed as yet. I heard a story on the journey here. It was a story that I would not countenance about a King of Laigin. I was told that you had rejected the native law and decreed that the punishment laid down in the new Penitentials from Rome should be enacted. Is it true that you have declared this thing?'

Fianamail was still smiling, though without warmth.

'Execution is the punishment decreed, Fidelma of Cashel. That much has been decided. In this I have been guided by both my spiritual adviser and by my Brehon. Laigin will lead the way in shaking off our old pagan ways. Let Christian punishments fit the crimes of this land. I am determined to show how Christian my kingdom of Laigin has become. Death it shall be.'

'I think you forget the law, Fianamail of Laigin. Even the Penitentials recognise the matter of appeal.'

'Appeal?' Fianamail looked astonished. 'But the sentence has been passed by my Brehon. I have confirmed it. There is no appeal to be made.'

'There is a judge higher than your Brehon,' Fidelma pointed out.

'The Chief Brehon of Éireann can be summoned. I think he will have much to say over this matter of the Penitentials.'

'On what grounds could you make such an appeal to the Chief Brehon of the five kingdoms?' sneered Fianamail. 'You have no knowledge of the case nor of the evidence. Besides, the execution is tomorrow and we cannot wait a week for the Chief Brehon to arrive here.'

His self-confident smile provoked anger in Fidelma and she fought to control it.

'Until I have investigated this matter, I would appeal to you for a stay of the implementation of the sentence on the grounds that Brother Eadulf of Seaxmund's Ham might not have been correctly defended; that his rights might not have been fully considered by the court that tried him.'

Fianamail leaned back in his chair with an expression of open derision.

'That sounds like the appeal of a desperate person, Fidelma of Cashel. You are clutching at straws. Well, you have no audience to appeal to now. Not like the audience you swayed at Ros Ailithir against me and Bishop Forbassach. I am the sole authority here.'

Fidelma knew she would not successfully appeal to Fianamail's sense of morality. The young man wanted vengeance on her. She decided to change her tactic and raised her voice sharply. ·

'You are a King, Fianamail, and whatever your antagonism to me and to Cashel, you will behave like a King for, if you do not, the very stones you walk on will cry out and denounce you as unjust and evil.'

Fianamail stirred uneasily at her vehemence.

'I speak as a King, Fidelma of Cashel. I am told that the Saxon was given every opportunity to defend himself,' he said grudgingly.

Fidelma seized upon the point. '*To defend himself?* Was he not provided with a *dálaigh* to plead for him – to plead the law on his behalf?'

'That is a privilege granted to few foreigners. However, it is true that as he spoke our language and apparently knew something of law, he was allowed to offer a defence. He received no less a treatment than we extend to any wandering religious.'

'Then Brother Eadulf of Seaxmund's Ham did not tell you of the rank he held?' Fidelma demanded, beginning to see a faint ray of hope.

Fianamail stared at her, not understanding what she was driving at.

'The man is a religieux, a *peregrinatio pro Christo*. What other rank would he have?'

'He is a *techtaire*, not merely a travelling religieux. As a *techtaire*, one should observe the advice of the *Bretha Nemed*, for Eadulf travelled under the protection of King Colgú as a member of his household.'

The young King was slightly bewildered. He was no *dálaigh* or Brehon. He did not know the law to which Fidelma referred.

'Why would the Saxon be under the protection of your brother's house?'

Fidelma sensed a hesitation in his youthful arrogance.

'That's easy to understand. Theodore of Canterbury, archbishop and adviser to all the Saxon kingdoms, sent Eadulf as his personal emissary to my brother. Therefore, he comes with the honour price of eight *cumals*, half the honour price which you yourself hold as King of Laigin. He has the rights and protection of an embassy. And he is entitled to half the honour price of the man he serves. In returning to Theodore of Canterbury, and bearing messages from my brother, Eadulf continues to bear the same honour price and is therefore in my brother's service. The law is clear about the protection it affords to members of an embassy.'

'But he committed a murder,' protested Fianamail.

'So your courts have claimed,' agreed Fidelma. 'But the circumstances have to be examined, for doesn't the *Bretha Nemed* claim that the officers of a King may carry out acts of violence in self-defence during the course of their duties without liability? Is it known what reasons lay behind his offence? It may well be that he carried immunity from prosecution. Was this considered?'

Fianamail was clearly confused by her technical knowledge. He was unable to argue and admitted it.

'I have not your proficiency in law, Fidelma of Cashel,' he confessed. 'I must seek advice on this matter.'

'Then send for your Brehon now; let him stand here before me and argue precedents.'

Fianamail rose, shaking his head, and went to pour himself a glass of wine at the table.

'He is not here at this time. I do not expect him to return until tomorrow.'

'Then you must make your judgment without him, Fianamail. I do not lie to you about the law. On my honour as a *dálaigh* with or without the advice of your Brehon, if this kingdom has given a false or a mistaken judgment, then you may find that you are deemed to be no true King and you will answer to a greater court which will judge you. No King is higher in authority than the law.'

Fianamail was struggling to see how best he should proceed. He raised his hands in a hopeless gesture and let them fall to his side.

'What is it you seek?' he asked, after he had hesitated for a moment or so. 'Are you telling me that you claim immunity for the Saxon? That I will and shall not accept. His crime was too odious. What do you want?'

'Ultimately, I would plead with you to return to the laws of our country,' Fidelma replied. 'The foreign Penitentials have no place in our thoughts. Killing for the sake of vengeance is not our law . . .'

Fianamail held up a hand to stay her eloquence.

'I have given my word to Abbot Noé, my spiritual adviser, and to Bishop Forbassach, my Brehon, that the punishments decreed by the Faith will be carried out – a life for a life. Address your argument for an appeal in this matter of the Saxon but do not attempt to change my edict on the law.'

Fidelma felt a quickening of her pulse as she sensed a breach in his determination.

'I am asking you to defer the execution so that the facts of this case may be examined to ensure that the law has been served.'

'I cannot overturn my Brehon's judgment; that is not in the King's power anyway.'

'Allow me a period to investigate this crime of which you claim Brother Eadulf is guilty and let me examine the facts based on a possible submission that he acted under protection as a *fer taistil*, an officer of the King's court under immunity. Give me your authority to carry out such an investigation.'

She used the legal term *fer taistil* which, while meaning literally a 'traveller', meant specifically an emissary between kings.

Fianamail returned to his chair. His brow was furrowed as he considered the matter. It was clear that he was worried by acceding to her demands but was unable to find reasons to counter Fidelma's arguments.

'I do not wish to quarrel with your brother again,' he admitted at last. 'Nor do I wish to do anything which contradicts the protocols and justice of my kingdom.' He paused and rubbed his chin ruefully. After a while he gave a long, deep sigh. 'I will give you time to look into the crime of which this Saxon has been found guilty. If you can see anything in the conduct and judgment of our courts which is not in order, then I will not challenge your right of appeal on those grounds.'

Fidelma suppressed a small sigh of relief. 'That is all I ask. But I will need your authority.'

'I will call for quill and vellum and set it down,' he agreed, reaching forward. He took a small silver hand-bell and rang it.

'Good.' Fidelma felt a weight dissolving from her shoulders. 'How long will you give me to make my examination?'

A servant entered and was instructed to bring the writing materials. The young King's eyes were cold.

'How long? Why, you have until noon tomorrow when the sentence on the Saxon is to be carried out.'

Fidelma's momentary surge of relief was halted as she realised the restriction Fianamail had placed on her.

'There you are,' Fianamail smiled. 'You cannot claim that I am disobeying the customs of our land. I have allowed you time to prepare an appeal. That is what you sought.'

The servant re-entered with the writing materials and the King scribbled swiftly on the vellum. Fidelma took time to recover her voice.

'Are you giving me no more than twenty-four hours? Is there justice in that?' She spoke slowly, trying to stop her surging anger from erupting.

'Whatever justice it is, it is still justice,' replied Fianamail vindictively. 'I owe you no more.'

For a moment Fidelma was silent, trying to think of some other appeal she could make to him. Then she realised that there was nothing more she could say. The young man held the power and she had no greater power to overturn his desire for vengeance.

'Very well,' she said at last. 'If I find the grounds for an appeal, will you halt the execution pending the arrival of Barrán, the Chief Brehon, to hear the case?'

Fianamail sniffed slightly. '*If* you find grounds for an appeal and they are considered worthy by my own courts of justice, then I shall allow a delay until the Brehon Barrán can be summoned. Those arguments of grounds for such an appeal must be substantial and not merely suspicions.'

'That goes without saying. Will you also allow me to go without let nor hindrance where I will during these next twenty-four hours in pursuit of my enquiries?'

'It is covered by this.' The King held out the vellum to her. She did not take it.

'Then you must append your seal of authorisation showing that I act with your consent and authority.'

Fianamail hesitated. Fidelma knew a piece of vellum giving consent for her to ask questions was worth nothing without the King's seal.

The King wavered, once again undecided as to how he should act.

'The killing of a *techtaire* is a serious offence before the Chief Brehon and High King,' observed Fidelma firmly. 'The death of a King's messenger, whether by murder or by execution, has to be answered for. It is wise that you should authorise me to investigate the matter.'

Fianamail finally shrugged and took from the writing box a piece of wax, melted it over a candle onto the vellum and pressed his signet ring firmly into it.

'You now have that consent. It cannot be said 'that I did not allow every possible avenue to be explored.'

Fidelma was satisfied and took the authorisation.

'I would like to see Brother Eadulf immediately. Is he being held here in your fortress?'

To her surprise, Fianamail shook his head. 'No, not here.'

'Where then?'

'He is held over at the abbey.'

'What is he doing there?'

'It was there that his crime was committed and there he was tried and sentenced. Abbess Fainder has taken a personal charge of this matter, for the victim was one of her own novices. It was in the abbey that the Saxon stood trial and where he will be executed tomorrow.'

'Abbess Fainder? I thought the Abbey of Fearna came under the jurisdiction of Abbot Noé?'

'As I told you, Abbot Noé is now my spiritual adviser and confessor . . .'

'Confessor? That is a Roman concept.'

'Call him a "soul friend" if you like to stick to the quaint old-fashioned ways of the Church. I have given him jurisdiction on religious matters throughout my kingdom. The Abbey of the Blessed Máedóc is now under the guidance of Abbess Fainder. Her stewardess is actually a distant cousin of mine, Étromma.' He suddenly seemed apologetic. 'A poor branch of the family with whom I have few dealings but who, I am told, is good at running the day-to-day affairs of the abbey. However, it is the abbess herself who has demanded that the Penitentials be used to guide us in our Christian Faith as well as in our daily lives and to be the instrument of the Saxon's punishment.'

'Abbess Fainder?' Fidelma reflected. 'I have not heard of her.'

'She has but lately returned to this kingdom from several years' service in Rome.'

'And so she supports the Penitentials of Rome against the wisdom texts of her own land?'

Fianamail inclined his head by way of an affirmative reply.

'I see,' Fidelma said. 'You mentioned that Brother Eadulf was charged with causing the death of a novice in the abbey. Just who is it that he was supposed to have killed?'

Fianamail regarded her in mock reproof. 'For someone who comes riding post haste from Cashel determined to prove the Saxon's innocence, I would have thought you might have known of what he was accused,' he said slyly.

'Murder, of course. But who is he supposed to have murdered?'

Fianamail was almost pitying. 'I suspect, Fidelma of Cashel, that you have rushed into this mission with your heart instead of your head.'

Fidelma coloured hotly. 'My reason is to let justice be served,' she replied stiffly. 'Now who was he supposed to have killed?' she asked again.

'Your Saxon friend raped a young girl and then strangled her,' the King said tonelessly, watching her face. 'She was a novice at the abbey . . . *and she was only twelve years old.*'

Even after she had been conducted from the King's chamber, Fidelma still felt a numbness in her. Of all the crimes, the very idea that Eadulf could have been accused of raping a twelve-year-old girl and then murdering her was abhorrent. How could Eadulf have been adjudged guilty of such a thing? It was something so alien to the nature of the man she knew.

In the courtyard of the fortress, Fidelma, waiting until there were no Laigin warriors within earshot, turned to Dego, Aidan and Enda.

'I need one of you to ride to Tara and seek out the Chief Brehon, Barrán,' she said quietly. 'It will be a dangerous journey through hostile Laigin territory, but needs to be done with all speed.'

Aidan stood forward immediately.

'I am the best rider here, lady,' he said simply. It was not a boast and neither Dego nor Enda wasted time by disagreeing with him. Fidelma accepted the truth of his statement without further ado.

'I need you to persuade Barrán to return with you immediately, Aidan. Explain the situation so far as you know it. Plead in my name if you have to. And, Aidan . . . be very careful. There may be people who would not want you to reach Tara, let alone return here with Barrán.'

Aidan was confident.

'I understand and will have a care, lady. It will not take me long to reach the territory of the southern Uí Néill. They are no friends to the Laigin and as soon as I am there, I shall be safe enough. With good fortune I shall return within a few days.'

'All that falls to me is to prevent this execution tomorrow. Then hope that you can return in time with Barrán to hear what mystery lurks here,' she said.

Aidan spoke hesitantly. 'Are you sure that there is a mystery to be uncovered, lady? I mean, could it be . . .?' He lapsed into silence under her disapproving scrutiny.

Dego intervened; he was anxious.

'If you expect Aidan to leave here in broad daylight, lady, it will not give him much of a chance if, as you appear to believe, Laigin warriors will be watching our movements.'

'We will give them something to watch then,' Fidelma replied with a sudden burst of her old confidence. 'We will go into the township to find accommodation for our stay here. Once among the crowds of the town, Aidan will leave us. If he rides west for the Slaney, it might appear as if he is simply heading back to Cashel. There are woods enough near the river and he can use the cover of them to strike north. Agreed?'

'Agreed,' Aidan confirmed. Then he paused: 'I am sorry, lady, that I questioned . . .'

Fidelma reached out a hand and laid it on his arm.

'You have a right to be suspicious, Aidan. The unthinkable might even be true – Eadulf could be guilty; let us not prejudge matters. But also let us remember that we know the man.'

Dego exchanged glances with his companions.

'We are with you, lady. Shall we leave now?'

'At once. Let us walk our horses from the gate, slowly and casually down the hill and once we are in among the houses, hidden from the eyes in this fortress, then Aidan can mount up and ride westward.'

They ordered their horses from the stable and the guard commander came forward as the stable boys were leading them out.

'Are you not staying here, lady?' he enquired in surprise. It was usual for visiting dignitaries to be offered hospitality at the King's court.

'We will find accommodation within the town,' she assured him. 'It is better that I and my escort do not impose ourselves on the hospitality of your King.'

The man looked perplexed. It was unusual but he knew something of the enmity between Fearna and Cashel and put their departure down to this reason.

'Very well, lady. Is there any further service that I can render?'

'Perhaps you could recommend an inn in this town.'

The guard commander replied immediately. 'There are several, lady. I have a sister who runs the Inn of the Yellow Mountain just beyond the main square. It is named after the place we came from, seven kilometers north-east of here. Her place is clean and quiet. She allows no rowdiness there.'

'We shall look out for it then,' Fidelma assured him with a smile of gratitude.

'She is called Lassar. Tell her that her brother recommended the inn.'

The four of them, reins held over their arms, walked their horses through the fortress gate and down the sloping path to the sprawl of buildings below. It was midday and the streets were thronging with people. There was a market in the main square around which everything centred, crammed with food stalls selling all manner of fish, poultry and meats as well as fruit and vegetables. The noise of the traders trying to outbid each other in attracting custom made an ear-splitting cacophony of sound to rise over the township.

Fidelma led the way through the crowded square and across to the entrance of a side street, where she glanced round. They were out of sight of the sentinels' posts on the fortress and she turned to Aidan.

'You know now what you must do?'

The young man grinned and sprang up into his saddle. 'I will see you here within a few days and bring Barrán with me, lady. If I do not return, it will be because I am dead.'

'Then make sure that you return.'

He raised a hand in salute and dug his heels into the sides of his horse.

They watched him move along the street as rapidly as the people allowed. Then he disappeared beyond the buildings. Fidelma sighed deeply and turned to her two remaining companions.

'Where to now, lady?' asked Dego. 'Will we go to the abbey to find Brother Eadulf?'

'Firstly, we should take up the suggestion of the commander of the guard and find his sister's inn,' smiled Fidelma. 'Then I shall go to the abbey.'

'Isn't that a dangerous thing? I mean, going to an inn recommended by a Laigin warrior?' Enda asked.

'Perhaps not. The connection might prove useful. I do not think that the recommendation was made through any guile. I believe the man was honest.'

'A Laigin warrior . . . honest?' Dego sounded as if he doubted such a thing could be so.

Fidelma did not expand on her opinion but instead hailed a passer-by with an enquiry as to where the Inn of the Yellow Mountain might be found. It turned out to be but a street away, just off the main square but protected from the hubbub of sound by other buildings. The Inn of the Yellow Mountain announced itself by a signboard bearing the image of a yellow triangular shape which was clearly meant as a mountain. The inn was large; a two-storey wooden structure with its own yard and stables. It seemed popular for there were several people coming in and out of it.

They led their horses into the yard and Dego took Fidelma's reins as she moved forward to the door of the inn. A large woman came bustling out as Fidelma approached. She had a kindly face and Fidelma could see some resemblance between her features and those of the guard commander.

'Rooms for the night?' greeted the woman. 'We have the best prices in Fearna, Sister. And you will certainly do better here for comfort and food than seeking free lodgings at the abbey . . .'

She broke off with a frown as she suddenly recognised the accoutrements of the two warriors as being those of Muman.

'Are you Lassar?' asked Fidelma pleasantly, claiming her attention once more.

'I am.' The woman turned back, a look of suspicion on her face as she scrutinised her questioner.

'It was your brother, the warrior at the fortress, who recommended your inn to us, Lassar.'

The woman's eyes widened with some respect. 'You have been to Fianamail's fortress?'

'My business brought me here to speak with Fianamail,' Fidelma confirmed. 'Have you rooms for my companions and myself?'

Lassar glanced dubiously at the warriors again before turning back to Fidelma.

'I have a room that they can share and a small room that you can use on your own – but it will cost more than sleeping in a shared room,' she added defensively.

'That is no problem.'

Lassar raised a hand and, as if from nowhere, a stable boy appeared and took charge of their horses. Dego retrieved the saddlebags from the steeds before they were led away.

The fleshy-faced woman gestured them inside. 'So, Mel recommended the inn, eh?'

'Mel?'

'My brother. I thought that he might be too grand to think of my business, now that he is commander of the guard at Fianamail's palace.'

'Now?' Fidelma picked up on the slight emphasis. 'He has only just become commander there?'

'Oh yes. He has only just been raised to the guard as well as made captain of it.'

Lassar led them up the stairs to the second storey and conducted them to a door, which she flung open with the air of someone about to reveal a priceless treasure beyond. It was a dark, narrow little room, with a tiny window. It looked fairly claustrophobic.

'There is your room, Sister.'

Fidelma had seen worse and at least it appeared warm and the bed was comfortable.

'And the room for my companions?'

Lassar pointed along the corridor.

'There is one they can share down there. Will you want food as well?'

'Yes, although our plans might change.'

Lassar frowned slightly. 'Then you plan to be here for some time?'

'For about a week, probably,' Fidelma replied. 'What are your prices?'

'Since there are three of you, and if you can guarantee me a week, then I will charge you a *pinginn* each a person. That is a *screpall* a day. For that you have the freedom of the inn, coming and going as you like and meals as you like. There will be hot water for baths in the evenings. So you see, I am not wrong. You will do better by staying here and not seeking the hospitality of the abbey.'

It was the second time that the woman had referred to the abbey in disparaging tones and it drew Fidelma's interest. It was true that a travelling religious would normally expect to obtain free lodgings at an abbey. But Lassar's opinion of the abbey and its hospitality seemed surprisingly low even for an innkeeper who must see the abbey as a rival.

'What makes you say that?' she asked.

The fleshy-faced woman grimaced defiantly. 'It is clear that you are a stranger here.'

'I have not denied it.'

'Times have changed, Sister. That is all I say. The abbey has turned into a place of misery. Once I was hard pressed to attract travellers to the inn here, for many sought the hospitality of its walls. Now, no one wants to enter. Not since . . .' She suddenly paused and shuddered.

'Not since . . .?' pressed Fidelma.

'I will say no more, Sister. A *screpall* a day for all three if you want the rooms.'

Fidelma realised that Lassar would not be forced to say anything more about her views on the abbey.

'A *screpall* a day is fine,' she agreed, glancing at Dego and Enda. 'I will give you three *screpalls* in advance for the rooms and we would like to wash first and have a meal as soon as possible.'

'If you wish for a cold wash, then there is no problem. Hot water, as I say, is only provided at night for a bath. I have little help here now that my brother has become so grand a person up at the palace.'

'There is no problem,' Fidelma assured her, taking out some coins from her *marsupium*, the leather purse at her waist, and handing them to her.

The woman paused for a moment as if counting the coins in her hand. Then she smiled in satisfaction.

'I will send water to your room and you may come down and eat when you like. It will only be cold fare. Hot meals may be had in the evening because . . .'

Fidelma smiled indulgently. 'I know. We appreciate your help, Lassar.'

The innkeeper disappeared down the stairs. Dego let out a breath of relief.

'What now, lady?' he asked. 'What shall we do next?'

'After we have refreshed ourselves, I suggest that you make yourselves inconspicuous around the town and see what gossip you can pick up with regards to the events here. Find out what people feel about the imposition of the Penitentials as law and punishment instead of our native laws.'

'What will you be doing, lady?' asked Enda. 'Should we not go with you?'

Fidelma shook her head. 'I am going to the abbey. I want to see Eadulf.'

Chapter Four

The Abbey of Fearna seemed even more forbidding close to than it had from a distance. A baleful atmosphere clung to the building, as tangible as cobwebs to its walls. The feeling was insubstantial, almost ethereal, but it was there like a cold mist hanging over everything. There were two great dark oak doors, hinged with iron, which were the main gates. On the right-hand door a large bronze image was fixed. Fidelma realised that this was the famous figure of an angel wrought by Máedóc, for it seemed to have intricately decorated wings and held a sword in its right hand. The face was circular, the eyes wide, round and socketless, giving it an appearance almost of malignancy. She had heard that this image was called 'Our Lady of Light' and meant to be a symbol of protection.

Fainder, Abbess of Fearna, was equally impressive and forbidding; that fact Fidelma had to admit, although she took an inexplicable and instant dislike to the woman. From the moment she was shown into the room where the abbess sat, upright in a tall oak-carved chair before a long wooden table which served her as a desk, Fidelma felt the aura of her presence. Haughty and belligerent. Even sitting, she gave the impression of stature, of leanness which added to her height. Yet when she rose to greet Fidelma, the impression was not confirmed. Fidelma, who was considered tall, towered over the woman who was only of medium height. The perception of height was simply one given by her personality, her bearing and nothing else.

The hand that she held out to greet Fidelma was strong, the bones prominent, her skin rough with calluses – these were associated more with those used to working in the fields than with a religieuse. She was dark-haired and Fidelma estimated that she was in her thirties. Her face was symmetrical; however, there was something hard about the features. The black eyes were deepset and one held an odd cast. Yet it was not this that made her appearance sinister, but the fact that she seldom blinked. The dark eyes, even with a cast, seemed to fix on Fidelma like gimlets and did not look away. Had Fidelma been of lesser character she might have dropped her gaze in discomfiture.

When Abbess Fainder spoke her voice was soft, modulated and almost soothing, lulling one into a deceptive feeling of security. Only Fidelma, her sensitivity to people's personalities developed over many years, was attuned to the strong tones behind the gentle articulation. Fainder would tolerate no disagreement with her opinions; of that, Fidelma was absolutely certain.

From the way the abbess held out her hand, Fidelma realised that she was supposed to bow and kiss her ring of office, Roman style. However, Fidelma took the hand and inclined her head only a fraction in the manner of the Irish Church.

'*Stet fortuna domus*,' she intoned.

Abbess Fainder's eyes glinted for a moment, the annoyance gone so quickly that only a careful observer might have noticed it.

'*Deo juvante*,' she replied shortly, resuming her position and motioning Fidelma to sit on a chair before the table. Fidelma did so.

'So, you are Fidelma of Cashel?' The abbess smiled; it was no more than a parting of her thin, bloodless lips. 'Your name was spoken of in Rome when I was there.'

Fidelma did not answer. There was no comment she could make. Instead she motioned to the piece of vellum bearing Fianamail's order and seal.

'I have come on most urgent business, Mother Abbess.'

The abbess did not acknowledge the vellum placed before her. She was sitting upright in her chair, hands on the table, palm downwards, resuming the same position as when Fidelma had been shown into her room.

'You have a reputation as a *dálaigh*, Sister,' Fainder continued. 'Yet you are a religieuse; I am told that you took it upon yourself to leave the Abbey of Kildare because you disagreed with its abbess, Abbess Ita.'

She paused in expectation of a reply but the comment had been phrased as a statement. Fidelma gave no response.

'When one becomes a religieuse, Fidelma of Cashel,' the abbess laid an emphasis on the title which acknowledged that Fidelma was a princess of the Eóghanacht, 'one's first duty is obedience to the Order, to the Rule of Saints. Obedience is the first rule for it is the duty of the religieuse not to disagree in mind, not to speak as one pleases and not to travel anywhere with entire freedom. Attention to the Rule is the manifestation of a Godly life.'

Fidelma waited patiently until the abbess had ended her homily before speaking clearly and deliberately.

'I am here in my capacity as *dálaigh*, Mother Abbess, and with the authority of my brother, Colgú, King of Cashel. That which I have placed before you is an authority of Fianamail, King of Laigin.'

Abbess Fainder's voice hardened and still she did not glance at the vellum.

'You are now a religieuse in the abbey of Fearna – *my* abbey – and all religieuse have a duty to obedience, Sister.'

'This is not Rome, Mother Abbess,' replied Fidelma with a voice that was quiet yet betrayed a sharpness that gave clear warning. 'I understand that you have only recently returned from there and may be forgiven for a lapse of memory as to the laws of this land. I am here as a *dálaigh* of the level of *anruth*. Surely I do not have to remind you of the law of rank and privileges?'

Holding a degree which was only one lower than the highest that the secular and ecclesiastical colleges could bestow, Fidelma, in law as well as her position as sister to a king, outranked an abbess.

Fainder blinked for the first time. It was an oddly menacing movement, like a snake that hoods its eyes for a fraction of a second.

'In this abbey,' Fainder spoke softly, 'the rules of the Penitential govern our life. Thanks be to God that we also have a progressive King in Fianamail who has seen the wisdom of extending the Rule of the Penitentials to all his people as the Christian Duty of Life.'

Fidelma stood up, leaning forward and deliberately retrieving the unread vellum from Abbess Fainder's desk. Her patience was exhausted.

'Very well. I take it that this is a refusal to obey the authority of the Council of the Chief Brehon and of the High King. You bring a disservice on your abbey, Fainder. I am surprised that you wish to incite the wrath of a judicial enquiry by disregarding my authority and the warrant of your King, Fianamail.'

Fidelma had turned to the door when Abbess Fainder's voice, an odd-sounding staccato, stayed her.

'Stop!'

The abbess was still sitting in the same position, hands palm downward on the table. It seemed to Fidelma that her face had become like a mask; every line sharp and graven.

Fidelma waited at the door.

'Perhaps,' the abbess seemed to struggle for a formula of words to escape from the corner in which she found herself by Fidelma's refusal to be intimidated, 'perhaps I did not choose my words as well as I might have. Let me see the authority of Fianamail.'

Fidelma returned to the desk and placed it once more before the austere woman. She said nothing. Fainder read it quickly, a frown momentarily passing over her features. Then she looked up at Fidelma.

'I can raise no objections to the authority of the King. I only inform you of the way this abbey is governed and my aspiration to keep it governed by the Penitentials.'

Having found a formula of words which suited her, Fainder's voice was now back to its gentle reassuring level. Fidelma distrusted the tone immediately.

'Then I have your leave to see Brother Eadulf and conduct my enquiry?'

Abbess Fainder waved to the seat which Fidelma had recently vacated.

'Reseat yourself, Sister, and let us discuss the matter of this Saxon. Why does he concern you?'

'Justice concerns me,' replied Fidelma, hoping that the hotness she felt in her cheeks was not mirrored by a flush of embarrassment at the question.

'So you know this Saxon? Of course,' again came the parting of the lips in a smile. 'I heard that in Rome you were in the company of a Saxon Brother. Ah, perhaps he was the same person?'

Fidelma reseated herself and regarded the abbess with an even gaze.

'I have known Brother Eadulf since the conference at the Abbey of Whitby. This last year he has served as an emissary from Theodore of Tarsus, the Archbishop of Canterbury in the land of the Saxons, to my brother, the King of Cashel. I was sent by my brother to conduct his defence.'

'Defence?' Abbess Fainder sniffed. 'You must have been informed that he has been found guilty and will be punished under the retribution laid down for his crime? The Penitentials prescribe execution which will be at noon tomorrow.'

Fidelma leaned forward a little.

'As he was an emissary of a King and a Bishop, he has rights under our laws which may not be violated. I have been given leave to investigate the case against him to see if there are grounds for appeal in law, although obviously no appeal can be made against the desire I seem to feel in this place for vengeance.'

Again Abbess Fainder's face was set, controlling any reaction she might have had to Fidelma's thrust.

'Perhaps you do not know the nature of the terrible crime of which this Saxon has been found guilty?'

'I have been told, Mother Abbess. The Brother Eadulf that I know could not have done the thing of which he has been accused.'

'No?' The dark face of Abbess Fainder was mocking. 'How many mothers, sisters . . . *lovers* . . . of murderers have said as much before now?'

Fidelma stirred uncomfortably. 'I am not . . .' she began. Then she raised her chin defiantly, determined not to be provoked. 'I would like to start my enquiry as soon as possible.'

'Very well. Sister Étromma is the stewardess of the abbey and she will assist you.'

She reached out towards a hand-bell. Its clamour had scarcely died away when a religieuse entered. She was a short, fair-haired woman who was pleasantly featured but moved with quick, bird-like motions. She scurried rather than walked, hands concealed in the folds of her robes. It was the same woman who had greeted Fidelma at the abbey doors and conducted her to the Abbess Fainder's chambers. Abbess Fainder addressed her.

'Sister, you have already made the acquaintance of our . . . our distinguished visitor,' Only the momentary hesitation indicated the irony in the abbess's voice. 'She is to be given all the assistance she needs in these next twenty-four hours. She is investigating the crimes of the Saxon to make sure that we have not transgressed any laws.'

Sister Étromma glanced at Fidelma with wide-eyed surprise and then turned back to the abbess with a swift jerk of her head.

'I shall see to it, Mother Abbess,' she muttered. Then, after a moment's pause, she added: 'It is unusual, isn't it? The Saxon has already been judged.'

'You will see to it, Sister Étromma,' snapped the abbess, 'for she bears an authority from Fianamail which, it seems, we are obliged to obey.'

The little stewardess lowered her head. '*Fiat voluntas tua*, Mother Abbess.'

'I will doubtless see you later, Sister Fidelma; perhaps in the chapel for devotions?'

Fidelma inclined her head to the abbess but ignored the question.

Sister Étromma hastened from the room before her. Outside the abbess's chamber the stewardess seemed to relax visibly.

'How may I serve you, Sister Fidelma?' she asked in a less breathless voice than the one she used to address her superior.

'I would like to see Brother Eadulf immediately.'

Sister Étromma's eyes widened. 'The Saxon? You want to see him?'

'Is there a problem? The abbess has said that I am to be given all assistance.'

'Of course.' Sister Étromma looked confused. 'I was not thinking. Come, I will show you the way.'

'Have you been stewardess here long?' asked Fidelma as the religieuse began to lead her through the gloomy vaulted corridors of the abbey.

'I have been *rechtaire* here for ten years. I came to this abbey when I was a child, along with my brother.'

'Ten years as *rechtaire*,' Fidelma reflected. 'That is a goodly time. Have you known Abbess Fainder long? I know she has but recently returned from Rome, but did you know her before she went there?'

'When she came to the abbey three months ago,' Sister Étromma said, 'she was a stranger to most of us here. Noé was our abbot before her. We are a mixed house, you see. Like Kildare.'

Fidelma smiled a brief acknowledgement.

'I know. Why did Abbot Noé decide to resign as abbot here?'

'It was the King himself who required Noé to be his spiritual adviser, or so we were told. He still has chambers in the abbey but stays mainly in the King's palace. The running of the abbey has passed to Fainder who was then appointed as our abbess.'

Did Fidelma detect a slight bitterness in her tone?

'Why was Fainder appointed if she was not formerly of this community?'

Sister Étromma did not reply.

'As *rechtaire* at the abbey for ten years it might be considered that you had a better claim to the office?' Fidelma pressed.

'She was a protégée of Abbot Noé in Rome.'

'I did not know that Noé had ever been a religious in Rome.'

'He only went there on a pilgrimage and did not remain for any length of time. He met the abbess there, I believe, and brought her back to be his successor. It was when he returned that he announced his retirement from the abbey.'

'That is unusual,' remarked Fidelma. Then she realised another possibility. 'Is Fainder related to Noé, perhaps?'

Nepotism was not unknown in the religious houses and often abbots and abbesses and even bishops took office following the same successional system as kings and their nobles. As well as being of blood descent they were elected by their *derbhfine* which usually comprised three generations of the family descending from a common great-grandfather. Often sons, grandsons, nephews and cousins, were appointed to be abbots in place of a previous abbot or abbess in much the same way as kings were appointed or other chiefly heads.

When Étromma did not respond, Fidelma posed another question.

'Are you happy with the way the abbess runs this community? I mean, are you happy with Fainder's commitment to govern by the Penitentials and the Roman form of administration? I am surprised that Abbot Noé blessed this new departure for I always thought that he was an adherent of the Rule of Colmcille.'

Sister Étromma halted a moment, causing Fidelma to halt also, and the stewardess looked round as if in search of eavesdroppers before replying.

'Sister,' she dropped her voice to a whisper, 'it is wise not to mention such conflicts in this place. The differences between the Irish Church and that of Rome are not a subject for discussion here. Since Fainder has become our abbess she has grown powerful and rich. It does not do to voice criticism.'

'Rich?' queried Fidelma.

Sister Étromma shrugged. 'The abbess does not dismiss material wealth, even though she expounds the austerity of the Penitentials to others. She seems to have acquired much wealth since her arrival. Perhaps one should look towards the rich and powerful who patronise her. But it is not for me to voice criticism.'

It was clear to Fidelma that the stewardess was resentful of the abbess.

However, Fidelma did not wish to pursue the matter of sister Étromma's prejudices. She was more concerned about hearing how Eadulf was faring.

Sister Étromma moved quickly on along the corridor.

'Do you know what happened concerning Brother Eadulf?' Fidelma allowed a short silence before raising the subject.

'He is to be executed tomorrow.'

'I mean the facts leading to his trial.'

'I know that when he first arrived here, he seemed pleasant enough and spoke our language well.'

'So you met him when he arrive here?'

'Am I not the *rechtaire* of the abbey? It is my duty to greet all travellers, especially those wishing for hospitality within our walls.'

'So when did he arrived here?'

'About three weeks ago. He came to the gate and asked for a night's lodging. He said that he was planning to take a boat downriver to Loch Garman. He was going to look for a ship to take him back to the land of the Saxons. There are plenty of Saxon ships putting into Loch Garman these days.'

'So what happened?'

'There is little I know. He arrived late one afternoon, as I say, and I gave him a bed in the guests' hostel. He attended devotions and ate a meal. During that night I was awakened by the abbess. It seemed that the body of a young novitiate had been found on the quay outside the abbey. The girl had been discovered by a captain of the watch. There is frequent theft from the boats that tie up there. A lot of trade passes through the township. That's why a permanent watch is employed on the quays.

'It seems that the young girl had been assaulted and then strangled. An alarm was raised. I was asked by the abbess to lead the way to where the Saxon was sleeping.'

Fidelma frowned. 'Why the Saxon? What made the abbess single him out?'

Sister Étromma was dispassionate. 'Simple enough. He was identified.'

'Identified? By whom and how?' Fidelma tried not to show her dismay.

'The captain of the watch had informed the abbess that the Saxon was responsible. I led the abbess, the captain of the watch and some others into the guests' hostel. The Saxon was in bed, pretending to be asleep. When he was forced from the bed he was found with blood on him and a torn piece of the dead novitiate's robe.'

Fidelma suppressed a groan. This was becoming worse than she had imagined.

'That's bad enough, but you have not told me how he was identified.

I am puzzled to know how the captain of the watch was able to claim the Saxon was responsible when, as you tell me, he was not caught on the spot but was asleep in his bed in the guests' hostel. What is the name of this captain, by the way? I shall want to see him.'

'His name is Mel.'

Fidelma's eyes widened at the information.

'The same Mel who is commander of the guard at the palace of Fianamail? The brother of Lassar, the innkeeper at the Inn of the Yellow Mountain?'

Sister Étromma looked surprised. 'You know of him then?'

'I am staying at the Inn of the Yellow Mountain.'

'His success in capturing the Saxon caused the King to appoint him one of his commanders. He used to be a captain of the watch on the quays.'

'A good promotion then,' Fidelma commented drily.

'Fianamail can be generous to those who serve him well,' agreed the stewardess. Did Fidelma detect a slight note of cynicism in her voice?

'Let me ask the question again; what led the captain of the watch so unerringly to the bed of Brother Eadulf, who just happened to have the incriminating evidence still on him?'

Sister Étromma grimaced. 'It was reported that a religieux had been seen running from the quay to the abbey just before the body was discovered.'

'How many religieux does the abbey of Fearna hold? One hundred? Two hundred?' Fidelma could not keep the note of scepticism from her voice.

'Closer to two hundred, Sister,' agreed Sister Étromma evenly.

'Two hundred? Yet the trail led straight to the Saxon. It seems a fine piece of detection on the part of the captain of the watch.'

'Not really. Were you not told?'

Fidelma steeled herself for another revelation. 'There are many things that I have not been told. To what do you now refer exactly?'

'Why, there was a witness to the actual attack.'

Fidelma was silent for a moment or two. 'A witness?' she asked slowly. 'An eye-witness to the rape and murder?'

'Indeed. There was another novitiate who was down on the quay with the one who was killed.'

'Are you saying,' Fidelma said, 'that this novitiate ... what is her name?'

'The girl who was witness?'

'Yes.'

'Fial.'

'And the name of the girl who was killed?'

'Gormgilla.'

'Are you saying, then, that Fial actually saw the rape and murder of her friend Gormgilla and identified Brother Eadulf as the man responsible?'

'She did.'

'And she clearly identified the attacker? There was no doubt as to who she identified?'

'She was absolutely clear. It was the Saxon.'

Fidelma felt an overwhelming sense of despair. Until now she had been thinking that this matter must be some silly mistake. Even when she heard the extent of the charges against Eadulf, of rape and murder, especially of a young girl of twelve – a girl under the age of choice – she had not changed her mind for she had an implicit belief in Eadulf. It was just not in his character to do such a thing. It had to be a silly mistake in identification or wrong interpretation.

Now she was confronted with overwhelming evidence. Not just the physical evidence of bloodstains and torn clothing but, above everything, the evidence of an eye-witness. The case against Eadulf now appeared devastating. What would Barrán, the Chief Brehon, say when he came to Fearna at her demand only to find that she had no case to offer him? Could it be, in spite of her faith in him, that Eadulf was guilty after all? No! Surely she knew Eadulf too well?

Sister Étromma took her through an arched door into a large quadrangle. Following, Fidelma caught sight of a wooden platform. She did not need to ask what the gruesome apparatus was. The body of a young monk hung inert from the rope suspended from the gibbet. There was no one about.

For one awesome moment, during which her blood seemed to turn to ice, Fidelma thought that the body was that of Eadulf; that, in spite of the assurances she had been given, she was too late. She halted abruptly and stared, her senses numb.

Sister Étromma, seeing that she was not following, stopped and turned back. She wore an unhappy expression and did her best to avoid looking at the corpse.

'Who is that?' demanded Fidelma, having registered that the corpse wore the tonsure of St John and not the tonsure of St Peter as Eadulf did.

'That was Brother Ibar,' the stewardess replied quietly.

'For what reason has he been executed?'

'Murder and theft.'

Fidelma's mouth compressed for a moment. 'Is this punishment by the Penitentials going to be the fashion now in this abbey?' she asked bitterly. 'Do you know the details of his crime?'

'I attended the trial, Sister. The entire community were ordered to do so by Abbess Fainder. It was the first trial that led to execution under the new Penitential laws and he was a member of our community.'

'You spoke of murder and theft?'

'Brother Ibar was found guilty of killing a boatman and robbing him down on the abbey quay.'

'When was this?'

'A few weeks ago.'

Fidelma was studying the gently swinging corpse.

'There seems much death on the abbey quay,' she reflected. An idea occurred to her. 'You say that Ibar killed a boatman on the quay and robbed him a few weeks ago? Was it before or after the crime of which Brother Eadulf was accused?'

'Oh, after. The very day after.'

'Unusual, isn't it? Two murders on the same small quay within two days and now two Brothers of the Faith condemned to die, one dead already.'

Sister Étromma frowned. 'But there was no connection between the two events.'

Fidelma gestured distastefully towards the corpse.

'How long does he have to hang there?'

'Until sunset. Then he will be cut down and taken out to be buried in unconsecrated ground.'

'How well did you know him?'

'Not well. He was a newcomer to the community. I believe he came from Rathdangan, to the north of here. He was a blacksmith by trade. He worked in that capacity in the community.'

'Why did he kill the boatman and rob him?'

'It was judged that he was spurred on by greed. It was a purse of gold coin and a gold chain that he took, having stabbed the man.'

'Why would a blacksmith who works in this abbey need money? A blacksmith is respected enough that he can name his own price for his art. Why, his honour price is ten *seds*; the equivalent of an *aire-echta*, a Brehon of lower qualification.'

Sister Étromma shrugged expressively. 'The air is chill here, Sister,' she said. 'Let us move on.'

Fidelma turned after her and they continued across the quadrangle, with the buildings towering on all sides, and through another small door. Sister Étromma went up the stone steps which rose two storeys to an upper floor. The building was dank and musty. Fidelma felt an overwhelming sense of despondency. The gloom and foreboding which hung depressingly about the place in no way gave her a sense that she was in the house of a community devoted to the Christian life. There was an atmosphere of impending menace which she found hard to explain.

Sister Étromma led her along the dingy corridor, after she had allowed Fidelma time to pause and let her eyes grow accustomed to the gloom. Along this corridor stood a small oak door with iron bolts.

A huge shadow suddenly appeared in the darkness from the end of the corridor.

'Who is it?' demanded a guttural voice. 'Is it you, Étromma?'

'It is,' replied the stewardess. 'This is Sister Fidelma, a *dálaigh* who has permission from the abbess to question the prisoner.'

Fidelma caught a smell of onions on the breath of the burly figure as he came forward and peered closely at her.

'Very well,' came the harsh tones. 'If it is all right with Étromma, you may enter.' The figure seemed to recede back into the darkness.

'Who was that?' whispered Fidelma, slightly awed by the size of the guard.

'That was my Brother Cett who now acts as gaoler,' replied Étromma.

'*Your* Brother Cett?' Fidelma asked, wondering about the prefix 'my'.

Sister Étromma's voice was distant. 'Both brother in flesh as well as in Christ. Poor soul, my brother is a simple man. We were caught in a raid by the Uí Néill when we were children and he received a wound to the head so that now he only does menial tasks, and those involving the need for strength.'

Sister Étromma withdrew the iron bolts from the cell door.

'Call me when you are ready to leave. Brother Cett or I will be in earshot.'

She drew open the door and Fidelma entered the cell beyond, standing for a moment blinking in the beam of light which came through the barred window in the opposite wall.

A startled voice exclaimed: 'Fidelma! Is it really you?'

Chapter Five

As the door swung shut behind her, and the bolts rasped in their sockets, Fidelma stepped to the centre of the small room and held out her hands to the young man who rose swiftly from the stool on which he had been sitting. Brother Eadulf took her hands in his and for a moment the two stood gazing at each other; no words passed between them but their eyes met and spoke silently of their concern and anxieties for each other.

Eadulf looked haggard. He had not been allowed to shave regularly and, as a result, a stubble covered his cheeks and jowl. His brown curly hair was untidy and matted and his clothing was dirty and rank. Eadulf saw her expression of dismay at his condition and he grinned in apology.

'I am afraid that the hospitality in this place has not been of the best, Fidelma. The good abbess does not believe in wasting soap and water on one who is not destined to stay long in this vale of tears.' He paused. 'But I am so glad to see you once again before I depart.'

Fidelma made a sound, inarticulate, it could even have been a small sob. Then she grimaced, making the contortion of her features an attempt to disguise her feelings.

'Are you well otherwise, Eadulf? You have not been ill-treated?'

'Roughly handled . . . at first,' confessed Eadulf lightly. 'Emotions can run high, due to the nature of the crime of which I am accused. It was a young girl who was raped and killed. But how are *you*, Fidelma? I thought you were on a pilgrimage to Iberia? To the Tomb of St James?'

Fidelma made a small dismissive gesture with her hand.

'I returned as soon as I heard the news. I hurried here to be your counsel.'

Eadulf smiled brightly for a moment and then he grew serious again.

'Have they not told you that it is all over? The so-called trial did not last long and tomorrow I have an appointment in the quadrangle down there,' he jerked his head to the window. 'Did you see the gibbet?'

'I have been told.' Fidelma glanced round and chose to sit on the stool which Eadulf had vacated.

Eadulf took his seat on the bed. 'I forget my manners in this place, Fidelma. I should have invited you to sit.' He tried to sound humorous but his voice was hollow and flat.

Fidelma sat back, hands clasped in her lap, and gazed inquisitively at Eadulf.

'Did you do this thing that they accuse you of?' she asked abruptly.

Eadulf's gaze did not falter.

'*Deus miseratur*, I did not! You have my word on that, though I am afraid my word does not count in this matter.'

Fidelma nodded slightly. If Eadulf gave his word then she accepted it.

'Tell me your story. I left you at Cashel when I went to take the pilgrim ship for Iberia. Take up your story from there.'

Eadulf was silent for a moment, gathering his thoughts.

'My story is not complicated. I decided to accept your advice and return to Canterbury, to Archbishop Theodore. I have been away for a year now. There was nothing to stay in Cashel for, anyway.'

He paused but Fidelma, though she shifted her position slightly on her stool, did not comment.

'Your brother had messages for me to take to Theodore and to the Saxon kings.'

'Verbally or in writing?' queried Fidelma.

'One message, to Theodore, was in writing. The other messages, to the kings, were verbal ones, mere salutations and expressions of friendship.'

'Where is the written message now?'

'My personal belongings were confiscated by the abbess.'

Fidelma thought for a moment. 'Did you have anything to identify you as a *techtaire*?'

Eadulf knew the word and smiled.

'He gave me a white wand of office. Now that I think of it, I believe I removed that and the written letter from my travelling bag and hid them for safekeeping under the bed in the guests' room.'

'So that they would have been removed by now and put with your other belongings?'

'I expect so. Your brother offered me the loan of a good horse. However, not knowing when and how I could return that kindness, I took the offer of a place on the wagon of a merchant who was travelling here to trade. I knew that I could get a passage in a boat going downriver where I could expect to find a Saxon merchant ship on which to get passage home. The journey to this place was without incident.'

He paused for a moment as though to put the events in sequence before recounting them.

'I arrived at the abbey in the late afternoon and, naturally, I came asking for hospitality for the night, thinking to find a boat the next morning. I spoke to the *rechtaire*, Sister Étromma, who asked me my business. I told her that I was on my way back to Canterbury. I did not think it worth mentioning that I was bearing messages to the archbishop. She offered me a bed in the guests' dormitory. There was no one else staying that night. I attended devotions, had a meal and went to bed. Oh, and Sister Étromma introduced me to Abbess Fainder . . . but the abbess seemed preoccupied, or else she does not like Saxons. She more or less ignored me.'

'What then?'

'I was in a deep sleep. It must have been early morning, perhaps an hour before dawn, when I found myself being dragged out of bed. There was shouting all around me and I was punched and pummelled. I did not know what was happening. I was dragged here and thrown in a cell . . .'

Fidelma leaned forward with interest.

'Did anyone explain to you what was happening? Did anyone accuse you of anything or say why you were being dragged from your bed at such an hour?'

'No one said anything except to scream abuse at me.'

'When did you first know what you were being accused of?'

'Not for a long time. I would say that it was about midday when that giant, Brother Cett, came into this cell. I demanded to be told what was going on, but almost immediately, Abbess Fainder entered with a young girl. The girl was dressed in the robe of a novitiate although she seemed very young.'

'What then?'

'The girl simply pointed at me. Nothing was said and then she was led from the cell.'

'She did not say anything? Anything at all?' pressed Fidelma.

'She just pointed at me,' repeated Eadulf. 'Then the abbess took her away. Nothing was said at any time and Brother Cett withdrew and locked the door.'

'When were you actually informed of the crime of which you were being accused?'

'It was not until two days later that I was told.'

'You were left here for two days without anyone telling you anything?' Fidelma's tone rose angrily.

Eadulf grinned ruefully. 'And without food and water,' he added. 'I told you that the hospitality of this abbey was not of the best.'

Fidelma stared at him in consternation. 'What?'

'It was two days later that Brother Cett came in again and allowed me to wash and eat something. An hour afterwards, a tall man, cadaverous-looking with a brittle voice, came and told me he was the King's Brehon.'

'Bishop Forbassach!'

'Indeed, Bishop Forbassach was his name. Do you know him?'

'He is an old adversary. But go on.'

'It was this same Forbasssach who told me that I was accused of raping a young novitiate of the abbey and then strangling her. I was speechless. I told him that I had come to the abbey for food and a bed for the night. That I had been awakened and assaulted and thrown in this cell for two days.

'He told me that I had been found in bed with blood on my clothes and a piece of the novitiate's torn and bloody robe.' He pursed his lips. 'I thought I was being clever for I said, sarcastically, to the bishop, that I thought he had said the girl had been strangled, so if I had been found with blood all over me it was miraculous. It was then that the bishop told me where the blood had come from. The novitiate was a twelve-year-old virgin. As the final blow, the bishop informed me that there was an eye-witness to my attack.'

'I am afraid it is pretty damning evidence, Eadulf,' Fidelma said. 'Do you have any explanation as to how it was come by?'

Eadulf lowered his head. 'None. I thought I was having a bad dream,' he muttered.

'Was it true that there was blood on your clothes?'

Eadulf held out his hand. She could see dark stains on it.

'I noticed the blood on my robe soon after I was thrown in here. I thought it was simply my own blood, having been punched and kicked by those who dragged me here. I did have a cut on the face.'

Fidelma could see a small, healing scar. 'What of the piece of torn robe?'

Eadulf shrugged. 'That I knew nothing about until a piece of cloth was presented at the formal hearing. I had no knowledge of it.'

'And the eye-witness?'

'The young girl? She was either lying or mistaken.'

'Had you seen her before? Before she accused you, that is?'

'I don't think so. I presumed that it was the same young girl who was shown into the cell and pointed to me. I must admit that I was not very alert after my beating. She appeared at the trial and was called Fial.'

'You say that you attended devotions and a meal before going to bed? Did you see this girl, Fial, at that time?'

'Not to my knowledge, though she might have seen me. The strange thing is that I could not remember any young novitiates at all in the chapel; at least, not as young as she was. Fial was no more than twelve or thirteen years old.'

'Did you talk with anyone at all, apart from the stewardess and the abbess?'

'I did talk a short while to a young Brother. His name was Ibar.'

Fidelma raised her head sharply. '*Ibar?*' She glanced automatically towards the window, thinking of the body of the hanging monk.

'They say he killed a boatman the day after I was supposed to have killed the young girl,' confirmed Eadulf. 'They hanged him this morning.' He suddenly shivered. 'There is something vile here, Fidelma. I think you should leave immediately lest anything happens to you. I could not bear to think . . .'

Fidelma reached forward and laid her hand on his arm reassuringly.

'Whatever evil it is, Eadulf, they would not dare to harm me for fear that it might bring down a retribution they are unable to contend with. Whoever "they" are. Have no fear for my safety. Besides, I have a couple of my brother's warriors with me.'

Eadulf shook his head stubbornly. 'Even so, Fidelma, there is little assurance of safety in this place of darkness. Some evil stalks this abbey and I would rather you abandon me and go back to Cashel for your own safety.'

Fidelma's jaw came up dangerously. 'No more talk like that, Eadulf. Here I am and here I stay until we have sorted this matter out. Now, concentrate. Tell me about your trial.'

'Time passed; I lost count of it. Brother Cett fed me irregularly and allowed me to wash when it took his fancy. He likes inflicting hardship, that one. An evil man. Have a care of him.'

'I was told that he is somewhat simple.'

Eadulf grinned crookedly. 'Simple? Yes. He obeys orders and cannot understand anything complicated. But when he is told to inflict pain, he enjoys it. He was the executioner for . . .' Eadulf spread a hand towards the window leaving it to Fidelma to assume the rest.

She wrinkled her nose in repugnance. 'A member of the religious as an executioner? God have mercy on his misguided soul. But you were about to tell me of the trial.'

'I was taken down to the chapel and Bishop Forbassach sat in judgment with Abbess Fainder. They were joined by a man who looked as grim and stony-faced as Forbassach. He was an abbot.'

'Abbot Noé?'

Eadulf nodded affirmatively. 'Do you know him as well?'

'Both Bishop Forbassach and Abbot Noé are my antagonists of old.'

'Bishop Forbassach repeated the charges: I denied them. Forbassach said it would go hard with me as I was wasting the time of the court. I denied them again; what else could I do but speak the truth?' Eadulf was silent a moment, contemplating. 'Sister Étromma was called as a witness. She told how she had welcomed me to the abbey. Then she identified the body of the murdered girl as one Gormgilla, who was entering the abbey as a novitiate . . .'

Fidelma interrupted him sharply.

'Just a moment, Eadulf. What were her exact words? About Gormgilla, I mean.'

'She said that Gormgilla was a novitiate . . .'

'That is not what you said. You said "who was entering the abbey". Why did you use that form?'

Eadulf shrugged diffidently. 'I think that was the way she said it. What does it matter?'

'It matters a lot. But continue.'

'That was all Sister Étromma had to say, apart from the fact that this Gormgilla was but twelve years old. Then the other girl was called . . .'

'The other girl?'

'The one who had entered my cell and pointed at me.'

'Ah yes, Fial.'

'She identified herself to the court as a novitiate in the abbey. She said that she had been a friend of Gormgilla. She also said that she had arranged to meet her on the quay just after midnight.'

'Why?'

Eadulf stared blankly at Fidelma. 'Why?' he echoed.

'Was she asked why she was going to meet a young novitiate on the quay after midnight? We are speaking of twelve-year-olds here, Eadulf.'

'No one asked her. She simply said that she went to the quay and saw her friend struggling with a man.'

'How did she see?'

Eadulf looked bewildered; Fidelma was patient.

'It was after midnight,' she explained. 'One presumes that it was dark. How could she see all this?'

'I presume that the quay is lit with torchlight.'

'Was this checked? And could the features of a man's face be seen clearly by torchlight? Was she asked how close she was and where the light was situated?'

'Nothing was said. All she told the court was that she had seen her friend struggling with a man.'

'Struggling?'

'She said that the man was strangling her friend,' he went on. 'The man rose from her body and ran for the abbey. She then identified me as that man. She said she had recognised the man as the Saxon stranger staying at the abbey.'

Fidelma frowned again. 'She used the words "Saxon stranger"?'

'Yes.'

'And you claim that you had not seen her before? That you had not spoken to her?'

'That is so.'

'How did she know that you were a Saxon then?'

'I suppose that she must have been told.'

'Exactly. What else was she told?'

Eadulf looked at her mournfully. 'A pity that you were not at the trial.'

'Maybe not. You have not mentioned who represented your legal interests at the trial.'

'No one.'

'*What?*' The word exploded from her in anger. 'You did not have the services of a *dálaigh*? Were you offered such services?'

'I was just taken into the court. I was not given the opportunity to ask for some legal representative.'

Fidelma's face was beginning to take on an expression of hope for the first time.

'There are many things wrong here, Eadulf. Are you sure that Bishop Forbassach did not ask if you wished to be represented or if you would represent yourself?'

'I am sure.'

'What other evidence was offered against you?'

'A Brother Miach gave evidence. I understand he is the physician here. He came forward to give details of how the girl had been sexually assaulted and strangled. Then I was asked if I still denied the matter and I said I did. It was then that Forbassach said that the matter was being judged under the ecclesiastical code and not the laws of the Brehons of Éireann. I was to be hanged. The sentence would be referred to the King himself to confirm. A few days ago the King's confirmation came and so, tomorrow, I am to meet Brother Cett on that platform down there.'

'Not if there is justice, Eadulf,' replied Fidelma firmly. 'There are too many questions to be asked based on what you have told me.'

Eadulf pursed his lips ruefully. 'Perhaps it is a little late to ask them now, Fidelma?'

'Not so. I will put forward an appeal.'

To her surprise Eadulf shook his head.

'You don't know the abbess. She has great influence over Bishop Forbassach. People here walk in fear of her.'

Fidelma looked interested. 'How do you know this?'

'Having been incarcerated in here for some weeks, I have become attuned to that communication I do possess. Even that unspeakable Brother Cett can supply me with information in his monosyllabic way. If this abbey is a spider's web, then the abbess sits at its centre like a hungry black spider.'

Fidelma smiled, for it seemed an apt description of Abbess Fainder.

She rose slowly to her feet and glanced about the cell. It contained nothing apart from a stool and a cot with a straw mattress and a blanket. The only clothes Eadulf had were those which he was wearing.

'You said that the abbess must have your travelling bag and the wand and letter from Colgú to Theodore?'

'If they have not been left under the bed in the guests' hostel.'

Fidelma turned to the door and banged upon it, calling for Sister Étromma. She turned her head to Eadulf and smiled encouragement.

'Have hope, Eadulf. I will seek out the truth here and try to find justice.'

'You have my support in that but I have come to expect nothing in this place.'

It was the burly, sinister Brother Cett who opened the door and stood aside to let Fidelma pass into the dark corridor beyond. He slammed the cell door shut and threw the bolts.

'Where is Sister Étromma?' demanded Fidelma.

The big man did not answer but simply raised his hand to point along the corridor.

Fidelma followed his directions and found Sister Étromma waiting in a seated recess by a window at the head of the stairway. The window gave a view of the river beyond. Boats were moving on it. It seemed a busy stretch of waterway. So intent was Sister Étromma on examining this vista that Fidelma had to cough to attract her attention.

She turned and came to her feet at once.

'Your talk with the Saxon was satisfactory?' the stewardess of the abbey asked brightly.

'Satisfactory? Hardly. There is much that is *un*satisfactory about the proceedings. I hear that you were a witness at the trial?'

Sister Étromma's features became defensive. 'I was.'

'I heard that you also identified the victim, Gormgilla. I had not realised that you knew her.'

'I did not.'

Fidelma was perplexed. 'Then how did you identify her?'

'I told you before, she was a young novitiate in the abbey.'

'Indeed. So am I to presume that you, as *rechtaire* of the abbey, greeted her among the novitiates when she arrived at this abbey? When did she join this community?'

There was a look of uncertainty on Sister Étromma's face.

'I am not sure exactly . . .'

'It is exactness that I am seeking, Sister,' Fidelma snapped waspishly. 'Tell me, *exactly*, when you first met the dead girl, Gormgilla.'

'I . . . I only saw her after her body was brought to the abbey mortuary,' the *rechtaire* confessed.

Fidelma stared at her for a moment in astonishment. Then she shook her head. Perhaps she should grow used to being astonished in this case.

'You saw her for the first time only *after* she was dead? Then how could you identify her as a novitiate at the abbey?'

'I was told that she was by the abbess.'

'But you had no right to identify her in evidence before a court if you did not personally know her.'

'I would not doubt the word of the abbess. Besides, Fial said that she was her companion and came to the abbey with her to be a novitiate.'

Fidelma felt it pointless to lecture the *rechtaire* on the rules of being a witness.

'Your testimony is worthless in the court. Who did see this girl before her death? She surely did not simply appear in the abbey?'

Sister Étromma was defiant. 'The abbess told me and I tell you. Besides, the mistress of the novitiates greets all the newcomers and trains them. She would have seen the girl.'

'Ah. Now we are getting somewhere. Why didn't the mistress of the novitiates give evidence? Who is this woman and where do I find her?'

Sister Étromma hesitated. 'She has gone on a pilgrimage to Iona.'

Fidelma blinked. 'And when did she do that?'

'A day or so before the murder of Gormgilla. Therefore it was natural that I, as stewardess of the abbey, came forward to give evidence. It was from the mistress of the novitiates that the abbess probably knew that the girl was one of her charges.'

'Except that your testimony in law is without any foundation. You are only repeating what you have been told, not what you know.' Fidelma was angry; angry that normal legal procedures seemed to have been totally disregarded. There were certainly enough discrepancies of legal practice to put forward an appeal.

'But Fial was also a novitiate and identified her friend,' protested Sister Étromma.

'Then we must find Sister Fial, for it seems her testimony is more than crucial to this entire affair. Let us do so now.'

'Very well.'

'Also I want to see the other witnesses to this matter. There is a Brother Miach, I believe?'

'The physician?'

'The same – but perhaps he, too, has gone on a pilgrimage?' she added sarcastically.

Sister Étromma did not react to the barb.

'His apothecary is on the floor below. I will leave you with him while I go to find Sister Fial.'

She turned and made her way down the steps, with Fidelma following.

Fidelma's mind was racing. Never in her years as a *dálaigh* had she encountered such flagrant breaches of legal procedures. She believed that she already had sufficient grounds on which to base an appeal to have the trial re-heard. She could scarcely believe that the Brehon of Laigin could have officiated over this farce. He surely knew the rules of evidence.

Obviously, the main problem was the eye-witness testimony of the young novitiate, Fial. That would be the main obstacle in any move to seek an acquittal for Eadulf. Her eye-witness evidence was disastrous for Eadulf. Yet the saga of events sounded bizarre.

There were many questions she must ask Fial. Why had she and her friend arranged to meet on the quay in the middle of the night? And, in the darkness of that night, how could she have seen the features of the killer of her friend so clearly that she could identify him? Who told her that he was a Saxon stranger? If one accepted Eadulf's word, he had neither seen nor spoken to Fial before. Had he been pointed out to her? If so, by whom?

Fidelma sighed deeply, knowing that while she might pick at points and challenge the legal procedures, the main facts remained. Eadulf had been identified by an eye-witness. He had been found with his robe bloody and with a torn piece of the girl's clothing on him. How could she refute that evidence?

The apothecary was a large, stone room with wooden doors and shuttered windows which opened onto a herb garden. Dried herbs and flowers hung in bunches from wooden rafters and a fire burnt in a hearth at one end of the room, above which a large black iron cauldron hung. In it steamed a noxious-smelling brew. Jars and boxes were stacked along the surrounding shelves.

An elderly man turned as Sister Étromma entered. He was slightly stooped, his grey-white hair merging with a flowing beard. His eyes were light grey and had a cold, dead quality.

'Well?' His tone was high-pitched and querulous.

'This is Sister Fidelma from Cashel, Brother Miach,' Sister Étromma announced. 'She needs to ask you some questions.' She spoke to Fidelma. 'I will leave you here while I find Sister Fial.'

Fidelma found the elderly physician glaring suspiciously at her.

'What do you want?' he snapped. 'I am very busy.'

'I will not keep you long from you work, Brother Miach,' she assured him.

He sniffed disdainfully. 'Then state your business.'

'My business is as a *dálaigh*, an advocate of the courts.'

The man's eyes narrowed a fraction. 'And what is that to do with me?'

'I want to ask you some questions about the trial of Brother Eadulf.'

'The Saxon? What of it? I hear that they are hanging him, if they have not done so already.'

'They have not hanged him yet,' Fidelma assured him.

'Ask your questions then.' The old man was impatient and temperamental.

'I understand that you gave evidence at the trial?'

'Of course. I am the physician of this abbey. If there is a suspicious death then I am asked for my opinion.'

'Tell me, then, of your evidence.'

'The matter is over and done with.'

Fidelma replied harshly: '*I* will say when it is over and done with, Brother Miach. You will answer my questions.'

The old man blinked rapidly, apparently unused to being spoken to in such tones.

'They brought me the body of a young girl to examine. I told the Brehon what I had found.'

'And that was?'

'The girl was dead. There were bruises around her neck. Clearly she had been strangled. Moreover, there were obvious indications that she had been raped beforehand.'

'And how did those obvious indications manifest themselves?'

'The girl had been a virgin. Not surprising. She was only twelve, so I am told. The sexual intercourse had caused her to bleed extensively. It needed no great medical knowledge to see the blood.'

'So there was blood on her robe?'

'There was and around the area where you would expect to find it in the circumstances. There is no doubt as to what happened.'

'No doubt? You say it was rape. Could it have been otherwise?'

'My dear . . . *dálaigh*,' the old physician was pitying in his tone. 'Use some imagination. A young girl is strangled after having intercourse; does it seem likely that it could be anything else but rape?'

'It is still more of an opinion than true medical evidence,' Fidelma said. The old physician did not reply and so she passed to her next question. 'Did you know the child?'

'Gormgilla was her name.'

'How did you know that?'

'Because I was told.'

'But you had never seen her in the abbey before she was brought to you in death?'

'I would not have seen her unless she had been ill. I think it was Sister Étromma who told me her name. Come to think of it, I would have been seeing her sooner rather than later, had she not been killed.'

'What makes you say that?'

'I think she was one of those religieuses who like to punish themselves for what they think are their sins. I noticed that she had sores around both wrists and around one ankle.'

'Sores?'

'Signs that she had used bonds on herself.'

'Bonds? Not connected with her rape and murder?'

'The sores had come from the use of constraints which she had obviously worn some time prior to her death. The sores had nothing to do with her other injuries.'

'Were there signs also of flagellation?'

The physician shook his head. 'Some of these ascetic masochists simply use bonds to expiate the pain of what they deem as sins.'

'Did you not find that this masochism, as you define it, was strange in one so young?'

Brother Miach was indifferent. 'I have seen worse cases. Religious fanaticism often leads to shocking self-abuse.'

'Did you also examine Brother Eadulf?'

'Brother Eadulf? Oh, the Saxon, you mean. Why would I do that?'

'I am told that he was found with blood on him and in possession of a piece of the girl's torn robe. Perhaps it would have been appropriate to have examined him to show whether there was any consistency in his appearance with the idea that he had carried out an attack on the girl.'

The physician sniffed again. 'From what I hear, it needed no words of mine to convict him. As you say, he had blood on him and a piece of the girl's bloodstained robe. He was also identified by someone who saw him do the killing. What need for me to examine him?'

Fidelma restrained a sigh. 'It would have been . . . appropriate.'

'Appropriate? Pah! If I spent my life doing what was appropriate, I would have let a hundred suffering patients die.'

'With respect, that is hardly a comparison.'

'I am not here to argue ethics with you, *dálaigh*. If you have done with your questions then I have work to do.'

Fidelma ended the interview with a brief word of thanks and left the room. There was nothing else to pursue with the physician. There was no sign of Sister Étromma returning. She waited outside the apothecary for several minutes before a thought came to her. One of the gifts Fidelma possessed was an almost uncanny ability to find her way in any place once she had been there before. She knew by means of retained memory and instinct just how to find her way back to the places in the abbey through which she had been led. So instead of continuing to wait for Sister Étromma, she turned along the passageways and began to retrace her steps towards the chamber of Abbess Fainder.

She opened the door onto the silent courtyard of the abbey and crossed it slowly. The body of the monk was still hanging from the wooden gibbet. What was his name – Brother Ibar? Strange that he should have murdered a boatman and robbed him on the same quay just a day after the rape and death of Gormgilla.

She suddenly halted in the middle of the courtyard's quadrangle.

This was one of the two people in the abbey to whom Eadulf had spoken at any great length on the evening that he had arrived.

She turned back and rapidly made her way up the stairs to the dank corridor which led to Eadulf's cell. Brother Cett had gone; another religieux was standing guard in his place.

'What do you want?' he muttered rudely, emerging from the gloom.

'Firstly, I would like to see you use better manners, Brother,' Fidelma replied curtly. 'Secondly, I would like you to open the door to this cell for me. I have authority from the abbess.'

The figure took a step back in the gloom as if in surprise.

'I have no orders . . .' came his sullen tone.

'I am giving you the orders, Brother. I am a *dálaigh*. Brother Cett had no problem when I came here earlier with Sister Étromma.'

'Sister Étromma? She said nothing to me. She and Cett have gone down to the quay.'

The religieux considered the matter while Fidelma fretted impatiently for several long seconds. She thought that she would be met with a stubborn refusal. Then, almost reluctantly, he moved forward and threw the bolts back.

'I will call you when I am ready to leave,' Fidelma told him in relief, entering the room.

Eadulf looked up in surprise.

'I did not expect to see you again so soon . . .' he began.

'I need to ask you a few more questions. I want to know more about this Brother Ibar. We may not have long as they don't know that I have come back to see you.'

Eadulf shrugged. 'Little enough to tell, Fidelma. He sat next to me in the refectory for the evening meal on the day that I arrived here. We spoke briefly there. I never saw him again – well, not until this morning, down here.' He nodded towards the courtyard.

'What conversation passed between you?'

Eadulf looked at her with a frown.

'He only asked me where I came from. I told him. He said he was from the north of this kingdom, a blacksmith by trade. He was proud of his trade although disappointed that the abbey couldn't make better use of his talents than to ask him to turn out constraints for the animals. He had been unhappy here since Abbess Fainder's arrival. I recall that I pointed out that many communities needed animals by which to feed themselves and every task was worthy of the labourer. He said . . .'

'You spoke of nothing else? You spoke only of such general matters?' Fidelma tried not to sound disappointed.

'Oh, he also asked me about some Saxon customs, that's all.'

'Saxon customs? Such as what?'

'Why Saxons kept slaves. A curious thing to ask, I thought.'

'Nothing else?'

Eadulf shook his head. 'He just seemed unhappy with the work that he was asked to do. He seemed preoccupied with it right to the end. In fact, the last thing I heard the poor fellow cry was "ask about the manacles". I think he had gone out of his mind by then. It's a terrible thing to face, is a hangman's rope . . .'

Fidelma was clearly disappointed and did not notice the falter in Eadulf's voice. She had hoped that the late Brother Ibar might have made some remark which would prove to be the thread that could unravel and disentangle this curious web. She forced a smile at Eadulf.

'No matter. I will see you again and soon.'

She banged on the door.

The surly Brother had been waiting outside, for the door immediately swung open and she was let out.

Chapter Six

Sister Fidelma was crossing the courtyard again when Sister Étromma caught up with her.

'I asked you to wait at the apothecary,' she admonished irritably. 'You might have become lost, for this abbey is no small country church.'

Fidelma did not bother to explain that she had a facility for remembering her way to and from a place once she had been shown. Neither did she mention that while the abbey was, indeed, large by comparison to many houses in the five kingdoms, she had seen greater abbey complexes at Armagh, at Whitby and in Rome.

'I was told that you had been called down to the quay,' she said.

The stewardess appeared to be taken aback. 'Who told you that?'

Fidelma did not want to confess that she had seen Eadulf again and so continued: 'I was on my way to find Abbess Fainder. 'I have a few more questions for her. Did you find the novitiate, Sister Fial?'

Sister Étromma looked uncomfortable for a moment.

'No, I have not been able to find her.'

'Why on earth not?' Fidelma was exasperated.

'No one appears to have seen her for some time.'

'Exactly how do you quantify *some* time?'

'I am told that she has not been seen for several days. We are still looking for her.'

Fidelma had a dangerous glint in her eye. 'Before we see the abbess, I would like you to show me the guest hostel – the place where Brother Eadulf slept.'

It did not take long for the stewardess to guide Fidelma to the hostel. The dormitory of the guests' quarter was not large; there were only half a dozen beds in it.

'Which bed did Brother Eadulf occupy?' asked Fidelma.

Sister Étromma pointed to the farthest placed bed in a corner of the room.

Fidelma went to it and sat on its edge. She gave a cursory glance underneath the bed. There was nothing there.

65

'Naturally it has been used several times since the Saxon was here,' the stewardess explained.

'Naturally. And has the mattress been changed?'

Sister Étromma appeared puzzled. 'The mattresses are changed as and when they need to be. I don't think that we have changed it since the Saxon slept here. Why?'

Fidelma pulled away the blankets to reveal the straw-filled mattress. It was the usual thin palliasse type. She reached forward tentatively and prodded it here and there.

'What are you looking for?' demanded the *rechtaire*.

Fidelma did not respond.

She had felt a slight hardness amidst the straw and her eyes detected the hole at the side of the mattress where the stitching had become undone. She smiled. She knew Eadulf better than he knew himself. He was a cautious man and the upheavals of the last weeks had caused him to forget just how cautious he had been.

Fidelma reached into the mattress and her slim fingers caught the small rod of wood. Next to it she felt the soft roll of vellum. She withdrew them swiftly and held them up to Sister Étromma's astonished gaze.

'You will bear me witness, Sister,' Fidelma said as she stood up. 'Here is the white wand of office which Brother Eadulf carried showing that he was an official messenger from the King of Cashel. Here is a letter in the hand of the same King, to Archbishop Theodore of Canterbury. Brother Eadulf had put them for safekeeping in the mattress.'

Sister Étromma's face bore a curious expression, of which uncertainty seemed predominant.

'These had best be taken to Abbess Fainder,' she said eventually.

Fidelma shook her head and deliberately placed them in her *marsupium*, the leather pouch she always wore at her waist.

'These will remain with me. You saw from where I retrieved them? You will be my witness. These plainly show that Brother Eadulf was a *fer taistil*, a *techtaire*, a king's messenger, and therefore part of the king's household with rights of protection.'

'It is no use telling me the law,' protested Sister Étromma. 'I am no *dálaigh*.'

'Just remember that you bear witness to my finding these items,' insisted Fidelma. 'And now . . .'

She began to move towards the door with Sister Étromma trailing unhappily in her wake.

'Where do you want to go now, Sister?' she asked. 'To see the abbess again?'

'The abbess? No, I will see her later,' replied Fidelma, changing her mind. 'Show me first where the girl Gormgilla was attacked and killed.'

Sister Étromma seemed troubled as she conducted Fidelma along more corridors to another tiny courtyard on the far side of the abbey which, from the aromas that permeated the air, Fidelma guessed to be an adjunct to the abbey kitchens and presumably to its storerooms. On one side of the small courtyard were two tall wooden gates and Sister Étromma went immediately to them. She did not attempt to move the great heavy iron bolts that secured them for there was, set in one of the large gates, a small door through which one person at a time might squeeze. She opened the door and pointed at it wordlessly.

When Fidelma had climbed through – for one had to step over the bottom of the door – she found herself facing the broad stretch of river. Immediately before the gates, running along the abbey walls, was a well-used track wide enough for wagons to pass along. Beside the track lay an earthen embankment from which a wooden quay had been constructed, for the river itself was parallel to the track at this point. Next to the quay, a sizable river boat was tied up. Several men were unloading barrels from it.

'This is our own quay, Sister,' Sister Étromma explained. 'Goods for the abbey are landed here. You will see, further along the river, other quays where the merchants of the town conduct their business.'

Fidelma stood for a moment, bathing her face in the sun. It was warm, in spite of the gentle breeze, and refreshing after the mustiness and gloom of the abbey building from which she had emerged. She closed her eyes momentarily and relaxed, breathing deeply. After a pause, she looked around her. The stewardess was right. Along the river there were several boats tied up to the quays. Fearna, she reminded herself, was the centre of trade as well as being the royal centre of the Uí Cheinnselaigh dynasty which ruled Laigin.

'Where was this murder committed?'

Sister Étromma pointed towards the abbey's quay. 'Just here.'

A bell began to toll in the abbey. Fidelma glanced towards the sound in surprise. It was surely not a call to prayer? A moment later, one of the religieux came running from the gates towards Sister Étromma.

'Sister, a messenger has arrived from upriver. One of the river boats has sunk in midstream. He thinks that it was the boat which just left the abbey quay.'

'Gabrán's boat?' Étromma had gone pale. 'Is he sure? Is everyone safe?'

'No, he is not sure, Sister,' replied the Brother. 'And he has no further knowledge.'

'Then we must go to see what can be done.'

She was turning for the abbey when she suddenly remembered that Sister Fidelma was standing looking on and she hesitated.

'Forgive me, Sister. It seems that one of the boats that regularly trades with the abbey might have sunk. As stewardess, it is my duty to attend to this matter. The river is a dangerous place.'

'Do you want me to come with you?' asked Fidelma.

Sister Étromma shook her head distractedly. 'I have to go.'

She joined the Brother who was already hurrying along the track by the abbey walls. Fidelma watched her leave, bemused by her departure. Then she was distracted by a male voice calling her by name. Fidelma turned to see a familiar figure strolling along the river bank towards the abbey quay.

It was the warrior, Mel, the very person who Sister Étromma said had found the body of the murdered girl and then tracked her death to Eadulf. It was a stroke of good fortune that he had appeared at this moment, saving her going in search of him. She turned towards him and walked slowly across the path to the edge of the quay as Mel climbed up onto the wooden boarding.

'We meet again, lady.' He greeted her with a broad smile as he halted before her.

'Indeed, that we do. I am told that your name is Mel.'

The warrior nodded pleasantly. 'I heard that you accepted my recommendation and that you and your companions are staying at my sister Lassar's inn. I thought there was a third man with you? Lassar tells me that only you and two others are staying there.'

Fidelma realised that the warrior's perception was acute and she had to be careful what she said.

'There were, indeed, three warriors with me. One had to return to Cashel,' she lied.

'Well, I trust that the accommodation is to your liking. My sister provides good food and comfortable beds.'

'My companions and I are indeed very comfortable at the Inn of the Yellow Mountain. But it is good to see you here.'

The warrior frowned slightly. 'Why so, lady?'

'I have just spoken with those at the abbey concerning the recent murder of the young novitiate,' replied Fidelma. 'They told me that you were a key witness at the trial of Brother Eadulf.'

The warrior gestured deprecatingly. 'I was not exactly a key witness. I was merely the captain of the watch on this very quay on the night that the killing took place.'

'Will you tell me exactly what happened? I presume that you know my interest in this matter?'

The warrior looked uncomfortable for a moment before nodding.

'Gossip travels swiftly in this town, lady. I know who you are and why you are here.'

'How did you happen to be on the quay that night?'

'That is simple enough. I was on watch, as I have said. There were four of us on duty here that night.' He waved his arm expansively to take in the entire collection of wooden quays which served the township of Fearna.

'Is there much crime here to justify such a watch?' enquired Fidelma.

Mel gave a boastful laugh.

'Not much crime at all – *because* of the watch. As the principal city of the Laigin kings, we are an important upriver trading post. It helps the traders rest easy that their boats and cargoes appear to be safely guarded.'

He paused but she urged him to continue with his story.

'Well, as I say, there were four of us on patrol that night. I was the captain. Each man had his allotted section of the quays. I suppose it was well after midnight that I was walking from . . .' he turned to point to a small quay further down from the abbey. 'One of my men was stationed there. Another of the watch was further along here. So I was making a normal check of my men, walking from that point along the quays checking on my watch.'

'What sort of night was it?'

'The weather was fair, not raining,' he reflected. 'But it was a cloudy sky which made it dark. We did have torches,' he added.

'But the visibility was impaired?' Fidelma pressed eagerly. 'You cannot see that far even with a torch.'

'True enough,' he agreed. 'That's why I almost stumbled over the body of the girl before I saw it.'

Fidelma raised her eyebrows. 'You stumbled over it? You mean that you actually *discovered* it? I thought that there was a witness to this murder?'

Mel hesitated. 'So there was. It is a little complicated, Sister.'

'Is it? Then tell the story as plainly as you can.'

'I was walking along, holding my torch high. It was, as I say, a very dark night. I came down the river path here and was about to cross this quay.'

'Were there any boats tied up to the quay?' Fidelma interrupted as the thought suddenly struck her.

'Yes, there was one of the trade boats that puts in here regularly. It was in darkness and no one was on deck. They wouldn't be, not at that hour in the morning. They were probably all below, asleep, or in a drunken stupor.' He grinned, contemplating the idea. 'As I came along, I saw a figure on horseback.'

'Where was this figure?' demanded Fidelma. 'On the track there?'

'No. It was just here. At the start of the quay.'

'What was this figure doing?'

'When I first saw it, the figure was still, so still I did not notice it until I saw the movement of the horse. They had no torch but sat in the darkness. That was how I discovered the body.'

Fidelma suppressed an impatient sigh. 'Please explain – and with more detail.'

'When I saw the figure, I raised my torch in order to challenge it but before I could do so, I was challenged to identify myself. It was the Abbess Fainder who sat on the horse.'

Fidelma's eyes widened slightly. 'Abbess Fainder?' she echoed, stupidly. 'She was sitting on horseback here by the body in total darkness?'

'That is what I have been telling you,' Mel nodded. 'As soon as I identified myself, she said: "Mel, there is a body here. Who is it?" That is what she said. I stumbled forward in the dark and peered down. It was lying in the dark shadows of the bales and that was how I nearly tripped over it. I saw at once that it was a young girl and that she was dead.'

'What bales? Show me exactly where the body was positioned.'

Mel pointed to where some bales and a few boxes were piled nearby on the quay.

'It lay just there.'

Fidelma frowned as she scrutinised the spot.

'Are you saying that those boxes and bales are the same as on that night?'

'I did not mean to imply that. They are different but similar boxes, and bales stood there on that night. I would swear that they stood almost in the same position.'

Fidelma glanced at him swiftly. 'You would swear, even though it was dark?'

'It was my task to examine the spot in daylight to show the Brehon.'

'What did you see of the body by your torchlight?'

'You could see hardly anything in that light. The girl had a dress on but not the robes of a religieuse.'

'I see. So it was only later that she was identified as a novitiate at the abbey?'

'I suppose it was.'

'What was Abbess Fainder doing all this time while you were examining the body?'

'She waited until I had finished. There being nothing that I could do for the poor lass, I stood up and told the abbess that the girl was dead. She instructed me to bring the body to the abbey and said that she would go on to find the physician, Brother Miach. So I—'

'Wait one moment,' Fidelma interrupted. 'Did Abbess Fainder tell you why she was here, sitting on her horse in the darkness and within feet of a dead body?'

Mel shook his head. 'Not at that time. Later on I think she told the Brehon, Bishop Forbassach, that she had been returning to the abbey from some distant chapel and was about to enter the gate when she saw the dark shadow of the body and rode towards it just as I appeared.'

Fidelma pressed her lips tight for a moment, glancing from the gates of the abbey to the spot which Mel had indicated and measuring the distance.

'Yet you could hardly see it in the shadows of the bales even though you were carrying a torch and were right next to it? I will have to speak further with the abbess,' she muttered. 'Well, continue. I am confused as I was told that there was an eye-witness to the killing.'

'There was, indeed. I shall come to that,' continued Mel. 'When the abbess went into the abbey, I realised that I would need some help in the task; I also needed to let my men know where I was. So I waved my torch as a signal to my comrade who was on watch at the next quay, and he came to join me. It was then that I heard a sound behind the bales. I called out and raised my torch. The light illuminated a young girl standing behind the bales.'

'Had you noticed her before?'

'Not in the darkness. Nor had the abbess noticed her. I demanded to know who she was but she was in a distressed condition, shivering and frightened. It was some time before we learned that her name was Fial and that the dead girl was her friend Gormgilla. She told me that they were novitiates at the abbey. Apparently, she had come to the quay to meet her friend, and saw Gormgilla struggling with the figure of a man. She stood rooted to the spot in fear and in that moment, the man rose from her friend and ran off in the direction of the abbey. The girl said that she recognised him as a Saxon religious who was staying there.'

'Why wasn't this girl noticed before?'

'I told you, it was dark.'

'You had a torch and had stood some time on this quay.'

'Torches do not cast a great amount of light.'

'There was enough light for the abbess to see the dead body from horseback at a distance of several metres and ride over to it. Now it seems there was enough light for this girl, Fial, to recognise the killer. And presumably recognise him from a distance. Was she ever asked why she didn't scream or come forward to help her friend?'

'I think that she might have been asked at the trial. She was probably too frightened to move. It can happen.'

'It can. But why did she not come forward when the abbess rode up, or when you arrived? Why did she not cry out to the watch to help her?'

Mel considered the question before replying with a shrug.

'I am not a *dálaigh*, lady. I am a simple captain of the watch . . .'

Fidelma shot him a glance and smiled. 'No longer. You are now a commander of the palace guard. How did you receive your promotion?'

Mel was not abashed.

'I was informed that the King was pleased with my vigilance and I was to become a commander of the guard at the palace. Bishop Forbassach recommended me.'

Fidelma was silent for a moment or two.

'So, this girl, Fial, appears out of nowhere . . .'

'From behind the bales on the quay,' corrected Mel.

'She says that she has seen everything in the darkness and yet did nothing,' mused Fidelma with cynicism in her voice. 'Did she confirm Abbess Fainder's story?'

Mel looked startled. 'I did not know that the evidence given by the abbess needed confirmation.'

'Everything concerning an unnatural death needs confirmation, even the evidence of a saint,' replied Fidelma shortly. She glanced at the bales, walked across to them and looked towards the abbey gates.

'Let us consider this,' she began quietly. 'Fial and the dead girl are novitiates at the abbey. Fial says that she has arranged to meet her friend here on the quay. We will leave aside the fact that it is a very curious hour to meet – in the dead of night.

'Fial tells us that she arrived and saw her friend in the process of being attacked by a man whom she identifies as Brother Eadulf; he then ran back to the abbey. Is that right so far?'

'That is the story as I was told it by the girl.'

'And yet, in order to take up a position hiding behind these bales – and I presume you have identified their position correctly – Fial must surely have *walked by her friend* while she was being attacked. Only if she had arrived *before* her friend, or *with* her friend – and then remained hidden while Gormgilla was attacked – does her story make any sense.'

Mel frowned and examined the position she had pointed out, as if for the first time realising the implication of Fial's account.

'It was dark,' he hazarded. 'Perhaps in the dark she walked past her friend and the attacker?'

Fidelma smiled thinly. She did not have to say anything for him to recognise how weak his suggestion was. After a moment she turned to the obvious anomaly.

'There is a very curious time-lapse between the murder being committed, being witnessed by the girl and then her coming forward. One must presume that the murderer had fled from the scene before Abbess Fainder arrived. His only path back to the abbey gates from this quay would have been blocked by the abbess who had halted her horse at the end of the quay. Do you agree?'

Mel nodded silently, following her logic.

'So Fial had waited behind those bales for a long time. She had witnessed the murder; she observed the murderer leave the scene – running back to the abbey, according to her testimony; she watched Abbess Fainder arrive; she saw your arrival and examination of the body; she waited while the abbess returned to the abbey and you summoned your comrade. *Not until then does she come forward.* Was she ever asked why she stood there in the darkness and waited so long?'

'I did not think of it at the time,' Mel said. 'I carried the body into the abbey; my comrade brought the girl Fial along. Abbess Fainder had aroused the physician and the stewardess, Sister Étromma. They were present when I questioned Fial. That was when she identified the Saxon Brother as the man who attacked and killed her friend. Fial was left in the charge of one of the Sisters while we all went—'

'We?' queried Fidelma.

'The Mother Abbess, Sister Étromma, a Brother called Cett, myself and my comrade . . .'

'Perhaps you should name this comrade?'

'Daig was his name.'

'Was?' Fidelma caught the inflection.

'He was drowned in this river only a few days after these events.'

'It seems that witnesses in this case have a habit of disappearing or dying,' Fidelma said dryly.

'We were led by Sister Étromma to the guests' hostel. The Saxon monk was there, pretending to be asleep.'

'Pretending?' she asked sharply. 'How can you be so sure that he was merely pretending?'

'What else would it be but pretence, when he had just come from the quay, having murdered someone?'

'*If* he had just come from the quay having murdered someone.' Fidelma rephrased the sentence with heavy emphasis on the first word. 'Could it be that he had not, in fact, done the murder and was genuinely asleep?'

'But Fial identified him!'

'Much depends on what this Fial saw, doesn't it? So the Saxon was found in the bed in the dormitory?'

'He was. Brother Cett was the one to arouse him. It was pointed out in the lamplight that there was blood on the fellow's clothes and a piece of torn cloth was found on him. It was later discovered that the cloth was from Gormgilla's robe. It, too, was bloodstained.' Mel's face lightened. 'That proves the truth of what her friend Fial said, for how else had the Saxon's clothes become bloodstained and how else had he come into possession of the torn robe?'

'How else, indeed?' muttered Fidelma rhetorically. 'Did you question Brother Eadulf?'

Mel shook his head. 'At that point the Abbess Fainder said that she would take charge of the affair as it was a matter concerning the abbey. She asked me to assist Brother Cett in removing the Saxon to a cell in the abbey. This was done and the Brehon, Bishop Forbassach, was sent for. That is all I know of the situation until I was, of course, called for to give this evidence at the trial.'

'Were you entirely happy with the trial?'

'I don't understand.'

'Did you not think that these events as you relate them are inconsistent and raise questions?'

Mel pondered the question for a moment.

'It was not my place to think once the authorities had taken over,' he said finally. 'If there were questions to be asked, then it was the task of the Brehon, Bishop Forbassach, to do so and to point out anything which was wrong.'

'But Forbassach raised no questions?'

Mel was about to say something when he suddenly frowned, his gaze moving beyond Fidelma's shoulder. She turned quickly to see what the object of his scrutiny was and had no difficulty in recognising the figure of Abbess Fainder, in spite of her long black robe, astride a sturdy horse, cantering away along the track by the abbey walls having, presumably, just emerged from the abbey gates.

Fidelma grimaced in annoyance.

'I was hoping to have a word with her just now. Annoying woman! Time is at a premium. But presumably she is going to see about the sunken boat.'

Mel glanced up at the position of the sun.

'Abbess Fainder always goes for a ride about this time,' he observed. Then an expression of bewilderment crossed his features. 'Sunken boat? What sunken boat?'

Fidelma ignored him for a moment for she was thinking it strange that an abbess would leave her abbey to go riding on a regular basis. Religious usually forswore horses, taking vows of poverty especially in transport, unless they were of certain social rank. Fidelma's position as a *dálaigh* of the rank of *anruth* allowed her the privilege of travel by horseback which being a religieuse would have been denied her.

'Where does she go every day at this time?' she asked.

Mel was indifferent to her question.

'Sunken boat?' he asked again. 'What do you mean?'

Fidelma told him of the message Sister Étromma had received, and how she had hastened off to see what help she could render.

She was mildly surprised when Mel, looking serious, began to make hasty excuses to leave.

'You'll forgive me, Sister. I should go to see what the problem is. It is part of my duties to be informed of such occurrences. We would not want the river blocked so that other vessels cannot pass. Forgive me.'

He turned and hurried off along the bank in the direction that Sister Étromma and her companion, as well as Abbess Fainder, had all taken.

Fidelma did not waste time puzzling about their concerns. Instead she stood on the quay and looked about her, examining the scene carefully, before letting out a low sigh. She did not think that any further secrets would be revealed by staying any longer at this place and she began to make her way back to the inn.

Chapter Seven

On her arrival back at the Inn of the Yellow Mountain, Fidelma sought out Dego and Enda. They had returned from their excursion around the township but had little to report. They had found a very divided population. Some people were clearly shocked at the King's decree that the Penitentials should now form the law for *all* citizens – and cease being simply the rules by which some religious communities conducted their life. Others, more fanatical in their belief in the new faith, supported the extreme measures of the Penitentials. Dego and Enda could only base their opinions on the few conversations they had had with traders and merchants in the market square, for they had to proceed carefully. Even so, it was clear that news of Fidelma's arrival and the purpose of it was spreading through the township. What was the ancient saying? Gossip needs not a horse to carry it.

Fidelma, in return, sketched the basis of her findings at the abbey. The faces of Dego and Enda grew long as she told them of the evidence against Eadulf.

'I have to return to the abbey to speak again with Abbess Fainder,' she said. 'There is the matter of the missing Sister Fial, whose evidence I find hard to believe. Fainder intrigues me, however. If we discount Fial's motives, it is the impetus of the abbess which has wrought this change to the law. There is something very disturbing about her.'

'Even so, lady,' Enda said reflectively, 'there is this testimony of Sister Fial. She says that she actually witnessed Eadulf rape and kill her friend. That is clear enough in any law.'

Dego was grim-faced in agreement with his comrade. 'Do you think that you can shake her testimony?' he asked.

'I think I might, on what I have been told so far, but only if I have a chance to speak with her. It seems convenient that she has disappeared.'

Dego and Enda exchanged a glance.

'Do you suspect a conspiracy to hide her?' Enda said.

'All I say is that the disappearance of Sister Fail is coincidental.' Fidelma paused thoughtfully. 'However, I should be able to raise enough questions on the conduct of the trial to cause any unbiased judge to delay the enactment of this penalty pending further investigations. After I have seen the abbess again, I will demand that King Fianamail keep his word and hear my grounds for an appeal. We simply need to buy a week of time. I'd be happier pleading my case before Barrán than a Laigin Brehon who might be influenced by Bishop Forbassach.'

'What shall we do in the meanwhile?' Dego asked.

'There is something,' Fidelma said slowly. 'I have found that the Abbess Fainder regularly leaves the abbey on horseback each afternoon and apparently goes on mysterious journeys, sometimes returning very late. I'd like to know where she goes and who she sees.'

'Do you believe that the abbess is involved in this case in some way?' Enda demanded.

'Possibly. At the moment, I find that there are so many mysteries in this place that it is probably best to clarify each one in turn. Maybe it is of no importance, maybe it is. It was when she was returning from such a journey, after midnight, that she was seen next to the body of the murdered girl. Was that merely a coincidence?'

'Enda and I will keep a watch on the fine abbess and her travels then, lady,' smiled Dego. 'Leave that to us.'

It was some time before Mel returned to the inn. Fidelma had finished her midday meal and was preparing to go back to the abbey. Dego and Enda had set off on their tasks again. Fidelma had realised, with growing frustration, that she had nothing to do until the Abbess Fainder returned to the abbey or Sister Étromma found Sister Fial. She was restless and annoyed for she was very conscious of the onward rush of time and the fact that Eadulf had so little of it left to spare. She forced herself to sit in the main room of the inn, before the crackling fire, and tried to contain her growing agitation. It was not in her nature to sit still when there was so much to do. The words of her mentor, the Brehon Morann, calmed her: *Whoever has no patience has no wisdom.*

She also sought refuge in the art of the *dercad*, the act of meditation by which countless generations of Irish mystics had achieved the state of *sitcháin* or peace, calming extraneous thought and mental irritations. Fidelma was a regular practitioner of this ancient art in times of stress although several members of the Faith, such as Ultan, Archbishop of Armagh, had denounced its usage as a pagan art because it had been practised by the Druids before the coming of the New Faith. Even the Blessed Patrick himself, a Briton who had been prominent in establishing the Faith in the five kingdoms two centuries before, had expressly forbidden several of the meditative arts of self-enlightenment. However, the *dercad*, while frowned upon, was not yet forbidden. It was a means of relaxing and calming the riot of thoughts within a troubled mind. Fidelma used it regularly.

Time passed and finally she heard Mel coming into the inn. She snapped out of her meditation with ease and greeted him as he entered.

'Was it bad?' she asked directly.

He looked startled, not immediately observing her sitting in the shadowy corner by the fire. Then he shook his head as he realised to what she was referring.

'You mean the river boat accident? No lives were lost, thanks be.'

'And was it Gabrán's boat?'

The question seemed to have an electrifying effect on Mel. He started back in surprise.

'What makes you ask that?' he demanded.

'Only that Sister Étromma seemed concerned when it was reported that it might have been his boat because the man traded with the abbey.'

'Oh?' Mel paused a moment as if to think on the matter and then shook his head. 'It was some old river barge that should have been broken up for firewood a long time ago. The timbers were rotted. It is reckoned that it will take only a few hours to drag the wreck to the riverbank out of the way of the main passage.'

'So Sister Étromma's concern was without foundation?'

'As I told you, being a river trading post, it is a concern to us all if there is any danger of the river becoming impassable.'

'I understand.'

Mel was about to continue on his way but she stayed him.

'A few other questions occur to me, if you don't mind answering them. I will not keep you long.'

Mel sat down before her. 'I am happy to help you, lady,' he smiled. 'Ask your questions.'

'What were the circumstances of the drowning of your comrade – the one who was with you on the night of the murder of Gormgilla?'

Mel seemed surprised by the question.

'Daig? He was on watch on the quays one night, as usual, and it seems that he slipped off the boards of the quay, probably on the wet wood, and struck his head on something, perhaps a timber support. He was unconscious in the water and drowned before anyone knew it. His body was found the next day.'

Fidelma considered this for a moment.

'So his death – his name was Daig, you say? – so Daig's death was just a tragic accident. There was nothing suspicious about it?'

'It was an accident right enough, and tragic enough, for Daig was a good member of the watch and knew this river like the back of his hand. He was brought up on the river boats here. But if you think there was some connection with the murder of Gormgilla, I can assure you there was not.'

'I see.' She stood up abruptly. 'Do you know if Sister Étromma has returned to the abbey?'

'I believe so.' The warrior followed her example, rising slowly.

'What of Abbess Fainder? Has she also returned?'

Mel shrugged. 'I don't know – I doubt it. When she leaves the abbey she is usually gone for some time.'

'Did the abbess go to see the sunken boat?'

'I did not see her there. It would be unusual. The abbess regularly goes riding alone during the afternoon. I think she goes up into the hills.'

'Thank you, Mel. You are most helpful.'

When Fidelma returned to the abbey, she was greeted at the gates by Sister Étromma.

'Well, Sister,' Fidelma said, 'have you any word on the missing girl, Sister Fial?'

Sister Étromma's face was impassive.

'I have only just come back to the abbey myself. I will make more enquiries. I did instruct one of our community to make a search through the abbey.'

'Has Abbess Fainder returned? There are further questions that I need to put to her.'

Sister Étromma was confused. 'Returned?'

Fidelma nodded patiently. 'From wherever the abbess goes riding in the afternoon. You do not happen to know where that is, do you?'

The *rechtaire* of the abbey was dismissive.

'I would not know about the personal habits of the abbess. Follow me. I believe she is in her chambers.'

She conducted Fidelma once more through the gloomy corridors of the abbey towards the chambers of the abbess. They had to cross a small cloistered area at the back of the chapel to reach them.

Fidelma heard the raised voices from across the cloisters. She recognised the voice of the abbess, strident in its effort to quell the hard masculine tones which were raised in interrogation. Beside her, Sister Étromma halted and coughed nervously.

'It seems that the abbess is busy. Perhaps we should return when she is less . . . preoccupied,' she muttered.

Fidelma did not pause in her stride.

'My business will not wait,' she said firmly. She walked along the cloistered path towards the abbess's door, with Sister Étromma trotting at her heels, and paused to knock upon it. It was partially open and the voices continued unabated as if the speakers had not heard her knocking.

'I tell you, Abbess Fainder, it is an outrage!' The man who was speaking was an elderly man whose clothing distinguished him as someone of rank and influence. He had snow-white hair falling to his shoulders and a silver circlet around his forehead. He wore a long green woven cloak and carried a wand of office.

Abbess Fainder was smiling in spite of her strident tone. On closer inspection it was simply a mask, a taut assembly of her facial muscles. An attempt to demonstrate her superiority.

'Outrage? You forget to whom you speak, Coba. Besides, my actions have been approved of by the King, his Brehon and his spiritual adviser. Do you dare to say that you are more competent to judge matters than they are?'

'That I do,' replied the elderly man, unabashed. 'Especially if they ignore the principles of our laws.'

'*Our* laws?' sneered the Abbess. 'The laws recognised in this abbey are those governing the Church of which it is part. We recognise no other law. As for the rest of the kingdom, why – we must not allow it to wallow in ignorance any longer. We must turn to Christian law as given by Rome otherwise we are cursed for eternity.'

The man addressed as Coba took an almost threatening step closer to the table of the abbess. Fainder did not flinch as he bent forward in anger across it.

'It is strange to hear those words coming from a learned woman, especially one in your position. Do you not recall the words of Paul of Tarsus to the Romans? "When Gentiles, who do not possess the law, carry out its precepts by the light of nature, then, though they have no law, they are their own law, for they display the effect of the law inscribed on their hearts." Paul of Tarsus had more sympathy with our law than you do.'

Abbess Fainder's eyes were dark with anger.

'You have the effrontery to lecture me on the Scriptures? Do you dare tell the religious, who are your superiors in the Faith, how to interpret the Scriptures? You forget yourself, Coba. You have a duty of obedience to us who are appointed to govern you in the Faith; you will obey and not question me.'

The elderly man looked down pityingly at her.

'Who appointed you to govern me? I certainly did not do so.'

'My authority comes from Christ.'

'As I recall in the first letter of the Apostle Peter from the same Scriptures, and he was Christ's appointed leader of the Faith, it says to "Tend the flock of God whose shepherds you are, and do it not under compulsion but out of sheer devotion; not tyrannising over those who are allotted to your care, but setting an example to the flock." Perhaps you should remember those words before you demand unquestioning obedience?'

Abbess Fainder almost choked in frustration.

'Have you no humility, man?' Her voice rose, cracking in anger.

Coba laughed coldly. 'I have humility enough to recognise when I lack humility.'

The abbess suddenly caught sight of Fidelma standing at the door, witnessing the argument with an expression of amused interest on her face. Abbess Fainder's features immediately dissolved into a cold mask. She turned back to the elderly man.

'The Brehon and the King have agreed on the matter of punishment, Coba. It will be carried out. That is all I have to say. You may go.' She turned again to Fidelma and her voice was icy. 'Now, what do *you* want, Sister?'

The elderly man had turned to the door as soon as he was aware of Fidelma's presence. He made no effort to obey the abbess's summary dismissal.

'I give you fair warning, Abbess Fainder,' he said, eyes on Fidelma and cutting across any reply that she was about to give to the abbess. 'I shall not let this matter drop. You have slaughtered one young Brother already and now you intend to kill the Saxon. That is not our law.'

Fidelma addressed herself to him rather than the abbess.

'So, you have come to protest against this sentence of death?' she asked, regarding the elderly man with interest.

The man called Coba was not friendly.

'That I have. If you call yourself a religieuse, then you will do likewise.'

'I have already made my protest known,' Fidelma assured him. 'Who are you?'

It was Abbess Fainder who reluctantly intervened.

'This is Coba of Cam Eolaing of which place he is *bó-aire* and not an *ollamh* of law nor of religion,' she added spitefully. A *bó-aire* was a local magistrate, a chieftain without land whose wealth was judged by the number of cows he owned, hence he was called a 'cow-chief'. 'Coba, this is Sister Fidelma from Cashel.'

The elderly man's eyes narrowed in scrutiny as he turned to examine Fidelma.

'What is a religieuse of Cashel doing in Fearna? Simply to protest at the actions of its abbess, or do you have another purpose?' he demanded.

'The abbess failed to mention that I am a *dálaigh* of the courts with the rank of *anruth*,' she replied. 'Also, I am a friend of the Saxon who lays under the threat of death. I have come here to help defend him from any injustice.'

The elderly chieftain relaxed a little.

'I see. And I suppose that you have not been able to persuade the abbess to desist from her evil intention?'

'I have not been able to change the sentence which has been confirmed by the King and his Brehon,' Fidelma admitted, wording her answer cautiously.

'Then what do you propose to do? A man was murdered this morning and another is to be murdered tomorrow. Vengeance is not our way.'

Abbess Fainder made some inarticulate sounds but Fidelma ignored her.

'It is not our way,' she conceded. 'I agree. But we can only follow the path of law to fight injustice. I have been given permission to see if there are matters which may form the basis of an appeal.'

The elderly man almost spat. 'Appeal! Nonsense! The Saxon's life is to be taken tomorrow. His release must be demanded. There is no time for legal niceties.'

Abbess Fainder's eyes narrowed. 'I must warn you, Coba, that demands will be met with resistance. If you try to interfere with the law . . .'

'Law? Savagery! Those who support this judicial taking of life have an affinity with murderers and cannot call themselves civilised.'

'I warn you, Coba, your views will be brought to the attention of the King.'

'The King? A querulous youth who has let himself be misled in these matters.'

Fidelma laid a hand on the old man's arm.

'A querulous youth with power,' she warned him gently. The chieftain seemed too outspoken for his own good.

Coba laughed dryly at her concern. 'I am too old and have lived too full a life to be frightened of people with power, whoever they are. And throughout that life, young woman, I have supported our law, our culture and philosophies. No new savagery can replace my principles without my voice being raised in protest.'

'I can understand your feelings, Coba,' Fidelma agreed. 'I share them. But you, as a local magistrate, must know that the only way to challenge and change things is by doing it through the medium of the law.'

Coba stared at her for a moment, his eyes deep set and dark.

'Your great Christian teacher, Paul of Tarsus, once said that the law was the schoolmaster. What do you think he meant by that?'

'And which law did he mean?' snapped Abbess Fainder. 'Not pagan law but the law the Faith brings.'

Coba ignored her and spoke directly to Fidelma: 'The most characteristic feature of our law is the procedure by means of which rights and wrongs are respectively vindicated or redressed. The most obvious effect of a crime, any crime, is the infliction of an injury on some other person and the natural consequence that this should bring down on the wrongdoer. In any well-regulated society, the principle is that the wrongdoer must compensate the victim for the injury.'

'That is the law of the Brehons,' agreed Fidelma. 'You sound as if you have studied that principle well.'

Coba nodded absently. 'In the five kingdoms we have a system of honour prices which, according to the nature of the injury and the status of the person injured, compensation and fines are judged. The philosophy of the Brehons was to make the law a schoolmaster; to teach the wrongdoer that the loss which is then inflicted on him is the loss that he has inflicted on the injured person.'

Abbess Fainder interrupted him again.

'I believe that the Roman way of punitive redress, that is "an eye for an eye", is the deterrent and reflects the natural instinct of man. The natural retaliation for murder is to take reprisal from the wrongdoer by killing him also. Isn't this what combative children do when they fall out? One hits another and the reaction is to strike back.'

The elderly chieftain waved his hand in dismissal of her argument.

'That is a system based on fear. Violent reprisal for a crime leads to a fierce resentment which determines the wrongdoers to inflict even more violence as vengeance; that leads to more reprisals and the production of more fear and more violence.'

Abbess Fainder was flushed with indignation at this challenge to her authority.

'We came out of the primitive barbarism. Some remain in it. If we want to prevent crime then we must use means that primitive barbarian minds understand. Spare the rod and spoil the child. The same applies with adults. Once they understand that the penalty of wrongdoing is death then they will not transgress.'

Fidelma thought it time to intervene in the heated argument.

'Such a debate, interesting as it is, is leading us nowhere. I have come to ask you some questions, Abbess Fainder. With your permission I would request that Coba withdraw so that we may discuss the matter in private.'

Coba was not offended.

'My business with the abbess is done. I need to speak with your *rechtaire*, Abbess Fainder.' He turned and smiled shortly at Fidelma. 'I wish you luck, Sister Fidelma. If you need someone to support your plea against the enactment of these barbarous Penitentials, then I am your man. Assuredly so.'

Fidelma inclined her head in acknowledgment.

After Coba had left, Fidelma came straight to the point.

'You did not tell me that it was you who found the body of the murdered girl.'

Abbess Fainder did not alter her expression.

'You did not ask,' she replied evenly. 'Besides, it is not exactly true.'

'Then tell me what is the truth.'

Abbess Fainder sat back reflectively, her hands palm down in what Fidelma realised was a characteristic position.

'As I recall the matter, that night I was returning to the abbey . . .'

'A curious time for the abbess to be returning to her abbey. It was after midnight, or so I am told.'

The other woman shrugged. 'I know of no rule which forbids an abbess to leave her abbey.'

'Where had you been?'

For a moment Abbess Fainder's eyes narrowed in aggravation. Then she relaxed and smiled again.

'That is none of your business,' she said without malice. 'Suffice to say that it has nothing to do with this affair.'

Fidelma realised that she could hardly press the point without further knowledge.

'I am told you were on horseback.'

'I was returning along the riverbank to the gates which overlook the abbey's quay on the river. Our stables are just there.'

'I have seen the place,' Fidelma assured her.

'I was riding along the path . . .'

'Was there moonlight?'

The abbess frowned for a moment. 'I don't think so. No, it was a cloudy night and dark. I was about to turn into the gate when something attracted my attention.'

'Which was?' pressed Fidelma after she had paused.

'I think on reflection it was a sound near a pile of bales and boxes that had been landed from one of the trading boats which had arrived that day.'

'A sound?'

'I do not know exactly. But something attracted my attention and I eased my horse near to the bales. That was when I saw the huddled shape of the body.'

'Yet it was cloudy and dark. You had no torch. How could you see that it was a body in such conditions?'

Abbess Fainder pondered the question.

'I don't recall. There must have been some light from somewhere. I just know that I saw the huddled form and knew it was a body. Perhaps the moon came out momentarily from the clouds. I don't know.'

'What then?'

'I sat for a moment and then Mel, the captain of the watch, came out of the darkness. I did not recognise him at first and so I called out to ask who he was. When I saw it was Mel, the captain of the watch, I asked him to examine the body. He did so and told me that it was a young girl: she was dead. I instructed him to bring the body into the abbey and I went to rouse Brother Miach, our physician.'

'I see. And the body was brought in by Mel?'

'It was.'

'By Mel alone?'

'No, by Mel and one of his comrades.'

'Do you recall his name?'

'It was a man called Daig,' she said shortly.

'When the body was laid out, I presume that you recognised it as one of your young novitiates?'

'Not at all. I had never seen her before. It was the girl who had also been brought in, Fial, she who witnessed the attack by your Saxon friend, who identified her,' the abbess said viciously.

'You had never seen either of those girls before that night. Isn't that strange?'

'There is no mystery there for I do not greet all the novitiates, as I have said before.'

'So you heard from Fial that she had apparently witnessed the rape and murder of her companion?'

'By this time, Sister Étromma had been found and she led us to where the Saxon was pretending to be asleep. He was dragged from his bed. There was blood on his robe and we found a torn piece of the dead girl's robe in his possession.'

Fidelma stroked the side of her nose with a slim forefinger, brows drawn together.

'Didn't you think that was odd?'

'How so?' demanded the abbess belligerently.

'That after such a crime, the attacker would tear a piece of his victim's clothing off and take it with him to bed as incriminating evidence? And the fact that he had not attempted to clean the blood off his own robe – isn't that odd?'

Abbess Fainder shrugged. 'It is not my place to delve into the motivations of a sick mind. People behave strangely, you must know that. One explanation is that your Saxon friend had no time, having realised a hue and cry had been raised. He simply hoped he would not be noticed.'

'I concede that you have a point but I would not accept that it is not our place to delve into the motivations of sick minds. Isn't that what we are here for, Mother Abbess, to give comfort and succour to the sick and distressed by our understanding?'

'We are not here to make up excuses for the evil-minded, Sister. "Whatever a man soweth that shall he also reap" – you should remember Paul's Epistle to the Galatians?'

'There is a fine line in discovering reasons and making up excuses.' Fidelma swung abruptly towards the door then she paused and glanced back. 'I also came to give you notice, Abbess Fainder, that I am going to proceed with an appeal based on the evidence that I have heard so far.'

For a moment Abbess Fainder looked startled.

'Are you saying that you have grounds on which to appeal on behalf of the Saxon?' she demanded.

At that moment the door swung open and Coba re-entered without knocking.

Abbess Fainder rose from her chair in quiet anger. 'Have you taken leave of your manners, to come bursting into my chamber without knocking,' she said icily. 'I am . . .'

'I came to warn you,' he interrupted, though there was dry humour in his tone.

'Warn me?' Abbess Fainder was astonished.

'The King is approaching the abbey,' the *bó-aire* told her. 'The Brehon, Bishop Forbassach, is with him.'

'Then I am saved a journey to the King's fortress,' smiled Fidelma. 'I shall now make my appeal on behalf of Brother Eadulf.'

'This is good news,' Coba cried enthusiastically. 'It would be better news if you could stop this madness that has entered our kingdom. We must get these Penitentials thrown out before they displace our entire system of government.'

The abbess suddenly relaxed and reseated herself, reaching for her hand-bell to summon her stewardess.

'So Fianamail is coming? Then, perhaps, he and Forbassach will put an end to this nonsense. Our abbey routine has been disturbed enough. We will receive the King and his Brehon, formally, in the chapel.' She shot a hostile glance at Fidelma. 'We will see how far you will get with your appeal then, Sister.'

It was Coba who addressed the abbess.

'Even at this late stage your voice could be raised for mercy and be listened to. Return to the law of this land!'

'I have heard no reason, so far, to change my mind either in this specific case or in terms of the wider philosophy of punishment,' the abbess bristled.

'Have my arguments not moved you to reconsider the effectiveness of the implementation of compensation and rehabilitation on society rather than the imposition of fear to create a moral society?'

'We want to create an *obedient* society,' snapped Abbess Fainder. 'No, I am not moved at all. If a child steals, then the child is punished and fear of punishment creates obedience.'

Coba made a final, desperate attempt to demonstrate his philosophy.

'Let us use that child analogy. How many have said that their child steals? "We have told the child that it is wicked to steal and we have beat him or her for stealing. Yet still they steal. Why is this?" The answer depends on the individual child. Some are cowed into submission by punishment or the threat of punishment, but not all. Indeed, punishment of a physical nature often leads to a strengthening of resolve for vengeance on the figure of authority or the society that the figure represents. It can lead to increasing violence instead of preventing it.'

'Doing nothing at all increases that violence,' sneered the Abbess. 'You are an old and foolish man, Coba.'

'What our law seeks to do is to solve the problems of the attitude of wrongdoers. The best corrective measure is to make the child understand that stealing involves pain to someone, by taking away something belonging to the child every time they commit a theft. Most children respond to this rather than to a smack or physical pain. Thus we have a law system by which the naughty child can learn. If they have any capacity for sympathy, then they realise the pain they have inflicted and further, they may be led into changing their ways.'

'I cannot stand here arguing this nonsense, Coba. Your laws and their punishments have failed otherwise we would now live in a society free from all crime.'

Fidelma felt a strong desire to enter the argument again.

'Every breach of law is effectively an injury to another, and if a man is brought to the realisation of that injury then his soul is saved; when he has been so rehabilitated he may go on to lead a worthwhile life. Thus the law is a work of moral education by being a curative punishment, as well as a compensatory and preventative punishment.'

Coba nodded in approval at her explanation.

Abbess Fainder turned to them both with an expression of cynicism.

'You will not persuade me to change my mind. The Saxon has been judged and tomorrow he will hang for the crime he has committed. Now let us go and greet the King.'

Chapter Eight

It was late evening when the appeal court finally assembled in the great hall of the fortress of Fianamail of Laigin. It had taken some insistence on Fidelma's part to force Fianamail and his Brehon, Bishop Forbassach, to agree to the hearing during their meeting in the chapel of the abbey. Bishop Forbassach and Abbess Fainder argued strongly against any such hearing but Fidelma pointed out that the young King had given his word that if Fidelma could discover legal objections to the conduct of the trial apart from objections to punishment under the Penitentials then he would order a consideration of those objections. Bishop Forbassach immediately demanded to know what the objections were but Fidelma pointed out that the arguments could not be revealed unless it was done during a formal hearing.

It was with reluctance that Fianamail realised that he would have to abide by his promise. Clearly, the abbey was no place to hold the appeal as several scribes and officials needed to be summoned to attend. The great hall of the fortress was deemed the only suitable place at such short notice.

The hall was lit by flickering torches, balanced in their iron holders on the walls, and warmed by a central fire. Fianamail took the central position on a dais in his carved oak chair of office. At his right side sat Bishop Forbassach, Brehon of Laigin.

Abbess Fainder was in attendance and, as her support, she had brought her *rechtaire* Sister Étromma and, strangely – or so Fidelma thought – the villainous-looking Brother Cett. Brother Miach accompanied them. There were several religious, scribes and some of the King's household and warriors including Mel. Seated among the others, Fidelma had spotted Coba, the local chieftain, who was so against the introduction of the Penitentials. Dego and Enda sat at the rear of the chamber to watch the proceedings.

It was not a true court of law in the sense that in an appeal to stay a sentence, the defendant did not have to be present, there was no prosecutor, nor were witnesses usually called. The arguments to stay the sentence rested on the ability of the *dálaigh* to raise questions about the procedures of evidence heard at the previous trial or even present questions on the inappropriate severity of the sentence.

Fidelma had taken a seat before the dais. A stillness descended when Bishop Forbassach rose and called the assembly to order.

'We are here to hear the plea of the *dálaigh* from Cashel. Proceed,' he instructed Fidelma before he resumed his seat.

Fidelma rose reluctantly to her feet. She had been growing puzzled at the sight of Forbassach apparently about to moderate over the court.

'Am I to understand that you are presiding at this hearing, Forbassach?' she demanded.

Bishop Forbassach stared coldly at his old antagonist. He was a man with an unforgiving nature and she sensed his enjoyment at her confusion.

'That is an odd opening for your plea, Fidelma. Do I need to answer such a question?'

'The fact that you presided over Brother Eadulf's trial must surely exclude you from sitting in judgment on your own conduct of that trial.'

'Who has a greater legal authority in this kingdom than Bishop Forbassach?' intervened Fianamail irritably. 'A lesser judge has no authority to pronounce criticism of him. You should know that.'

Fidelma had to admit that this was true and a matter she had overlooked. Only a judge of higher or equal rank could overturn a judgment made by another. Yet for Forbassach to judge this matter would clearly be a further injustice.

'I had hoped that Forbassach might have sought the advice of other judges. I see only Forbassach sitting here and not even a qualified *dálaigh* to adjudicate the evidence with him. How can a judge be judge of their own judgments?'

'I shall note your objections, Fidelma, if you wish to register them.' Bishop Forbassach's smile was triumphal. 'However, as Brehon of Laigin I acknowledge no other person to have authority to preside in this court. Should I remove myself it could be argued that I was admitting that I have been guilty of prejudice in this matter. Such objections from you are overruled. Now I will hear your appeal.'

Fidelma's mouth compressed and she glanced across to where Dego was sitting, a bemused spectator. He caught her eye and grimaced, a small gesture of support. She realised now the bias against her even before she began her plea. There was nothing else to do but proceed as best she could.

'Brehon of Laigin, I wish to make a formal appeal to you to postpone the execution of the Saxon, Brother Eadulf, until such time as a proper enquiry and a new trial can be arranged.'

Forbassach continued to regard her with an unchanging sour expression. Fidelma found his attitude almost contemptuous.

'An appeal must be backed by the weight of evidence of irregularities of the first trial, Fidelma of Cashel,' Forbassach acknowledged dryly. 'What are the reasons for your appeal?'

'There are several irregularities in the presentation of evidence at the trial.'

Forbassach's disagreeable expression seem to deepen.

'Irregularities? Doubtless you are suggesting that such irregularities are due to the fact that I, who presided at that trial, am responsible for them?'

'I am well aware that you presided at the trial, Forbassach. I have already made my objection known to your judging your own conduct.'

'So what are you charging me with? What exactly?' His voice was cold and menacing.

'I am not charging you with anything, Forbassach. You know enough of the law not to misinterpret my words,' snapped Fidelma. 'An appeal is merely to lay facts before the court and put forward questions, the answers are left to the court to pursue.'

Bishop Forbassach's eyes narrowed at her barbed response.

'Let me hear your so-called facts and you may also ask your questions, *dálaigh*. It cannot be said that I am not a fair man.'

Fidelma felt as if she were beating against a wall of granite and tried to gather some inner strength.

'I appeal on the grounds of irregularities of law. I would present the following specific points.

'Firstly, Brother Eadulf was a messenger between King Colgú of Cashel and the Archbishop Theodore of Canterbury. He had the protection and privilege of the rank that entails. This rank was not taken into account during the proceedings. He carried a written letter and the white wand of an *ollamh*, a messenger who had immunity from legal proceedings.'

'A white wand of office? A message?' Bishop Forbassach sounded amused. 'They were not presented in evidence.'

'Brother Eadulf was not allowed the opportunity. I present them now . . .' Fidelma turned to pick up the objects from the bench on which she had placed them. She held them out for examination.

'Retrospective evidence is no evidence,' Bishop Forbassach smiled. 'Your evidence is inadmissible. Bringing such items with you from Cashel . . .'

'I found them in the guests' hostel of the abbey where Brother Eadulf had left them,' Fidelma retorted, angry at Forbassach's attempt to dismiss them.

'How are we to know that?'

'Because Sister Étromma was with me when I found them in the mattress of the bed which she identified as that which Brother Eadulf had used.'

Bishop Forbassach turned his gaze to where Sister Étromma was sitting.

'Stand forward, Sister. Is this true?'

Sister Étromma was clearly nervous of Bishop Forbassach and also cast a frightened glance towards the abbess as she stood up.

'I accompanied the Sister into the guests' hostel and she bent over the mattress and then produced those items.'

'Did you see her actually find the items?' pressed the Brehon.

'She had her back towards me and turned from the bed to show me.'

'Then she may well have been carrying the items on her person and only pretended to find them?' suggested Bishop Forbassach with a note of satisfaction. 'The evidence cannot be submitted.'

Fidelma was outraged.

'I protest! As a *dálaigh*, I am sworn to uphold the law and your insinuation besmirches my honour!'

'As a Brehon, I have also sworn the same oath and yet you dare question my judgments!' snapped Forbassach. 'What is sauce for the goose will also be sauce for the gander. Continue with your case.'

Fidelma swallowed hard, trying to keep control of her emotions. Losing her temper would benefit no one, least of all Eadulf.

'Secondly, Brother Eadulf was awaken from his sleep, assaulted and taken to a cell without being told of what he had been accused. He was kept in the cell for two days without food or water. It was only when Forbassach came and told him the nature of the crime of which he was accused that he knew why he was being detained. No advocate, no *dálaigh*, was appointed in his defence, neither was he allowed to question the evidence. He was asked only to admit his guilt.'

'If he had been innocent, he could have presented his evidence,' grumbled Bishop Forbassach. 'All of what you say, anyway, is merely based on the word of the Saxon. These claims are denied. Proceed.'

Fidelma went on stubbornly.

'Then let us refer to the irregularities of the witness statements. Sister Étromma came forward to identify the dead girl. How could she identify her when she had never seen her before she was confronted by her dead body? She had been told that she was a novitiate in the abbey. Yet she did not know that fact at first hand.'

'The mistress of the novitiates told her.'

'She had already left on a pilgrimage. Even if she had, you know the law, Forbassach. She did not know the girl from her own personal experience. Étromma's evidence was not valid according to the rules of the court.'

'That is a matter for the judge,' replied Bishop Forbassach tightly. 'I judged that the matter of identification was not important; so long as the girl was identified it does not matter by whom.'

'We are talking of rules of law,' Fidelma responded. 'But let us continue to the next witness – the physician, Brother Miach, who examined the body. He swore that the girl had been forcibly raped. True, she was a virgin who had had intercourse just before her death. That much, as a physician, he should have told us. But our physician brings opinion into his evidence and his opinion was that the girl had been raped. Now, I am not saying that she wasn't, just that an opinion is not evidence and should not have been accepted as such. The evidence does not indicate beyond question the type of intercourse which happened before the girl's death. Was it the crime of *focloir* or *sleth*; forcible rape, or rape by persuasion? This should have been pointed out and considered.

'Now comes the evidence of Sister Fial who is the key witness . . . an eye-witness. She says that she is a friend of the dead girl. They became novitiates in the abbey at the same time. They were both under the age of choice. Sister Fial says that she had made an arrangement to meet the dead girl on the quay outside the abbey at a time which must have been well after midnight. No one has asked why at the trial, or for what purpose. Is it not strange that twelve- or thirteen-year-old novitiates are wandering outside the abbey at such an hour? Are these important questions dealt with? No, they are not.

'Next, Fial says that in the darkness, down on the quay, she sees a man attacking and strangling her friend. She must have walked within a metre of where the attack was happening. What does she do in response to the sight? She simply stands by the bales and watches while her friend is assaulted and strangled. She sees the man running back to the abbey and entering it. *All in the dark*. She stands undecided what to do – how long, we are not told. We cannot even ask her because Sister Fial seems to have disappeared from the abbey. She stands, making no attempt to go to her friend. The abbess comes along and still she continues to remain in the silent shadows while Mel examines the body. It is a long time before she emerges to tell her story.'

She paused; a total silence had descended.

'Then we have the evidence of Mel, the captain of the watch, who, coming to the quay, sees the figure of the abbess, Abbess Fainder, on horseback looking down at the body. Yet at no time was the abbess called to give evidence as to her role in this business. She points the body out to Mel. It is Mel and his comrade, Daig, who take charge and are eventually told by the girl, Fial, our missing witness, that she identifies the attacker as the Saxon monk staying at the abbey.

'Eadulf is found in bed. He conveniently has a piece of the murdered girl's bloodstained robe in the bed with him, making no attempt to hide it.'

Forbassach grinned dourly.

'I think you have scuppered your own arguments, *dálaigh*. The evidence shows clearly that the Saxon was in bed with such bloodstained clothing as demonstrates beyond question that he was the guilty party.'

'I believe that the irregularities outweigh that evidence and those irregularities must be clarified before the matters of the bloodstains can be taken into account. I have already dealt with the circumstances of his detention which are, I say again, not in accordance with the law. He is detained in the abbey. We know the results. What is not known is how our missing witness, Fial, identified the Saxon Brother. Indeed, how does she know that he was a Saxon Brother when Brother Eadulf has said that at no time did he lay eyes on the girl when he came to the abbey. He spoke to very few people – the abbess, Sister Étromma and a Brother called Ibar. Only they knew him to be a Saxon for he speaks excellent Irish. No one asked the girl how she could recognise the Saxon in the darkness. There are too many questions that have not been asked in this case, let alone answered.'

Fidelma paused for a moment, as if taking breath.

'On these grounds, Brehon of Laigin, I appeal directly to you with the request that the sentence on Brother Eadulf be suspended until such time as a proper impartial investigation has been made and a fair and just trial be held.'

Bishop Forbassach waited for a moment, as if giving her a chance to continue, and then he asked sharply: 'Do you have any further arguments to put before me, *dálaigh* of Cashel?'

Fidelma shook her head. 'Given the time that I was allowed, that is all I can bring forward at the moment. I think it is enough for a stay of the execution for a few weeks at least.'

Bishop Forbassach turned and held a hurried whispered conversation with Fianamail. Fidelma waited patiently. The bishop turned back to her.

'I will make the decision known in the morning. However,' he glanced sourly at Fianamail, 'if the decision were mine alone I would say it fails.'

Fidelma, usually so self-controlled, took a step backward as if someone had pushed her in the chest. If she admitted the truth to herself, she had realised from the outset that Bishop Forbassach had decided to protect his initial judgment and sentence. However, she had hoped that he might delay the execution for a few days for the sake of appearances. It appeared that Fianamail was more conscious of keeping to the façade of justice than Forbassach. Fidelma was not prepared for such a blatant demonstration of injustice.

'Why do you say that you would fail my appeal, Forbassach?' she asked, after she had recovered her voice. 'I am interested to know the argument. Would the learned judge tell me on what grounds he is dismissing this appeal?'

Her tone was quiet, subdued.

Bishop Forbassach misinterpreted the timbre as an acknowledgment of defeat. There was something of triumph in his expression.

'I told you that the decision will be announced tomorrow. However, firstly, I was the judge at the trial of the Saxon. I say that he was accorded every respect and facility. He says that this was not so. You have his word, that of a stranger to this land, against mine. I speak as the Brehon of Laigin. There is little doubt whose word should be taken.'

Fidelma's eyes narrowed angrily. Her temper rose.

'You reject my appeal because you were judge at that first trial? I did not ask you to be judge at this appeal. I see that you are merely safeguarding your own interests . . .'

'Fidelma of Cashel!' It was Fianamail who stopped her. 'You are addressing my Brehon. Even your relationship to the King of Muman does not give you the right to insult the officers of my household.'

Fidelma bit her lip, realising that she had let her temper run away with her.

'I withdraw those words. From the outset, however, I find a judge judging himself . . . unusual, that is all. I would like to know, apart from the unwillingness of a judge to admit to any mistake that he might have made, what other grounds there are for dismissing this appeal?'

Bishop Forbassach leaned forward.

'I would dismiss it because you have no facts. You have merely asked a lot of clever questions.'

'Questions that cannot be answered at this time,' snapped Fidelma. 'That is the basis of my plea, a plea to stop the sentence until those questions *can* be answered.'

'Unanswerable questions do not bear on the original decisions of the trial. You say this Saxon was a messenger. Where was his white wand of office? You now produce it like a conjurer and your only witness cannot swear that she saw you take it from the spot from which you claimed you took it.'

'I can produce—'

'Anything that you can produce,' interrupted Bishop Forbassach, 'is invalid as evidence, for who knows but that you brought it to this place yourself. It is not evidence, for we do not know that the Saxon carried it. As to the witnesses, you impute both their knowledge and integrity.'

'I do not do so!' protested Fidelma.

'Ah.' Bishop Forbassach smiled triumphantly. 'Are you withdrawing the remarks which you made about them?'

Fidelma shook her head. 'I do not do so.'

'Then you must impute their testimony.'

'I do not. I have put forward a number of questions that they should have been asked at the trial.'

'We heard their testimony at the original trial and saw no reason to cross-examine them,' Forbassach said decisively. 'They are all of upstanding character and, in our judgment, have told the truth. The witness, Sister Fial, clearly saw the Saxon. She was an eye-witness to his heinous crime. You would dare to impute the credibility of a thirteen-year-old child who has just witnessed the rape and murder of her even younger friend? What justice is that, Fidelma of Cashel? We obviously have different values here, in Laigin, to your courts of Cashel where it is said you entertain the crowds with sharp wit and legal niceties. Here we consider that truth is not games of legal *fidchell*.'

Fidchell was a wooden board game, a game of intellectual skill, on which Fidelma prided her proficiency.

Fianamail laid a hand on Bishop Forbassach's arm and whispered urgently into his ear. The Brehon grimaced sourly and nodded. The young King abruptly stood up.

'This hearing is now ended. In fairness, my Brehon, Bishop Forbassach, has asked to discuss the case with me so that any judgment we may make may be seen to be completely fair. He will announce our adjudication on this appeal at dawn tomorrow. These deliberations are now ended.'

Fidelma felt a moment of black despair as she dropped back into her chair.

'The courts of Laigin have descended into darkness!' cried a strident male voice. She barely noticed that it was the elderly *bó-aire*, Coba, who rose and stormed from the room.

Fianamail hesitated, angered at the demonstration and then, with a scowl on his face, he swept from the chamber. Bishop Forbassach stood, undecided for a moment, and then the abbess went to join him. His features broke into a look of triumph as he turned to her and they left together. As the others began to disperse Dego rose and came forward and placed a hand awkwardly on Fidelma's shoulder in an effort to comfort her.

'You did your best, lady,' he muttered. 'They are determined to see Brother Eadulf die.'

Fidelma raised her head, aware that there were tears glistening in her eyes, and unashamed of them.

'Dego, I do not know what else I can do now legally to save him. There is no time.'

'But they will not give judgment until tomorrow. There is still hope that they will find for your appeal.' There was no conviction in his voice.

'You heard how the Brehon Forbassach hectored me. No; he will uphold the sentence he has passed.'

Dego agreed reluctantly. 'You're right, lady. That Bishop Forbassach has demonstrated his bias. Did you see the way he went off with Abbess Fainder and both of them smiling and his hand on hers? There is some collusion in this matter.'

'The only hope left is if the Chief Brehon of Ireland, Barrán himself, arrives and orders a halt to this foul injustice,' Fidelma said.

Dego shook his head sadly. 'Then there is no hope, lady. It would take at least three more days before young Aidan could find Barrán and bring him here; probably a full week and that if luck were on our side.'

Fidelma rose, trying to regain her composure.

'I must go back to the abbey and tell Eadulf to prepare for the worst.'

'Would it not be better to wait until the decision is formerly announced in the morning?'

'I cannot fool myself, Dego, nor can I fool Eadulf.'

'Do you want me to come with you?'

'Thank you, but no, Dego. This is something I'd best do alone. I think Eadulf will wish to see some friendly faces tomorrow when this terrible thing is done. At least he can die in the company of friends as well as enemies. I will seek permission to attend as soon as the judgment is given. Will you and Enda join me?'

Dego did not hesitate.

'We will. God forgive them if they do ignore your plea, lady. It is many a brave man that I have seen die in battle: I have killed many myself. But in the fury of the battle, in hot blood, men who were free, with a sword or spear in hand to defend themselves; a fight that was man to man, equal to equal. But this . . . this is a foul thing, reducing men to the dignity of a poor calf at the slaughterhouse. It leaves one with a sense of shame.'

'It is not our way of punishment,' Fidelma conceded. Then she sighed deeply. 'I suppose one can argue that the person who does murder, who inflicts suffering and death on another, does not need our sympathy, but . . .'

'No reason why we should descend to the level of a murderer and enact cold-blooded rituals to disguise our murder,' Dego interrupted. 'And, surely, you are not saying that you now accept Brother Eadulf is guilty of this crime?'

Fidelma was trying hard to fight back the emotion she felt and shook her head rapidly. She hoped that her eyes were not too bright.

'I do not *know* at this time whether Eadulf is guilty or not. I *believe* he is innocent. I accept his word. But words are not enough in law. All I say from knowledge is that there are too many questions that should have been answered and now . . . now it seems too late. Go back to the inn, Dego. I will join you and Enda there soon.'

She walked slowly across the township towards the abbey, her mind oppressed by gloomy thoughts. She did not know what to say to Eadulf. She could only tell him the truth. She felt that she had utterly failed him. She had no doubt in her mind that, in spite of Fianamail's attempt to play at diplomacy, Bishop Forbassach would deny the appeal. The belligerent way he had countered all her questions indicated that he was intent on carrying through the demands of Abbess Fainder to enact these cruel new punishments.

If only she had more time! There were too many implausible aspects to the evidence. Yet Bishop Forbassach did not seem to care about pursuing them. Time! It all came down to time. And tomorrow, when the sun was at its zenith, her good friend and companion would have his life extinguished because she had not succeeded.

As she approached the gates of the abbey she determined not to let anyone see that she had lost confidence; after all, it only needed something, some little thing, to cause a delay. Her chin came up in a defensive posture.

When Sister Étromma came to the gate, she was looking strangely anxious. She had left the King's hall and hastened back to the abbey as soon as Bishop Forbassach had announced his opinion.

'I am sorry, Sister. I could only answer the truth. You did have your back to me when you found those items and I could not truly swear I saw you take them from their hiding place. Bishop Forbassach was so fierce in his questioning that I . . .'

Fidelma held up a hand to placate the anxious stewardess. She did not blame her. Had she supported Fidelma, Bishop Forbassach would doubtless have found some other means of questioning the evidence.

'It is not your fault, Sister. Anyway, no decision has been announced as yet,' Fidelma replied, trying to make her voice as indifferent as possible.

Sister Étromma continued to look distraught.

'But you must know that it is a foregone conclusion?' she pressed. 'Bishop Forbassach has said as much.'

Fidelma tried to appear confident.

'It is in the hands of the King and his advisers. In spite of Forbassach,

I still say that there are questions that should be addressed, and any impartial judge would know that a life could not be taken until those questions are answered.'

Sister Étromma lowered her head. 'I suppose so. Do you really believe that there might be a delay in the execution of the Saxon?'

Fidelma's voice was tight. She chose her words carefully.

'I hope there will be. Yet it is not up to me to predict a judge's decision.'

'Just so,' muttered the *rechtaire* of the abbey. 'This is not a happy place now. I look forward to the coming day when I shall go to the Isle of Mannanán Mac Lir and retire from the anxieties of this abbey. But I expect that you will wish to see the Saxon?'

'I do.'

She turned and let the way through the abbey again and into the main courtyard. The sun was well down now and darkness enshrouded the abbey. However, the courtyard was lit by numerous torches. Two men, watched by two others, one of them a religieux, were cutting down the body of Brother Ibar from the wooden gibbet. They looked up from their gruesome task and one of them grinned at her.

'Making room for tomorrow,' he called; a coarse-faced man in working clothing. Nearby was some sacking laid out on the flagstones of the courtyard ready to receive the body. No wooden coffin for Brother Ibar, observed Fidelma, but a sackcloth and probably a swiftly dug hole in the marshland along the riverbank. The two black-clad workmen reminded her of ravens picking over the bones of their victim rather than morticians preparing a corpse for a funeral.

Fidelma hesitated in mid-stride and her gaze fell on the face of the religieux who was acting as an overseer. It was the burly, pugnacious figure of Brother Cett. He stared lopsidedly at her, displaying a row of cracked and blackened teeth. She had rarely seen a man so resembling a brute before. She shivered. Next to him was a small, wiry-framed man whose clothing proclaimed him to be a boatman. His leather trouser and jerkin and linen scarf were commonly worn among the river boatmen. This man did not bother to look up as they crossed the courtyard.

'We are going to the Saxon's cell, Cett,' called Sister Étromma as they passed.

The big man grunted, perhaps signifying agreement but the sound could have meant anything. It seemed that the *rechtaire* took it for assent for she passed on with Fidelma following swiftly.

She led the way up the stairs to the cell, outside which another religieux was seated on a wooden stool under a flickering brand torch, engaged in contemplation of his crucifix, which he held in both hands before him in his lap. He sprang up as they approached and recognised Sister Étromma immediately. Without a word, he drew back the bolts on the cell door.

Sister Étromma turned to Fidelma. 'Call when you wish to leave. I have other business to attend to so cannot remain.'

Fidelma passed into the cell. Eadulf rose to greet her. His face was grim.

'Eadulf . . .' she began.

He shook his head swiftly. 'You do not have to tell me, Fidelma. I saw you and the other Sister crossing the courtyard from the window here and I can guess the outcome. Had the appeal been allowed I would imagine Bishop Forbassach would have come with you and not sent you ahead with such a dismal look on your face.'

'It is not certain,' Fidelma said weakly. 'The result of the appeal will be announced by Forbassach tomorrow morning. There is still some hope.'

Eadulf turned to the window. 'I doubt it. I told you all along, there is some evil in this place which determines my end.'

'Nonsense!' snapped Fidelma. 'You must not give up.'

Eadulf glanced over his shoulder and smiled bleakly.

'I think that I have known you too long, Fidelma, for you to keep secrets from me. I can tell it from your eyes. You are already mourning my death.'

She quickly reached out a hand and touched his. 'Don't say that!'

For the first time he heard the brittleness in her voice and knew she was close to tears.

'I'm sorry,' he muttered, feeling awkward. 'A stupid thing to say.' He realised she needed as much support as he did to face the coming ordeal. Eadulf was not an emotionally selfish man. 'So, Bishop Forbassach will pronounce on your appeal tomorrow morning?'

She nodded, not trusting herself to speak.

'Good. Then we will take it as it comes. In the meanwhile, could you ask Sister Étromma to ensure that I have soap and water? I would like to look my best for whatever the morning brings.'

Fidelma felt the tears stinging her eyes. Suddenly Eadulf reached forward and wrapped his arms around her, squeezing hard and then thrusting her away almost brutally.

'There! Off you go, Fidelma. Leave me to my meditations. I will see you in the morning.'

She took the cue; there was too much between them for her to remain. Another few seconds and they both would be without any control of their emotions. She turned and called harshly for the Brother. A moment later the bolts rasped and the door swung open. She did not look back into the cell as she left.

'Until tomorrow, Eadulf,' she muttered.

Brother Eadulf made no reply as the cell door slammed shut behind her.

Fidelma did not return to the inn immediately but went for a walk along the riverside, finding a deserted corner at the end of the quays and a log to sit on in the gloom. The moon was brilliant white, casting its eerie dancing lights on the waters. She sat quietly, her cheeks wet with hot tears. She had not cried since she was a young girl. She did not even attempt the meditation technique of the *dercad* to quell the raging emotion within her. She had tried to keep her emotions in check ever since she had learnt of Eadulf's peril. She could not help him by giving way to sentiment. She had to be strong; divorced from emotion so that she could see logically.

Yet she felt torn between a terrible sense of despair and an explosive feeling of outrage. Since she had known Eadulf she had tried to keep her feelings hidden, even from herself. She had been oppressed by a sense of duty; duty to the Faith, to the law, to the five kingdoms and her own brother. Now, just as she had finally ceased to deny her feelings and had begun to admit just how much Eadulf meant to her, he stood in danger of being taken away from her for ever. It was . . . so unfair. She realise how banal the phrase was, but could think of no other expression for all her reading of the ancient philosophers. The old philosophers would excuse such outrageous fortune by saying that the gods willed otherwise. She could not accept that. Virgil wrote: *Fata viam invenient* – the gods will find a way. She had to find a way. She had to.

Chapter Nine

Fidelma stirred in her uneasy sleep.

She was dreaming; dreaming of the corpse of the religieux swinging at the end of the taut rope from the wooden gibbet. Behind the corpse were gathered a group of cowled figures, laughing and jeering at the dead man. She was trying to reach forward, hands outstretched, towards the hanging form, but something was pressing her back. Hands were holding her. She turned to see who it was and the face of her old mentor and tutor – the Brehon Morann – appeared behind her.

'Why?' she screamed at him. 'Why?'

'The eye hides what it does not wish to see,' the old man smiled enigmatically.

She pulled away and turned back to the hanging male form.

There was a crashing noise. At first she thought that it was the gibbet breaking up, the wood splintering and scattering.

Then she realised that she had been awakened and the crashing noise was a reality outside her room; heavy footsteps were pounding up the stairs of the Inn of the Yellow Mountain. She had barely time to sit up in the bed before the door was smashed open without any further warning.

Bishop Forbassach pushed through the door, a lantern in his hand. Behind him, with drawn swords, came half a dozen men, among them a large, burly figure which was familiar to her. It was Brother Cett.

Before she could fully recover her wits, Bishop Forbassach, holding the lantern high, had begun to search her small room, dropping to his knees and peering under her bed.

One of the men stood with a drawn sword pointing at her chest in silent menace.

Fidelma was shocked. She gazed at them firstly in bewilderment and then with a sense of growing outrage.

'What does this mean?' she began.

There came another interruption, the sound of a scuffle beyond the door. Some of the men turned to help their comrades behind them and then Dego and Enda were dragged into the room, arms pinioned behind them. They had apparently come running, swords in hand, at the sound of the disturbance. They were overwhelmed by numbers and disarmed, their arms twisted unmercifully high behind their backs so that they were almost bent double between Forbassach's men.

'What is the meaning of this outrage, Forbassach?' Fidelma demanded coldly, the icy tone disguising her seething fury. She ignored the menacing sword that was held against her. 'Have you taken leave of your senses?'

The bishop, having examined the corners of the room, turned back to her, lantern still in hand. His face was a mask of threatening animosity.

'Where is he?' he snarled.

Fidelma stared back at him with equal dislike.

'Where is who? You have much to explain for this unwarranted intrusion, Brehon of Laigin. Do you know what you are doing? You have transgressed all laws of—'

'Silence, woman!' muttered the man who held the sword at her chest, giving it a jab to emphasise his order.

Fidelma felt the pinprick. She did not even glance at the warrior but remained with her gaze fixed on Forbassach.

'Tell your bully who I am, Forbassach, and do you remember it also. If blood is drawn from the sister of the King of Colgú who is a *dálaigh* of the courts then blood will answer for blood. You know the law. There are some things that no allowances can be made for. You have passed beyond my patience.'

Bishop Forbassach hesitated at the ice-cold rage in her voice. Yet he had difficulty in controlling his own temper and stood for what seemed a long time before he succeeded.

'You may put your sword down,' he said in clipped tones to the man. Then he turned back to Fidelma. 'I ask you again, where is he?'

Fidelma regarded the intimidating figure of the Brehon of Laigin with cold curiosity.

'And I ask *you* again, who is it to whom you refer?'

'You know well enough that I am referring to the Saxon.'

Fidelma blinked rapidly in astonishment as she realised the implication of his question but forced herself not to show her feelings.

Bishop Forbassach grimaced with irritability.

'Don't pretend that you have no knowledge of Brother Eadulf's escape.'

Fidelma's eyes did not leave his.

'I do not pretend. I have no idea what you are talking about.'

The bishop turned to his little army.

'You men remain,' he gestured to those holding Fidelma's companions. 'Keep hold of those two. The rest of you will search this inn and search it thoroughly, outbuildings as well. Check to see if any horses are missing.'

Fidelma was aware of Lassar appearing behind the men looking terrified. She wished that she could reassure the woman. However, her own heart was beating rapidly. She knew that she must not allow Forbassach to dominate the situation.

Then a thin, whining masculine voice, slurred by alcohol, rose above the hubbub and confusion.

'What's this noise? This is an inn and I paid for a good bed and a night's sleep.'

Behind the crowd at the door a small man pushed his way forward. He had clearly been roused from an alcohol-induced sleep; his hair was dishevelled, a cloak wrapped around him for decency's sake.

Bishop Forbassach turned, vexed by the interruption.

'What is happening is no concern of yours, Gabrán. Get back where you belong!'

The little man moved forward a step, almost like a terrier squaring up to a hound. He squinted almost short-sightedly at the bishop and then recognised him. He started to mumble apologies and backed away in confusion. Forbassach turned to Fidelma once more.

'So, you were claiming that the Saxon is not here?'

Fidelma's eyes were bright in anticipation.

'I am not claiming anything: I am telling you that he is not. It seems that he has escaped?'

Bishop Forbassach greeted her question with a sneer. 'As if you do not know.'

'I do not know.'

'He is not in his cell in the abbey. He has escaped and Brother Cett here was knocked unconscious by those who aided him in that escape.'

Fidelma took a sharp inward breath as he confirmed her deduction. A sudden breath of hope. She gave Forbassach a hard look.

'You accuse me of helping him escape? I am a *dálaigh* and constrained by the laws of the courts of the five kingdoms. I knew nothing of this until you told me this moment. Why do you break into my room in the middle of the night with a use of force and threaten me and my companions?'

'For obvious reasons. The Saxon made no attempt to escape until you arrived and it was clear that he did not escape on his own account.'

'On my *dálaigh*'s oath, Forbassach, I have had no hand in this matter. This much you could have learnt from me without your dramatic entrance and use of unnecessary force. Nor is it necessary for you to continue in your violence to my companions.'

Bishop Forbassach turned to where Dego and Enda were still bent double in excruciating pain in the hands of his men.

'Let them up,' he reluctantly ordered.

The men holding the two Cashel warriors loosed their holds. Forbassach gave them a moment to recover their breath.

'Well, accepting your word that you had no hand in the matter, perhaps your men acted in your stead. Speak, you!' He pointed abruptly to Dego.

The warrior's eyes narrowed and doubtless he would have attacked the arrogant Brehon had he not been aware of the muscular Brother Cett at his side.

'I know nothing about this escape, Brehon of Laigin,' he replied in a measured tone but there was no respect in his voice which the rank of the Brehon should have commanded.

Bishop Forbassach's face mirrored his anger.

'And you?' he demanded, turning to Enda.

'I was in bed until your bullies disturbed my slumber by attacking the sister of my King,' he said defiantly. 'I came to defend her from your assault. You may have to answer to the consequences of that attack later.'

'Perhaps we might persuade you to reflect on your memories,' smiled the bishop unpleasantly.

'This is an outrage, Forbassach!' cried Fidelma, horrified by his insinuation. 'You will not lay hands on my men. Remember, they are trusted warriors of my brother, the King of Cashel.'

'Better we lay hands on them than we should lay hands on you, woman,' broke in the surly Brother Cett.

'There will be blood between Cashel and Fearna if you let this matter get out of hand, Bishop Forbassach!' warned Fidelma harshly. 'You know that even if your bullies do not.'

'I can vouch that these two warriors have not been out of the inn this night, my lord bishop.'

The interruption came from a man who was standing outside the room and now pushed his way in.

Fidelma saw that it was Mel, the commander of the palace guard.

Bishop Forbassach looked up at him in surprise.

'What makes you so sure of this, Mel?' he demanded.

'Because this is my sister's inn, as you know, and I have been staying here this night. My bed is in the room next to where these men sleep. I am a light sleeper and I can vouch for the fact that they have not stirred until your men burst in here.'

'You have been a long time in coming to tell me,' observed Forbassach. 'If you are so light a sleeper, why have you taken all this time to come to see me?'

'Because your men started to search my sister's inn and I thought it wiser to go with them to ensure that they were not too enthusiastic in their search and damaged her property.'

The bishop stood as if puzzled how next to proceed. It was clear that the unexpected support from the Laigin warrior had left him without room to manoeuvre. While he stood undecided, one of his men came hurrying back.

'The inn and all the outhouses have been searched. There is no sign of the Saxon. No sign of anything at all.'

'Are you sure? Have you searched everywhere thoroughly?'

'Everywhere, Forbassach,' replied the man. 'Maybe the Saxon stole away on a boat towards Loch Garman to get a ship back to his own lands?'

Bishop Forbassach turned back to Fidelma with lips compressed angrily. Fidelma decided to seize the advantage.

'My companions and I will accept your apology for this unwarranted intrusion, Forbassach. However, you have stretched the laws of hospitality to their limits and beyond. I will accept your apology only because it is clear that you are under some stress.'

Bishop Forbassach's face clouded in anger for a moment and he seemed about to make a verbal attack again. Instead he hesitated and then motioned to his men to leave. His fiery eyes did not leave Fidelma's ice-cold gaze.

'Let me warn you, Fidelma of Cashel.' He spoke slowly, as if he had trouble formulating his thoughts in words. 'This matter of the Saxon's escape is a serious one. It is known that you are a friend of his. You came here to defend him. The fact that he has escaped at this moment is no coincidence. You and your companions may have outwitted us and been able to hide him from our search. Doubtless you knew that we would come here first. I warn you, Fidelma, this will be your undoing. By taking the law into your own hands you will never be able to practise the profession of law again.' He laughed shortly. 'And here is an amusing thought to ponder on, Fidelma. I was actually going to defer the execution of the Saxon for a week, to please the concerns of King Fianamail, so that we might find some answers to those clever questions which you put forward. The escape of the Saxon is now a clear confession of his guilt. As soon as he is recaptured, he will be hanged. We will have no more appeals.'

Fidelma met Bishop Forbassach's smouldering gaze evenly.

'You are wrong to accuse me of aiding Brother Eadulf's escape, Forbassach. I have, unlike some in this kingdom, maintained strict compliance to the laws of the five kingdoms and have not discarded my faith in them for any other law. Remember that, Forbassach. Nor would I interpret his escape as a confession of guilt. Every innocent person has the right to self-defence. The escape might just as easily be interpreted as a defence from a judicial murder.'

The bishop made to reply, changed his mind and left the room without another word.

Dego came forward with a look of concern on his face.

'Are you all right, lady? They have not harmed you?'

Fidelma shook her head. She put a hand up to her shoulder where the tip of the warrior's blade had pricked it.

'A scratch, no more. Pass me my robe, Enda,' she instructed quietly and when the young man did so, she swung out of the bed. She regarded the two young warriors carefully.

'Now we are alone, tell me, and speak the truth. Did either of you have any hand in Eadulf's escape?' She asked the question swiftly, breathlessly.

Dego answered immediately with a negative gesture. 'I swear it, lady.' Then he smiled crookedly. 'However, had such an idea occurred to us, I think we might well have considered participation in it.'

Enda agreed solemnly. 'That is about the size of it, lady. The idea did not occur to us and now that someone else has carried out the plan it puts shame on us.'

Fidelma pursed her lips in rebuke. While her heart agreed with them, her rational thought did not.

'It would put a shame on you to break the law,' she admonished.

'Not break the law, lady,' insisted Enda, 'just bend it a little to buy time for the Brehon Barrán to arrive.'

She looked up as Lassar entered, followed by her brother Mel. They had apparently made sure that Bishop Forbassach and his men had left the inn.

'This is a bad business, Sister,' fussed Lassar. 'It is difficult to run an inn these days but if I have offended the bishop who is a Brehon, the abbess and the King all at once, I shall have no hope in continuing to run the inn. No hope at all.'

Mel put his arm around his sister's shoulders to comfort her.

'It is a bad business, lady,' he echoed uncomfortably. 'We have come to ask you, openly and honestly, whether you have a hand in this business.'

'We have not,' Fidelma assured them. 'Do you want us to leave the inn?'

'Forgive us, lady. This is naturally upsetting for my sister. It would be unjust to turn you from the inn when there are no grounds for doing so.'

Lassar sniffed and dabbed at her eyes with an edge of her shawl.

'You are welcome to stay here. I just meant . . .'

'And you are right to point out your position,' Fidelma interrupted firmly. 'I can assure you that if our staying here becomes a matter of compromising your livelihood then we will depart. If you feel happy with our staying then we shall stay. We have done nothing wrong in the eyes of the law of this land, in spite of Bishop Forbassach's suspicions. That I can assure you.'

'We accept your word, Sister.'

'Then the only thing we can do now is to try to get some sleep during whatever is left of the night.'

Lassar and her brother left the room together but Fidelma motioned Dego and Enda to hold back.

'Now that we are assured that none of us are involved, this does bring up a problem,' she whispered softly.

Dego inclined his head in agreement.

'If we did not help Eadulf to escape, who did and for what purpose?' he asked.

'For what purpose?' echoed Enda, puzzled.

Fidelma smiled gently at the young warrior.

'Dego has seen the point. I have observed that several people involved in these events have disappeared – key witnesses at the abbey. Is it at all possible that Eadulf has been induced to "disappear" also in the same manner?'

The possibility made her feel uneasy but it was one which had to be faced, as far-fetched as it seemed, but then, on reflection, it was no more far-fetched than the other mysteries connected with this business. There was a silence while the three of them thought about the implication.

'Well, there is little we can do now in the middle of the night,' Fidelma admitted reluctantly. 'What is clear, however, is that we must find Eadulf before Bishop Forbassach and his men do.'

Once alone, Fidelma did not know whether to give way to the feeling of wild elation which had been her first response to the news that Eadulf had escaped the gibbet, or to allow the nagging depression to overtake her thoughts – the fear that he might have escaped into a worse fate. She could not regain her state of sleep. Surely things were not as bad? She had been certain that Eadulf was facing death that morning. Now he had escaped. Had Brehon Morann been too cynical when he had once advised her that any time things appeared to be going better, it meant that something had been overlooked? What had she overlooked?

She sought vainly for sleep in the art of the *dercad* but her thoughts were too clouded with her new fears for Eadulf. It was dawn before she fell into an exhausted slumber. It was a sleep from which she awoke with no dream memories but only foreboding that all was not well.

Eadulf had not gone to bed that night. Knowing that it was likely to be his last night on earth had somehow made the idea of sleeping it away seem a senseless act. He sat on his bed, the only comfortable seat, gazing through the bars of his cell window at the little patch of night-blue sky. He tried to form his random, panic-stricken thoughts into one cohesive stream of thought, but try as he might those thoughts rebelled. It was not true, as the sages claimed, that a man faced with imminent death could concentrate more clearly. His thoughts kept leaping here and there. To his childhood, to his meeting with Fidelma at Whitby, to his further meeting in Rome and then his coming to the Kingdom of Muman. His mind kept rambling through memories, bittersweet memories.

The sound was muffled. A grunt. Something falling. He was standing up, looking towards the door, when the bolts rasped open.

A dark figure stood in the doorway. It wore a cowled robe.

'It . . . it can't be time already,' Eadulf protested, horrified by the thought. 'It is not yet daylight.'

The figure beckoned in the gloom. 'Come,' it whispered urgently.

'What is happening?' Eadulf's voice was a protest.

'Come and do not speak,' insisted the figure.

Eadulf moved reluctantly across to the cell door.

'It is imperative that you do not say anything. Just follow us,' the cowled figure ordered. 'We are here to help you.'

He realised that there were two other men in the corridor. One held a candle. The other was dragging the recumbent form of Brother Cett into the cell that he was vacating. Eadulf's heart began to beat faster as he saw what was happening.

He stepped quickly after them; his reluctance had vanished. The cell door was shut and secured.

'Raise your hood, Brother,' whispered one of the cowled figures. 'Head down now.'

He obeyed immediately.

The small group walked smartly along the corridor and down the stairs, Eadulf content to follow where they led, through a maze of corridors and suddenly, without meeting any impediment, they were outside the walls of the abbey, through the gates by the riverbank. Another figure was there holding the reins of several horses. Without a word, the leading figure helped Eadulf to mount while the others were already springing into the saddles of their horses. Then they were trotting rapidly away from the abbey gates, along by the moonlit silver waters of the river.

They reached a clump of trees and the leader caused them to halt, raising his head as if in an attitude of listening.

'No sounds of pursuit,' the man muttered. 'But we must be vigilant. We will ride hard from now on.'

'Who are you?' asked Eadulf. 'Is Fidelma among you?'

'Fidelma? The *dálaigh* from Cashel?' The spokesman laughed softly. 'Save your questions yet awhile, Saxon. Can you keep up if we maintain a gallop?'

'I can ride,' replied Eadulf stiffly, yet still bewildered at who these men might be if they had not been sent by Fidelma.

'Let us ride!'

The leader dug his heels into his horse's flanks and the beast leapt forward. Within a second, the other horses were following. Eadulf felt the exhilarating breath of the cold night wind on his cheeks and in his hair, blowing the cowl from his head, his hair ruffling and tousling in its grip. For the first time in weeks he had a sense of levity, of excitement. He was free with only the elements to constrain and caress his body.

He lost count of time as the body of horsemen thundered along the riverside road, turning into woods, up a narrow track that snaked in and out of shrubland and open spaces, across marshland and up small hills. It was a dizzy, whirling ride, and then they went through a cleared area of land to a peak on which an old earthwork fortress rose; its ditches and ramparts must have been dug in ancient times. On top of the ramparts rose walls of great wooden logs. The gates stood open and, without even pausing, the body of horsemen thundered in, across a wooden bridge stretching through the ramparts.

They came to a halt so swiftly that some of the horses reared and kicked out in protest. Then the men were sliding from their mounts and figures with torches were rushing out to take charge of the lathered animals, leading them away to stables.

For a moment Eadulf stood, breathless, regarding his companions in curiosity.

They had now dropped their cowls and in the light of the torches and lamps Eadulf realised that none of them were religious. They all had the look of warriors.

'Are you warriors of Cashel?' he asked after he had recovered sufficient breath. This drew forth laughter and they all drifted off into the darkness leaving Eadulf alone with their leader.

In the light of a nearby brand torch, Eadulf saw that he was an elderly man, with long flowing silver locks. He took a step forward with a smile and shook his head.

'We are not from Cashel, Saxon. We are men of Laigin.'

Eadulf frowned in total bewilderment now. 'I don't understand. Why have you brought me here? Indeed, where is here? Was it not at the instructions of Fidelma of Cashel?'

The elderly man chuckled softly. 'Do you think a *dálaigh* would disobey the law to the extent that they would snatch you from the jaws of hell, Saxon?' he asked in amusement.

'Then you are not from Fidelma? I am at a loss . . . Are you letting me free to continue my journey home?'

The elderly man came forward and pointed to the walls of the fortress, for such was the place to which Eadulf had been brought.

'These walls are the boundaries of your new prison, Saxon. While I do not agree with the idea of taking life for life, I believe that our native laws must be upheld. I will not submit to the Penitentials of Rome but I will uphold the laws of the Brehons.'

Eadulf was more confused than ever. 'Then who are you and what is this place?'

'My name is Coba, *bó-aire* of Cam Eolaing. See the walls? These are the walls of my fortress. These are now boundaries of your *maighin digona.*'

Eadulf had never heard the term before and said so.

'The *maighin digona* is the precinct of sanctuary allowed by the law. Within these walls I am empowered to extend my protection to any stranger flying from unjust punishment, flying from a hue and cry. I have effectively saved you from the violent hands of your pursuers.'

Eadulf took a deep breath. 'I think I understand.'

The old man glanced keenly at him. 'I hope that you do. I have only extended this sanctuary to you until such time as you are summoned before a senior judge and given justice under our native law. Let me warn you, this sanctuary is not inviolate, for if you are guilty under our law you will not escape that justice. If you escape from here before you are judged again then I myself would incur your punishment. I am allowed to avert violence but not to defeat justice. Only death will await you outside these walls if you attempt to leave before further legal judgment.'

'For that I am grateful,' Eadulf sighed. 'For I am truly innocent and I hope my innocence can be proved.'

'Whether you are innocent or not, that is no concern to me, Saxon,' the old man said sternly. 'I simply believe in our law and shall ensure that you will answer to our law. If you escape, then the law holds me, as being the one extending sanctuary to you, responsible for your original offence and I must take your punishment upon myself. Therefore, I shall not let you escape the law. Do you understand what I say, Saxon?'

'I do,' Eadulf agreed quietly. 'You make it very clear.'

'Then praise God that this dawn,' the old man pointed to the reddening eastern sky, 'will not be your last but merely heralding the first day of the rest of your life.'

Chapter Ten

'Are you the woman who was in trouble with the Brehon of Laigin, Bishop Forbassach, eh?'

The thin, reedy voice seemed vaguely familiar.

Fidelma glanced up from her breakfast to see a scrawny-looking individual leaning over her. There was no one else in the main room of the inn for she had come down to an early breakfast.

She frowned at the man's unprepossessing appearance. He was clad in the garb of a boatman. It was a moment or two before she recognised him as the little man who had been drinking and had started to complain at having his sleep disturbed when Forbassach had burst into the inn. Yet anyone so untypical of the usual idea of a boatman she had yet to see. He was a wisp of a man, angular with long, lank brown hair. In spite of his beak of a nose, thin red lips and dark, almost fathomless eyes, it was clear that in his youth he might have been handsome; now, however, his weatherbeaten features were moulded not so much by age but by dissolute experience.

'As you see, I am in no trouble,' Fidelma replied shortly, returning her attention to her plate.

The boatman sat down without invitation, seemingly unabashed at her unfriendly response.

'Don't give me that,' he sneered. 'I saw what I saw last night. A Brehon does not come out in the middle of the night with a half-a-dozen warriors if there is no cause. What did you do?' He smirked, showing a line of blackened teeth. 'Come on, you can tell me. Why, I might even be able to help you. I have quite a lot of contacts in Fearna – influential contacts – and if you make it worth my while . . .'

The boatman suddenly let out a sharp exclamation, and the next moment it seemed that he was rising unwillingly from his seat, his head bent to one side. Holding him by the ear was Dego whose tight grasp was expertly applied.

'I believe that you are annoying this lady.' Dego's voice was soft but menacing. 'Perhaps you would like to move on?'

117

The man twisted and attempted to struggle before realising that his antagonist was a muscular young warrior. His reed-like voice rose to a wail in protest.

'I was not insulting her. I was offering my help and—'

Fidelma waved her hand casually.

'Let him go, Dego,' she sighed, adding firmly to the boatman: 'I do not want your help. Certainly, I do not wish to pay for any help that you might be offering. Now, I suggest that you follow the advice of my comrade and move on.'

Dego let go of the man's ear and the boatman, clutching it, staggered back a step or two.

'I will not forget this,' he whined, keeping out of reach of Dego. 'I have friends and you will pay for this. You think that you can get the better of me? Others have tried. They have learnt better.'

Lassar had entered to attend to Fidelma's wants and heard the man's complaint.

'What has happened?' she demanded.

Dego smiled vindictively and seated himself in the chair which the boatman had just vacated.

'It was my mistake,' he told Lassar with a smile. 'I had the impression that this little man,' he jerked at thumb at the boatman, 'was pressing his unwanted attentions on Sister Fidelma. I have apologised for misunderstanding.'

The man had been standing rubbing his ear. He stopped when he heard her name, clearly recognising it. Fidelma wondered why.

'I am sure this fellow accepts your apology, Dego, and has no wish to cause any more trouble,' Fidelma said firmly.

The boatman hesitated for a moment and then jerkily inclined his head.

'A person is entitled to make a mistake. Isn't that the truth?' he muttered.

Fidelma's eyes narrowed suddenly as a memory came to her.

'I've seen you before, haven't I?'

The little man scowled. 'No!'

'I have it! You were in the abbey courtyard watching them take down the body of Brother Ibar.'

'Why shouldn't I have been? I do a lot of trade with the abbey.'

'Do you have a morbid interest in the grotesque, or was the fate of Brother Ibar of particular interest to you?' Fidelma asked the question out of instinct rather than logic.

Lassar, who had been standing by, puzzled at the exchange, intervened helpfully.

'Gabrán does do a lot of trade up and down the river. Isn't that right?'

The man merely turned and left the inn without replying to either question. Lassar smiled apologetically.

'I think you may have hurt his feelings. If you want to know, Sister, it was one of Gabrán's men who was killed and robbed by Brother Ibar.'

Dego grimaced towards Fidelma. 'Did I do wrong in intervening?'

She shook her head and turned towards Lassar who was putting freshly baked bread on the table.

'He does not look much like a boatman or river man to me, apart from his clothing.'

The big woman shrugged. 'Yet he is a river man, Sister. He runs his own boat called the *Cág*, trading along the river. Now and then he stays here in the inn when he has had his fill of drink and cannot find his way back to his boat. He was here the night his man was killed.'

'The *Cág*? Isn't *Jackdaw* a strange name for a boat?'

Lassar was indifferent to the nuance of the name. 'Each to their own, I say.'

Fidelma smiled shortly. 'A wise saying. What do you know of the murder of his crewman?'

'I know nothing at first hand.'

'You must have heard some gossip about it, though,' Fidelma pressed.

'Gossip is not always truth,' replied the woman.

'You are right in that. Yet sometimes, prejudiced knowledge is very helpful in discovering truth. What did you hear?'

'All I know is that the boatman was found on the quay the day following the murder of the young girl by the Saxon. A day later Brother Ibar was caught with some of the boatman's belongings and so he was tried and convicted for the crime.'

'Who heard the case against him?'

'The Brehon, of course, Bishop Forbassach.'

'Do you know if Brother Ibar ever admitted that he was guilty?'

'Not during the trial nor afterwards, so I am told.'

'And the evidence was that he had the belongings of this boatman on him?'

'To confirm those facts you would have to ask someone who attended the trial. I have work to do.'

119

'One moment! Would it be your brother, Mel, who was involved in catching Ibar? He was captain of the watch, wasn't he?'

To her surprise, Lassar shook her head.

'Mel had nothing to do with the case of Ibar. It was one of his watch, though. Daig was the man's name.'

Fidelma considered this fact in silence and then observed softly: 'There seems to be much death on that quay by the abbey. It seems an unhappy, dark place.'

Lassar grimaced as she picked up some dishes. 'There is truth in that. You have met Sister Étromma and her half-wit brother, haven't you?'

'Cett? I have. What have they to do with it?'

'Nothing. I mention them as an example of unhappiness. Would you believe that Sister Étromma was a descendant of the royal line of Laigin, the Uí Cheinnselaig?'

Fidelma tried to recall why it came as no surprise. She was sure that she had been told before.

Lassar grew confidential. 'Did you know that when the Uí Néill of Ulaidh raided the kingdom when Étromma was a child, she and her brother were taken as hostages. They say that this was when Cett received a wound which has made him simple. A sad tale.'

'Sad, indeed, but not unique,' agreed Fidelma.

'Ah, but what *was* unique was the fact that although Étromma was of the royal house, the King, Crimthann it was who ruled at that time, refused to pay the ransom money and left the two children to the tender care of the Uí Néill. Étromma's branch of the family were poor and could not afford the ransom.'

'What happened?' asked Fidelma, interested.

'After a year, Étromma and her brother managed to escape from the north and return here. I think she was very bitter. They both entered the service of the abbey. So you are right, there is much sadness there.'

Lassar gathered the dishes and left the room. Fidelma sat in thought for a moment before finally rising. Dego looked up questioningly.

'Where to now, my lady?' he asked.

'I am going back to the abbey to see what further information I can pick up,' she told him.

'Do you think that Bishop Forbassach was right and Brother Eadulf had help to escape?' asked Dego.

'I think it would be hard to escape from the cell in which he was incarcerated without any outside assistance,' she agreed. 'But who helped him and why is the mystery we must solve. There is one person who might have helped him and that is a chieftain called Coba. He certainly upholds the Laws of the Fénechus against the Penitentials which Fainder is so fond of. But perhaps it would not do to approach him directly just in case I have been misled. While I am at the abbey, find out what you can about Coba. Don't make it obvious, though.'

Dego inclined his head in agreement. 'Eadulf has done a dangerous thing, lady. Do you think he will attempt to contact us?'

'I hope so,' Fidelma said fervently. 'I would want him to stand before Barrán to clear his name. Bishop Forbassach is right in that escape can be interpreted as the sign of a guilty man.'

'Yet had he not escaped he would have been a dead man,' Dego reminded her dryly.

For a moment Fidelma felt a surge of bitterness.

'Do you think I have forgotten that I was helpless to aid Eadulf for all my knowledge of law?' she snapped at the warrior. 'Maybe I should have done what someone else has now done.'

'Lady,' Dego said swiftly, 'I meant no criticism of you.'

Fidelma reached out to lay her hand on his arm.

'Forgive my temper. I am at fault, Dego,' she said contritely.

'If Eadulf can avoid capture for the next few days then there is a chance that Aidan will return with Brehon Barrán,' Dego said reassuringly. 'If so, that retrial you wish for can be held.'

'But if he is a free agent now, where will he go?' mused Fidelma. 'He might try to take ship and sail for the lands of the Saxons, back to his own country.'

'Leave this land without telling you, lady? He would not do that now he knows that you are in Fearna.'

This did not comfort Fidelma.

'He may not have a choice, but I hope he does not delay on my account. Rather he should take to the mountains or woods and wait until the hue and cry has abated.' She paused, uncomfortably; a *dálaigh* should not be considering how best the law could be avoided. 'Where is Enda, by the way?'

'He went out early. I thought he said he had a mission to perform for you?'

She could not recall instructing Enda to go anywhere but she shrugged and said: 'If I do not see you before, I will try to meet you both back here, at the inn, sometime after noon.'

She left Dego finishing his breakfast and walked purposefully through the streets towards the abbey.

It was clear that the news of Brother Eadulf's escape had spread in the township for, as she walked along, people glanced with undisguised interest at her, some stopping to whisper to their neighbours. Their expressions ranged from hostile to simply curious. Only once or twice did a few people express their suspicions of her by shouting abuse. She ignored them. No one in Fearna, it seemed, remained ignorant of her identity, nor of her connection with the Saxon who had been due to hang at midday.

Within her, Fidelma still felt an intensity of different emotions about the situation. She realised that if she was to achieve anything now, she must keep those emotions in check. She had to make a tremendous effort of will and sweep all sentiment from her mind. If she thought of Eadulf in any other way than someone who desperately needed her help and experience, then she could go mad with the anguish that bubbled just below the surface of her calm exterior.

At the gates of the abbey, Sister Étromma greeted her with deep suspicion.

'You are the last person I expected to see,' she said rudely.

'Oh? Why so?' demanded Fidelma innocently, as the *rechtaire* grudgingly let her through the gates.

'I would have thought that you would be returning to Cashel rejoicing. The Saxon has escaped. Isn't that what you wanted?'

Fidelma regarded her seriously.

'What I wanted,' she replied with heavy emphasis, 'was that Brother Eadulf should have justice and be cleared of the charge against him. As for returning to Cashel rejoicing, I will not leave here until I find out what has happened to Brother Eadulf and, indeed, until after I have cleared his name. Escape does not absolve people before the law.'

'Escape is better than death,' the stewardess of the abbey pointed out, almost echoing the words of Dego.

'There is truth in that but I would rather that he was cleared than became a fugitive, in which case any man can treat him as one who is without the law and act accordingly.'

'Everyone in the abbey thinks that you had a hand in the escape. Did you?'

'You are direct, Sister Étromma. No, I did not help Eadulf to escape.'

'It will be difficult to convince people of that.'

'Difficult or not, it is the truth. Nor am I interested in wasting time trying to convince people.'

'Here you may find that lies win you friends but truth only begets hatred.'

'Speaking of hatred, you do not like Abbess Fainder much, do you?'

'It is not a requirement for a stewardess to like the abbess whom she serves.'

'Do you like the way she governs the abbey? I refer to this business of the Penitentials.'

'The Rule of the Abbey has been pronounced. I have to obey it. But I can see where you are leading, Sister. Do not attempt to persuade me to condemn the attitude of the abbess, nor of Bishop Forbassach. Whether punishment be by the Penitentials or by the Law of the Fénechus, remember that the Saxon was found guilty of rape and murder. For that crime, punishment under law must be made – whatever the law. Now, I am busy. There is much to be done in the abbey this day. What is the purpose of your visit?'

'I would firstly like to see the abbess.'

'I will be surprised if she agrees to see you.'

'Let us put that to the test then.'

Abbess Fainder did see Fidelma. She sat behind her desk as usual, looking austere, her dark eyes suspicious.

'Sister Étromma tells me that you have denied any knowledge of the Saxon's escape, Sister Fidelma. You do not expect me to believe that?' was her sharp opening remark.

Fidelma smiled softly and seated herself without being asked, conscious of the flicker of annoyance on the face of the abbess, but this time Abbess Fainder was too wise to object.

'I do not expect you to believe anything, Mother Abbess,' Fidelma replied calmly.

'But you want to plead your innocence of knowledge to me?' sneered the abbess.

'I do not have to plead anything before you,' Fidelma said. 'I have come merely to seek your consent to continue to ask questions among the members of this community.'

Abbess Fainder sat back with a surprised expression.

'For what purpose?' she demanded. 'You have asked all the questions and have made your appeal to the court. The truth was known when the Saxon fled from his cell.'

'Yesterday I did not have time to ask all the questions that I wanted to ask concerning the matter of the charges levelled against Brother Eadulf. I would like to resume today.'

For the first time Abbess Fainder looked totally bewildered.

'You will be wasting your time. Anyway, as I understand it, Forbassach will be investigating any involvement that you might have in the Saxon's escape. To me this escape is a clear indication of his guilt. He will be dealt with when he is caught. Those who have helped him escape will also be punished. Remember that, Sister Fidelma.'

'I am fully aware of all the legal procedures, Mother Abbess. And until Brother Eadulf has been recaptured, I have time to resume my task. That is, unless you have something which you do not want me to discover.'

Abbess Fainder went white and was about to retort when there was a noise at the door and it opened before she could protest.

Fidelma swung round.

To her surprise, it was the thin, reedy river boatman named Gabrán who stood in the doorway. He paused and then his eyes fell on her and he looked uncomfortable.

'I am sorry, lady,' he muttered to the abbess. 'I did not know you were engaged. The stewardess said you wanted to see me. I will return later.'

He left the room, closing the door, without acknowledging Fidelma.

Fidelma turned back to Abbess Fainder with a slight look of amusement on her features.

'Now that is a fascinating thing. I have not seen a boatman with such a free run of an abbey that he may come and enter the abbess's private chamber without knocking.'

Abbess Fainder looked embarrassed. 'The man is a boor. He has no right to presume to enter here,' she said after a hesitation. Her tone was not convincing. 'Anyway, who are you to question me on such matters?'

Sister Fidelma smiled gently but did not comment.

Abbess Fainder waited for a moment and then shrugged.

'The man trades with this abbey, that is all.' She sounded defensive. Fidelma remained silent, sitting as if waiting for Abbess Fainder to continue.

'Bishop Forbassach was coming to see you last night,' began the abbess. 'As soon as it was discovered that the Saxon had escaped, or – rather – *had been helped* to escape, I called for the bishop. He felt it was obvious that if the Saxon was anywhere, you would know. He seems to have missed you.'

'He did not,' replied Fidelma. 'He woke me from my sleep in the middle of the night in a fruitless search for Brother Eadulf.'

Abbess Fainder's eyes widened. She had obviously not had a report about Forbassach's midnight call.

'He searched your room and discovered nothing?' She frowned uncertainly.

'You sound surprised. No, he did not discover Brother Eadulf under my bed, if that is what you mean, Mother Abbess. Nor, if he had intelligence, would he have expected to do so. Bishop Forbassach found nothing.'

'Nothing?' Abbess Fainder's tone was incredulous and she sat deep in thought as if considering the news. Then her haughty attitude seemed to collapse. She became subdued. 'Very well; if you need to ask more questions then ask away. I am sure that everyone in this abbey suspects the identity of those who helped the Saxon escape.'

Fidelma rose casually. 'Thank you for your cooperation, Mother Abbess. It is good to know that everyone in the abbey suspects those who helped Eadulf to escape.'

Abbess Fainder looked startled. There was a question in her eyes as she peered at Fidelma.

Fidelma decided to answer.

'If everyone in this abbey has some idea who helped Brother Eadulf escape, then perhaps they will be able to inform me so that we can swiftly resolve this mystery. They might even know who really killed the young girl whom he was falsely accused of murdering.'

Abbess Fainder recovered her disdainful attitude.

'In spite of everything, are you still claiming the Saxon is innocent?'

'I will even now avow it is so.'

The abbess shook her head slowly. 'I will say this, Sister Fidelma, you are tenacious in your faith.'

'I am glad that you have discovered that much about me, Mother Abbess. You will also learn that I never give up until the truth has been discovered.'

'Truth is mighty and will prevail,' quoted Abbess Fainder sarcastically.

'A good saying, except that it is not always true. However, it is an ideal to work for and I have spent my life doing so.' She suddenly reseated herself and leaned forward across the table. 'While I have the opportunity, I need to ask you some questions.'

Abbess Fainder was astonished at her change of direction. She made a gesture with her hand as if inviting Fidelma to do so.

'I presume that Sister Fial is still missing?'

'I have not heard that her whereabouts has been discovered. It appears that she has decided to leave the abbey.'

'What can you tell me about Sister Fial, this mysterious young novitiate?'

Abbess Fainder grimaced in annoyance.

'She was twelve or thirteen years old. She came from the mountains to the north of here. I believe that she said that she and Gormgilla came together to join the community here.'

'Twelve or thirteen years is lower than the age of choice,' pointed out Fidelma. 'They were rather young to consider joining a community on their own. Or did their parents bring them?'

'I have no idea. Sister Fial was very emotional, which was natural after witnessing the death of her friend. She refused to speak further other than to recount the details of the events of that night. I do not find it surprising that she has left us. She has probably returned to her home.'

Fidelma suddenly let out a cry as a thought came to her. The abbess looked startled.

'A child under fourteen has no legal responsibilities. They must be of the age of choice.'

Abbess Fainder waited politely. Fidelma pressed the point with annoyance.

'What this means in law is that a child of that age cannot give evidence in a court. I should have made mention of this in my appeal. All Fial's evidence was actually not admissible in court.'

The abbess seemed amused. 'That is where you are wrong, *dálaigh*. It was explained to me by Bishop Forbassach: the evidence of a young child in its own household may be used against a suspect.'

Fidelma was confused. 'I do not understand that interpretation of the law. How can this child, Fial, possibly be in her own household?'

Fidelma was well aware of the fact that, in law, the testimony of a child below the age of maturity was allowed in certain circumstances –

if the child gave evidence about something which had happened in their own home of which they had personal knowledge, for example. Only then was their evidence taken into account.

Abbess Fainder replied, smiling with superior knowledge: 'This community was judged by Forbassach to be the household of its members. The child was here as a member of the community. This was her home.'

'That is nonsense!' snapped Fidelma. 'That perverts the meaning of the law. She had arrived here as a novitiate and, from what has been said, was in the abbey only a few days. How was this abbey judged as her own home, her community, within the spirit of that law?'

'Because Bishop Forbassach so judged it. I would argue this law with him and not with me.'

'Bishop Forbassach!' Fidelma compressed her lips in irritation. The Laigin judge had done a lot of bending of the law. The idea of an under-age child giving evidence had never occurred to her until now; yet if Forbassach was willing to bend the law so much, it was no wonder he was determined to protect his previous judgments. If only Barrán had been hearing the appeal, Eadulf would have been free by now, and . . .

Abbess Fainder had flushed at her sneering tone.

'Bishop Forbassach is a wise and honest judge,' she replied protectively. 'I have every faith in his knowledge.'

Fidelma noted the sincerity in the abbess's voice as she defended the Brehon.

'You seem to require the services of Bishop Forbassach often in this abbey,' Fidelma observed quietly.

The abbess's face, if anything, went an even deeper crimson.

'There have been several incidents that have been disturbing to our peace in this abbey in recent weeks. Besides which, Forbassach is not only a Brehon but a bishop and has his apartments in the abbey.'

'Forbassach lives in the abbey? I did not know that,' acknowledged Fidelma swiftly. 'Well, it is a curious place where several people have been killed and others are now missing. I have already presumed that this is not usual?'

Abbess Fainder ignored the irony in her voice.

'You have presumed correctly, Sister Fidelma,' she replied coldly.

'Tell me about Brother Ibar.'

The abbess's eyes hooded for a moment. 'Ibar is dead. He has received his just punishment on the very day you arrived here.'

'I know that he has been hanged,' Fidelma conceded. 'I am told he killed and robbed a boatman? I would like some details of that crime.'

Abbess Fainder was hesitant. 'I cannot see that it has any connection with your Saxon friend,' she said.

'Indulge me,' invited Fidelma. 'I find it unusual that we have three deaths on that quay within a short space of time.'

Abbess Fainder looked shocked. '*Three* deaths?'

'The girl Gormgilla, the boatman and then a watchman named Daig.'

The abbess frowned. 'Daig's death was an accident.'

Fidelma wondered why the abbess's mouth had become slightly pinched.

'Daig was also the member of the watch who caught Brother Ibar and who was himself later found dead.'

'It wasn't like that at all!' The abbess's voice was sharp, almost cracking.

'I thought that I had merely stated the facts. What was it like? I would like to know.'

Again there was hesitation before the abbess spoke.

'The boatman named Gabrán trades regularly with this abbey. That is the man who came to my door just a moment ago. It was one of his crew who was killed. I can't remember the name of the man.'

'That is sad,' Fidelma commented icily.

'Sad?'

'That the name of a person whose death led to the execution of one of your community remains unknown.'

Abbess Fainder blinked, not knowing whether Fidelma was being sarcastic or not.

'Sister Étromma will doubtless know the name if it matters so much to you. It is her task as *rechtaire* to know such things. Shall I send for her?'

'No matter,' replied Fidelma. 'I can speak with her later. Continue.'

'It is a sordid story.'

'Unnatural death is seldom anything other than sordid.'

'The boatman was drunk, I am told. He had been drinking at the Inn of the Yellow Mountain and was making his way back to Gabrán's boat. It had been moored there for two days. At the quay he was struck from behind with a heavy piece of wood: his skull was smashed in. Some money and a gold chain were taken from the body by his killer.'

'Were there any witnesses to this attack on the man?'

Abbess Fainder shook her head. 'None actually saw the attack.'

'Then how does Brother Ibar enter the picture?'

'Daig was captain of the watch. He captured Ibar.'

'Captain? Wasn't that the position held by Mel?'

'Fianamail had already promoted Mel to command his palace guard.'

Fidelma pondered a moment. 'I was told the killing of the boatman happened on the next day after the death of Gormgilla?'

'That is so. Fianamail was pleased by Mel's prompt action and promoted him that very morning.'

'Mel was promoted before Brother Eadulf's trial?' Fidelma shook her head in amazement. 'A Brehon might interpret that as giving inducements to witnesses.'

Abbess Fainder coloured again. 'Bishop Forbassach did not. He advised the King to promote Mel. I have noticed that several times you have impugned the morals and actions of the Brehon of Laigin. You should remember that he is a bishop of the Faith who is your superior in both creed and law. I would have a care if—'

She caught sight of the sparkle in Fidelma's eyes, that had seemed to change colour from green to cold ice blue.

'Yes?' asked Fidelma quietly. '*Yes?*'

Abbess Fainder's chin came up. 'It seems to me unethical behaviour to attack such a respected figure as Bishop Forbassach, especially when you are not even of this kingdom.'

'The law of the Brehons is the law regardless of which of the five kingdoms of Éireann one is in. When the High King Ollamh Fódhla first ordered the law to be gathered together nearly a millennium and a half ago, it was enacted that the laws of the Fénechus would apply to every corner of this land. When the judgment is wrong it is the duty of all, from the lowest *bó-aire* to the Chief Brehon of the five kingdoms himself, to demand that the errors be explained and corrected.'

Abbess Fainder's features grew tight before the intensity in Fidelma's voice. Wisely, she said nothing further.

'Now,' Fidelma said, sitting back, 'you were saying that Mel had been promoted and Daig was now captain of the watch on the quay. How did he capture Brother Ibar? You used the word "capture". That word implies that Brother Ibar was resisting or attempting escape.'

'That was not the case. When the body of the boatman was discovered by Daig, Daig knew it was a crewman from Gabrán's boat. He called Gabrán to identify the man and it was Gabrán who noticed that the gold chain, which the man usually wore, was missing, as well as some coins recently paid him in wages. Lassar, the innkeeper, gave testimony that the boatman had just left her inn with plenty of money on him. Gabrán had apparently just paid his wages in the inn. Hence the reason for the man's drinking. It was clearly a robbery.'

'Very well, So how did the path from the attack on the boatman, without any witnesses, lead to Brother Ibar?'

'It was a day later that Ibar was caught. He was found trying to sell the boatman's gold chain in the market square. The irony was that he tried to sell the chain to Gabrán himself who then called Daig, after which Ibar was arrested, charged, found guilty and hanged.'

Fidelma grew unhappy at this recital.

'It was a stupid thing to do if Brother Ibar was guilty,' she reflected. 'I mean, to attempt to sell a gold chain that belonged to the victim to the very man who was his captain? Surely, if Gabrán was well-known for his trading at the abbey, Ibar would have been aware that Gabrán might recognise the chain? He would have sought out a less dangerous method of disposing of it.'

'It is not up to me to guess what went on in Ibar's mind.'

'Gabrán, as you have pointed out, had been trading with this abbey for some time. How long had Brother Ibar been here?'

The abbess shifted uncomfortably in her seat.

'I think he had been here some time. Before I came here, anyway.'

'Then my point is valid. What did Brother Ibar say in answer to the charge?'

'He denied everything. Both the killing and the theft.'

'I see. How did he explain the possession of the chain?'

'I really can't remember.'

'Why would Brother Ibar want money so desperately – if we accept that he did kill and rob the boatman?'

The abbess shrugged and did not reply.

'And what happened to Daig? How did he get killed?'

'I told you that it was an accident. He was drowned in the river.'

'A captain of the river watch, drowned?'

'What do you insinuate?' demanded Abbess Fainder.

'I am merely making an observation. How could someone qualified enough to be captain of the watch among the quays have such an accident?'

'It was dark. I believe he slipped and fell from the quay. As he did so, he knocked his head against a wooden pile and was therefore unconscious, drowning before anyone could help him.'

'Was there any witness to that accident?'

'None that I am aware of.'

'Then who told you those details?'

Abbess Fainder frowned in annoyance. 'Bishop Forbassach.'

'So he investigated that death as well? How long after Brother Ibar's trial did this accident happen?'

'How long? As I recall, Daig met his death before the trial.'

Fidelma closed her eyes for a moment. She should cease being surprised at the curiosities connected with the events at the abbey.

'Before? Then Daig's evidence was not presented at the trial?'

'There was little evidence needed. Gabrán was the main witness. He was able to identify the murdered man. He told of the circumstances of the missing money and also identified the gold chain which Ibar had tried to sell him.'

'It all seems very convenient. This Gabrán was the only one who put forward the motive of robbery for the boatman's murder; he was the only one who claimed the items had been stolen and was the only one who then linked Brother Ibar with the crime. And, on that one man's testimony, Brother Ibar was hanged. Doesn't that worry you?'

'Why should it worry me? Bishop Forbassach had no difficulties in accepting that evidence. Besides, it was not simply on Gabrán's testimony. When Daig was told that Ibar had tried to sell the gold chain, he caused a search to be made of Ibar's cell here in the abbey and it was there that the chain and money were found. Anyway, the matter of Ibar has nothing to do with the Saxon, Sister. What are you trying to prove? I would have thought that your duty as a *dálaigh* now lay in helping us try to recapture the Saxon.'

Fidelma stood up abruptly. 'My duty as a *dálaigh* is to seek the truth in this matter.'

'You have heard the facts and the facts are many.'

'Falsehood often goes further than the truth,' Fidelma said, remembering a comment from her mentor, the Brehon Morann.

There came the distant chiming of a bell, tolling the midday Angelus. Abbess Fainder also rose to her feet. 'I have duties to perform.'

'One more question first; where might I find the chambers of Abbot Noé?'

'Noé?' Abbess Fainder seemed surprised at the question. 'This is no longer the abbot's main residence, although he keeps an apartment here. He now has chambers in the palace of the King, but you will not find him there. He left Fearna yesterday morning for the north. He is not expected to return for a while.'

'For the north?' Fidelma was disappointed. 'Do you know where he has gone?'

'The bishop's movements are not my concern.'

Fidelma inclined her head and left the abbess in her chamber. When she reached the small quadrangle, some instinct made her pause in the shadow of a stone recess. After a moment, the abbess emerged from her chamber and went hurrying across the quadrangle. She did not go in the direction of the chapel where the members of the community were gathering for midday prayers, but left through a side gate.

Fidelma followed at a distance. On opening the wooden gate she found it was a connecting door into another quadrangle, the very one whose gates led out onto the quay. She quickly drew back behind the gate, leaving it slightly ajar, because the abbess was in the middle of the courtyard mounting a horse. No one else was about. Then the abbess walked her horse through the gates. Fidelma was amazed that the abbess would leave her abbey when the Angelus bell was ringing, calling the community to its devotions. She wondered what was so important to draw her away.

Fidelma walked swiftly across the courtyard to the still-open gate which led onto the quays. She looked up and down but there was no sign of the abbess and her horse. Once beyond the gate, the abbess must have sent the horse into a canter, so quickly had it disappeared. However, to her surprise, Fidelma then saw Enda, on horseback, emerge from the shadow of the abbey walls and send his mount trotting along the riverbank in a leisurely fashion. He was clearly following the abbess.

A broad smile came to her face. She had almost forgotten that she had asked Dego and Enda to attempt to find out where the abbess went riding, and she had not rescinded that order. At least Enda would be able to follow and resolve the mystery.

Chapter Eleven

Fidelma was still thinking about Abbot Noé after she had returned to the Inn of the Yellow Mountain. She was surprised that he had not made a point of being in Fearna during this time. As both abbot and spiritual adviser to Fianamail, Fidelma had expected him to figure more prominently in the proceedings. Eadulf had told her he had sat at the original trial. Apart from his alleged role in supporting the cause of the Penitentials, he had not, however, been prominent in any of the subsequent events.

Why Fidelma found Abbot Noé a subject for her thoughts she could not really say. From the little she knew of the irascible abbot, she was surprised that he had appointed someone to take charge of his former abbey who sought to change the laws of the land. As she remembered Abbot Noé, he had been supportive of the Fénechus law system. Yet she knew from her past experience with him that he was a devious man and given to intrigue. She could not help wondering if he had played a major role in this mystery.

She sat in the main room of the inn turning the matter over in her mind. Then, eventually, she returned to the matter of Eadulf's disappearance from the abbey. She was careful in her choice of the word 'disappearance' because she did not trust either Forbassach nor the abbess. Had he really escaped? Too many people seemed to have 'disappeared' who were key witnesses in the events. She shivered suddenly. What was she saying? That Eadulf had simply disappeared along with the others?

The warmth of the fire and the fact of her disturbed night caused a drowsiness to overcome her and, almost reluctantly, she found herself lulled by her thoughts, slipping into inertia. Before she knew it, she was fast asleep.

She did not know how long it was before the sound of a door opening awakened her. Enda was entering: he looked satisfied with himself. She smothered a yawn, stretched, and greeted him.

'Well, Enda?'

The young warrior came immediately to her side and took a seat. He lowered his voice, having glanced quickly around to make sure they were alone, and said: 'I followed the abbess without her observing me. She rode north . . .'

'*North?*'

'Yes – but for no more than five or six kilometres. Then she went up into the hills. There is a settlement there called Raheen. She went to a small cabin and was greeted by a woman there. They seemed very friendly.'

Fidelma raised an eyebrow slightly in query. 'Friendly?'

'They embraced each other. Then the abbess and the woman went inside the cabin. I waited for an hour or so before the abbess came out.'

It was then that Fidelma realised that the best part of the afternoon had gone. She had slept several hours.

'Go on,' she said, trying to hide her annoyance at the wasted time. 'What then?'

'While she was there, she was joined by our friend, Forbassach. The woman left the two of them alone for a while. Then Forbassach departed and, a short time later, so did Fainder. She began to ride back towards Fearna so I did not bother to follow her.'

'What did you do instead?'

'I thought that you would want to know who the woman was, the one whose cabin they visited.'

Fidelma smiled in approval. 'You learn quickly, Enda. We'll make a *dálaigh* of you yet.'

The young man shook his head, taking her light-hearted comment seriously.

'I am a warrior, the son of a warrior, and when I am too old to be a warrior I shall take to my farm.'

'Did you discover who this woman was?'

'I decided not to ride directly to her cabin but to make some enquiries from other inhabitants in the vicinity. I was told that her name was Deog.'

'Deog? Did you discover anything else?'

'Only that she was recently widowed. Her husband was a man called Daig.'

Fidelma was silent for a moment or two. 'Are you sure that was his name?'

'That was the name I was given, lady.'

'If she is recently widowed, he must be the same man.'

Enda looked uncertain. 'I am not sure that I understand.'

Fidelma found that she did not have the time to explain to him. Why would Abbess Fainder and Bishop Forbassach be visiting the widow of the watchman who was drowned? Fainder had given Fidelma the impression that she had hardly known the man, so why visit the widow? Not only that but, as Enda reported, they seemed good friends. Now here was yet another mystery.

'I don't suppose you asked if the abbess was a frequent visitor to the woman, Deog, did you?' she asked.

Enda shook his head. 'I did not want to attract too much attention,' he explained. 'So I did not press too many questions.'

In that, Enda had behaved correctly, Fidelma conceded. Too many questions might put people on their guard.

'How far from here did you say this woman lived?'

'Less than an hour's swift ride, lady.'

'It will be dark in a few hours,' mused Fidelma, looking thoughtfully up at the sky. 'Nevertheless, I think I should speak with this Deog.'

'I know the path now, lady,' Enda said eagerly. 'We should have no problems riding there nor returning even in the dark.'

'Then that is what we shall do,' Fidelma decided. 'Where is Dego?'

'I think he was in the stables rubbing down the horses. Shall I go and fetch him?'

She shook her head. 'The sooner we leave the better. We will go to find him.'

It was true that Dego was rubbing down Enda's horse after its journey. He looked up as they entered. He appeared nervous as he greeted Fidelma.

'I came back to the inn just after noon, lady,' he said, 'just as you instructed. However, I saw you fast asleep by the fire. I thought you might need your sleep more than hearing that I had nothing to report anyway. I hope I did right in letting you sleep on.'

For a moment Fidelma did not know what he was talking about until she remembered that she had said that she would meet him at the inn after her return from the abbey to decide on the next strategy. She smiled apologetically at his worried features.

'You did right, Dego. I am the better for the sleep. Enda and I are going for a ride. We shall probably be gone some hours.'

'Should I come with you?'

'It is unnecessary. Enda knows where we are going. While we are away I want someone here just in case Brother Eadulf tries to make contact with us.'

Dego helped her saddle her horse while Enda re-saddled his mount.

'Where shall you be,' Dego asked, 'just in case anything happens?'

'We are visiting a woman called Deog who lives in a place called Raheen some six kilometres north from here. But do not let anyone know.'

'Of course not, lady.'

They mounted, setting off at a brisk walk through the streets of Fearna. Enda led the way underneath the towering grey walls of the gloomy abbey buildings, past the walls along the banks of the river as it twisted northwards. Then he took a fork in the road which led up a slow incline over a hill and through a small wooded area, no bigger than a copse.

Here Fidelma called on Enda to halt for a moment. She turned back to the edge of the trees and shrubs which afforded a view of the road behind them and waited quietly for some time, leaning forward in the saddle, just behind the foliage of the trees.

Enda did not have to ask what she was doing. If anyone was following them they would soon be seen from this position. Fidelma waited a long while before letting out a sigh of relief. She smiled at Enda.

'It seems my fears are groundless. No one is tracking us at the moment.'

Without a word, Enda turned and set off again through the copse and then along a track between a series of cultivated fields towards a more densely forested area which covered the rising hills beyond.

'What is that big hill in front of us, Enda?' asked Fidelma, as they moved upwards on the track.

'That's the very hill after which our host's inn is named. That is the Yellow Mountain. We turn more easterly in a moment and come round the shoulder of the hill before turning north again towards Raheen. It stands at the head of a valley and is not a long ride away at all.'

Within a short time, as the bright autumnal sky was beginning to cloud and grow dark, showing that late afternoon was creeping on, Enda halted and pointed. They were at the head of a valley stretching southwards towards the river. Here, dotted across the hillside, were several cabins with dark smoke ascending. It was obviously a farming community.

'Do you see that far cabin, lady?'

Fidelma followed the line of his pointing finger.

A small cabin clung to the precipitous slope of the hillside. It was not an impoverished place but neither did it speak of any degree of wealth or position. It was made of thick grey granite stone and covered by a heavy thatch that was badly in need of renovation.

'I see it.'

'That is the woman Deog's cabin; the cabin that Abbess Fainder and Bishop Forbassach visited.'

'Very well. Let us see what Deog has to contribute to our enquiries.'

Fidelma nudged her horse forward and, with Enda following, she rode directly for the cabin that he had indicated.

The occupant of the cabin obviously heard their arrival, for as they were dismounting and hitching their horses to a small fence which marked the boundaries of a vegetable garden in front of the building, the door opened and a woman came out. She was preceded by a large hound who ran towards them but was checked by a sharp command from the woman. She was not yet of middle age but her face seemed so etched with lines of worry and concern that at first glance she seemed older than her years. Her eyes were pale, probably grey rather than blue. She was dressed simply, as a countrywoman, and her appearance was that of someone hardened to the elements. To Fidelma there seemed something curiously familiar about the features. But Fidelma's scrutiny was swift and also encompassed the dog who, she discerned, was elderly but keen to defend his mistress.

The woman came forward in concern as her eyes fell on Fidelma.

'Have you come from Fainder?' she demanded without preamble, obviously taking in the fact that Fidelma wore the robes of a religieuse.

Fidelma was surprised at the anxiety in her voice.

'Why would you imagine that?' she parried.

The woman's eyes narrowed. 'You are a religieuse. If Fainder has not sent you here, who are you?'

'My name is Fidelma. Fidelma of Cashel.'

The woman's features visibly hardened and her mouth tightened. 'So?'

'It seems that you have heard my name,' observed Fidelma, interpreting the other's reactions correctly.

'I have heard your name spoken.'

'Then you know that I am a *dálaigh*.'

'That I know.'

'It is growing dark and cold. May we come into your cabin and speak with you for a while?'

The woman was hesitant but finally inclined her head in invitation to the cabin door.

'Come in then, though I am not sure what we can speak about.'

She led the way into the large single living room of the cabin. The hound, seeing no danger threatened, went quickly before them. A log fire snapped and crackled in the hearth at the far corner of the room. The old hound spread himself before it, head resting on his paws, but a half-closed eye was still fixed warily on them.

'Sit yourselves down,' invited the woman.

They waited until she had chosen a seat by the fire and then Fidelma sat opposite her while Enda perched uncomfortably on a stool near the door.

'Well now, what do you wish to talk about?'

'I am told that your name is Deog?' Fidelma began.

'I will not deny it for that is the truth of it,' replied the woman.

'And was Daig the name of your husband?'

'May the good Lord be merciful to his soul, but that was his name. What business had you with him?'

'He was one of the watch on the quays in Fearna, I believe?'

'Captain of the watch, he was, after Mel received promotion to the royal guard of the King. Captain of the watch, though he did not live long to enjoy it.' Her voice caught and she let out a sniff.

'I am sorry for your trouble, Deog, but I need to have some answers to my questions.'

The woman controlled herself with an effort. 'I have heard that you have been asking questions. You are a friend of the Saxon, I am told.'

'What do you know about . . . about the Saxon?'

'I know only that he was tried and sentenced for killing a poor young child.'

'Nothing else? Not whether he be guilty or innocent?'

'Would he be innocent when he has been condemned by the Brehon of Laigin?'

'He *was* innocent,' Fidelma replied shortly. 'And there seem to be too many deaths on the quays by the abbey to be a coincidence. Tell me about the death of your husband, for example.'

The woman's face was immobile for a moment or two and her pale eyes searched Fidelma for some hidden meaning to her words. Then she said: 'He was a good man.'

'I do not question it,' replied Fidelma.

'They told me that he had drowned.'

'They?'

'Bishop Forbassach.'

'Forbassach told you, in person? You move in illustrious circles, Deog. Exactly what did Bishop Forbassach say?'

'That during the night watch, Daig slipped off the wooden quay and fell into the river, catching his head on one of the piers and knocking himself unconscious. He was found next morning by a boatman from the *Cág*. They said that he . . .' her voice caught and then she went on, 'that he drowned while he was unconscious.'

Fidelma leaned forward a little. 'And were there witnesses to this?'

Deog regarded her in bewilderment. 'Witnesses? Had anyone been nearby, then he would not have drowned.'

'So how are these details known?'

'Bishop Forbassach told me that it must have been that way, for that is the only way it could have happened consistent with the facts.' She said the words as a formula and it was clear that she was repeating what the Brehon had told her.

'But what do *you* think?'

'It must have been so.'

'Did Daig ever talk with you about what happened on the quays? For example, about the death of the boatman?'

'Fainder told me that they executed poor Ibar for that crime.'

Fidelma frowned. '*Poor* Ibar? Did you know the Brother then?'

She shook her head. 'I know his family. They are blacksmiths on the lower slopes of the Yellow Mountain. Daig told me how he had found him out.'

'How was that? What exactly did Daig tell you?' Fidelma asked eagerly.

'Why do you want me to tell you what Daig told me about the killing?' Deog looked at Fidelma nonplussed. 'Didn't Fainder tell you? Not even Bishop Forbassach wanted to know the exact details.'

'Indulge me,' Fidelma smiled. 'I would like to hear and if you can manage to, keep the words as close to your husband's own as possible.'

'Well, Daig told me that he had been patrolling along the quay near the abbey around midnight, when he heard a cry. Daig was carrying a brand torch and raising it, he gave an answering shout, beginning to move forward in the direction of the sound. Then he heard some footsteps running across the boards of the quay. He came upon a huddled form. It was the body of a man, a boatman. Daig recognised him as one of the crew of Gabrán's boat which was even then tied up alongside the quay. The man's head had been smashed in and there was a wooden club lying nearby.'

'A club?'

'Daig told me that he thought it was one of those wooden sticks used on boats.'

'A belaying pin?'

Deog shrugged. 'I am not acquainted with them but I think that was the term he used.'

'Go on.'

'He told me that the boatman was clearly dead and so he left the body and ran on in the direction of the running steps. But he soon realised that the night had concealed the culprit and so he returned to the body . . .'

'Did he tell you in which direction the sound of the steps went? Was it, for example, in the direction of the abbey gates?'

Deog considered the question thoughtfully.

'I do not think that it was in the direction of the abbey gates for he said the sound of the footsteps was swallowed up into the night. There are usually two torches lit at the gates of the abbey during the night. If the culprit ran to the gates, Daig would have seen him illuminated by them.'

'Two lit torches?' Fidelma was silent for a moment digesting this information. 'How do you know this?'

'Fainder told me.'

Fidelma hesitated a moment and then decided not to be side-tracked.

'We will come back to that later. Continue with the story Daig told you.'

'Well, he returned to the body of the boatman and raised the alarm. Another sailor from Gabrán's boat, roused from his sleep, told Daig that Gabrán was at the Inn of the Yellow Mountain and the last time he had seen the dead man, he was also there. The man had apparently gone to the inn to collect some money Gabrán owed him.

'Daig went to the inn and found Gabrán. He had been drinking heavily and so it was a while before some sense could be made of the situation. Lassar, who owns the inn, told Daig that Gabrán had been joined by the boatman and there was some sort of argument. Gabrán paid him off and they became friendly again. The boatman drank there for while and then returned to the boat. Lassar was asleep by then, as it was late, but was awakened when Daig arrived to question Gabrán.'

The woman paused in her recitation.

'Is this truly what you want to know, Sister?' she asked, frowning. 'Bishop Forbassach thought it was all irrelevant.'

'Go on, Deog. What else did Daig tell you?'

'Gabrán confirmed that he had just paid the man some wages that he owed him.'

'Did he explain the argument?'

'It was to do with the money. Daig said the cause was not important. What was important was that no money was found on the sailor. There was another thing. When Gabrán was told the money was missing he asked about a gold chain that the man usually wore around his neck. That was gone as well.'

'I presume no money or chain was found on the body.'

'That was what worried Daig. You see, after he had made his futile attempt to chase the footsteps he had heard receding into the night, he came back and searched the body.'

'It worried him? Worried him in what way?'

Deog was frowning as she tried to recall what Daig had told her.

'It was . . . and he thought that he might well have been mistaken . . . it was . . .'

'Take your time,' advised Fidelma as she hesitated, trying to remember.

'When he first saw the body, before he started to chase after the sound of the footsteps, Daig was sure that he caught sight of the gold chain around the neck of the dead man. He thought it glinted in the torchlight.'

'But the chain had gone when he returned to the body, is that it?'

'That's what caused him concern. It was not there when he returned.'

'Did he mention this to anyone?'

'To Bishop Forbassach.'

'I see. What happened? What did Forbassach do?'

'I don't think it was ever mentioned again. After all, Daig was not absolutely sure. Lassar confirmed that the man had been given the money and she knew that he usually wore a gold chain. She knew him as a regular member of Gabrán's crew who came to the inn several times. He always boasted that the gold chain had been won in some battle against the Uí Néill.'

Fidelma was silent for a moment as she turned over the information in her mind.

'I know that the question of the gold chain began to worry him,' Deog added.

'Did Daig tell you how he managed to follow the trail to Brother Ibar?'

'Indeed he did and he felt it was an amazing coincidence. Gabrán himself came to Daig the next day and said that he had been in the market square when a religieux approached him and tried to sell him a gold chain. He had immediately recognised it as that belonging to his dead crewman.'

'Rather an odd coincidence,' observed Fidelma dryly.

'Yet coincidences do happen,' replied Deog.

'Did Gabrán know the religieux?'

'He knew he was a member of the abbey community.'

'So he says he bought the chain?'

'He pretended to be interested and arranged to meet the man later. Then he followed this Brother straight back to the abbey. He asked the *rechtaire* what his name was – it was Ibar, of course – and then he went to Daig and told him the whole story. Daig went to the monastery and explained matters to Abbess Fainder. Together with the *rechtaire*, Daig made a search of his cell. They found the chain and a purse of money under Brother Ibar's bed.'

'What then?' queried Fidelma.

'The chain was identified by Gabrán who also said that the purse of money approximated to that which he had given his crewman for his wages. Fainder sent for Bishop Forbassach, and Brother Ibar was formally accused.'

'I am told that he denied the accusation?'

'He did. He denied the killing, he denied trying to sell the chain to Gabrán, and he denied all knowledge of the money hidden under his bed. He called Gabrán a liar. Yet in view of the overwhelming evidence there was only one conclusion to be reached. Yet Daig was worried about the coincidence – just as you said, he felt it was an amazing coincidence. He was also worried by his memory of having seen the chain on the neck of the victim *after* the killing.'

'But you said that he told Bishop Forbassach of his concern?'

'Yes.'

'Did he do anything further about all this? Did he pursue the matter with Gabrán?'

'You are a *dálaigh*. You should know well enough that Daig was just a watchman. He was no lawyer to pursue such enquiries. He told Forbassach and, from then on, it was his task. Bishop Forbassach was content with the evidence.'

'But nothing of this came out at Ibar's trial?'

'Not as far as I know. My Daig drowned before the trial, so he was not able to raise his questions.'

Fidelma sat back in her chair to reflect on what Deog had told her.

'Bishop Forbassach appears as both accuser and judge again. That is not right.'

'Bishop Forbassach is a good man,' protested Deog.

Fidelma regarded her with curiosity. 'There is one thing I find fascinating, Deog,' she observed. 'For a countrywoman, and one who does not live in Fearna, you have a lot of knowledge of what goes on there and seem intimate with some influential people.'

Deog sniffed deprecatingly. 'Wasn't Daig my husband and didn't he keep me informed? We often talked about what he did down in Fearna. Isn't it thanks to that fact that you have now learnt answers to the questions that you asked?'

'Indeed. But you know more than what your husband has told you. I understand that you are visited by Bishop Forbassach and Abbess Fainder.'

Deog was suddenly nervous. 'So, you know that?'

Fidelma smiled thinly. 'Exactly so. Abbess Fainder rides out to see you regularly, isn't that so?'

'I will not deny it.'

'With respect, why would Abbess Fainder ride out here so regularly? Why would she feel the need to tell you, the widow of a member of the river watch, a man she told me that she hardly knew, the details about Brother Ibar's trial?'

'Why shouldn't she?' demanded Deog defensively. 'Fainder is my young sister.'

Chapter Twelve

It was some moments before Fidelma recovered from the unexpected reply.

'Abbess Fainder, the Abbess of Fearna, is your young sister?'

Deog gave a swift affirmative gesture.

'Does it surprise you that a powerful, rich abbess should have such a poor relation?' she demanded, a note of belligerence in her voice.

'Not at all,' Fidelma assured her. 'Talent and ability deserve important rewards, although it does occur to me to ask you – is Abbot Noé related to your family?'

Deog looked bewildered. 'Why should he be?'

'Are you sure that he is not related to you? Or is any other member of his family so related?' she pressed.

'He is not related. I do not see why you should ask such questions.'

'Just idle curiosity, that's all,' Fidelma assured her. 'Now, you were telling me that the abbess has wealth?'

Deog seemed mollified. 'My sister has made a good life for herself.'

'To be a servant of the Faith is not a usual way of gaining riches.'

'Perhaps not. But as abbess in the King's capital, she has to mix with rich and powerful people and it would not be seemly that she should go abroad in threadbare attire. I presume the abbey ensures that she has sufficient for her needs.'

Fidelma decided not to pursue the matter.

'Why did Abbess Fainder pretend not to know your husband? Why was that? Did she not like her brother-in-law?'

'We agreed that things were best kept from people until Fainder was settled firmly in her office. You see, she had only returned from Rome three or four months ago to become abbess. That was why she rode covertly each day to meet with me. This was where we both grew up. Luckily, she had been away for so long that many people had forgotten her. We thought it better that way until she had established her position.'

'Are you saying that Fainder was fearful that she would lose her authority as abbess if it were known that you were her sister?'

Deog hesitated, embarrassed at the truth, then raised her head defiantly.

'It is not so unusual, is it? If you sit on the council of the kingdom with the King, then the fact that your sister's husband is merely a watchman could undermine your authority.' Then: 'Fainder was too long in Rome, perhaps. She had adopted their ways and not our ways,' confessed Deog. 'I am told that the great lords do not mix with peasants there, nor do the great church-leaders come from the peasant people. Apparently it is the position of the family which dictates what a child will be in those lands. Alas, Fainder has become imbued with that snobbery.'

'But not so much that she turned her back on you.'

Deog smiled cynically. 'There is an old saying. The thing which grows in the bones is hard to drive out of the flesh.'

'Tell me about your sister.'

'You should ask her such a question.'

'You are her older sister. You will know her best.'

For a moment Deog's expression softened.

'It's true. I am five years older than Fainder. When I was fifteen our father was killed in one of the wars against the Uí Néill and soon after my mother died of grief. I was of the age of choice then and took charge of this cabin and the little bit of land. Fainder remained with me until she reached the age of choice and then she went into the abbey at Taghmon to become a religieuse. I did not see her until she was eighteen years old when she came to me and said she was going away. She was joining a party of religious who were going to Bobbio where Columbanus had built his religious house.'

'A bird flies away from every brood,' quoted Fidelma.

'A fine saying, although there is another; a bird had little affection that deserts its own brood.'

'Go on. You felt that Fainder had little affection for her home and family?'

'When she left, it was the last that I heard of Fainder until a few months ago. Then she came riding up to my door and announced that she had returned and that she was Abbess of Fearna.'

'You had not seen her since she was eighteen years old?'

Deog smiled sadly. 'She had been ten years at Bobbio and then moved south to Rome. It was at Rome that she attracted the attention of Abbot Noé who happened to be on a pilgrimage there. It was he who invited her back to Fearna and persuaded her to become the abbess.'

Fidelma was perplexed. 'Abbot Noé actually persuaded Fainder to return to Laigin to become abbess in charge of the abbey in his stead?'

'So she told me and so I tell you.'

'I believed that Noé was of the creed of Colmcille but Fainder seems to have adopted many of the ways of Rome.'

'She has become zealous for Rome,' agreed Deog. 'She has adopted the austere, high and mighty ways of the Roman clerics. But, I think, that is only on the exterior. She is certainly zealously committed to bringing the ways of our church into communion with the rules of Rome.'

'Are these executions a manifestation of that determination?'

Deog looked unhappy and did not reply.

'She seems to have exerted her will over Bishop Forbassach and over the King in his turn,' observed Fidelma after a while. 'She has persuaded them that the kingdom should adopt the Penitentials.'

'She has become a very powerful person,' agreed Deog. 'I do wish, however . . .'

'Yes?' prompted Fidelma.

'This harshness, it can be too excessive. Many people – and I have tried to warn her about this – many people are becoming afraid of the abbey of Fearna. That a Brother of the Faith has been executed there, and the punishments that we have heard of . . .'

'Punishments?'

'There was a Brother who was flogged there a few weeks ago.'

'*Flogged?*'

'It is claimed that he lied and so Fainder had him stripped to the waist and flogged with birch rods. I, too, find it hard to believe.'

'Do you know the name of the Brother who was flogged?'

Deog replied with a shake of her head.

'You say that people are becoming afraid of the abbey. What are they saying?'

'They say the abbey has become evil. Have you noticed the statuette, the one of the angel, outside the main abbey door? It is the one that the Blessed Máedóc is said to have made with his own hands.'

Fidelma replied that she had.

'That used to be called our Lady of Light, and people would make offerings before it. Now it is called by another name.'

'Which is?' Fidelma asked.

'Our Lady of Darkness.'

'Have you spoken to your sister about the things people are saying?'

'Oh yes.' Deog was bitter. 'She told me to tend to my garden and that I should not speak about religious matters which I did not understand.'

'Does she not realise that she is causing alarm among the people? Does she not realise the harm she is doing to the Faith?' pressed Fidelma.

'I do not think so. She is so used to the ways she learnt abroad, particularly the pitiless forms of punishment and unremitting harshness of life there, that she thinks that it is we, here, who are at fault; who are lax and living without morals. She is determined to impose the rule of the Penitentials over us all.'

'And the innocent must suffer with the guilty?'

'Do you believe Brother Ibar was innocent?'

'Didn't your husband, Daig, think so?'

'Daig had his reservations. He felt that there were questions which needed to be asked.'

'And Daig died before he could ask them at the trial.'

For a moment Deog turned two large shocked eyes on Fidelma.

'What are you saying?' she whispered. 'That Daig . . . that Bishop Forbassach, the Brehon . . .?' She raised a hand to cover her mouth.

Fidelma said swiftly, 'I am not drawing any conclusions, I am only making an observation on the facts. It seems that Gabrán has some questions to answer. Why didn't Forbassach ask them?'

'Bishop Forbassach will do what Fainder tells him to,' the woman said softly.

Fidelma examined her cautiously.

'Is there a particular reason why Bishop Forbassach meets with Fainder in your cabin?'

Deog laughed bitterly. 'Do you really think my haughty and powerful sister comes here most days simply to visit humble little me?'

Fidelma was quiet. She had begun to suspect something of the sort but she wanted Deog to spell it out.

'My cabin is no more than a convenient place for their assignations.'

'Did your husband know while he was alive?'

Deog shook her head. 'I was sworn to secrecy on pain of my immortal soul, by Fainder. Now I see the path that she is intent on, I realise that it is not *my* immortal soul that is imperilled.'

'There should be no need for secrets. It is not an offence for religious to live together and marry, at least not yet, although there is a faction in Rome who argue for celibacy. Was it such people Fainder was scared of?'

'It was Bishop Forbassach, not Fainder, who demanded secrecy. He is already married,' Deog admitted. It suddenly occurred to her just how far the conversation had gone. 'I thought that you had come here to free the Saxon? Fainder told me that you were attempting to prove him innocent but he showed his guilt by escaping last night. Why are you asking me all these questions about Daig, Fainder and Bishop Forbassach?'

'I would not say that escaping from the abbey showed guilt,' Fidelma replied sourly. 'Especially after all that you have told me. It merely showed that he had no desire to be executed like Ibar.'

'I don't understand.'

'Your husband, Daig, was also involved in the apprehension of Brother Eadulf in the abbey.'

'He was. But then it was Mel who was captain of the watch that night and Daig was only following his orders. That was when the young girl was raped and killed.'

'A young girl killed, a boatman killed and then Daig drowned . . .' mused Fidelma. 'In every case it seems that Forbassach has been persuaded not to ask the right questions and thus ignore the evidence. Is that a matter for concern, I wonder?'

Deog did not understand what she was driving at.

It was Enda who, having sat quietly through all the exchanges, suddenly spoke up, his eyes excited.

'Didn't you tell me that Gabrán's boat was tied up on the abbey quay the night the girl was killed? Isn't there a link there?'

Fidelma turned to him in annoyance but saw the young warrior was so eager that she felt she could not reprove him for pointing out a fact that she had completely overlooked.

'We will speak of that later, Enda,' she said. It was then Fidelma realised that the room had grown dark, apart from the warm light cast by glowing embers of the fire.

Deog stood up and lit a tallow candle and then threw some more wood onto the fire. There was a crackle and soon flames licked at the dry wood, causing a brighter light to chase the gloom.

'We'd better head back to Fearna,' Fidelma announced, rising regretfully. She turned to Deog. 'I am most grateful for everything that you have told us, Deog. I am sorry to awaken any chords of anguish in your heart. Sometimes it is best to discuss things so that grief can be exposed rather than bottled up.'

Deog grimaced. 'I do not mind speaking of my husband. He was a good man and sought to do his best for the community. My great sadness was that he did not get on with my sister. Nor did she like him. Alas, her years in religion have seen her grow bitter with life and harsh in her judgments of people. Yet she does not see her own faults. This relationship with Bishop Forbassach will end unhappily.'

Fidelma raised a hand and touched the woman comfortingly upon the shoulder.

'They are truly good who are faultless, Deog. Alas, who among us is without faults?'

Deog looked pleadingly at Fidelma. 'You will not tell anyone about Fainder?'

Fidelma looked impassive. 'I cannot promise that, Deog. You know that for I, too, have sworn an oath to pursue truth.'

'Fainder will never forgive me.'

The woman was clearly distressed at the idea of what her sister might do if the truth became known. Fidelma squeezed her shoulder again.

'Fainder must live with the consequences of her own actions and prejudices. You need not mention the substance of our discussion to her. I promise you this, I will not reveal Fainder's relationship with Forbassach nor with yourself unless it becomes necessary.'

'Becomes necessary? I don't understand.'

'If this fact needs to be brought to light in the course of my enquiries, then I shall bring it to light. If it is simply irrelevant, then it shall remain a secret between the two of us. Isn't that fair?'

Deog, sniffing, nodded her head in agreement. 'I suppose it will suffice.'

'Good. Now, it is dark and we must return to Fearna.'

They left the woman in her cabin and went to where they had tethered their horses.

The night was dark and chill, the clouds, chasing one another across the night sky, obscured the stars and the moon for the most part, making it almost impossible to see far.

'It's best to give the horses their heads,' advised Enda. 'In that way, they may tread the path homeward more carefully.'

Fidelma smiled in the shadows. She had ridden almost before she could walk and knew the habits of horses well enough. She rode with a loose rein allowing the horse to pick its way along the track, guiding gently only now and then to keep the beast moving in the right direction. She rode behind Enda, a dark shadow in front of her, knowing that the young warrior was keenly aware of his surroundings, attuned to any sense of danger.

The late autumn evening was really cold. Instinctively she knew that there would be a frost that night, the first frost of the oncoming winter. She hoped that Eadulf was not sleeping out in the open. She shivered at the thought. Yet if he were not hiding in the surrounding forests or hills, where was he? Who would be sheltering him?

She had pondered long on the problem of how he had managed to effect his escape from his cell in the abbey. Time and again she had come back to the conclusion that he must have been helped by an outside force. But who? And why?

'Not that path, lady!' called Enda from the darkness ahead.

Fidelma blinked.

She realised that she had fallen so deeply into her thoughts that she had given her horse too much head. As they reached a fork in the track, the horse, with free rein, had begun to turn down the left-hand path. Fidelma hauled quickly on the rein and turned the animal's path towards the shadow of Enda.

'Sorry, I wasn't thinking,' she called. 'Do you know where that path leads? It seems to go directly south.'

'It leads to a place called Cam Eolaing. I was told that it is on the same river that passes by the abbey but it is a longer route to Fearna if we go down to Cam Eolaing and turn along the river track.'

'Cam Eolaing?' Fidelma wondered why the name seemed familiar to her. She had heard it recently but could not place where and in what context. 'And this is the quickest way?'

'It is. We shall be—'

It was Enda who heard the danger a split second before the cry caused Fidelma to start. Three or four shadows burst through the woods and brush at the side of the road, attempting to grab their horses' heads. Instinctively Fidelma jerked the reins of her mount, causing it to rear up on its hind legs and lash out with its forelegs in protest as the bit tugged at the corner of its mouth. It was this that caused its flying hooves to connect with the body of one of the forms, knocking it backwards with a harsh scream of agony.

The figures were men and they were wielding weapons; not sticks or staves but swords, so far as the darkness allowed her to identify them. She tugged at her horse again, as it seemed the only means of protection.

In front of her, Enda had drawn his sword and smashed it down on another attacker.

'Ride, lady, ride!' the young man yelled.

It was as she dug her heels into the animal's flanks to spur it forward, that the clouds parted for a second or so and the bright white winter moon shone down, causing the scene to be lit with an ethereal brilliance. She glanced down and for a moment time stood still.

It was the face of the boatman, Gabrán, which stared up at her in anger.

Then her horse surged forward and she was tearing along the darkened track with Enda at her side.

It was only after a kilometre had passed that they drew rein to allow their snorting mounts to recover from the swift gallop. They were lucky that the track was straight, its surface fairly even, otherwise the precipitous gallop through the darkness might have been extremely dangerous.

Enda replaced the sword that he had drawn. 'Robbers!' he snorted in disgust. 'This country is filled with robbers!'

'I don't think so,' rejoined Fidelma.

Enda's head came up sharply. 'What do you mean, lady?'

'The moon came out for a second behind the cloud and I recognised their leader. It was Gabrán.'

'Gabrán?' Enda's tone displayed his astonishment, mingled with some satisfaction. 'Didn't I say that he was the connection?'

'You did. I had quite forgotten that his boat had been moored at the quay on the night the girl was killed. Then the next night, one of his crew is killed. You were right to point it out. *Agnus Dei*!' she ended with an exclamation.

Enda was startled. 'What is it, lady?'

'Gabrán's boat was also there when Daig was found drowned. Didn't Deog tell us that a boatman from a boat called the *Cág* found his body? The *Cág* is Gabrán's boat.'

Enda let out a low whistle. 'Are you sure that you recognised him, lady? It was dark.'

'The moonlight was full on his face long enough for me to recognise the man, Enda. His is a face that one does not forget.'

'Then we'd better push on to Fearna in case they have mounts and ride behind us,' he said uneasily. 'What do you think his game is, lady?'

They began to walk their mounts quickly along the track, side by side.

'I've no idea. You have done well in making this connection, Enda. It was staring me in the face and I did not see it. There is a big mystery here. It grows each moment and always, as you say, we find Gabrán close by.'

Enda was silent for a moment. Then he said: 'I must confess that I am at a loss, lady, as to why Gabrán attacked us. Surely he must think we know more than we do?'

Fidelma had been thinking the same thing, turning over the facts as she knew them.

Usually, facts were like a string of beads. There was always a connecting thread between them even if many of the beads were missing and had to be sorted out; there was always some inevitable connection. But this time there was no thread that Fidelma could see; no connection to the facts that she had garnered so far – none except this curious fact that the thin little river boat man was always near-at-hand in every event. Moreover, he traded with the abbey and seemed to have unrestricted access to Abbess Fainder's rooms, as she had witnessed. He also stayed at the Inn of the Yellow Mountain. Was he the thread that linked everything together? But how?

As they joined the track along the river and came up by the grim, dark walls of the abbey, Fidelma raised her head from her contemplation.

'We will have to find out more about Gabrán,' she finally spoke aloud, realising immediately that she was stating the obvious.

'Do you think he realised that you recognised him?' asked Enda.

'I am not sure. See if his boat is still alongside the abbey quay. I suspect it is not. It would probably be moored close to the spot where we were attacked. But it is worth a look.'

They were passing the quays now and Enda swung down and handed his reins to Fidelma while he went to check on the river boats.

'His boat was called the *Cág*, wasn't it?' Enda asked.

'The *Jackdaw*, that's right.'

Enda went to where there was a dark shadow of a boat tied up on the abbey quay. She saw a shadow emerge on the deck and heard voices. Then Enda came back, shaking his head.

'Was that Gabrán's boat?' Fidelma asked.

'No, lady,' Enda said, remounting. 'The man said that the *Cág* pulled out earlier in the evening, heading upriver.'

'Did the man know where Gabrán comes from?'

'I asked him that. He did not. But surely Lassar, at the inn, will know where his home port on the river is. She seemed to know him well enough.'

'I suppose that you are right.'

They skirted the abbey walls and rode into the township straight to the Inn of the Yellow Mountain.

A stable lad came to take their horses and, as they entered the warm main room of the inn, Dego came across to them. He seemed relieved to see them.

'I was going to ride out in search of you both,' he said. 'It has been dark for ages and this is not the countryside to ride freely about in the dark.'

Fidelma was reassuring.

'I think that we would agree with you, Dego. Let us find a table near the fire and see what food Lassar can offer us this evening. Not that I feel particularly hungry tonight.'

Lassar had come bustling out of an inner room with a tray of drinks. She saw them, served her customers, and then came across with a smile of welcome.

'I was wondering whether you would be back for an evening meal, Sister. You are late this evening. Have you been searching for the Saxon? I am told there is no news of him at all.'

Fidelma pulled off her travelling cloak and indicated a table near the large fire that was now crackling away in the hearth.

'We have been out riding,' she confirmed shortly. 'We'll sit there and you may tell us what you can offer us this chilly night.'

Lassar followed them to the table and waited as they seated themselves.

'For the main dishes, there is a choice tonight of *lonlongin*, the gullet of an ox filled with minced meat and cooked like a sausage. It is a delicacy of the area. Or there is fish – salmon – or I still have some sea-calf which I serve with *duilesc* and butter.'

'This meat pudding sounds fine for me,' Enda said enthusiastically.

Fidelma wrinkled her nose a little in distaste. 'I'll have salmon and the *duilesc*.' She had a liking for the red, edible seaweed.

'There is the hair-onion, leek, if you like it, with goose eggs and cheese,' added Lassar.

'I'll remain with the salmon but the hair-onion sounds good.'

Dego decided to accompany Enda with the *lonlongin* served with root vegetables. For the next half an hour or so, a silence fell on their company. For Fidelma, each mouthful was an ordeal as her thoughts returned to Eadulf and how he might be faring that cold night. Concentration was better when she had some task to fulfil; some objective. Left to her own thoughts, she fell into a morbid frame of mind. She broke the silence by turning to Dego.

'Did you find out any more about Coba?'

Dego paused while taking a sip of wine. 'Not really. He has a fortress not far from here, a place called Cam Eolaing. He is a minor chieftain and magistrate, well-respected and not a supporter of Fianamail's introduction of the Penitentials.'

Fidelma was irritable. She could have told Dego as much.

'But would he go against Fianamail to the extent that he might help Eadulf escape?' she asked.

Dego shrugged but was silent.

'We will go to see this chieftain tomorrow,' Fidelma decided.

When Lassar reappeared to collect their dirty plates, Fidelma took the opportunity to ask her about Gabrán.

'Gabrán? Why do you ask about him?' The woman looked suspiciously at her.

'I am interested in this river-boat trade, that is all.'

'He has gone away for a few days now.'

'Gone?' asked Fidelma innocently. 'Back to his home port? Where is it that he comes from – somewhere upriver?'

'Not far from here – Cam Eolaing. Beyond that place the river is not really navigable for any length.'

Chapter Thirteen

Eadulf had not slept well. The pre-dawn chattering of the birds finally caused him to give up the idea of sleep and splash his face in the bowl of cold water which stood by his bed. As he towelled himself he felt a new strength of purpose. He had been left alone for an entire day since the old man, Coba, had brought him to the fortress. He was free to wander around but always within the confines of the walls and there were always guards nearby who answered him in monosyllabic tones and politely refused to elaborate on any of his questions. When he had asked to see Coba he was told that the chieftain was unable to see him. True, he had been fed well, but he was irritated that no one would explain what was happening. He wanted information.

Why had Coba given him sanctuary? Did Fidelma know where he had been taken and what his position was in law? While Eadulf had heard of this *maighin digona* he was not sure that he entirely understood it although he did realise that sanctuary was an ancient custom. Coba had said that he had disagreed only with the punishment handed out to him because it was not in accordance with the law of the Fénechus. But would a man really stand against his King and the highest authorities in the kingdom to such a point that he would rescue a foreigner from his death cell in total defiance of them? Eadulf was uncomfortable and suspicious of the motivations of the chieftain.

As if in answer to his thoughts, there was a sound outside his door and it opened. Eadulf threw the towel on the bed and found himself face to face with a small, wiry and thin-faced man whom he had never seen before.

'I am told that you understand our language, Saxon,' the man said abruptly.

'I have a knowledge of it,' admitted Eadulf.

'That is good.' The man obviously believed in brevity. 'You may go.'

Eadulf frowned, uncertain that he had heard him correctly. 'Go?'

'I am to tell you that you are free to leave this fortress. If you go down to the river you will find a religieuse from Cashel waiting for you.'

Eadulf's heart beat faster and his face lightened. 'Fidelma? Sister Fidelma?'

'I am told that is her name.'

Eadulf felt a surge of relief and joy. 'Then she has cleared me? She has won the appeal?'

The thin-faced man's features were immobile. His eyes dark and deep set.

'All I am asked to convey to you is what I have already done. I know no more.'

'Then, my friend, I shall leave you with my blessing. But what of the elderly chieftain? How may I express my thanks to him for his kindness in bringing me here?'

'The chieftain is not here. There is no need to thank him. Go quickly and silently. Your friend is waiting.'

The man's tone was without emotion. He stood to one side and made no attempt to take Eadulf's extended hand.

Eadulf shrugged and glanced round the room. He had nothing to take with him. All his possessions were at the abbey.

'Tell your chieftain, then, that I owe him a great debt and will ensure that it is repaid.'

'It is of no consequence,' replied the foxy-faced man.

Eadulf left his room and the man followed him outside. The fortress seemed deserted in the cold white light of the crisp autumnal dawn. A frost still lay on the ground making it slippery beneath his leather sandals. His breath came like puffs of smoke and he realised just how cold it was.

'Is it possible to borrow a cloak?' he asked pleasantly. 'It is cold and my cloak was confiscated at the abbey.'

His companion seemed impatient.

'Your companion has clothing for your journey. Do not delay. She will be growing impatient.'

They had reached the gate of the fortress. A second man stood there; a sentinel who began to unlatch the wooden bolts and swing open the portal.

'Can't I express my thanks to anyone for giving me this sanctuary?' Eadulf thought it churlish to leave the fortress in such a fashion.

His companion seemed about to make some sharp comment and

then a curious smile flickered over his cadaverous features.

'You will be able to thank him soon, Saxon.'

The gate swung open.

'Your friend will meet you down by the river,' the man repeated. 'Now you may go.'

Eadulf thought he was a surly fellow but smiled his gratitude all the same and hurried on through the gate. Before him stretched a sloping path from the small hillock on which the fortress stood, winding down towards a wooded area through which he could see the grey ribbon of water a few hundred metres away.

He halted and glanced back to the man at the gate.

'Straight down there? Is that where Sister Fidelma is waiting?'

'Down by the river,' echoed the man.

Eadulf turned down the frosty path. It was slippery beneath his feet but the only alternative was to walk in the centre of the path where horses had churned it into a muddy mess. He stuck to the side of the path, its angled level causing him to move more quickly than he wanted. It was only a few moments later that the inevitable occurred. He suddenly slipped and fell.

That was what saved his life.

As his legs shot out from under him, causing him to fall backwards, two arrows flew by, one embedding itself with a hard thud in a nearby tree.

For a split second Eadulf looked at the arrows in stupefaction. Then he rolled swiftly on his side and glanced back.

The thin-faced man who had told him to go stood in the act of placing another arrow to his bowstring. He had been joined by the second man who looked every inch a professional archer for he was just releasing his second shot. Eadulf rolled again, this time into the side of the track and then he scrambled to his feet in an ungainly movement, throwing himself immediately into the underbrush. He heard the soft whine of the wood pass by his ear.

Then he was running; running for his life. He had no thoughts as to how or why; he did not try to work out what had happened. Some animal instinct for self-preservation overcame all his thought processes. He was pushing through the woods, while some small part of his brain uttered a prayer of thanks that they were mainly evergreen trees and shrubs which thus shielded him from his attackers. However, the frost was not on his side. He knew he was leaving tracks and he prayed for the sun to rise and allow the frost to disperse. Failing that, he must find some ground where the frost had not taken.

Inevitably he made his way towards the river. He knew that air near running water was sometimes warmer. Would Fidelma be there, waiting for him?

He gave a sardonic laugh.

Of course not. It had simply been a ruse to kill him. But why? He suddenly realised that the men had law on their side. What was the ruling of the *maighin digona*? He had been given sanctuary provided he kept within the bounds of the grantee's land. The owner of a sanctuary was bound not to allow a fugitive to escape, for the owner would then be held responsible for the original offence.

Eadulf groaned in anguish as he ran through the brush. He had fallen for a trick. He had been told to go but now could be shot down as a fugitive who had broken the laws of sanctuary. He had given them the legal opportunity to kill him, but who were they? Was this some ruse of Coba himself to kill him? If so, why rescue him in the first place? It did not make any sense.

He came to the riverbank and, as he had anticipated, the air was warmer here near the water and the frost was vanishing. The pale sun was climbing upwards in the sky and soon it would be dispersed. He paused and listened: he could hear the sounds of his pursuers. He began to hurry along the bank of the river, eyes searching for cover. He knew that his pursuers would soon break out of the trees behind him. He could not afford to stay on the bank any longer.

Ahead he saw some small juniper trees and then a patch of densely growing holly with its thick, waxy green leaves rising into a narrow conical shape with several proclaiming their feminine gender by their red berries. Eadulf was well aware that the sharp spines on the lower leaves, nature's design to protect the trees from browsing animals, were going to hurt, but there was no other means of concealment to hand.

He could hear the two men tracking him shouting to one another now. They were very close. Eadulf left the river bank and jumped into the juniper coverage, falling to the ground, before pushing and hauling his way under the uncomfortable screen of the holly trees. He flung himself flat under their cover and lay on the hard, cold ground, heart beating wildly from its recent exertions. He could see a little stretch of the riverbank from his position, and from this vantage point he saw his pursuers come to a halt.

'God's curse on the wily Saxon!' he heard the thin-faced man declare.

His companion looked around. His voice was morose. 'He could have gone either way, Gabrán. Up or downriver. It's your choice.'

'God rot him!'

'That's no answer. Anyway, I can't see why we had to wait until he was out of the fortress to shoot him down. Why couldn't he have been killed while he slept?'

'Because, Dau, my good friend,' the other explained with a sarcastic tone, 'it had to be made to look as though he had fled the sanctuary, that's why! Also, we had to get him out of Coba's fortress quietly before the household awakened. The death of the guard that I had to silence will be put down to the Saxon. Another murder to his account. Anyway, you go upriver and I'll look downriver. My boat is moored below. I shall have to bring it upriver before noon. I do not like this. All the while the Saxon is alive, he is a danger to the whole scheme of things. It would have been best had he been left to hang at the abbey.'

The thin-faced man left his companion and began to move off rapidly along the river bank, his eyes searching the ground for signs of Eadulf's tracks. His companion halted a while and examined the surrounding countryside and then began to walk slowly in the opposite direction. Then he paused. Eadulf shifted nervously. Had the man spotted where he had left the bank and pushed through the juniper trees?

He looked desperately round for some means of defence. Near at hand lay a discarded blackthorn stick, torn from a nearby tree. Eadulf reached tentatively forward and eased it towards himself with his fingertips. Then he grasped it firmly and rose carefully, trying not to catch the sharp leaves of the holly.

The warrior who had been addressed by the name Dau had kept an arrow in his hand, holding it in the same fist as his bow, and was now peering round as if searching for tracks.

It was at that moment that Eadulf suddenly realised that he had no choice as to his next move. The man was going to kill him. He was not sure why but that did not matter at the moment. His task was to save his own life. Eadulf moved carefully, trying to remember the skills he had once been taught as a youth by his father when hunting in his own country, the land of the South Folk. Avoiding the entwining branches, he moved slowly inch by inch around the holly tree and through the junipers to come up behind his adversary. With each footstep, he swore that the man must surely hear him.

The bowman stood looking irresolutely before him into the trees and shrubs, even as Eadulf crept forward, raising the stick in both hands. It took one swift blow to knock the man down. He fell with an almost imperceptible grunt. For a moment Eadulf stood over the inert form still holding his blackthorn stick ready to strike again. There was no further movement.

'Forgive me for I have sinned,' he muttered as he genuflected and knelt down by the unconscious man. He removed his adversary's leather boots, throwing them into the river, swiftly followed by his bow and quiver of arrows. He removed and placed the man's hunting knife in his own belt. He also removed the man's sheepskin cloak, realising that he needed it if he was taking to the open country. At least, when the archer came around, he would not be thinking in terms of pursuit for a while, not without his boots, warm cloak and weapons. Eadulf glanced skyward, trying to remember the lines from John: 'If we confess our sins, He is faithful and just.' He hoped that the divine powers would understand his actions.

Then he stood up, swung the heavy cloak around his shoulders and started to walk towards the rising hills. He was unsure which way he should go. He realised that he ought to put enough distance between the fortress of Cam Eolaing and himself before he started to make any decisions on his ultimate destination. Certainly, he had realised that Fidelma was not any part of this strange plot to kill him. It would probably be a waste of time to go in search of her now. The best thing to do might be to head eastward to the coast and try to find a ship that would take him to either the land of the West Saxons or one of the other Saxon kingdoms? Well, there was plenty of time to think about it. He must find shelter, and some food, before he started to make decisions.

Fidelma glanced up at the knock on the door. It was Lassar, the innkeeper. She looked tired and somewhat nervous.

'It is the Brehon, Bishop Forbassach, again. He wishes to speak with you.'

Fidelma had just finished dressing and was about to descend to the main room of the inn for breakfast.

'Very well. I'll come immediately,' she told the innkeeper.

Downstairs, seated by the fire and enjoying some of Lassar's hospitality was not only the Brehon of Laigin, Bishop Forbassach, but the elderly, white-haired man called Coba the *bó-aire* of Cam Eolaing.

She tried to disguise her astonishment at his appearance at the inn that morning. Immediately she became aware of a third man seated before the fire, an austere, elderly fellow with pinched features and a prominent nose. He was dressed in rich robes, the robes of a religieux with an ornate golden crucifix on a chain around his neck. He greeted Fidelma coldly and without approval.

'Abbot Noé.' Fidelma inclined her head towards him. 'I was wondering only last night whether I would meet you during my stay in Fearna.'

'It was, alas, an inevitable meeting, Fidelma.'

'I am sure it was,' she replied dryly and then, turning to Forbassach, 'Do you wish to search my room again for Brother Eadulf? I can assure you that he is not there.'

Bishop Forbassach cleared his throat as if in embarrassment.

'I have actually come to offer you an apology, Sister Fidelma.'

'An apology?' Her voice rose incredulously.

'I am afraid that I leapt to the wrong conclusion the other night. I now know that you did not help the Saxon to escape.'

'Really?' Fidelma did not know whether to be amused or concerned.

'I am afraid that it was I who aided that escape, Sister Fidelma.'

Fidelma swung round to Coba who had spoken slowly and with a note of regret.

'Why should you help Brother Eadulf?' she demanded in astonishment.

'I have just arrived from Cam Eolaing this morning to confess my deed. I found Abbot Noé had arrived back at the abbey and was in conference with Bishop Forbassach. We spoke of the matter and came here to support Forbassach in his apology to you.'

Fidelma raised her arms in a helpless gesture. 'I do not understand.'

'Alas, it was simple enough. You know already where I stand on the infliction of punishment under the Penitentials. I could not stand by and see another of these punishments carried out when I claim that they are opposed to the basis of our legal system.'

'I agree with your concerns,' Fidelma acknowledged. 'But how did that lead you to take the law into your own hands and help Eadulf escape?'

'If I am at fault, I shall be punished.'

Bishop Forbassach scowled at the man. 'You will have to pay compensation for this action, Coba, and you will lose your honour price. No more can you claim to exercise magisterial powers in this kingdom.'

Fidelma was impatient to know if her suspicion that Coba had given Eadulf shelter was correct.

'What has happened to Brother Eadulf?'

Coba glanced nervously at Abbot Noé.

'It would be wise if you tell Sister Fidelma all,' the abbot advised brusquely.

'Well, being against the punishment, I decided that I would offer the Saxon sanctuary – the *maighin digona* of my fortress . . .'

'Sanctuary does not involve helping someone escape from incarceration,' muttered Forbassach.

'Once in the confines of my fortress, the sanctuary applies nevertheless,' snapped Coba.

Fidelma considered the argument.

'That is true. However, the person seeking sanctuary usually finds the territory of the *maighin digona* by themselves before requesting sanctuary. Nevertheless, the sanctuary rule applies once inside the boundaries of the chieftain willing to provide it. Are you confirming my suspicion that Brother Eadulf is now receiving shelter and sanctuary in your fortress?'

She had been feeling confident, having assumed that Eadulf was safe in Coba's fortress and could remain there until Barrán arrived. Her spirits began to drop however as she realised how sombre Coba's features were.

'I informed the Saxon of the conditions of the sanctuary. I thought he had understood them.'

'The conditions being that he remain within the confines of the fortress and make no attempt at further escape,' Bishop Forbassach intervened pedantically, for Fidelma knew well what the restrictions were. 'If he attempts to escape then the owner of the sanctuary has the right to strike him down to prevent that escape.'

A cold feeling crept through Fidelma's veins. 'What are you saying?'

'Early this morning, when I awoke, I found the Saxon was not in his room,' Coba stated quietly. 'The gates of the fortress were unbarred and he was gone. One of my men was found near the gate. He was dead. Struck down from behind. I only have two watchmen there at night for no one has ever attacked the fortress of Cam Eolaing before. The other guard, Dau, was later found by the river, unconscious. He had been robbed of his cloak, boots and weapons. When he recovered, he told my men that he had attempted to pursue the Saxon and recapture him. He had been on the bank when he had been hit from behind. It is clear that the Saxon is trying to make good his escape into the countryside.'

Bishop Forbassach was nodding impatiently. He had heard the story before from Coba.

'Coba has done a foolish thing in believing that the Saxon had any morals and would obey the rules of the sanctuary. He will be heading east towards the sea and a ship for the Saxon lands.'

He turned to Fidelma, suddenly looking awkward again.

'I just wanted to tell you that I am sorry that I thought you were involved in his initial escape. I want to make clear to your brother, the King of Cashel, that I have apologised for any insult to you. I also wanted to let you know, however, that the Saxon has tied the noose about his own neck now.'

Fidelma was preoccupied with her thoughts and only caught the last part of his sentence.

'What?'

'It is clear that he fled from Cam Eolaing because he was guilty.'

'You said that when you claimed that he had fled from the abbey. It was not so then. It may not be so now.'

'Why flee from the safety of the sanctuary of Cam Eolaing if he were not guilty? He could have remained there indefinitely.'

'He could only have remained there for as long as sanctuary was granted, not indefinitely,' she corrected pedantically.

'The fact remains that he fled. Now he can be hunted down and killed without further ado. Anyone can kill him and do so in accordance with the law.'

At that moment Mel entered the room. He started to apologise and was about to leave when Bishop Forbassach, in irritation, waved him to remain.

'I might need you, Mel. It is a matter of the King's business.'

Meanwhile Fidelma had lowered herself wearily into a seat as she realised that what Forbassach had said was true. A convicted murderer who broke the rules of *maighin digona* and fled from the sanctuary could be treated as one already dead. She found herself clenching her teeth together to contain her anguish for a moment.

Bishop Forbassach was moving to the door. 'I must alert the warriors of the King. Come with me, Mel.'

'Wait!'

The Brehon turned back at Fidelma's call.

'Since you are here, I have a complaint to lodge against Gabrán. He and his men attacked me last night.'

'The river-boat man?' Bishop Forbassach seemed bewildered. 'What has this to do with the matter we are discussing?'

'Perhaps nothing, perhaps a lot.'

'Gabrán comes from Cam Eolaing, of which I am chieftain,' Coba intervened. 'What did he do?'

'Last night, one of my companions and I were returning to Fearna. Gabrán and some of his men attacked us. They used swords.'

There was a silence.

'Gabrán?' Coba's voice was hollow. 'How would you know that it was Gabrán who attacked you? It was a dark night.'

Fidelma swung round to him with narrowed eyes.

'You forget that even on a dark night, the moon still hangs in the sky, and sometimes even the heaviest clouds are obliging.'

'But why would he attack you?'

'That is my question. Do you know anything more about his personal life, his allegiances and values?'

Coba gestured indifferently.

'He lives outside of the settlement, across the river from it, in fact, on the east side of the valley. I do not think that he has any special allegiances except to that of his trade. So far as I know, he lives alone. He has no wife.'

Bishop Forbassach was following the conversation though with suspicion on his face.

'Are you sure about this, Sister?' demanded Abbot Noé, entering the conversation. 'Gabrán has had a long trading association with the abbey here and is considered most trustworthy.'

'I am sure it was Gabrán who attacked us,' affirmed Fidelma.

'Where do you say that this attack took place?' asked Bishop Forbassach.

Fidelma looked carefully at him and held his gaze.

'We were returning from a place which I think you know well. We were on the way back from a cabin at a settlement called Raheen. The attack took place on the road just above Cam Eolaing. My companion Enda and I were lucky to escape with our lives.'

Fidelma was not disappointed by Forbassach's reaction at the mention of the name Raheen. The Brehon's face went pale and it took him some time before he found his voice.

'Often there are robbers on the highways around Fearna, catching unwary travellers,' he offered, his voice nervous.

'It was Gabrán,' repeated Fidelma.

Coba was rubbing his chin thoughtfully.

'I would have thought that Gabrán made enough money from his boat. He is often transporting goods up and down the river as far south as Loch Garman, taking cargoes to the ocean-going ships that sail to Britain and to Gaul.'

'What sort of cargoes does he run?' asked Fidelma curiously.

'What does that matter?' Bishop Forbassach replied impatiently. 'Are we here to talk about Gabrán and his business or the escape of the Saxon?'

'At the moment I would like to know why Gabrán attacked me.'

The Brehon seemed concerned in spite of his attitude. He knew the serious implications which might result from an attack on a *dálaigh*, let alone a King's sister. That was the very reason he had come to apologise to Fidelma for his previous behaviour.

'Are you charging this man, Gabrán, with an attack on you, Sister Fidelma?' he demanded.

'I am.'

'Then I shall order that he be arrested to answer this charge. Do you hear this, Mel?'

The commander of the guard nodded thoughtfully.

'Then you and I will go in search of Gabrán when we leave here,' Forbassach announced. 'We can be making enquiries about the Saxon at the same time. The search for the Saxon absconder must be uppermost in our minds. In that matter, Fidelma of Cashel, I must warn you that you also stand in danger if you have helped him evade the justice of this kingdom.'

Fidelma's eyes flashed momentarily.

'I am aware of the law, Forbassach! I did not help Brother Eadulf to escape, nor did I offer him sanctuary. In the meantime, I intend to continue to investigate the mysteries which surround this matter . . . mysteries which have led me along the road to Raheen.'

Coba was not aware of the sharpness in her tone and the pale look on Bishop Forbassach's face.

'I regret the Saxon played me false by escaping,' he said, 'but I do not regret my action in seeking to prevent his execution under the Penitentials. He should be punished under the native laws of our land.'

Bishop Forbassach had recovered something of his old self and scowled at the *bó-aire*.

'You are in a minority in the council of the King of Laigin, Coba. You made your views known when the King and I made our decision on the validity of the punishments asked for by Abbess Fainder. That should have been an end to it.'

'That could not have been an end to it,' Coba replied spiritedly. 'The matter should have been held over until the next great festival of Tara when it could have been raised in the convocation on the law of the five kingdoms. The decision should have been left to the kings, lawyers and laymen of all five kingdoms as every other major law is laid before them and debated before being enacted.'

Abbot Noé intervened quietly. 'My brothers in Christ, calm yourselves. It will not benefit anyone to waste time in debate. Surely you both have business to attend to? If you do not, then I surely do.'

Bishop Forbassach glowered for a moment before giving them a curt farewell, hurrying from the inn followed by the warrior Mel, who managed to give Fidelma an apologetic glance as he left.

Coba regarded Fidelma sadly.

'I thought I was doing the right thing, Sister Fidelma.' He sounded sheepish.

'Are you sure that Brother Eadulf knew the limitations of the *maighin digona*?' she asked. 'Although he has spent much time in our land, he is still a stranger and our ways may be confusing to him.'

Coba shook his head sympathetically.

'I cannot hold out that explanation for his actions, Sister,' he replied. 'When we arrived at my fortress yesterday, I explained to him most carefully the consequences that would follow should he attempt to leave it. I followed the procedure carefully and sent a messenger to the abbey last night to inform the abbess of what I had done.'

'The abbess knew last night that Eadulf had been taken to your fortress?' broke in Abbot Noé.

'I told you,' repeated Coba, 'I followed the procedures of the law most carefully. I am certain that the Saxon understood. I only wish I could give you comfort in that matter, Sister.'

Abbot Noé muttered: '*Ignorantia legis neminen excusat.*'

Coba glanced at the religious. 'But surely, ignorance of the law in a foreigner may be argued as a mitigation?'

'It is unlike Eadulf to take such an action,' Fidelma said softly, almost speaking to herself.

Abbot Noé's face was grim.

'According to you, Sister, it is unlike the Saxon to have raped and murdered a young novitiate. Perhaps you do not know this Saxon as well as you like to think you do?'

Fidelma raised her head to meet the eyes of her old antagonist.

'Perhaps there is a truth in that,' she admitted. 'But if there is no truth in it, as I do believe, then there is something curious happening in this place. I mean to reveal every aspect of this matter.'

The abbot smiled but without humour.

'Life *is* curious, Sister. It is the cauldron of God in which we are placed to test our souls. *Ignis aurum probat, miseria fortes viros.*'

'Fire tests gold, adversity tests the strong,' repeated Fidelma softly. 'The line of Seneca has much wisdom in it.'

Abbot Noé suddenly rose and moved to stand in front of Fidelma. He peered at her with an intense expression in his eyes.

'We have clashed in the past, Fidelma of Cashel,' he observed softly.

'That we have,' she agreed.

'The guilt or innocence of your Saxon friend aside, I want you to know that I care about the Church in this kingdom and do not want to see it damaged in any way. Sometimes the Abbess Fainder can be overly enthusiastic in the cause of the Rule of the Penitentials; she is a zealot, if you like. I say this in spite of the fact that she is a distant cousin of mine.'

His statement caused Fidelma to glance up in curiosity.

'Abbess Fainder is your cousin?'

'Of course, that is why she is qualified to be in charge of the abbey. Anyway, she sees things in simple terms of right and wrong; of white and black, without any subtle shades of grey. You and I both know there is more in life than such extremes.'

Fidelma frowned at him.

'I am not sure that I know what you mean exactly, Father Abbot. If I recall correctly, you were never a supporter of Rome's rules.'

The thin-faced abbot sighed momentarily and inclined his head.

'A man can be won to an argument,' he admitted. 'I have spent many years in contemplation of the arguments. I followed the debate at Whitby very carefully. I believe that Christ gave the keys of heaven to Peter and told him to build his Church and that Peter built that Church in Rome where he suffered martyrdom. I now make no pretence of that. What I am saying is that people may choose different paths to their objective. Sometimes people have to be won by argument and not by order. I was won by years of meditating on the arguments. Others should follow the same path and not be ordered to change. Alas, I am a lone voice in these councils.'

He left the inn without another word.

Coba stood looking confused for a moment and then he glanced at Fidelma.

'I must return to my fortress. I have organised a search for the Saxon. I am sorry about your friend, Sister. In trying to help, I have only made matters worse. There is the old saying that friends should keep clear of an unfortunate man. We may be well advised to heed that saying. I am truly sorry that things have turned out this way.'

After he had left, Fidelma heard a gentle cough behind her.

Dego and Enda had come down the stairs.

'Did you hear all that?' she asked.

'Not all,' confessed Dego, 'but enough to know that the elderly man, Coba, gave Brother Eadulf sanctuary and now he has fled from that sanctuary. That is not good.'

'No, it is not,' agreed Fidelma solemnly.

'What about Gabrán?' demanded Enda. 'What was said about him?'

Fidelma quickly repeated what she had been told about the river-boat man.

They breakfasted for the most part in silence. There was no one else in the inn or at least no one who came to breakfast while they were there.

Chapter Fourteen

It was midday and Eadulf began to feel a gnawing pang of hunger. It was still very cold but the frost had dispersed, and the morning sunshine spread a pleasant warmth in the unshaded areas. The warmth was deceptive however because the moment a cloud crossed the face of the sun, or a tall tree blocked its rays, the cold became sharp again. Eadulf eased the cloak around his shoulders and thanked God that he had had the sense to remove it from his assailant.

He had followed the banks of the broad river north through a valley for about a kilometre or so, away from Cam Eolaing, until the river began to narrow. The hills rose steeply on all sides, black, brooding peaks in spite of the pale sun. A little further on he came to a curious intersection of waters. The river was fed on either side, though not exactly at the same point, by two gushing smaller rivulets; one flowed from the south-east and the other from the west, tumbling down from the surrounding hills through smaller valleys.

Eadulf looked cautiously around before deciding to rest a moment, perching himself on a fallen tree. The log was bathed in the bright rays of the sun.

'It is time for decisions,' he muttered to himself. 'Which way to go?'

If he crossed the main river and headed through the easterly valley, he presumed that he would eventually strike the sea. It could not be more than ten kilometres away. At the coast he could seek safety on a ship sailing for home. It was very tempting to head that way, to find a ship and leave Laigin – but Fidelma was uppermost in his thoughts.

Fidelma had hurried back from her pilgrimage to the Tomb of St James when she had heard of his troubles, and she had come to defend him. He could not leave her now; leave without seeing her, leave and let her think that he did not . . . He frowned. Think that he did not – what? He felt confused at the complexity of his own thoughts. Then he made up his mind. Fidelma was still in Fearna. He had no choice: he must return and find her.

'*Ut fata trahunt!*' he muttered, standing up. The Latin literally meant

171

'as the fates drag', an expression that recognised that he had limited control over his destiny. It was the only way that he could explain the decision that he felt had already been made for him.

He turned and began to walk along the bank of the rivulet, facing the flow of its gushing waters and moving up towards the hills. A few kilometres in the distance, the tall peaks began to rise more steeply in a line, their rounded tops stretching like a barrier before him. He had no plan; he did not know how he would contact Fidelma once he returned to Fearna. Indeed, having heard of his removal from the abbey, Fidelma might have already left town. The thought niggled at him. Yet he could not leave without making the attempt to contact her. He left it to the mercy of destiny.

Dego and Enda exchanged an anxious glance.

Since finishing her breakfast, Fidelma had fallen into a silent meditation. The two young warriors became impatient.

'What now, lady?' Dego finally ventured, in a loud voice. 'What should we do?'

Fidelma stirred after a moment. She looked blankly at Dego before registering his question in her mind. Then she smiled wryly at her companions.

'I am sorry,' she said contritely. 'I have been turning over the facts in my mind and I seem to be getting no nearer to discovering a thread which links the events, let alone finding a motive as to why these people have been killed.'

'Is knowing the motive so important?' asked Dego.

'Know the motive and you usually know the culprit,' affirmed Fidelma.

'Did we not agree the other night that Gabrán appeared to be the thread?' Enda reminded her.

'It was precisely his role in this mystery that I have been attempting to analyse.'

'Why don't we seek Gabrán out and ask him?' returned Enda.

Fidelma chuckled softly at his directness.

'While I am wasting my time in trying to put those pieces into some order, you come straight to the point. You have reminded me that I am ignoring my own rule; that of not making assumptions before gathering the facts.'

Dego and Enda rose together eagerly.

'Then let us find this boatman, for the sooner he is found, lady, the sooner you will have your facts,' Dego said.

Smoke was rising from a small copse a little distance ahead of Eadulf: it must be smoke from someone's fire. Hunger, cold and weariness made Eadulf's decision for him. He moved on through the small wood and found a large clearing beyond, in which was situated a cabin by a tiny stream. It was a sturdy, stone-built affair; low-roofed and thatched. He paused for he realised that there was something curious about the clearing. It was flat and seemed to have been raked free of any obstacles except, at various points surrounding the cabin, and at unequal distances from it, heavy posts had been driven into the ground. It was as if they formed a pattern. On the top of each post were notches that had been chipped into them.

Eadulf had been long enough in the five kingdoms of Éireann to realised that the notches were Ogham, the ancient writing named after the old god of literacy and learning, Ogma. Fidelma could read the old script easily but he had never mastered it, for it represented words that were archaic and obscure. He wondered what these posts symbolised. He had, at first, thought he was coming to a woodsman's cabin but he had never seen one with such a curious structure of posts around it.

He took a few steps forward, noting the dead and dying autumnal leaves which seemed to be scattered in profusion at a certain distance from the cabin and then, curiously, everything was swept clear of leaves all around the cabin within this border. Eadulf was perplexed and took another step forward, feeling the crunch of leaves underfoot.

'Who is it?' demanded a strong masculine voice, and a man appeared in the door of the cabin.

Eadulf saw that he was of medium height with long straw-coloured hair. His face was in the shade of the doorway but Eadulf saw that he was a well-muscled man with a warrior's build and, indeed, the impression seemed to be confirmed by the balance of his body, the way he stood poised as if ready to meet any threat.

'Someone who is cold and hungry,' answered Eadulf lightly, taking a step forward.

'Stay still!' snapped the man in the doorway. 'Keep on the leaves.'

Eadulf frowned at the request. 'I am no threat to you,' he offered, wondering whether the man was deranged in some way.

'You are a stranger – a Saxon, by your accent. Are you alone?'

'As you can see,' replied Eadulf in growing puzzlement.

'*Are* you alone?' insisted the man.

Eadulf became irritated. 'Don't you trust the evidence of your own eyes?' he asked sarcastically. 'Of course I am alone.'

The man in the doorway inclined his head a fraction and in that movement the shadow left his face. It had been a handsome face but there was an old burn mark across his brow and eyes, searing the flesh.

'Why, you are blind!' Eadulf ejaculated in surprise.

The man started back, nervously.

Eadulf held up a hand, palm outwards in a gesture of peace, and then, realising the futility of the gesture, let it fall.

'Have no fear. I am alone. I am Brother . . .' he hesitated. Perhaps his name might have travelled through this kingdom even to the blind. 'I am a Saxon Brother of the Faith.'

The man tilted his head to one side.

'You seem unwilling to give me your name. Why is that?' he asked sharply.

Eadulf glanced round. The place seemed isolated enough and surely this blind man could do him no harm.

'My name is Brother Eadulf,' he said.

'And you are alone?'

'I am.'

'What are you doing alone in this area? It is bleak and isolated. Why would a Saxon Brother be travelling through these hills?'

'It is a long story,' replied Eadulf.

'I have plenty of time,' returned the other grimly.

'But I am weary and, moreover, cold and hungry.'

The man hesitated as if making a decision.

'My name is Dalbach. This is my cabin. You are welcome to a bowl of broth. It is fresh made from badger meat and I have bread and mead to complement it.'

'Badger meat? Now that is good fare, indeed,' observed Eadulf, knowing that many of the people of Éireann considered it a choice dish. In the ancient tale, didn't Molling the Swift, as a sign of esteem, promise to procure a dish of badger meat for the great warrior Fionn Mac Cumhail?

'Over your meal you may tell me something of your story, Brother Eadulf. Walk forward now, directly to me.'

Eadulf walked towards him and Dalbach held out his hand in greeting.

Eadulf took it. It was a firm grasp. Still gripping his hand, the blind man raised his other to lightly touch Eadulf's face and trace his features. Eadulf was not startled by this for he remembered the case of Móen, the blind, deaf mute of Araglin whose method of 'seeing' was by touch. He stood patiently until the blind man was satisfied as to his investigation.

'You are used to the inquisitiveness of the blind, Brother Saxon,' he finally observed, dropping his hand.

'I know that you but wish to "see" my features,' agreed Eadulf.

The man smiled. It was the first time he had done so.

'You can tell much from a person's face. I trust you, Brother Saxon. You have sympathetic features.'

'That is a nice way of describing a lack of handsomeness,' grinned Eadulf.

'Does that trouble you? That you consider yourself not blessed with good looks?'

Eadulf realised that the faculties of the man were sharp and missed nothing.

'We are all a little vain, even the ugliest of us.'

'*Vanitas vanitatum, omnis vanitas*,' laughed the man.

'Ecclesiastes,' acknowledged Eadulf. 'Vanity of vanities, all is vanity.'

'This is my house. Come in.'

With that, the man turned and went into the cabin. Eadulf was impressed by the tidiness of it. Dalbach moved with unerring accuracy around the obstacles. Eadulf realised that the items of furniture must have been placed so that he could memorise their position.

'Place your cloak on the back of the chair and sit down, there at the table,' instructed Dalbach, while he went straight to a cauldron hanging over a glowing fire. Eadulf took off his sheepskin cloak. He watched as Dalbach, with dexterity, picked up a bowl from a shelf and ladled the broth into it. He moved directly back to the table and put down the bowl, almost in front of Eadulf.

'You will forgive any inaccuracy?' he smiled. 'Bring the bowl to you and pick up a spoon that should lie on the table. There is bread there, too.'

Indeed there was and Eadulf did not even wait to mutter a *gratias* before he was tucking in.

'You were not telling a lie then, Saxon,' Dalbach observed when he returned with his own bowl of broth. He held his head in a listening position.

'A lie?' mumbled Eadulf, between mouthfuls.

'You are, indeed, very hungry.'

'Thanks to your kind hospitality, friend Dalbach, the hunger is diminishing and I am also feeling warm again. It is a cold day out there. The Lord must have guided my footsteps to your cabin. Surely, though, this is an isolated spot for a . . . for a . . .'

'For a blind man, Brother Eadulf? Do not be nervous of the term.'

'What made you pick this lonely spot to live?'

Dalbach's mouth twisted cynically. The expression did not suit him.

'It chose me rather than I chose it.'

'I do not understand. I would have thought life in a town or village would be more easy with other people close by in case you needed assistance.'

'I am forbidden to live in them.'

'Forbidden?'

Eadulf looked at his host nervously. He knew that among his own people lepers were often forbidden to live in the towns and villages. Yet Dalbach did not appear to be suffering from leprosy.

'I am an exile,' explained Dalbach. 'Blinded and sent out from my people to fend for myself.'

'Blinded?'

Dalbach raised a hand to the scar across his eyes and smiled sardonically.

'You did not think that I was born like this, Brother Eadulf?'

'How were you blinded and why?'

'I am the son of Crimthann who ruled this kingdom thirty years ago. When he died, his Cousin Faelán claimed the crown . . .'

'The same King of Laigin who died last year, after which young Fianamail came to the throne?'

Dalbach inclined his head.

'I know your Saxon kingship succession is very different to ours. Do you know our Brehon law of succession?'

'I do. The man best suited among the royal family is elected by his *derbhfine* to be King.'

'Just so. The *derbhfine* is the electoral college of the family, three male generations from a common great-grandfather. I was a young man then, a warrior, and not long having reached the age of choice. Faelán was safe enough when he was elected but as the years went by he became obsessed with the idea that he might be challenged and he thought there was only one who could be that challenger. Me. He had me seized at night and a hot poker placed over my eyes, to give me a disability which would prevent the *derbhfine* from seriously considering me for any office in the kingdom. Then I was turned out to fend for myself, forbidden to dwell in any town or village throughout the kingdom of Laigin.'

Brother Eadulf was not surprised to hear of Dalbach's story. He knew that such things happened. Among the Saxon kingdoms, where the law was that the eldest male heir succeeded, the brutality in the scramble to the throne and power was just as bad. Brothers slaughtered each other, mothers poisoned sons, sons murdered fathers and fathers killed or imprisoned sons. Among the five kingdoms of Éireann it required only a physical blemish to prohibit someone from standing for kingship, so perhaps the brutality was not as bad as the Saxons' need to kill a candidate outright.

'It must have been hard to readjust to this life, Dalbach,' Eadulf commented in sympathy.

The blind man shook his head.

'I have supportive friends and even relatives. One of my cousins is a religieux in Fearna who frequently visits me to bring food or gifts, although his conversation is limited. My friends and relatives have helped me cope. Faelán is dead now and there is no danger. Besides, I lead an interesting life.'

'Interesting?'

'I have forsaken the sword to compose poetry, and I play the *cruit*, the small harp. I am well content with my life.'

Eadulf glanced doubtfully at the man's physique.

'You do not acquire such muscles by merely playing a harp, Dalbach.'

Dalbach slapped his hand on his knee and chuckled.

'You are observant, Brother. It is true that I continue to take exercise, for in these conditions one needs to be strong in body.'

'That is true . . . Ah!'

The blind man raised his head expectantly at Eadulf's sudden exclamation.

'What is it?'

Eadulf smiled ruefully.

'I have just worked out what the Ogham sticks mean around your cabin. They are a guide, aren't they?'

'You are observant, indeed, Brother Eadulf,' confirmed the other appreciatively. 'When I wander in the clearing, the posts are there to tell me at what point of the compass I am and guide me back to the cabin.'

'That is inventive.'

'One becomes inventive in such circumstances.'

'And are you not bitter? I mean about Faelán who did this terrible thing to you?'

Dalbach considered the idea and then he shrugged.

'I think the bitterness has evaporated. Wasn't it Petrarch who said that nothing mortal is enduring . . .?'

'. . . and there is nothing sweet which does not eventually end in bitterness,' finished Eadulf.

Dalbach chuckled in delight.

'Well, I admit, for some years I felt bitter towards Faelán. But when a man dies, what point is there in hating him? It is now the grandson of my Uncle Rónán Crach who rules the land. So it goes.'

'You mean Fianamail? He is your cousin?'

'The Uí Cheinnselaig are all cousins.'

A tone of wariness entered Eadulf's voice. 'And are you close to your Cousin Fianamail?'

Dalbach had picked up on the subtle change immediately.

'He ignores me and I ignore him. He has done nothing to recompense my sorrow. Why are you wary of him, Brother Eadulf?'

Eadulf was surprised by the abrupt question. He reminded himself that he was dealing with someone who was able to pick up every slight nuance and interpret it. Yet he found himself trusting this blind man.

'He wished to execute me,' Eadulf said, deciding that truth was the easiest course.

There seemed no change of expression on the face of Dalbach. He sat in silence for a moment or two and then sighed softly.

'I have heard about you. You are the Saxon who was to be hanged for raping and murdering a young girl. I thought your name was familiar and that was why you hesitated to give it.'

'I did not do it,' returned Eadulf swiftly. Then he realised that he should be surprised that Dalbach knew of him. 'I swear I am innocent of the charge.'

The blind man seemed to guess what he was thinking.

'I might be in a lonely place, but that does not mean to say that I am alone. I told you that I have friends and relatives who bring me news. If you are not guilty, why were you condemned?'

'Perhaps in the same way that you were condemned to blindness. Fear is a great motive for any unjust action. All I can say is that I did not do it. I would give anything to know the reasons behind the false accusation.'

Dalbach sat back in his chair thoughtfully.

'It is strange that debility in one sense is able to heighten the other senses. There is something in the timbre of your voice, Brother Eadulf, that has a resonance of sincerity in it. I might flatter myself but I think I know that you are not lying.'

'For that, I thank you, Dalbach.'

'So you have escaped your captors? Doubtless they are hunting for you. Are you making for the coast to escape back to your own country?'

Eadulf hesitated and Dalbach added quickly: 'Oh, you can trust me. I shall not give your plans away.'

'It is not that,' replied Eadulf. 'I had thought of making for the coast. The best course, though, is for me to remain and attempt to seek out the truth. That is what I intend.'

Dalbach was silent for a moment.

'That is a brave thing to do. You have confirmed my first impression of your innocence. Had you asked me to help you reach the coast, I would have become immediately suspicious. However, how can I help you to stay and seek out the truth?'

'I need to return to Fearna. There is . . . there is someone there who will help me.'

'That someone being Sister Fidelma of Cashel?'

Eadulf was utterly astonished. 'How do you know that?'

'The same cousin of whom I spoke. I have heard much of Fidelma of Cashel. It was her father, Failbe Fland, King of Muman, who slew my father when he was allied to Faelán at the battle of Ath Goan on the Iarthar Lifé.'

The man spoke without rancour but Eadulf's astonishment grew.

'Fidelma's father? But he died when she was a baby.'

'Indeed, he did. The battle of Ath Goan was over thirty years ago. Don't worry, Brother Eadulf. Battles between my father and his enemies no longer concern me. There is no enmity between me and any offspring of Failbe Fland.'

'I am pleased to hear it,' replied Eadulf fervently.

'So we must find a way of contacting this Fidelma of Cashel,'

Dalbach said. 'Do you have any plans?'

Eadulf shrugged before realising that it was a meaningless gesture.

'I do not, beyond getting back to Fearna and hoping that she will still be there. The problem is that I might be spotted immediately. Even with my cloak, I doubt that I could pass unnoticed for any length of time with this habit and the tonsure of St Peter on my head as well as a Saxon accent.'

Abruptly there came a nearby blast from a hunting horn. Its unexpectedness caused Eadulf to start.

'Don't be alarmed, Brother Eadulf,' Dalbach reassured him as he rose from his seat. 'That might be my cousin. I had word that he might be passing today or tomorrow to bring me some gifts.'

A figure appeared at the edge of the trees, halting before the clearing in front of the cabin.

Eadulf glanced through the window and then shot to his feet, knocking his chair backwards. He had no hesitation in recognising the small, wiry, thin-faced man who had roused him from his bed in the fortress of Cam Eolaing earlier that morning. It was the very man who had pretended to set him free and then had proceeded to try to shoot him down; to kill him.

Chapter Fifteen

'Gabrán?' Sister Étromma appeared surprised as she faced Fidelma at the gates of the abbey. 'What makes you think that I would know where he is?'

Fidelma was a trifle impatient with the stewardess.

'You are the *rechtaire* of the abbey. As Gabrán trades regularly with the abbey, I would expect that you might be the first person one should ask as to his possible whereabouts.'

Sister Étromma admitted reluctantly to the logic but spread her hands in a gesture denoting her inability to help.

'I am sorry, Sister. These are difficult times and since the Saxon's escape yesterday, the Mother Abbess has been particularly . . .' She hesitated and grimaced. 'Really, I don't know where he is.' Her voice was complaining. 'Suddenly, everyone seems so keen to find Gabrán. I do not understand it.'

'Everyone?' Fidelma asked the question swiftly, interested at the comment. 'I don't follow you.'

Sister Étromma reconsidered her statement.

'I mean that several people have asked me today if I know where he might be. The Mother Abbess, among others. I told her a short while ago that I was not his keeper.'

Fidelma raised a sceptical eyebrow at the idea of the bird-like, nervous stewardess saying anything so outrageous to the haughty abbess.

'So Abbess Fainder was asking for him this morning?' She was thoughtful.

'Asking if I knew where he was,' corrected the *rechtaire*.

'But you have no idea of his whereabouts?'

Sister Étromma exhaled in exasperation.

'The man lives on his boat unless he is too drunk to return to it. He comes from Cam Eolaing. His boat is not at the abbey quay so he could be anywhere along the river, anywhere between Cam Eolaing and Loch Garman to the south of here. I am not an augur so cannot tell you exactly where he is.'

Fidelma was surprised at the stewardess's irritability.

'Perhaps you can make a guess?' she enquired gently.

Sister Étromma seemed about to refuse and then she shrugged.

'Abbess Fainder chose to ride towards Cam Eolaing. Therefore I would imagine that is a good starting place to look for him.'

As Sister Étromma made to turn away, Fidelma stayed her. 'There are a few questions that I would like to ask in order to clarify some matters, Sister Étromma. It is obvious that you are hostile to Abbess Fainder. Why is that?'

The stewardess glared defiantly at her. 'I would have thought that was obvious.'

'Sometimes things can be so obvious that they are unseen.'

'I had ambition. A small ambition, true. Should I like the person who stole that ambition from me?'

'Then you must equally dislike Abbot Noé for bringing Fainder here and making her abbess over your head?'

Sister Étromma shrugged. 'I no longer care. I have already told you that I have other plans now.'

'What of this merchant, Gabrán?' Fidelma changed the subject. 'He seems to have a special relationship with the abbess. He entered her chamber without knocking the other day.'

Sister Étromma chuckled sourly. 'That can be put down to his churlish, uncouth attitude. But it is true that he seems to do some private trade for the abbess. He thinks it gives him a special, familiar relationship with her. He brings her merchandise like wine and other goods when he returns from the seaport at Loch Garman.'

Fidelma paused a moment before turning to another matter.

'The night the young girl Gormgilla was killed . . .'

'I told you what I know,' Sister Étromma interrupted quickly.

'I wanted to clarify something. When Fainder had her body brought into the abbey and sent for you, where were you exactly? Asleep?'

Sister Étromma frowned. 'No. As a matter of fact, I met our physician, Brother Miach, who had been summoned to examine the dead girl, when I was on my way from the *bibliotheca* to my chamber.'

'Why were you in the library so late at night?'

'Because of Abbot Noé. I had been delayed by the stable lads who had asked me if they should unharness Bishop Forbassach's horse . . .'

Fidelma was confused. 'I thought that you said that Abbot Noé . . .?'

Sister Étromma heaved an impatient sigh.

'Forbassach had arrived late at the abbey and left the stable in a hurry. He had not given instructions as to what should be done with his horse, whether he would be needing it again that night. He had obviously ridden some way in a hurry for it was sweating. I gave instruction to the stable lads and was making my way to my bed . . .'

'When had he arrived at the abbey? Was this before or after Abbess Fainder arrived?' demanded Fidelma. She felt it obvious that Forbassach and Fainder had ridden separately from Raheen but she wanted to be sure.

'He arrived some time before Fainder announced the discovery of the girl's body. I was told that she had only just arrived at the abbey when she had discovered it.'

Fidelma paused. Forbassach could well have arrived before the girl was murdered. She wondered if there was any significance in that fact. Then she continued: 'So you left the stable and went to your chamber?'

'No. I was on my way to my chamber when I heard a noise in the *bibliotheca*. I looked in and saw Abbot Noé. I asked him if I could help him. I am the *rechtaire*, after all.'

Fidelma tried not to show her reaction.

'So Abbot Noé was also in the abbey that night? I thought his apartment was in Fianamail's fortress.'

'He said that he was consulting some old books.'

'How long were you with him before you went to your chamber?'

'A few moments only. He told me, quite curtly, that he did not need my help.'

'And then?'

'Then I continued on towards my chamber until, as I have said, I encountered Brother Miach, who told me that the abbess had arrived back and a young novitiate of the abbey had been found dead. I went with him and the rest you know.'

Fidelma was silent for a moment or two. Then she found Sister Étromma gazing at her speculatively.

'Does that clarify matters for you?'

'It helps,' Fidelma conceded with a quick smile. 'It helps a lot.'

Fidelma returned hurriedly to the inn where she had left Dego and Enda saddling the horses in preparation to go in search of the boatman.

'Did you find out where he is?' Enda greeted her as she entered the stables.

'Not exactly. But we shall ride for Cam Eolaing for a start. It seems that Abbess Fainder is also looking for Gabrán and has gone ahead.'

'Abbess Fainder?' Dego was interested. 'I wonder why she would be looking for Gabrán?'

Fidelma was thoughtful as she mounted her horse. However, she had no answer for him.

Eadulf felt trapped. He knew that the approaching boatman meant him no good. Some tension in the atmosphere communicated itself to Dalbach.

'You know my cousin?'

'I know that his name is Gabrán and he tried to kill me this morning.'

'Oh, so it is Gabrán,' Dalbach said. 'He is not my cousin, though I know him. Gabrán is a merchant who sometimes passes by here. I do not understand why he should wish you harm, but I can tell that you fear him. Quick – you will find a ladder leading to the loft. Go up and hide – I will not betray you. Trust me. Do it now!'

Eadulf hesitated only a moment. He had no other choice. The foxy-faced boatman was almost at the door.

He grabbed his cloak from the back of the chair, setting it upright, and leapt for the ladder, scuttling up it. He knew his life now hung in the balance for the boatman was armed and he was defenceless.

He barely had time to stretch himself out on the wooden boards that constituted the floor of the loft, his head close to the hatch opening which gave him a view, albeit restricted, of the scene below, when the door of the cabin swung open.

'A good day to you, Dalbach. It is I, Gabrán,' the boatman called as he entered.

Dalbach moved towards him, hand outstretched.

'Gabrán, it is some time since you have stopped by my cabin. Good day to you. Come and sample some of my mead and tell me what brings you here.'

'That I will, gladly,' replied the other.

The man moved out of Eadulf's sight. He heard the noise of liquid being poured into an earthenware mug.

'Health to you, Dalbach.'

'Health, Gabrán.'

There was silence for a moment or so and then Gabrán smacked his lips in appreciation.

'I was expecting to meet a fellow merchant close by here who was bringing me some goods from Rath Loirc. I don't suppose you heard anything of strangers about here this morning?' came his next question.

Eadulf tensed, unsure whether his new friend would betray him or not.

'I have heard of no merchant here today,' replied Dalbach evasively.

'Well, I must return to my boat and send one of my men to search for him.' He paused and seemed to reconsider. 'Have any other strangers been this way? There is a hunt for an escaped Saxon murderer in these parts.'

'A Saxon, you say?'

'A murderer who escaped from my lord Coba's fortress, killing the guard who tried to prevent him and knocking unconscious another. Coba had given the man sanctuary and this is how his kindness has been repaid.'

Eadulf ground his teeth at the easy lies that came to the man's lips.

'That sounds a terrible thing.' Dalbach's voice was soft.

'Terrible it is. Coba has some men out searching for him. Well, as I say, I must return to my boat. If you do happen on my missing merchant . . . but you say that you have seen nobody?'

'I have *seen* nobody,' agreed Dalbach. Eadulf caught a note of solemn humour in his voice as he emphasised the word 'seen'. The blind man was not lying.

'Well, my thanks for the drink. I will send one of my men into the hills to find the missing merchant and my merchandise. If he does happen by here, tell him to wait for my man. I do not want to miss such valuable—'

The voice stopped abruptly. Eadulf, unable to see what was happening below, stiffened in alarm.

'If no one has been here, why are there two bowls on the table . . . the remains of two meals?' demanded Gabrán's voice, edged with suspicion.

Eadulf gave a silent groan. He had forgotten the stew that he had been eating. The remains were in full sight on the table.

'I did not say that no one has been here.' Dalbach's response was swift, assured. 'I thought that you had merely meant strangers. No one whom I consider a stranger has been here.'

There was a tense pause. Then Gabrán seemed satisfied at the explanation.

'Well, be warned. This Saxon may be glib of tongue but he is a killer.'

'I heard the Saxon was a religious.'

'Yes, but he raped and killed a young girl.'

'God have mercy on his soul!'

'God may have mercy but we will not when we have caught him,' came the testy reply. 'Good day, friend Dalbach.'

Eadulf saw the man move back into his line of vision and the door open.

'May you have success in finding your merchant friend, Gabrán,' Dalbach called. There was a muttered acknowledgement.

The door shut. Eadulf waited for a while and then eased himself up to his knees and moved across the floor to a small aperture. He saw the boatman, Gabrán, disappearing along the path into the woods. He suppressed a sigh of relief and returned to the ladder.

'Has he gone?' came Dalbach's whisper.

'He has,' Eadulf called softly down. 'I don't know how to thank you for not giving me away. Why?'

'Why?' echoed Dalbach.

Eadulf moved down the ladder to stand beside him.

'Why did you protect me? If this man Gabrán was your friend, why did you hide me from him? You heard what he had to say about me. I am a killer who apparently will stop at nothing to escape. Another man would feel threatened by my presence.'

'Did you do the things he claimed you did?' asked Dalbach abruptly.

'No, but—'

'Did you escape from Coba's fortress and kill a guard, as he said?'

'I knocked a bowman unconscious but I did not kill a guard. The man was trying to kill *me*. It was Gabrán himself who came and told me that I was free to leave. The moment I stepped beyond the walls of the fortress, he tried to shoot me down.'

Dalbach stood in silent thought for a moment or two. Then he reached out a hand and found Eadulf's arm.

'As I have said before, blindness does not rob men of their senses. Often, it causes other senses to awake. I told you that I trusted you, Brother Eadulf.' His voice was serious. 'As for Gabrán, perhaps "friend" was the wrong word to describe him. He is someone who travels through here now and then and calls to pass the time of day with me. I know him to be a merchant and sometimes he brings me gifts from friends. Now, be seated again, Brother Eadulf, and let us finish the meal and talk of your plan to return to Fearna.'

Eadulf reseated himself. 'My plan?' he asked, his mind distracted by the appearance of Gabrán.

'Before Gabrán turned up we were talking of your plan to get to Fearna and find your friend from Cashel,' Dalbach reminded him.

'Before we do so, I would like to know more of this man, Gabrán. You mentioned that he was a merchant?'

'Yes, he is a trader. He has his own boat and moves freely along the river.'

'I am sure that I once saw him in the abbey at Fearna.'

'No doubt. He trades regularly with the abbey.'

'But why did he come to Coba's fortress to tell me that I was free to go? I thought he was one of Coba's men.'

'Perhaps the chieftain of Cam Eolaing paid him to pretend to release you and then shoot you down,' offered Dalbach.

'That could be what happened,' Eadulf said, having given the matter thought. 'But why should Coba rescue me from the abbey in the first place if he merely wanted my death?'

'Gabrán's services are probably available to anyone who pays him, so maybe it was someone else. But that is a mystery which you must deal with. All I can tell you is that Gabrán is well-known along the river.'

'You said that he often comes this way.'

'I think that he must have family in the hills.'

Eadulf was interested in this deduction and said so.

'He often returns from his visits into the hills with young women. I presume that they are his relatives accompanying him back to the river.'

'You presume? Doesn't he introduce them?'

'He leaves them in the woods there when he comes to visit me, but I hear their voices at a distance. He stops for refreshment, you see – I always have mead on hand.'

'They never come with him to your cabin?'

'Never,' Dalbach confirmed. 'But what will you do about continuing your journey? Gabrán's arrival makes me suggest that you should not delay. I realise that if, instead of Gabrán, it had been my cousin from Fearna then you might not have escaped attention.'

'Perhaps it is wise not to stay longer than is necessary,' agreed Eadulf.

'Then you must take some clothes of mine and a hat to disguise you.'

'You are kind, Dalbach.'

'Not kind, although the sages tell us to have a kind look on another's misery. I glean my own satisfaction from making a small stand for justice.' He stood up. 'Now come with me and I shall show you where I keep some spare clothing and you may make the choice for your journey. Have you thought how you will approach Fearna?'

'How I will approach it?'

'The route which you will take there. I am told that the Brehon Bishop Forbassach is clever. He may deduce that you will attempt to make contact with your friend, Sister Fidelma, and mount a watch for you along the road from Cam Eolaing. It would be best to go north, across the mountains, and then approach Fearna from the northerly road. They would never expect you to come from that direction.'

Eadulf considered for a moment or so. 'It is a clever idea,' he agreed.

'It will be a cold night so do not attempt to stay on the mountains. There is a tiny sanctuary at the Church of the Blessed Brigid which lies on the southern slopes of the Yellow Mountain. Remember that place. The Father Superior, Brother Martan, is a kindly man. Mention my name and you will be given a warm bed and food.'

'I shall remember that. You have been a good friend to a friendless soul, Dalbach.'

'What is the cry – *justitia omnibus*. Justice for all or justice for no one,' Dalbach replied.

The bright autumn morning, with its sharp frost and clear skies, had begun to turn into a more typical dull, cheerless day. Cold, grey-white stormclouds had blown up from the south-west foretelling rain to come. At first the clouds had appeared very high, wispy as a mare's tail, developing into a lofty, milky sheet which, from Fidelma's knowledge, meant that the rain would arrive in twelve hours or less.

Fidelma, with Dego and Enda, had ridden along the river path towards Cam Eolaing and once or twice they had paused to hail passing boatmen in order to seek news of Gabrán. It seemed that his boat, the *Cág*, had not been seen passing downriver and so it was logical to assume that it was still moored at Cam Eolaing.

Cam Eolaing was a curious junction of rivers and rivulets set in a valley. At the spot where most of these waters intersected, they spread almost into a lake through which there were a series of islands not really inhabited for they were low and marshy. To the north and to the south, rose hills guarding this valley. On the northern shore, on a strategically placed hill, stood a fortress dominating the area. Fidelma guessed that this was Coba's fortress in which Eadulf had been given sanctuary on the previous day.

Beyond the lake, another ribbon of water flowed from the east, its origin shrouded among the rising hills. Cam Eolaing dominated the gateway through this hill countryside to the west. Below the fortress, mainly along the banks of the river, were several cabins, particularly along the north bank.

Fidelma indicated that they should halt for a while and Dego went to make enquiries about Gabrán and his boat from a blacksmith, who was engaged in preparing a fire in his forge as they approached. The brawny leather-jacketed man barely paused in his work but spoke gruffly and pointed across the river. Dego returned to them and explained.

'Apparently Gabrán usually keeps his vessel moored on the south bank of the river, lady. He lives just over there.'

The river was broad here and unfordable.

'We'll have to find a boat to take us across,' muttered Enda, pointing out the obvious.

Dego indicated along the bank to where there were several small boats drawn up.

'The smith says that someone along there will row us across.'

The blacksmith was right. They soon found a woodcutter who offered to take them across for a small consideration. It was decided that Enda would remain with the horses while Dego would accompany Fidelma to find Gabrán.

They were already in midriver when the woodcutter glanced over his shoulder and paused in his rowing.

'Gabrán is not there,' he announced. 'Do you still want to cross?'

Dego frowned sternly. 'Not there? If you knew that, why did you embark on this journey?'

The woodcutter glanced at him pityingly. 'I cannot see round corners, my fiery friend. It is only from here in midstream that I can see his moorings behind that islet. The *Cág*, that is his boat, is not at her moorings there. So Gabrán is not there. He lives on his boat, you see.'

Dego looked deflated at the explanation.

'Nevertheless, we shall continue,' insisted Fidelma. 'I see that there are other cabins by those moorings and someone may know where he has gone.'

The woodcutter silently bent to his oars again. He landed them at the empty mooring, and pointed out a cabin which belonged to Gabrán, although he explained that the boatman never stayed in it. Fidelma made him promise to wait and row them back when they had concluded their business. There was no one at the cabin, but a passing woman carrying a bundle of sticks slung on her back, halted at the sight of them.

'Are you seeking Gabrán, Sister?' she asked respectfully.

'I am.'

'He does not live there, although the cabin is his. He prefers to spend all his time on his boat.'

'I see. The fact that his boat is not here must mean that he is not here either?'

The woman agreed with her logic.

'He was here earlier this morning but he cast off very early. There was some excitement at the chieftain's fortress this morning.'

'Was Gabrán involved in it?'

'I doubt it; it was something to do with an escaped foreigner. Gabrán is more concerned with his profits than with what happens at the fortress of our chieftain.'

'We were told that the *Cág* had not sailed downriver today.'

The woman indicated north with her head.

'Then it went upriver. That's common sense. Is something amiss that so many people are seeking Gabrán today?'

Fidelma had been turning away when she paused and glanced back at the woman.

'So many people?'

'Well, I do not know her name, but there was a grand religieuse here. She was making enquiries after Gabrán not long ago.'

'Was it Abbess Fainder of Fearna?'

The woman shrugged. 'I wouldn't know her. I don't go into Fearna – it's a big, busy place.'

'You implied that other people have asked you about Gabrán today?'

'A warrior was here as well. He announced himself as a commander of the King's guards.'

'Was his name Mel?'

'He didn't say.' She shrugged again. 'He was here even before the grand religieuse.'

'He was looking for Gabrán?'

'In a great hurry, he was. Seemed most put out when I told him where the *Cág* had gone. Upriver? says he. Upriver? Then off he goes, racing away.'

'I see. I don't suppose that he mentioned why he wanted to find Gabrán?'

'Not he.'

'So we will find Gabrán somewhere upriver?'

'I have said as much.'

Fidelma waited but when no further information was forthcoming she asked: 'Yet this river appears to have two main arteries beyond those islands. Which one do we take?'

'You are a stranger here, Sister,' the woman chided. 'There is only one route for a boat. The eastern branch of the river is not negotiable for a boat the size of the *Cág*. Gabrán usually takes the northern route to some settlements along the way. He collects some merchandise there before he returns downriver where he sells it.'

Fidelma thanked the woman and turned for the woodcutter's boat with Dego following.

'It seems that we must ride further upriver after Gabrán, then,' she sighed.

'Why do you think the abbess was looking for him?' asked Dego, as they reached the boat. 'And now Mel? Are they all involved in this mystery?'

Fidelma shrugged. 'Let us hope that we shall discover that.' She found herself suddenly shivering. 'Today is bitterly cold. I hope that Eadulf has found some shelter.'

Back in the boat, the woodcutter was reclining, wrapped in a woollen cloak, looking comfortable in spite of the chill.

'I told you that Gabrán was not there,' he grinned, reaching out a hand to steady Fidelma as she climbed into the boat, causing it to rock a little.

'You did,' she replied shortly.

He rowed them back across the river in silence.

On the north shore, Dego gave the man the coin he asked for and they rejoined Enda.

'The *Cág* has gone upriver,' Dego told him. 'We shall ride after it.'

Enda's features were gloomy.

'I spoke to the woodcutter's wife while you were across there,' he offered. 'The northern branch of the river is not navigable beyond two or three kilometres from here, and the southern branch is not navigable beyond a kilometre or thereabouts.'

'Well, that is good news,' replied Fidelma, mounting her horse. 'That means we shall catch up with the *Cág* sooner rather than later.'

'The woodcutter's wife also said that there was another warrior here,' added Enda, 'who left his horse . . .'

'We know all about him; it was Mel,' Dego interrupted, hauling himself up into the saddle.

'Apparently he was with another man who waited for him on this shore while he went across the river.'

Fidelma waited patiently and then said with irritation, 'well – are you going to share your knowledge, with us Enda?'

'Yes, of course. It was the Brehon, the woman said. Bishop Forbassach.'

Eadulf had left his new-found friend Dalbach, and was climbing further up into the hills. The air was chill and a wind was whipping up from the south-east. He knew that bad weather was on its way. From his elevated position, he could see the dark shape of rainclouds gathering in the southern sky.

He was taking the track directly north which, Dalbach had advised him, would bring him into a valley at the eastern end of the northern mountains, somewhere beyond a peak where he could turn west and pick up the road to Fearna. In spite of his blindness, Dalbach seemed to recall the geography of his native land as well as any sighted man. Memories were seared into his mind. The countryside which Eadulf was travelling through was a desolate hilly landscape, and he was doubly grateful for Dalbach's hospitality and his loan of warm clothing and boots to replace his worn woollen habit and sandals. He was also glad of the woollen hat which Dalbach had provided; it complemented his sheepskin cloak, and fitted snugly on his head with the flaps covering his ears. The wind across the hillside was like a knife cutting frequently through the sensitive parts of the flesh.

He strode head down along a track which seemed to vanish now and then. Several times he had to pause to ensure that he was following it at all. It was not a well-frequented path; that much he could discern. Only now and again did he raise his head in an attempt to peer into the cold wind but it was easier to walk with his eyes on the ground before him.

It was during one of his brief glances ahead that he had cause to halt in surprise.

A man was standing a little way off on the path ahead of him.

'Come on!' the man shouted. 'I've been waiting for you.'

Fidelma and her companions had been riding for an hour along the north riverbank when Dego pulled on his reins and pointed in excitement.

'That must be the *Cág*! Look at that boat tied up by that jetty beyond those trees ahead.'

Fidelma's eyes narrowed. Not far ahead was a small group of trees, and a large river boat was tied up against the adjacent wooden jetty. By the jetty a horse was tethered. Fidelma recognised it straight away.

'That's Abbess Fainder's horse,' she told her companions.

'Then I presume that we have found Gabrán at last,' Enda observed.

The three riders moved on at a slow walk and halted where the abbess's horse stood quietly grazing. The wooden jetty was the only sign of any civilisation in the area. There seemed to be no houses or dwellings of any sort nearby. It was a curiously desolate spot.

From the *Cág* come no sound nor movement. Fidelma wondered where the crew were. She presumed that everyone was below and that no one had noticed their arrival. They tethered their horses and Fidelma led the way from the jetty onto the boat. It was a long, flat-bottomed vessel, used only for river navigation for it would be unstable and dangerous in open waters.

Fidelma paused on the deck; it seemed unnaturally quiet.

She made her way cautiously over to the main cabin, which was contained in the raised after portion of the vessel, with its door at deck level. She was about to knock when she heard a faint sound from within: she knew instinctively that something was wrong.

Glancing warningly at Dego and Enda, she put her hand to the catch and pushed it gently down before abruptly thrusting the door open.

Nothing had prepared her for the scene that was revealed within.

There was a great deal of blood in the gloomy cabin. The dark stains had leaked out from a body which lay sprawled on the floor. But it was the figure which was kneeling by the head of the body that shocked her. A figure with a bloodied knife in its hand.

The clothing indicated the identity of the corpse, even if Fidelma had not recognised the features twisted in a last moment of agony before death. It was Gabrán, the captain of the *Cág*. But the figure kneeling at his head, grasping the murder weapon, who now glanced up in frightened anguish towards her, was the Abbess of Fearna – Abbess Fainder.

Chapter Sixteen

'Come on. I've been waiting for you!' the man repeated as he leapt down from the rock to approach Eadulf.

Startled, Eadulf stood rooted to the spot and examined the man who had been standing on a jutting rock just above the path in front of him. He was dressed in rough country clothes. A brown, weatherbeaten skin denoted he was used to the outdoors. He was clad in a heavy leather jerkin over a thick woollen jacket and on his feet the tough boots that farmers usually wore.

Eadulf was not sure whether he should flee or stay and prepare to defend himself. Further along the track, he saw there was a cart already harnessed with a horse and realised that flight was pointless. He tensed his muscles for a fight.

The man halted and stared at him in disgust.

'Where's Gabrán? I thought he was coming in person this time?'

'Gabrán?' Eadulf glanced nervously behind him, uncertain what he should do. 'He's gone back to his boat,' he said, deciding to tell the truth. After all, that was what he had heard the river-boat captain tell Dalbach.

'Back to the river?' The man before him spat at the side of the path. 'Leaving you to come up here and make the collection, I suppose?'

'Leaving me to come up here,' repeated Eadulf, still truthfully.

'I've been hanging around here for two hours. It's cold and I wasn't sure whether he had said to meet him here at Darach Carraig or at Dalbach's cabin. Still, you are here now.'

'Gabrán did not tell me that I should have been here earlier,' Eadulf suddenly grew confident, realising that this must be the man with the merchandise whom Gabrán had been seeking when he came to Dalbach's cabin earlier. Obviously this fellow had been confused by the similarity of the names Darach and Dalbach.

'Just like him to get other people to do the work,' sighed the man. Then he frowned. 'You're a foreigner, aren't you?'

Eadulf stiffened slightly.

'A Saxon, I can tell by your accent,' went on the man suspiciously. Then he shrugged. 'No skin off my nose. I suppose you accompany the merchandise all the way from here to the lands of the Saxons, eh?'

Eadulf decided to make a non-committal sound.

'Well,' the man went on, 'it's cold and it's late and I don't want to hang about here any longer than I have to. There are only two this time. I think, in future, I must go further afield. I suppose you've left your cart at the bottom of the hill? Didn't Gabrán tell you that the track was traversable all the way up here? Well, you'll have no trouble with only two of them. I'll see Gabrán at Cam Eolaing when he returns from the coast but tell him, when you see him, that things are getting difficult. He can pay me when he returns. The price is going to increase though.'

Eadulf nodded as if in agreement. It seemed the only thing to do in this bizarre, confusing conversation.

'Good man. They are in the cave as usual. Gabrán has told you where it is located?'

Eadulf hesitated and shook his head. 'Not exactly,' he said.

The man sighed impatiently, turned and pointed. 'Two hundred metres along this path, my friend. Up the hill to your right you will see the short rock face, a small granite cliff. You can't miss the opening to the cave. That's where the merchandise is.'

The man glanced up at the sky and drew his collar up around his neck.

'It'll be raining soon. Maybe sleet will come with this cold. I'm off. Don't forget to tell Gabrán what I say. It's getting difficult.'

He went back to his cart, climbing quickly up onto the seat. He flicked the reins and turned the vehicle along a narrow, almost invisible track which branched off eastwards over the rolling hills.

Eadulf, shaken and confused, stood watching him go.

He had obviously been mistaken for one of Gabrán's men. What merchandise was the boatman collecting in this godforsaken spot, he wondered. Darach Carraig – the oak rock. A curious name. He glanced behind him in the direction from which he had come. Gabrán had mentioned sending another to look for the merchandise. Perhaps that man was close behind him? He'd better move on quickly in case he was overtaken.

He set off hurriedly along the path. He supposed that he had been mentally counting the two hundred metres for he paused after a few moments and glanced up the hill to his right. Not far above him he saw the cluster of large boulders and rocks strewn across the hill and the natural hill scooped out at that point forming a short granite cliff. He hesitated and felt an overwhelming sense of curiosity. He could at least see what Gabrán's peculiar merchandise was and why it had to be left in an isolated cave in an even more isolated part of the countryside. He glanced around. There was no sign of anyone in the bleak, darkening landscape.

Eadulf began to climb up towards the rocks and, as he did so, he saw that behind the larger of the granite boulders the almost cliff-like stretch of black rock appeared as if some hand had quarried it thus, it seemed so unnatural. As he drew closer, he was able to spot the dark entrance of a cave with a flat shelf of rock before it.

Reaching this, Eadulf paused for a moment to recover his breath from the short but steep ascent before taking a step forward. The cave was in semigloom. He peered into its dark recesses, standing waiting for his eyes to grow used to the shadows.

There was a sudden and unusual scrabbling sound which caused him to flinch, thinking some animal was within. Then he saw the source and his mouth dropped open in astonishment.

There were two human shapes on the ground at the far end of the cave, seated with their backs against the rocks. From the manner of their posture he saw they were bound hand and foot and, on closer inspection, he realised that they were also gagged. They were of slight build; that he could make out in the darkness, but beyond that he could see no other features.

'Whoever you are,' he declaimed loudly, 'I mean you no harm.'

He moved towards them.

Instantly there arose muffled, piteous moaning and the figure nearest him seemed to cringe away, although it could not move far because of its bonds.

'I mean you no harm,' repeated Eadulf. 'I must bring you to the light so that I may see you.'

Ignoring the animal-like sounds his movements provoked, he bent down and lifted the nearest squirming bound form and half-pulled, half-carried it to the cave entrance.

Two wide, frightened eyes stared at him from over the dirty rag that formed a gag.

Eadulf stepped away from the form in amazement.

It was the face of a young girl, no more than twelve or thirteen years of age, that stared back at him in utter fear.

'Well, Abbess Fainder,' Fidelma said slowly, as she examined the scene of carnage before her, 'I think that you have some explaining to do.'

Abbess Fainder returned her gaze almost uncomprehendingly. Then she looked down at the body of Gabrán beside her and at the knife in her hand. With a strange animal-like groan she dropped the knife and sprang to her feet. Her eyes were wild.

'He is dead,' she said hoarsely.

'That I can see,' agreed Fidelma grimly. 'Why?'

'Why?' the abbess echoed in a daze.

'Why is he dead?' pressed Fidelma.

The abbess blinked, staring at her as if she did not understand. It took a moment for her to gather her wits.

'How should I know?' she began and then stopped abruptly. 'You don't think that I . . .? I did not kill him!'

'With due respect, Abbess Fainder,' intervened Dego, peering over Fidelma's shoulder, 'we have just come aboard and, opening the cabin door, we find Gabrán dead. From the amount of blood it is clear that he has been knifed to death. You are kneeling at his head. Your clothes are smeared in blood and you have a knife in your hand. How are we to interpret this scene?'

The abbess seemed to be recovering herself. She glared angrily at Dego.

'How dare you! Who are you to accuse the Abbess of Fearna of common murder?'

Fidelma's mouth twitched in black humour as she considered the situation.

'No murder is common, abbess. Least of all this murder. It would take a fool not to point out the obvious. Are you trying to tell us that you had no hand in this murder?'

Abbess Fainder's face was white.

'I did not do it.' Her voice cracked with emotion.

'So you say. Come out on deck and explain it to me.'

Fidelma stood aside from the door and gestured for the abbess to leave the cabin. Fainder stepped out onto the deck and blinked in the daylight.

'There is no one else on board,' Enda reported with a note of malicious glee. He had made a cursory examination of the boat. 'You appear to be alone here, Mother Abbess.'

Abbess Fainder sat down abruptly on a hatch cover and, placing her arms around her waist, she bent over and seemed to hug herself, rocking a little to and fro. Fidelma sat down beside her.

'This is a bad business,' Fidelma said gently, after a few moments. 'The sooner we have an explanation the better.'

Abbess Fainder raised her anguished features to face her.

'Explanation? I have told you that I did not do it! What other explanation do you need?'

There was enough of her old spirit left in the voice for Fidelma's mouth to tighten impatiently.

'Believe me, Mother Abbess, an explanation is needed and it had better be one that I am satisfied with,' she snapped. 'Perhaps you had best begin by explaining how you came to be here.'

The abbess's features changed abruptly. The spark of her old arrogance burst out.

'I don't like your tone, Sister. Are you trying to accuse me?'

Fidelma was unconcerned. 'I don't have to accuse you. The circumstances speak for themselves. But if there is something that you wish to tell me, now is the time to do so. As a *dálaigh* I must report the evidence of my eyes.'

Abbess Fainder gazed at her as the shock of what she was saying registered. She opened her mouth, speechless for a moment or two.

'But I did not do it,' she said finally. 'You can't accuse me. You can't!'

'As I recall, Brother Eadulf said pretty much the same thing,' Fidelma told her, 'yet he was accused and found guilty of murder on much slimmer evidence. And here you are, actually found bending over the body, holding a knife, drenched in blood.'

'But I am . . .' The abbess's mouth snapped shut as if she realised the conceit of what she had been about to say.

'But you are the abbess whereas Brother Eadulf was merely a wandering foreigner?' concluded Fidelma. 'Well, Abbess Fainder? We are waiting for your story.'

A shudder went through the woman. Her haughty demeanour vanished and her shoulders slumped.

'Bishop Forbassach told me that you had accused Gabrán of attacking you last night.'

Fidelma waited patiently.

'Bishop Forbassach claimed that you would not lie over such a matter. So I came here to demand an explanation from Gabrán,' went on Abbess Fainder. 'I could not believe your story even if Forbassach did. Gabrán had . . .' She hesitated.

'Gabrán had . . . what?' prompted Fidelma.

'Gabrán is a well-known merchant on the river. He has traded with the abbey for many years, long before I became Abbess. Such an accusation brings an insult to our abbey and has to be challenged. I came here to see what Gabrán had to say.'

'So you came here hoping to prove my accusation against Gabrán false? Continue.'

'I finally found the *Cág* moored here. There was no one about. I came on board and called for Gabrán. There was no answer. I thought I heard a movement in the cabin so I went to the door and knocked. There was the sound of something heavy falling . . . I realise now that it was the body of Gabrán. Anyway, I called out again and went in. I saw the scene exactly as you saw it. Gabrán was dead and lying on his back in the cabin. There was blood everywhere. My first thought was for the man and I entered and knelt down. He was beyond help.'

'Presumably this is how you explain the fact that your clothes are stained with blood?'

'It is why my habit is bloody, yes.'

'Then what?'

'I was shocked by the knife-wounds that had been inflicted. I saw the knife . . .'

'Where was this knife?'

'Lying by the side of the body. I saw it and picked it up. I don't know what made me do that. Some unthinking reaction, I suppose. I just knelt there.'

'And then we arrived.'

To Fidelma's surprise, Abbess Fainder shook her head.

'There was something else before you came.'

'What was that?'

'It didn't mean much to me then but now it does.'

'Go on.'

'I heard a soft splash.'

Fidelma arched an eyebrow. 'A soft splash? What did you think it was?'

'I think it was the murderer leaving the boat.' The abbess shivered sightly.

Fidelma looked cynical. 'The boat was moored alongside a jetty. What would be the need for anyone to leave the boat via the river, especially in this icy weather. And if it was the murderer leaving the scene of this crime, then your horse was tethered nearby and presented a very effective means of escape. Isn't that so?'

Abbess Fainder stared blankly at Fidelma's remorseless logic.

'I am sure that someone was on this boat and left it by lowering themselves into the water,' she repeated stubbornly.

'It would certainly help your claim that you were innocent of this crime,' agreed Fidelma, 'but I have to say that it is unlikely in the extreme that someone, flying from this scene, would take that option. Look!'

She indicated the river side of the boat. The waters were flowing strongly at this point and the river was now more than five metres wide increasing the ferocity of the flow.

'Anyone attempting to swim in that river would have to be a strong swimmer. No one in their right mind would choose that route when all they had to do was step onto the riverbank on the other side of the boat.'

Fidelma suddenly frowned as a thought struck her.

'How could Gabrán navigate this boat up here against such a strong current?'

'Easy enough,' explained Enda. 'While I was looking around this boat I saw the harness attachments. It is common, lady, for a couple of asses to be used to pull river boats against the flow of the river where the current is strong. Otherwise, poles are used to propel the vessel. It is done all the time.'

Fidelma stood up and looked around. While Enda was obviously correct, there was still something wrong.

'So where are these beasts now? Who brought them here and who took them away? Indeed, where are Gabrán's crew, come to that?'

She returned to her seat on the hatch cover and closed her eyes for a moment in thought. She felt that she was overlooking something important. She wondered why the crew had left Gabrán on his own and taken the animals needed to bring the boat upriver to this spot? Abbess Fainder's story about merely happening on the boat and then finding Gabrán just at the moment of his slaughter seemed so far-fetched; as far-fetched as the idea of the killer escaping by jumping over the side of the boat into the swiftly flowing river. It was nonsense. But then, perhaps, Eadulf's story appeared equally nonsensical in face of the evidence of the girl Fial who claimed to have been an eye-witness to her friend's death. Fidelma expelled her breath in a deep sigh.

'Well, there is little we can do here for the time being,' she said, standing up. 'Dego, I want you to ride back to Cam Eolaing and find Coba, if he is there. He said that he was returning to his fortress and he is the *bó-aire* of this area. This matter needs to be reported to him. If you fail to find him at Cam Eolaing, ride back to Fearna and bring Bishop Forbassach here.'

Abbess Fainder was anxious.

'What do you mean to do?' She tried to sound commanding, but her voice trembled.

'I mean to follow the law,' Fidelma replied with grim humour. 'It will be up to the Brehon of this kingdom, I presume, as to whether that law will follow the punitive Penitentials, of which you are so fond, or whether you will be found guilty and punished by our own native system.'

Abbess Fainder's eyes widened with horror. 'But I did not do it.'

'So you have said, Mother Abbess,' Fidelma rejoined with a touch of well-deserved malice. 'Just as Brother Eadulf said that he did not do what *he* was accused of!'

Eadulf untied the gag on the young girl whom he had carried to the entrance of the cave. She continued to stare at him with eyes wide, round and dark, mirroring her fear. In spite of the tightness of her bonds she was trembling visibly.

'Who are you?' demanded Eadulf.

'Don't hurt me!' came the whimpering response. 'Please, don't hurt me.'

Eadulf tried a reassuring smile. 'I do not propose to hurt you. Who left you in this condition?'

The girl took some time to overcome her fear.

'Are you one of them?' she whispered.

'I do not know who "they" are,' Eadulf replied, and then, remembering the second bound form in the cave, he turn back and brought her out. She, too, was barely thirteen, a half-starved dishevelled little girl. He removed her gag and she sobbed in great breaths of air.

'You are a Saxon, so you must be one of them,' the first girl cried fearfully. 'Please do not hurt us.'

Eadulf sat down before them, shaking his head. He, too, was cautious, for he made it a rule never to loose the bonds of any person until he found out why they had been bound in the first place. He had once seen a young Brother killed by an insane woman when he had removed her bonds, thinking he was releasing her from a tormentor.

'I have no intention of hurting you, whoever you are. Tell me first, who are you, why are you bound and who bound you?'

The two girls exchanged a nervous glance between them.

'You must know, if you are one of them,' replied the first of the girls with some defiance.

Eadulf was patient. 'I am a stranger here. I do not know who you are nor who "they" are.'

'But you knew enough to come into the cave to find us,' pointed out the second girl, who seemed to have a quicker wit than her companion. 'No one would stumble on that cave by chance. You must be one of them.'

'If I am someone who means you harm, then you have nothing to lose in answering my questions,' Eadulf pointed out. The younger girl started to sob. 'However,' he added sharply, 'if I am simply a stranger passing by, then I might be able to help you in your plight if you tell me the reason why you have been bound and left in this cave.'

It was some time before the elder of the two came to a decision.

'We do not know,' she said after some thought.

Eadulf raised his eyebrows in disbelief.

'It is the truth that I tell you,' the girl insisted. 'Yesterday, we were taken from our homes by a man. He brought us to this place, bound us and left us. He said that someone would come to take us on a long journey and that we would never see our homes again.'

Eadulf stared hard at the girl trying to assess the truth of what she was saying. Her voice was dull, flat now, as if divorced from the reality of what she was saying.

'Who was this man?' he pressed.

'A stranger like yourself.'

'But not a foreigner,' added the second girl.

'I think that you had better explain further. Who are you and where do you come from?'

203

The girls seemed less nervous now as he drew them out of their first fear of immediate harm.

'My name is Muirecht,' said the elder. 'I come from the mountains to the north of here. Well over a day's riding.'

Eadulf turned to the younger of the two. 'And you?'

'I am called Conna.'

'And do you come from the same place as Muirecht?'

The girl shook her head.

'Not the same place,' Muirecht intervened, responding for her. 'I never saw her before we found ourselves together as prisoners. We did not know each other's names until this moment.'

'So what happened? Why were you made prisoners?'

The girls exchanged another glance and it seemed to have been silently agreed that Muirecht would speak for the two of them.

'It was yesterday morning, well before dawn, that I was awakened by my father . . .'

'And who is your father?' intervened Eadulf.

'A poor man. He is a *fudir*, although he is a *saer-fudir*,' she added this fact quickly and proudly.

Eadulf knew that the *fudir* was the lowest class of Irish society; a class scarcely little removed from the slaves of Saxon society. They were comprised not of members of the clan but were commonly fugitives, prisoners of war, hostages or criminals who had their civil rights removed as a form of punishment. The *fudirs* were divided into two sub-classes, the *daer-fudir* or unfree and the *saer-fudir*, who were not exactly free men but did not suffer the bondage placed on the lower rank. The *saer-fudir* were usually those who were not criminals and therefore could regain certain rights and privileges in society. They could work land that was allotted to them by their lord or king and on very rare occasions rise from the 'unfree' class to become a *céile*, a free clansman, and they might even reach to the rank of a *bó-aire*, a landless chieftain and magistrate.

Eadulf indicated that he understood.

'My father's plot of land is small,' went on Muirecht, 'but, in spite of that, the chief of the territory demands the *biatad*, the food rent. Twice a year my father had to repay the loans from the common stock.'

Eadulf knew the custom. Both free and unfree *fudir* could borrow cows, pigs, corn, bacon, butter and honey, from the common stock of the clan, provided that one third of the value of that which they took was paid back annually for seven years. At the end of that time the stock became their property without further payment. The free *fudir* was also obliged to give the Chief either service in time of war or service in an agreed number of days working the land of the Chief. Eadulf, coming from a society in which outright slavery was normal, always considered the idea of the non-free class of society being able to obtain such loans and work their way to freedom as a curious concept. He could see that, for a man with poor land and little ability to manage, the loan might, in certain circumstances, induce further poverty instead of raising him out of it.

'Go on,' he said. 'Yesterday morning your father awakened you before first light. Then what?'

Muirecht sniffed painfully at the memory.

'He was red-eyed. He had been crying. He told me to dress and be ready for a long journey. I asked him what journey. He would not answer. I trusted my father. He brought me out of the cabin. There was no sign of my mother nor of my young brother to bid me goodbye. But outside was a man with a cart.'

She hesitated, contemplating the scene in her memory.

Eadulf waited patiently.

'The same happened to me,' muttered the second girl, Conna. 'My father is a *daer-fudir*. I have no mother for she died three months ago. I was made to cook and clean for my father.'

Muirecht grimaced and the younger girl fell silent.

'Once out of the cabin, my father . . .' began Muirecht again and then she paused, tears in her eyes. 'He held me by the arms. The other man bound and gagged me and threw me in his cart. I saw, through a chink in the wood of the cart, my father receive a small bag with chinking metal in it. He grabbed it to his chest and hurried inside the cabin. Then the man climbed on his cart, threw brushwood over me and drove off.'

She suddenly began to sob long and loudly. Eadulf did not know how to comfort the girl.

'It was the same with me,' affirmed the younger girl. 'I was thrown into the cart and found this girl already there. We could not speak as we were both bound and gagged. And we have neither eaten nor had a drink since yesterday morning.'

Eadulf stared at them blankly, hardly able to take in the enormity of their story.

'What you are telling me is that both your fathers have actually sold you to the man with the cart?'

Muirecht had managed to control her sobbing and she nodded dismally.

'What else is there to believe? I have heard tell of poor families who sell their children to be taken to other lands to . . .' she fought for the words.

'To be a slave,' muttered Eadulf sadly. He knew the practice existed in many countries. Now he realised the sort of trade Gabrán must have been running along the river. He bought young girls from their families and transported them down to Loch Garman on the coast where they were sold as slaves to the Saxon kingdoms or to the land of the Franks. Poor people, to alleviate their impoverished circumstances, often resorted to selling one of their female children. He, personally, had never encountered such a trade among the people of the five kingdoms of Éireann because the law system seemed designed to keep anyone from utter destitution and the concept of one man holding another in complete servile bondage was alien. The revelation of the two girls came as a shock to Eadulf.

The sudden screech of a rook, taking off from a nearby high tree, caused Eadulf to start and glance up nervously, remembering that one of Gabrán's men was supposed to be coming into the hills to collect these girls.

'We must leave this place before these bad men come for you,' he said, bending forward and taking out his knife. He cut at the bindings that held the girls' ankles together and then released their hands. 'We ought to move on now.'

Muirecht was rubbing her wrists and ankles.

'We need a moment or two,' she protested. 'My hands and feet are numb from lack of blood.'

Conna was following her example in an attempt to restore the circulation.

'But we must hurry,' Eadulf urged, now that he had realised what dangers were involved.

'But to go where?' protested Muirecht. 'We can't go back to our fathers . . . not after what has happened.'

'No,' agreed Eadulf, helping them both to their feet. They stood and stamped their feet awhile to restore their circulation. Eadulf's brows were drawn together in perplexity. He could hardly take the two girls back with him to Fearna. Then he suddenly remembered that Dalbach had told him of the community on the Yellow Mountain. 'Do either of you know this area?' he asked the girls.

They shook their heads negatively.

'I have not been so far south ever,' Muirecht told him.

'There is a mountain called the Yellow Mountain,' Eadulf said. 'It lies to the west of here, overlooking Fearna. I am told that there is a church there dedicated to the Blessed Brigid. You will be given sanctuary there until it is decided what is for the best. Do you agree to accompany me there?'

The two exchanged another glance. Muirecht shrugged almost indifferently.

'There is nothing else that we can do. We will go with you. What is your name, stranger?'

'My name is Eadulf. Brother Eadulf.'

'Then I was right. You *are* a foreigner,' Muirecht sounded triumphant.

Eadulf smiled wryly. 'A traveller passing through this kingdom,' he added with dry humour.

As a flock of rooks began their cacophony in the valley below, Eadulf glanced down anxiously. Something was disturbing the birds; something or someone. It would not do to delay any longer.

'I think the man whom your captor was waiting for might be approaching. Let us move on as quickly as we can.'

Chapter Seventeen

Fidelma had left Abbess Fainder, with Enda in attendance, sitting on the hatch cover of the boat while she returned to Gabrán's cabin. She took a stand just inside the door, forcing her gaze on the scene of carnage within. The river-boat captain had been stabbed at least half a dozen times in the chest and arms. There was little doubt that it had been a wildly ferocious attack. Trying to avoid getting any blood on her clothing, she picked her way gingerly to the side of the body and began a careful examination.

The worst wound was a tear across the man's throat, as if his assailant had thrust the knife upwards, ripping it across the throat, using the entire length of the blade. The other wounds over the chest and arms seemed randomly thrust with the point of the knife. There was no pattern to them; they did not seem to have been aimed at any vital spot. The slashing of the throat had, however, been enough to bring about death for the rip was across the jugular vein. Every other blow seemed an expression of angry violence.

Could Abbess Fainder be capable of such an act? Well, everyone was capable of violence given the right circumstances, Fidelma knew that much. But what fury had driven Fainder? It was while she was contemplating this point that she realised she was staring at something without really seeing it. She concentrated. The slash across the throat had not been made by a knife. Certainly not with the same small blade that the abbess had dropped to the floor.

Fidelma forced herself closer. The slash had been made by a sword. She had no doubt of it, for the upward slash had not only ripped the flesh but shattered the jawbone and dislodged some teeth in the lower jaw by the power of its impact. To create such a wound would need a vigorous stroke.

Mentally reproving herself for initially missing the obvious, Fidelma glanced round but could see no weapon that might have made that terrible and mortal wound. She picked up the small knife which the abbess had held and compared its blade to the half dozen puncture marks over the man's chest and arms. It needed but a moment to confirm that the weapon could have made the more insignificant wounds but not the fatal one.

While she was bending down, another item caught her attention which, had she not bent close, she might have missed. It was a small clump of hairs. She realised that they were hairs from the head of Gabrán, for she compared them. It seemed that someone had grabbed a tuft of his hair and pulled it out by the roots, before dropping it to the floor. There were particles of blood still on the roots.

She replaced the knife and stood up but as she stepped back, her foot knocked against a jangling piece of metal causing it to scrape on the boards. She looked down and her eyes widened. The metal consisted of a pair of manacles. They were small and looked like wrist restraints. They had been lying discarded on the floor. The manacles were open and there was a key still in the lock which secured them.

She was about to turn away when something else caught her eye. There were some strands of material which had been caught on a protruding nail from a leg of a table which was one of the items of cabin furniture. Someone had swept by and the garment had caught against the nail. The strands were of brown dyed woollen homespun of the sort worn by most religious. Thoughtfully, she unhooked the fibres and placed them in her marsupium.

Fidelma then rose and considered the situation. These were several pieces in a puzzle. Each fitted to form a picture of Gabrán's last moments. If Abbess Fainder's denial of the killing was to be believed, especially the claim that she was outside the door when she heard Gabrán's body fall, it would mean the killer had still been in the cabin. That was patently impossible, otherwise Fainder would have seen the killer and been attacked in turn. Fidelma peered carefully around to see if there was anything else which would account for the sound of something as heavy as a body falling to the deck of the ship. There was nothing else apart from the body of Gabrán.

That meant either Fainder was lying for obvious reasons or that the killer had escaped from the cabin in the moments before the abbess had opened the door. Once more she gave the cabin a careful scrutiny.

The small hatch in the deck was not obvious; it was small and when she raised it and peered down into the darkness below, Fidelma realised that it was too small for her to squeeze through, nor could she see anything below in the darkness.

She took a lamp from a side table and returned to the main deck of the boat.

'Lift that hatch there, Enda,' she called as she approached. A quick glance at the abbess revealed that she was not wearing brown homespun but a richly woven black wool robe. Abbess Fainder rose from the hatch cover and moved to one side while the warrior lifted it with ease.

'What is it, lady?' Enda asked. 'Have you found something?'

'I am just having a look round,' she explained.

As she climbed down the steps leading from the hatch to the deck below she realised that there was already a lantern glowing there. The steps led into a large cabin which she found was separated from the main cargo hold by a bulkhead and hatchway. She glanced through this and saw that the hold was open to the sky and was devoid of any goods.

Fidelma turned to examine the cabin into which she had descended. It was obvious at first sight that this was where Gabrán's crew slept when they were on board.

There was another small bulkhead further back where the boat narrowed; this marked the position of Gabrán's cabin above. The area beyond was undoubtedly the recess into which the small aperture from Gabrán's cabin gave access. She lit her lamp from the small hanging lantern in the crew's quarters and opened the small door, noting at the same time that it had a lock on it but the key was on the inside. She noted with curiosity that three other keys of different shapes lay scattered on the floor inside, just by the threshold.

The next thing she noticed was the smell, which was even more vile than that in the crew's quarters. It contained the acrid stench of urine and the sweat of people living in close confinement. But the area was tiny, no larger than two metres by two-and-a-half metres. The space was devoid of any fixtures except for a couple of straw palliasses and an old leather slop bucket. Fidelma was too large to enter the narrow confines in comfort for the space was considerably less than two metres high. It was made even smaller by the intrusion of a small ladder leading to the hatch above.

She wondered what this space was used for. A punishment cabin? If so, for whom? For the crew who did not perform their duties? Fidelma knew that such punishments happened on seagoing ships but not on river boats where members of the crew could step ashore any time they chose. She raised her lamp high and her eyes fell on some splintered woodwork. Something had been gouged out of one of the thick wooden ribs of the boat to which it had been attached, and attached quite firmly. Peering down, Fidelma saw a length of chain on the deck and a sharp piece of metal. There was no doubt that the chain and its attachment had been dug from its wooden fixing by someone using the sharp metal. But why? And by whom? She was backing out of the door when she noticed the bloodstains on the inside of the hatchway. Smeared bloody footprints led across the cabin, growing fainter and vanishing before they reached the other side.

Fidelma did not say anything as she climbed back onto the deck and snuffed out her lamp. Enda and the abbess were waiting impatiently for her. She signalled to Enda to replace the hatch cover while she went to the side of the boat and gazed down at the swiftly flowing waters in perplexity. There was no sign of any smeared or bloody footprints on the deck.

Was it conceivable that Abbess Fainder was telling the truth? It did not make sense. Could someone have killed Gabrán and, being alarmed by the arrival of Fainder, retreated down into that gruesome little cabin below decks and then made their way through the larger cabin, up the ladder onto the deck and over the side? No; there was one thing wrong with that. The hatch cover had been closed and it needed someone of strength to pull it aside. It would also have made a noise which the abbess would have heard and commented upon. She turned, still thoughtful, and went to the main cargo hold and peered down. Of course, there was a ladder there. She conceded that someone could have come up on deck through that route.

For the theory to be convincing, the person who killed Gabrán and made their escape in such a manner would have to have been a dwarf, a tiny, slim person, in order to slip through the hatch from Gabrán's cabin down into the cell-like room below. Fidelma gave a shake of her head and turned back to where the Abbess Fainder had reseated herself on the hatch.

'Enda,' she addressed the warrior, 'will you check on the horses?'

He looked bewildered. 'They are safe enough, lady, and—' Then he saw the steely look in her eyes and realised that she wanted to be alone with the abbess. 'Very well,' he said, and moved off with a self-conscious air.

Fidelma stood before the abbess.

'I think that we should talk seriously, Mother Abbess, and leave aside any notions of arrogant pretensions of rank and duty. It will make my task easier.'

The abbess blinked up at her in surprise at her direct approach.

'I thought that we *had* been speaking seriously,' she countered, with a flash of irritation.

'Not seriously enough, it seems. Of course, you will wish to be represented by a *dálaigh* of your own choice . . .'

A look of concern crossed the abbess's features once again.

'I tell you that I am *not* involved in this death! You cannot believe that I will be charged with a murder that I did not commit?'

'Why not? Other people have been,' Fidelma replied with equanimity. 'However, I do not wish to know how you mean to instruct the *dálaigh* you choose but I now want you to answer some questions which I think are pertinent to the things which have been happening here during recent weeks.'

'If I refuse?'

'I am a witness, along with my men, to discovering you bending over the body of Gabrán with a knife,' Fidelma pointed out brutally.

'I have told you everything that you need to know,' the abbess fretted.

'Everything? I have talked with Deog, your sister.'

The effect on the abbess was startling. She paled and her lips parted in alarm.

'She has nothing to do with—' she began to protest, but Fidelma cut her short.

'Let me be the judge of the information necessary to my enquiries. Let us stop prevarications and let me, at last, have some answers!'

A sigh shook Abbess Fainder's shoulders and she bowed her head as if in submission.

'I know you came from a poor family at Raheen: your sister told me. And I believe that you were a novitiate at the abbey of Taghmon.'

'You have been busy,' the abbess replied bitterly.

'Then you decided to go to Bobbio?'

'I was sent on a mission there to Columbanus's foundation. I took some books as a gift to the library of Bobbio.'

'What persuaded you to support the Roman Rule?'

Abbess Fainder's voice momentarily took on the tone of a fanatic.

'When I reached Bobbio it was scarcely forty years since the death of Columbanus. Many of the religious there believed that the rules that he drew up, based on the rules of the Irish houses, were misguided.

Columbanus, as blessed as the man was, argued with many of his followers. The Blessed Gall left his service to set up his own foundation even before Columbanus crossed the Alps to Bobbio. I became one of the party which, having seen how communities of the Western church were governed, came to believe that we should give up the Irish Rule and adopt the rule of the saintly Benedict of Noricum.'

'So it was out of conviction that you did so?'

'Of course.'

'Then you went on to Rome?'

'The Abbot of Bobbio asked me to undertake a mission to Rome, to support a sub-house that we ran there as a hostel for pilgrims.'

'It sounds as though you did not go willingly?'

'At first I did not. I felt it was a way for the abbot to rid himself of the opposition to his administration. He was against the Rule of Benedict.'

'But you went?'

'I did. In fact, on a personal level, it was a time of happiness for me. I ran the hostel by the Rule of Benedict and lived and worked in the very centre of Christendom. It was there I came to study the benefits of the Penitentials.'

'How did you meet with Abbot Noé?'

'Easily enough. He stayed at my hostel while he was on a pilgrimage to Rome last summer.'

'You had not met him before nor were related to him?'

'No.'

'And yet he persuaded you to return with him to Laigin and become Abbess at Fearna?'

'He talked about Fearna,' The abbess was complacent. 'It was I who persuaded him to take me there.'

'How did that come about?'

'I suppose he appreciated the way I ran my house in Rome.' The abbess was guarded again.

'He knew your views on the Penitentials?'

'We discussed such matters long into the night. With all modesty, I converted him to my ideas.'

'Really? You must be a powerful advocate,' observed Fidelma.

'It is not surprising. Abbot Noé is a very progressive man. He shared my idea of a kingdom ruled by the Penitentials and we spoke of how he could become spiritual adviser to young Fianamail. To be adviser and confessor would give him influence in the matter.'

'So Abbot Noé suddenly developed this ambition. How was it that you were made his successor at Fearna when custom dictated that an abbot or abbess must be elected in the same manner as a chieftain or any other leader – that the candidate must be chosen from the *fine* or family of the previous abbot meaning either his community or his blood kin – and be elected by the *derbhfine*?'

Abbess Fainder flushed and said nothing.

'Your sister says that your family has no relationship with Noé's family or with his religious community at Fearna. Thus ecclesiastical organisation reflects the civil organisation of this land.'

'The sooner that is changed, the better,' snapped the abbess.

'In that regard, I might agree. The offices of bishops and abbots should not be kept in the same family for generations. But in dealing with the reality, how did Noé secure your election to the office?'

Abbess Fainder compressed her lips for a moment and then said, in a tight voice, 'He dropped hints that I was a distant cousin and no one dared question Noé's wishes.'

'Not even the *rechtaire*, the stewardess of the abbey? She must have known the truth. She is related to the King's family.'

The abbess grimaced, implying dismissal of Sister Étromma.

'She is a simple soul, content merely on running the business of the abbey.'

Fidelma gave the abbess a long, searching look.

'The reality was that you converted Noé by becoming his mistress, isn't that it?'

Her sharp, unexpected question caught the abbess off guard and her flushed face confirmed the answer to the question. Fidelma shook her head sadly.

'It is not my concern how the religious of Laigin govern their communities but how it impinges in the case of Eadulf. Does Forbassach know of your real relationship with Noé?'

'He knows,' whispered the abbess.

'As the Brehon of this kingdom, the bishop seems to accept a lot of bending of the law.'

'I am not aware of Bishop Forbassach breaking or bending the law,' protested the abbess.

'I think that you are *well* aware of it! Forbassach is also your lover, isn't that the truth of it?'

The abbess was silent for a moment, not sure how to answer and then she said defensively, 'I thought I loved Noé until I came here and met Forbassach. Anyway, there is no rule of celibacy in the Church.'

'True enough, save for those rules which you claim to follow. Your curious triangle is a matter for your own conscience as well as for the wife of Forbassach. I know him to be married. She must consider whether this relationship is grounds for divorce or whether she will meekly accept the situation. Does Noé know about Forbassach?'

'No!' Abbess Fainder was scarlet with mortification. 'I have been trying to break with him but . . .'

'It is difficult after he has made you abbess?' Fidelma was cynical.

'I love Forbassach.' She was almost defiant.

'But it will present a pretty scandal, especially among those who proclaim the cause of Rome and the Penitentials. As a matter of interest, why did you refuse to acknowledge Daig as your brother-in-law or Deog as your sister, come to that? I cannot believe it was a matter of protecting your social rank.'

'I visited Deog regularly,' Fainder protested.

'True, but in secret and because her cabin was a quiet place where you could meet with Forbassach.'

'You have already answered the question yourself. You would not understand because you have always had social rank. When you do not have it and manage to obtain it, you will do anything – *anything* – to defend what you have gained.'

Fidelma heard the vehemence in her voice.

'Anything?' she mused. 'It occurs to me that Daig's death was convenient in protecting your rank.'

'It was an accident. A drowning.'

'I presume you knew that he was only a witness against Brother Ibar because of Gabrán's word alone? It seems that the more he thought about the matter, the less sure he was about Ibar's guilt?'

Abbess Fainder seemed perplexed as Fidelma sprang from one subject to another.

'That is not so. It was Daig who caught Brother Ibar.'

'But only after Gabrán had told Daig that Ibar was guilty. Did Gabrán tell Daig the truth? And why, once Daig had made his deposition, did he so conveniently get killed?'

Fainder's face was drawn in anger now.

'It was an accident. He was drowned – I have told you. Nor has the matter anything to do with me.'

'Perhaps Daig could have cast more light on the matter. We don't know. And now another person who could have told us more about this business is also dead.' She gestured towards Gabrán's cabin.

Abbess Fainder stood up, facing Fidelma. She seemed to be trying to recover something of her old arrogance.

'I do not know what you mean nor what you imply,' she said coldly. 'I only know that you are trying to exonerate your Saxon friend. You are trying to accuse me and implicate Bishop Forbassach because we are lovers.'

'It would seem,' interrupted Fidelma evenly, 'that, whatever is going on at Fearna, people have a habit of either being killed or disappearing. I would think about that, if I were as innocent as you claim to be.'

Abbess Fainder stood staring at Fidelma with wide, dark eyes. Her face had grown pale. She took a step forward and, as she opened her mouth, a shrill cry of terror echoed from the woods on the bank.

For a moment both the abbess and Fidelma froze with uncertainty. The shriek, a shrill feminine scream, echoed once more.

Fidelma turned towards the bank, where she could see a small figure running through the trees. It seemed to be running blindly for it burst onto the bank and came to an abrupt halt, as if realising that the river barred the way. Then it twisted like a snipe, weaving and ducking and was away as fast as it could go.

'Enda! Quick!' cried Fidelma, running forward to the shore.

She had recognised the figure as a wisp of a girl, bedraggled and barefooted.

Enda plunged forward from his vantage position, which had been near to the spot where the girl had emerged out of the bushes; he was able to overtake her with ease. Within a few strides he was able to grab the girl by one of her thin arms and twist her around, sobbing, crying and beating vainly at him with her free hand.

Fidelma had already leapt onto the wooden jetty and she ran to Enda's aid.

As she reached his side she was aware of horses breaking through the trees and bushes along the pathway behind. She turned and found herself staring up at the surprised faces of Bishop Forbassach and Mel, the warrior, as they pulled rein on their snorting mounts.

She turned back to the dishevelled form in front of her.

217

'They've been after me! Don't let them kill me! Oh please, don't let them kill me!' screamed the girl. She was not much more than thirteen years old.

'Don't struggle then,' Fidelma said soothingly. 'We will not hurt you.'

'They'll kill me!' the girl was sobbing. 'They want to kill me!'

Fidelma was aware that Abbess Fainder had joined her for she felt her presence at her shoulder.

The abbess's voice was shocked. 'It is Sister Fial,' she breathed. 'We have been looking for you, Sister.'

Fidelma took in the bedraggled appearance of the young girl.

'Your dress is soaked,' she observed. 'Have you been swimming in the river?'

It had taken Eadulf and his two charges a considerable time to cross the hills; it was perhaps too generous to call them mountains for only a couple of them rose above four hundred metres. The problem was not the height but the bare, rocky countryside and the fact that the young girls were weak from their ordeal. Eadulf himself, after weeks of incarceration in a cell, and in spite of his attempts to keep fit, was also not in the best physical condition. They had to pause frequently for rest on their upward journey.

They had journeyed north, heading to the north-east end of the mountain range and then turned to continue their journey south-west. Eadulf could see the tall shadow of the Yellow Mountain in the distance and was confirmed in his plan that the main hope of passing the night in any degree of comfort and without inviting exposure was to follow Dalbach's advice and find sanctuary in the small religious settlement dedicated to the Blessed Brigid of Kildare, on the southern slopes. But the afternoon hours were speeding. It would be a long trek and one which would not be accomplished before nightfall.

Chapter Eighteen

Dego arrived back at the boat, in the company of Coba and several of his warriors, within minutes of the surprise emergence of Fial and her pursuers. Coba suggested that everyone should return to the comfort of his fortress at Cam Eolaing to discuss events. Fidelma had not been able to extract any sense from the still hysterical Fial nor from Bishop Forbassach and Mel, who suddenly seemed disinclined to explain themselves. The abbess had likewise grown quiet. Fidelma was undecided but Dego pointed out that the day was drawing on and it would soon be dark. The decision seemed to have been made for her.

Among Coba's men were warriors who knew the river well and they volunteered to bring Gabrán's boat downstream to the jetty below the fortress of Cam Eolaing. Two of the chieftain's men, together with Enda, took charge of the horses and rode back with them while Fidelma, with the others, took her place on the boat.

'When we reach your fortress, Coba,' Fidelma told the chieftain, 'I will examine these people in an attempt to find out what has happened. As a magistrate of the country, I think it would be fitting that you sat with me as the local representative.'

Bishop Forbassach, overhearing, immediately raised objections.

'Coba is no longer qualified to sit as a magistrate,' he complained tersely. 'In helping your Saxon friend escape, he lost his authority. You were there at the inn when I told him so.'

'Loss of rank must be pronounced and confirmed by the King,' Fidelma pointed out. 'Has Fianamail formally stripped Coba of his rank as *bó-aire*?'

Bishop Forbassach seemed irritated.

'The King had gone hunting with Abbot Noé in the northern hills when I went to see him about the matter of Coba's abuse of the law over the Saxon.'

'So, at this time, until Fianamail returns from hunting, Coba remains the *bó-aire* of this district, is that correct?'

Bishop Forbassach's look was contemptuous.

219

'Not in my eyes. I am Brehon of Laigin.'

'In the eyes of the law, Coba is still magistrate while you are too closely involved in this matter, Forbassach. He will sit with me while I make my examination.'

Coba's glance at Forbassach and the abbess contained not a little triumph in it.

'I shall do so willingly, Sister. There seems some collusion here.'

'We will discuss it at Cam Eolaing,' Fidelma assured him.

It was growing dark when the boat nudged against the wooden jetty below the fortress of Cam Eolaing. Torches had to be lit to illuminate the way up the track from the river to the gates of Coba's fortress. A small group of the chieftain's retainers had gathered once they heard that he was returning and that a body was being carried among his party. They grouped anxiously around the gates, concerned that someone from Coba's household had been killed.

Coba, leading the party to the fortress, halted briefly to identify the dead man to them. There was a murmur of surprise when they learnt it was Gabrán.

'Back to your duties now,' called their chieftain. 'Light the hall fires for my guests and prepare refreshments,' he instructed the house steward. Then, to the stable lads: 'Take the horses and see to their needs.' To those carrying Gabrán's body: 'Put that in the chapel.'

With half-a-dozen concise orders, Coba had organised an adequate reception for his guests, unwilling and willing. It was only after they had been washed, fed and rested, that they were called into the hall of Coba, where a fire blazed in the hearth and brand torches illuminated all the dark recesses.

Coba took his chair of office while Fidelma was offered a chair at his side.

She looked down at the expectant faces of Abbess Fainder, Mel, Enda and Dego, and the sullen, huddled figure of the girl named Fial. Then she frowned and glanced quickly round.

'Bishop Forbassach? Where is he?' She caught a gleam in Abbess Fainder's eyes.

Coba had turned to his chief warrior and the man hurriedly left the room.

Fidelma fixed Abbess Fainder with a cold stare.

'It would be easier for all of us if you told us where Forbassach has gone.'

'You presume that I know?' sneered the abbess.

'I know that you do,' replied Fidelma confidently.

'I have done nothing wrong,' replied Abbess Fainder, her jaw coming up aggressively. 'I refuse to accept the lawfulness of being held here and being questioned by you or the *bó-aire* of Cam Eolaing. Coba has shown himself to be my enemy. I am held here against my will.'

Fidelma saw from the set of her features that she was not going to get anywhere with the abbess.

'My men will search the fortress, Sister,' Coba assured her. 'We will find him.'

It was then that Coba's chief warrior returned to the hall and came straight to Coba.

'Bishop Forbassach has left the fortress!'

Coba looked startled. 'I posted a guard on the gate with strict instructions that no one was to leave unless I or Sister Fidelma said so. How can this be? Were my orders not obeyed?'

The man grimaced awkwardly. 'They were not, my chieftain. The gate stands open and Forbassach has taken a horse. Someone who saw him leave – they did not know that he had no permission to do so and so cannot be blamed – they saw him ride towards Fearna.'

Coba swore violently.

'*Aequo animo*,' murmured Fidelma, reprovingly.

'My mind is calm,' snapped Coba. 'Where is the guard who was at the gate? Where is he who let Bishop Forbassach through? Bring him to me!'

'He is gone also,' muttered the warrior.

Coba was puzzled. 'Gone? Who is this warrior who dares disobey me?'

'The man is called Dau. He has a bandaged head.'

Coba was suddenly thoughtful. 'The same man who was knocked unconscious when the Saxon fled from here this morning?'

'That is he.'

'Is it also known in which direction this man Dau has fled?' intervened Fidelma.

'The person who saw the bishop riding towards Fearna observed that another man rode with him, Sister,' the warrior replied. 'Doubtless, that was Dau. They have fled together.'

'Bishop Forbassach was not fleeing,' the abbess laughed scornfully. 'He rides to Fearna in order to bring the King and his warriors back here to make an end to your treachery, Coba, and an end to the false accusations of this friend of the Saxon murderer!'

'I am cold and hungry. I do not feel well. Can't we stop for a while?'

The complaint came from the young girl, Conna.

Eadulf drew to a halt and peered back to where the girl was lagging behind him and Muirecht in the gloom which was quickly descending over the mountain.

'This is too exposed – without shelter, Conna,' he replied. 'We must reach the religious community before nightfall or soon after. If we halt here, we will freeze to death.'

'I can't go on. My legs are giving out.'

Eadulf gritted his teeth. He knew that they were now on the southern slopes of the Yellow Mountain and must surely be near the sanctuary of which Dalbach had spoken. If they halted they would never get started again and, out here on the windy unprotected slopes of the mountain, they might soon perish of cold.

'We will continue a little further. We cannot be far off now. I thought I saw a wooded area down on the lower slopes a while ago when the sun was out. We will head in that direction. At least, if we don't find the religious settlement, then we will have some protection in the woods. We might even be able to get a fire going.'

'I can't move!' wailed the young girl.

'Leave her,' muttered Muirecht. 'I am cold and hungry too but I do not want to die this night.'

Eadulf was about to rebuke her for her callousness but decided to save his breath. He turned and walked back to where Conna had sunk to a seat on a boulder.

'If you can't walk,' he said firmly, 'I must carry you.'

The girl gazed up at him uncertainly. Then she bowed her head and rose unsteadily from her perch.

'I will try to go on a little further,' she conceded in a grumbling tone.

It was a long time before the stretch of trees appeared over a sinewy shoulder of the mountain, a gloomy dark outline, no more. It was not far off and Eadulf could see nothing beyond its dim vista which seemed to merge with the slope of the mountains.

'Come on!' Eadulf said. 'It will not be far now.'

They trudged on, the younger girl whimpering to herself now and then, the older one silent and angry.

The woods, when they reached them, were scarcely inviting in their dusk-shrouded blackness. Eadulf had trouble keeping to the track which led through them. Yet the fact that he had come on a well-used track was a good sign; it must mean that this was the way to the religious settlement. Nightfall came rapidly and there was no moon to light the way for the sky was cloudy and heavy.

After a while Eadulf sensed the thinning of the trees: they had emerged into open country again. The track split in two and it was lucky that he had his eyes to the ground trying to decipher which direction it would be best to take, otherwise he would have missed the fact that the path was diverging.

Muirecht suddenly gave a cry. 'Look! There is a light down there. Look, Saxon, below us!'

Eadulf raised his head. The girl was right. Some way down the darkened slope he could see the flicker of a light. Was it a fire or perhaps it was a lantern?

'There is another light just above us,' Conna pointed out peevishly.

Eadulf turned in surprise and peered through the darkness in the opposite direction. Above them he saw the faint light of a dancing lantern. It was closer than the lights below. He made a decision.

'We will go up towards that light.'

'It would be easier to go down,' protested Muirecht.

'And further to return here if we are wrong,' replied Eadulf logically. 'We will go up.'

He began to lead the way up the path towards the flickering light. It was further than he thought but at last they came to a flat area with several buildings, surrounded by walls, emerging from the darkness. A lantern hung above the gates and an iron crucifix was fixed to them marking the purpose for which the buildings were used.

Eadulf gave a sigh of relief. At last they had found the religious sanctuary recommended by Dalbach. He tugged on the bell rope outside the gate.

A young, fresh-faced religieux came to open up. He looked in astonishment at the strange trio who stood outside in the circle of light cast by the lantern.

'May I see Brother Martan?' Eadulf addressed him. 'Dalbach sent me here to seek shelter. I need food, warmth and a bed for myself and the little ones.'

The young religieux moved back and waved them inside.

'Come in, come in, all of you.' His welcome was enthusiastic. 'I will take you to Brother Martan and while you speak with him, I shall see that your daughters are cared for.'

Eadulf did not bother to correct the well-meaning young man.

Brother Martan was stocky and chubby-faced. He was a man of advancing years and he wore a perpetual smile.

'*Deus tescum*. You are welcome, stranger. I hear that you have come with Dalbach's blessing.'

'He told me that I might find a night's sanctuary from the elements in your house.'

'And Dalbach spoke truly. Have you come far, for your speech is that of a stranger to this land?'

The old man halted for Eadulf had automatically taken off his hat during the conversation.

'You wear the tonsure of Peter. So are you of the Faith?'

'I am a Saxon Brother,' admitted Eadulf.

'And you travel with your children?'

Eadulf shook his head and, without giving details of his own background, explained how he had encountered the girls.

'Ah, such a tragedy is not unusual,' sighed Brother Martan sadly, when Eadulf had finished. 'I have heard of such an evil trade in human flesh before. And you say that the name of Gabrán was mentioned in this foul enterprise? He is a man known to our brethren at Fearna. He is a trader along the river.'

'I shall be on my way to Fearna first thing in the morning.'

'And the two girls?'

'Could I leave them in your safekeeping?'

Brother Martan gave his approval. 'They can stay here for as long as it is necessary. Perhaps they can be offered a new life in a family community, since their own has rejected them. The Faith is always seeking novitiates.'

'That is a matter for them to decide. At the moment they have had a harsh experience. To be betrayed is one thing, but to be betrayed by your own parents . . .' He shuddered slightly.

'Come, Brother,' Brother Martan rose to his feet. 'I have kept you long enough from food and mulled wine. Then you must rest. You look completely exhausted.'

'I am,' agreed Eadulf. 'I nearly chose the wrong path when we came out of the woods. If I had made the wrong choice and wandered any longer on these slopes, I doubt whether I would have kept awake much longer.'

Brother Martan smiled uncertainly. 'Did you not see our lantern which we always keep burning outside the gates of our community?'

'Oh yes,' Eadulf agreed. 'However, I thought that the other light might mark your community.'

'The other light?' Brother Martan raised an eyebrow slightly and then smiled as understanding came to him. 'Ah! Down the mountain, a few kilometers from here, is one of the King's hunting lodges. When he or his huntsmen are resting there, there is often a fire and lights to be seen. Fianamail or one of his family are doubtless resting there now.'

Eadulf nearly groaned aloud in relief. Had he made the wrong choice, he knew how this day would have ended. Thankful, in more ways than one, Eadulf followed the kindly Father Superior to the refectory of the community.

In the hall of the fortress of Cam Eolaing, Fidelma had quietly taken charge again.

'Since Bishop Forbassach has fled from here,' she told her audience with a note of sarcasm, 'it might be interpreted – as he and others have interpreted similar actions in other people – as a sign of guilt.' She gazed in challenge at Abbess Fainder who coloured hotly but did not comment. 'However, we have much work to do with or without him.'

'I do not think you have time to do anything, Sister Fidelma. The bishop will return with the King's warriors soon,' Mel said provokingly.

Coba ignored his threat. 'Why were you and Bishop Forbassach trying to kill the young girl?' he demanded brusquely, without waiting for Fidelma to begin.

'We were doing nothing of the kind!' Mel responded coldly.

'The girl herself accuses you.'

'It is not so.'

'It is! It is!' Fial insisted, less hysterical now, and staring around at the company. 'You are all trying to kill me.'

Fidelma glanced at Coba before intervening, being technically a guest in his hall. The *bó-aire* gave silent consent.

'Let us put this another way, Mel. Why were you and Bishop Forbassach in pursuit of the girl?'

'It was well known that Sister Fial had gone missing from the abbey. All we were doing was trying to bring her back.'

'But how did you know where she was?' demanded Fidelma.

'I did not know where she was. I don't think Bishop Forbassach knew either until we came on her by accident.'

'You say that you came on her by accident? I think that I have missed something. How did you come here in pursuit of Sister Fial?'

'Why do you insist on calling me Sister?' the girl intervened in a petulant cry. She started to sob again.

Fidelma moved across and patted her on the arm.

'Be patient a little longer, my dear. We shall not be long in approaching the truth.' She glanced at Mel. 'Proceed with your story, Mel. How did you come here?'

'You must remember,' Mel said. 'You were there. I came down into the main room of my sister's inn. You were there with Coba, Bishop Forbassach and the Abbot Noé. You accused Gabrán of attacking you. Bishop Forbassach told you that he would investigate and instructed me to go with him.'

'That is why you were making enquiries about Gabrán at Cam Eolaing earlier?' intervened Fidelma.

Mel nodded affirmatively.

'Bishop Forbassach and I went first to the abbey. And when he had seen Abbess Fainder we rode out in search of Gabrán to see if there was any truth in your claim. The bishop could not believe that you had made up the story.'

Fidelma glanced towards Abbess Fainder. 'Did you tell Forbassach where Fial was?'

'I did not know where she was,' she protested.

'But you did see Bishop Forbassach this morning?'

'He came early, after he had spoken with you at the inn. He told me of your claim about Gabrán but did not tell me that he was going in search of him. That's why I went to find him myself.'

Fidelma turned back to Mel. 'And you tell me that you both left immediately in search of Gabrán? Are you claiming that you had only just arrived when we found you were chasing Fial?'

'That is when we arrived at Gabrán's boat, yes.'

Fidelma shook her head reprovingly. 'If you left the abbey when you claim that you did, and that seems to be confirmed by your early arrival at Cam Eolaing enquiring for Gabrán, how did you only just reach Gabrán's boat when we encountered you? We could not have passed so far ahead of you.'

'We were misled.' Mel was unabashed by the apparent inconsistency. 'We went up the wrong branch of the river and by the time we realised that it had become too narrow for Gabrán's boat to be anywhere along it, we had fallen some hours behind you. We had to come all the way back almost to Cam Eolaing again before setting off along the right path. Had we not made that mistake, we would have reached Gabrán's boat some hours ago, before you or the abbess.'

'Forbassach and you are local men. You must have known how the river divides.'

'Fearna is six or seven kilometres from here. Yes, I am a Fearna man, but I don't know every nook and cranny in the kingdom.'

Fidelma considered the explanation. While she found it questionable it was just possible. She decided that she could not pursue it without further information.

'Having been side-tracked and returned to find Gabrán's boat, what then?'

'That was when we encountered Sister Fial,' Mel explained. 'We were riding along the river path when, totally without warning, the girl leapt out of the bushes in front of us and skidded to a halt. I think she recognised us but she started to scream and run off. Bishop Forbassach and I gave chase. The next thing we knew was when we came on you . . .' He shrugged and gave a lopsided grin. 'Well, the rest you know, Sister.'

Fidelma pondered on his evidence for a while and then sighed deeply. She turned to the young girl, Fial. She had ceased sobbing but appeared ill and woebegone.

'Fial, I want you to know that I mean you no harm. If you are honest with me, I shall be honest with you. Do you understand?'

The girl did not reply but her eyes reminded Fidelma of a frightened animal. They had the same stark expression that an animal has when a predator closes in. Impulsively she went to place an arm around the girl's gaunt shoulders.

'There is nothing to be frightened of any more. I am not your enemy and I shall protect you from those who are your enemies. Do you believe me?'

There was still no response. Fidelma tried some direct questions.

'How long were you a prisoner on Gabrán's boat?'

The girl's silence continued.

'I know that you were there. You were held in a small cabin below and manacled.'

It was not a question but a statement. Finally, Fial shuddered and responded.

'I do not know how long I was there. This last time, I think it was two or three days. It was dark and I had no way of knowing.'

'You are putting words into the girl's mouth,' protested Abbess Fainder.

Fidelma took Fial's hands in both of hers and held them out for the rest of the company to inspect.

'Have I also made these marks on her wrists, Abbess Fainder?' she asked quietly. There were sores around the girl's wrists which showed where they had been constrained. 'I think Fial could also show you the sores around her ankles as well.'

Coba had already ascertained their existence.

'Were you bound, child, on the boat?' he demanded gruffly.

When the girl did not respond, Fidelma gently encouraged her by repeating the question. Fial dropped her head a little.

'I was.'

'How could anyone do this to a novitiate?' demanded Abbess Fainder, finally accepting the evidence of her eyes. 'Whoever did it, they have a lot to answer for.'

Fidelma shot her a look of cynicism.

'Gabrán has answered for it, Abbess, if you will recall. The same manacle marks were present on Gormgilla, according to your physician, Brother Miach.' Then she turned back to the girl. 'However, Fial was never a novitiate at Fearna nor any other abbey. Isn't that so?'

Fial shook her head.

'You told me—' Abbess Fainder burst out, but was silenced by a gesture from Fidelma.

'Let us hear your story, child. You and your friend Gormgilla were brought to Fearna on Gabrán's boat some weeks ago, weren't you?'

'We were not friends until we came to know each other after Gabrán took us as prisoners on his boat,' the girl replied.

Abbess Fainder stared angrily at her. 'This is not the story that you told the court during the trial of the Saxon.'

'There are many tales that were told to that court which need to be changed,' Fidelma replied waspishly. 'Let the girl continue. Where did you come from?'

'Our fathers both were *daer-fudir* and being only daughters it was our shame that they were enticed by Gabrán's gold to part with us.

Gormgilla and I spoke of this in the long dark periods we were together.'

'Are you claiming that Gabrán was buying young girls and selling them along the river – *to the abbey*?' cried Abbess Fainder aghast.

'Not to the abbey,' corrected Fidelma. 'Gabrán probably took the girls downriver to Loch Garman and sold them to slaver ships who took them God knows where.'

'But Gormgilla and this girl were supposed to be novitiates at the abbey,' protested the abbess. 'This girl herself claimed that she was a novitiate.'

'Fial has just told you that they were not. Tell us, Fial, about that night when Gabrán's boat arrived at the abbey while you were being taken downriver.'

The girl blinked rapidly but she had exhausted her tears now.

'Gormgilla was younger than me, only twelve. When we were brought aboard Gabrán's boat he singled her out and . . .' She let her voice trail off.

'We understand,' Fidelma assured her.

'We did not know where we were going because we were kept in the dark cabin and shackled all the time. I knew the boat had halted, and that it had lasted for some time. Gormgilla and I were nervous as to how long we would be shut up in that filthy-smelling place. Then the door opened and Gabrán came squeezing in. We could smell alcohol on him. He unlocked Gormgilla's shackles and she asked him where he was taking her.' Fial paused for a moment, remembering the scene.

'What did Gabrán say?' prompted Fidelma.

'He said that he was taking her to share some pleasure to help pass away the night. Then he dragged her struggling into the other, bigger, cabin and I was locked in darkness on my own. It was not long before I heard Gormgilla screaming. There were other sounds too – sounds like a struggle. Then all was silent.'

She paused again as if trying to come to terms with her memories before continuing.

'I do not know how much time passed. The hatchway opened suddenly. At first I thought it was Gabrán returning for me but it was another member of his crew – the same man who had brought us on board the boat. I do not know his name. He told me to be absolutely quiet and said that I would be free and rewarded if I did what I was told without question.

'He took me into the adjacent cabin where the other boatmen slept, although Gormgilla and I never saw them; we saw only Gabrán and this particular crewman. I don't think the others even knew that we were on board. In this cabin I saw Gabrán; he was stretched out on the deck and I thought he was in a drunken stupor – I had often seen my father in a similar way. I realised soon afterwards that there was blood on his clothes and he grasped a piece of bloody cloth in his hand. By him sat a man in the robes of the religious but with a heavy cowl over his face; in the darkness I could not see his features. He seemed nervous and one hand fumbled with his crucifix which hung around his neck beneath his robe.'

'Is this another tale to discredit my abbey?' Abbess Fainder's tone was one of disbelief at the entire story.

'I speak the truth,' the girl protested with some spirit. 'I can only say what I saw.'

Fidelma patted the girl gently on the arm in encouragement.

'You are doing well. What did he say to you, this religieux?'

'He said nothing. The sailor did all the talking. I was told that there had been an accident. That Gormgilla had been killed and it was essential that the right man should be punished. At first I thought that he was referring to Gabrán for I had no doubt then that it was he who had killed my poor companion.'

'But he did not mean Gabrán?'

'No. He told me that Gormgilla had left the boat to go onto the quay. He said that there was a Saxon staying at the abbey. He had raped and strangled Gormgilla. The Saxon would not be caught unless I testified that I had seen him kill her.'

'What?' Abbess Fainder appeared astounded. 'You say that you were told, with the approval of a religieux, to tell lies about something so important?'

'I knew it was all a lie but I also knew that unless I agreed to tell it, I would be dead as well. I was to say that I had stood behind some bales and had seen this Saxon attacking my friend. I could identify him by the fact that he wore a different tonsure to all other religious and this tonsure was described to me. I was also to say that I and Gormgilla were novitiates at the abbey.'

'How could you make that claim if it was not true?' sneered the abbess. 'My mistress of novitiates would have denounced such a deception.'

'Except that she had just gone on a pilgrimage to Iona,' Fidelma reminded her.

'I was told that no one would doubt my story,' added Fial.

Fidelma glanced at the abbess. 'As I recall, you supported the story, Fainder,' she said. 'You identified the girls to your stewardess as novitiates, didn't you?'

There was a silence before Fidelma asked firmly: 'Who else identified Fial as a novitiate?'

Abbess Fainder fell silent, frowning in thought.

Mel cleared his throat. He had been considering Fial's story.

'The girl did appear from behind the bales. She could have come from the boat. But she did tell me . . .'

'Indeed,' Fidelma interrupted impatiently. 'She had been on the boat the entire time. It makes sense of the points that I made to you about the inconsistency of her position on the quay. However, let her continue the story. When it was realised that Gormgilla's body had been found, some quick thinking had to be done.'

'Not by Gabrán, he was drunk. The girl said so,' interposed Coba with interest. 'Who do you think arranged this elaborate lie?'

'The person who employed Gabrán; the person in charge of this terrible trade in human suffering,' replied Fidelma confidently. 'It seems that by coincidence, that very person had arrived on the quay with one of Gabrán's crew just as Gabrán had killed Gormgilla. They grabbed the drunken man, probably knocked him unconscious to be able to manage him properly. Then they dragged him back on board and dumped him in a cabin to sleep it off. Then one or both of them returned to the body, thinking to dispose of it. Yet another coincidence . . . they were just about to remove the body when Abbess Fainder came trotting out of the darkness on her horse. They scurried back to the boat wondering what to do. Then Mel arrived.'

'Fainder has told her story of how she spotted the body,' Coba agreed. 'That fits into your theory.'

'Except that the Saxon's robes were covered in blood and he had a piece of . . .' Abbess Fainder did not finish as she remembered what the girl had said about Gabrán's state of clothing.

'What happened to the bloody cloth that was grasped in Gabrán's hand, Fial?' Coba asked.

'The boatman gave it to the religieux. He said that it could be put to good use if the religieux could get back to the abbey.'

'In other words, it was to be planted on Brother Eadulf,' muttered Fidelma. 'But let us not get ahead of the story. With the arrival of the abbess there was panic. They heard Mel hailing Abbess Fainder as he approached the quay. Gabrán's employer was cornered on the boat. They could no longer attempt to hide the crime. It therefore became imperative to allow Gabrán's employer to fade into the darkness and for Gabrán not to be suspected. Someone came up with the idea of forcing young Fial to give false evidence on the assurance that she would be freed. Is that so?'

Fial confirmed her surmise.

'I kept my part. I told everyone what I was instructed to say. I identified the Saxon by his unusual tonsure. They told me that I had to be locked in a room in the abbey for my own safety until after the trial. Days passed then, two days ago, a religieux came and let me out.'

'The same person who sat with the boatman who instructed you to identify the Saxon?'

'Not the same. I had not seen this man before. He took me to Gabrán's boat. Gabrán was on board. Before I could struggle, I was shackled as I was before. I heard the big man say to Gabrán, "You are to get rid of her"! That was all he said. Gabrán replied: "It shall be done." The religieux left and Gabrán pushed me down into the same small dark cabin that I had shared with Gormgilla. He grinned at me and said: "It shall be done but at a time of my own choosing".'

Fial started to sob again. 'I have been down there for all eternity. Gabrán came down last night and . . . and . . . he used me.'

Fidelma wrapped the girl's sobbing form in her arms and gazed towards Coba.

'It was, sadly, my arrival at the abbey and my enquiries that caused the poor girl to be taken from there and returned to Gabrán.'

Abbess Fainder, who was very pale, cleared her throat nervously.

'How can we be sure that she is telling the truth this time? She admits that she has lied before, so maybe she is lying now? It seems too grotesque a tale to be real.'

'Too grotesque to be made up by a thirteen-year-old child,' replied Fidelma sharply. She turned back to Fial. 'Just a few questions more, little one. While you were imprisoned in the darkness on the boat, you did not waste your time, did you?'

Fial looked at her questioningly. 'How did you know?'

'You managed to get a sharp piece of metal and you started digging out the fixture of the metal chain that bound your ankle.'

'I don't know how long it took me. Ages.'

'And when you were free . . .?'

'I could only free my leg iron. I still had manacles on my wrists.'

'Just so. But you were able to climb up through the small hatch into Gabrán's cabin? The hatchway into the main cabin was locked, of course.'

'So *she* killed him!' cried Abbess Fainder, realising where this was now leading. 'She stabbed him at the time that I came aboard. Why,' she paused, wondering, 'she must have been in the very process of killing Gabrán. I knocked at the cabin door and the girl slid back through the hatch. Then, while I was bent over the body, she escaped through the cabin and went over the side of the ship. That was the splash I heard.'

'You are nearly right, Mother Abbess,' agreed Fidelma.

'*Nearly* right?' The abbess was belligerent.

'When Fial climbed into the cabin she found that Gabrán was dead already. He had been killed by a sword blow which had been delivered with a terrific force. Am I right, Fial? Shall I continue?'

The girl seemed stunned by her apparent omniscience. When she did not speak, Fidelma continued: 'Fial knew where Gabrán kept his keys and released herself from the wrist manacles. She was about to leave when a desire came over her for revenge; revenge for the terrible injury that this brute had done her. It was, perhaps, an instinctive adolescent reaction. She grabbed a knife that lay nearby and pulling Gabrán up by his hair – she grasped the hair so tightly in her rage that some of it came out by the roots – she plunged the knife half-a-dozen times into his chest and arms. The wounds were superficial. Then the abbess knocked on the cabin door. Fial dropped the knife and let go her hold on the body. That, indeed, was the soft thud that Fainder heard.

'Fial knew that she had to escape. The only way lay below but the door was locked. She grabbed at some keys in Gabrán's cabin. There were four of them. She knew one of them had to fit the lock of her prison below. It was her only means to escape. She scuttled back into the cabin. The rest is obvious.'

Fidelma paused and placed her hands either side of the girl's face and drew it up so that Fial was forced to look directly into her eyes.

'Have I told it correctly, my dear? Is that how it happened?'

Fial let out a great sob.

'I would have killed him if I could. I hated him so – what he did to me! What he did to me!'

Fidelma dropped her arms around the child to comfort her.

Coba leaned backwards in his chair, closed his eyes for a moment and let out a long sigh.

'Do I understand this correctly? While the abbess was in Gabrán's cabin, the girl made her way up on deck and jumped into the torrent? The current of the river is strong there. Why not simply go ashore?'

'It was a point that confused me at the time,' Fidelma confessed. 'However, I did not take into account how strong fear is as a means of compulsion. Poor Fial was scared for her life. She did not know where she was. The last thing she wanted to do was draw attention to herself by walking off the ship onto a jetty. She did not know if her enemies were there. She obviously could swim well and took that route. Then shortly afterwards, on shore, when she encountered Fainder and Mel . . .'

'. . . She thought that we were part of this slave conspiracy,' Mel supplied.

'Conspiracy is a good word, Mel. For there are many mysteries here yet to be solved.'

Abbess Fainder sniffed disdainfully.

'That is very true, Sister. For if Fial did not kill Gabrán, and you finally seem to accept that *I* did not – then who did kill him?' Her eyes suddenly glistened. 'Or are we to conclude that your Saxon came looking for revenge?'

Fidelma's eyes flashed angrily.

'I hope this poor child's testimony has demonstrated that Brother Eadulf was *not* guilty of the rape and murder of Gormgilla, and that another hand guided that outrageous conspiracy!'

'Even so, Sister,' Coba interposed, 'where are you leading us? You say Gabrán was murdered but not by Fial nor by the abbess. I cannot see who else could have killed him, nor even why he was killed.'

'Gabrán was merely a tool. He was the means by which the trade in human beings was carried out, the means by which they were transported down to the sea port. Gabrán did not have the brains to plan and sustain this vile commerce. Have you forgotten Fial's words already? She spoke of the cowled religious who ordered her to falsely identify Brother Eadulf.'

Mel rubbed the back of his neck. 'She also mentioned another crewman who helped him when Gabrán was lying drunk. So who was the other crewman? Did *he* turn on Gabrán?'

Fidelma made a quick, impatient motion of her hand.

'No. Gabrán turned on *him*. That crewman was the man who was killed the next day – the one that poor Brother Ibar was wrongly executed for murdering.'

Abbess Fainder blinked rapidly. 'Are you saying that Ibar was innocent?'

'That is exactly what I am saying. Ibar the blacksmith was a convenient scapegoat and perhaps a necessary one. The day before he was killed, he had been complaining that all he was being employed to do at the abbey was to make animal shackles. Perhaps he did not realise, or perhaps he realised too late, that the shackles for animals were being used on human beings?

'Brother Eadulf told me that he heard Ibar crying, when he was being led to the gibbet, about manacles. "Ask about the manacles!" he called.'

'I would like to know, as Coba has already asked you, where you are leading us, Sister,' demanded the abbess. Her voice was suddenly tremulous and she seemed to have lost her strength.

Fidelma faced the abbess squarely.

'I would have thought that it was obvious, Mother Abbess,' she said quietly. 'This trade in young girls, selling them off to foreign slave ships, is being run by someone in Fearna, someone in the abbey – and that someone is a religious who bears a high rank there.'

Abbess Fainder's hand came up to clutch her throat, her face pale.

'No! No! she cried and then, without warning, she collapsed to the floor in a swoon.

Fidelma moved swiftly to her side and bent down, feeling for the pulse in her neck.

At that moment, one of Coba's warriors came bursting into the hall in a state of excitement.

'Bishop Forbassach has returned. He is outside with a large band of the King's warriors. He demands the release of the abbess and the warrior, Mel, and the surrender of the rest of us. What is the word, Chieftain? Do we surrender or do we fight?'

Chapter Nineteen

Eadulf awakened with a start as the door of his small chamber crashed open. He blinked in confusion at the figures crowding in the doorway. One of them was holding a lamp. His figure was very familiar. It was with a sickening sense of despair that Eadulf recognised Brother Cett. By his side stood the young, animated Fianamail. Eadulf was dimly aware of the anguished features of Brother Martan behind them.

Fianamail's features twisted into a smile of satisfaction as he gazed down at Eadulf.

'That is the man,' he affirmed. 'Well done, Brother Cett.'

Eadulf was dragged from the bed by Brother Cett and hauled upright. With expert ease, he found himself forced round; his hands were twisted behind him and he was bound. The hemp rope cut deeply into his wrists.

'Well, Saxon,' Brother Cett leered at him as he spun him back to face the young King. 'You thought that you had made your escape. Not so.'

He punctuated his sentences with a short, sharp rabbit punch which made Eadulf double over and retch at the pain.

'Brother!' cried Brother Martan in disgust. 'Forbear to use violence on a bound man, a man of the Faith at that!'

It was then that Eadulf heard a familiar voice.

'The Saxon has lost whatever Faith he adheres to, Father Martan. However, you are right to admonish Brother Cett. You need not treat a dying man so harshly, Brother. God will punish him before the day is out.'

Eadulf twisted round to see the sallow face of Abbot Noé swim into view. Realising the futility of his position, Eadulf forced a pain-racked grin at the dour religieux.

'Your Christian charity does you credit,' he gasped, trying to recover his breath.

Abbot Noé took a step forward and examined him carefully but his thin features were expressionless.

'There is no escape from the fires of hell, Saxon.' His voice was solemn.

'So I am told. We all eventually have to answer for our misdeeds; kings and bishops . . . even abbots.'

Abbot Noé simply smiled, turned and left the cell.

The young King Fianamail was impatient. He looked across the cell to the window and saw the diminishing darkness. It would be dawn within the hour. Brother Martan observed his restless glance.

'Will you leave at once for Fearna?' he asked. 'Or return first to your hunting lodge?'

'We will wait here until dawn and then ride directly for Fearna,' the King replied.

'Regretfully, we have no extra horse for your prisoner,' apologised the Father Superior.

Fianamail looked grim.

'The Saxon will not need one. There is a good strong tree outside the gates here. He has escaped our justice twice. He will not escape a third time. We will hang him before we depart.'

Eadulf felt a cold sensation in his stomach but he did his best not to show his feelings to those around him. He forced a smile. After all, death had to come to everyone, did it not? He had been facing death these last few weeks, although he had hoped that, with Fidelma's arrival, there might be some chance that the truth would be discovered. Fidelma! Where was she? He wished he could see her one more time in this world.

'Can that be within the law?' Brother Martan was staring askance at his King.

Fianamail turned on the man with a frown of displeasure.

'The law?' His voice was threatening. 'The man has had his trial. He was about to be hanged when he escaped. Of course it is legal! I act as representative of that law. Brother Cett will see to the arrangements and if you have moral qualms, Brother Martan, I suggest you consult the abbot.'

Brother Cett grinned sourly at Eadulf as Brother Martan left the cell.

'Now,' continued Fianamail, 'let me breakfast for the day is chill and I am hungry. To be awakened before dawn and have to come chasing outlaws is a tiring business.' He hesitated as if he had just thought of something. 'By the way, we will also take the two young girls with us to Fearna. In the circumstances, they will have a better chance of life in the abbey there than returning home or wandering the countryside.'

Brother Cett's sadistic expression broadened. 'It shall be as you say.'

The cell door slammed as Fianamail and the burly Brother Cett left Eadulf alone to watch the arrival of his last dawn.

The horses were trotting in a column, two abreast, towards Fearna. Dego was riding beside Fidelma while behind them rode Coba and Enda and behind them came Fial mounted on the same horse as Mel who, in turn, rode with Abbess Fainder. Bishop Forbassach was behind. In the front and at the rear came warriors of King Fianamail's guard. It was cold and dark but the leading horsemen seemed to know the road from Cam Eolaing to Fearna well and did not hesitate in keeping up a steady pace.

Dego finally glanced at Fidelma.

'Why did you persuade Coba to surrender, lady?' He demanded. His tone was slightly querulous. The question had been on his mind since Fidelma had urged the *bó-aire* not to resist the warriors whom Forbassach had brought with him. It was the first time since those hectic moments that Dego had been able to pose the question and he did so in a low voice, not wishing to be heard by the guards. 'We could have fought this bishop and his men.'

Fidelma returned his look in the gloom.

'And then what?' she asked gently. 'Taken satisfaction in making a futile stand or, had we been lucky enough to drive off Bishop Forbassach, the Brehon of Laigin and the King's warriors, would we have had satisfaction in bringing down a bloody conflict on both kingdoms in which truth and justice would have been entirely forgotten?'

'I don't understand, lady.'

'Say that Coba had refused to surrender? Bishop Forbassach is Brehon of this kingdom and has a legitimate right to demand the surrender of people held against their will.'

Dego remained silent.

'On what legal grounds did we have the right to refuse to surrender to the Brehon of this kingdom?'

'I thought that we were about to discover the reason. You had already proved that Brother Eadulf had been unjustly persecuted for crimes he did not commit. You showed that the abbess must have been involved in some terrible slave trade among young girls.'

'What I said,' replied Fidelma slowly, 'was that the abbey was a centre of passing young girls downriver and selling them to foreign slave ships. We had not yet gone into examining the details, far less discovering who is behind this trade.'

Dego felt bewildered.

'But now we have no chance of discovering anything, lady. By surrendering we have given ourselves no freedom of opportunity to continue our quest. At best, Bishop Forbassach will have us thrown out of the kingdom. At worst, he will have us imprisoned for . . . well, for something or other. I am sure he will dream up a suitable charge.'

'Dego, had Coba not surrendered, we might have all been slaughtered by the superior numbers of Forbassach's warriors; or, if by some miracle we had driven Forbassach off, how long would it have been before the King himself came with an army and burnt Cam Eolaing to the ground? We had no choice.'

Dego was reluctant to admit the logic of her argument. Indeed, Fidelma herself had only just supported her own logic, for emotionally she agreed with Dego. Her first instinct had been to fight, for there was a darkness and evil which pervaded the abbey and those associated with it. Yet, examining the situation coolly, she realised that there was no choice. The problem now arose as to how she could persuade Bishop Forbassach to allow her to continue the process that she had begun in Coba's hall. At least, she had shown that Brother Eadulf was not guilty and she now had the key witness to the event, the girl Fial.

Yet could she rely on Fial? She was young, still below the 'age of choice', and had already changed her version of events once. In law, her evidence was inadmissible. But that had not stopped Forbassach from finding a flimsy excuse to use it. Therefore, in an appeal, he must accept Fial's repudiation of it. But would he? Forbassach might easily dismiss her evidence if he so wished.

Any appeal to Fianamail was almost hopeless now. He was too young, without the maturity of years, to overcome his prejudices and his excessive ambition to leave his mark on his kingdom. Abbot Noé had apparently persuaded the young man to think of himself as 'Fianamail the Lawgiver', the King who changed the law system of Laigin by imposing the Penitentials to make it, as he thought, a truly Christian kingdom. Her heart sank as she turned over the possibilities in her mind.

While fighting Bishop Forbassach and his warriors had not been an option, each kilometre they drew nearer to Fearna produced no viable alternatives. At no time in her career had Fidelma felt so helpless through the lack of choice. Dego was probably right. Knowing Forbassach, the best she could hope for would be that the bishop would have her and her companions escorted to the border and expelled from Laigin. At worst he could lay charges against her for some conspiracy, for impeding justice, for false accusations, for abetting Coba in a 'rebellion' against the law. Forbassach was capable of all these things.

She sighed. Now she really hoped that Eadulf had absconded from the kingdom. Had he been wise, he would have made for the coast and picked up a ship to escape back to his homeland. Had he not done so, she shivered slightly at the thought of what might be his fate.

Dawn heralded a bright, chill morning. Brother Martan and two of his community stood with arms folded in their robes, and heads bowed under their cowls, at the gates of the tiny church and community of the Blessed Brigid, on the broad frost-covered slopes of the Yellow Mountain. The white frost stretched away like snow, southward towards the distant valley where the river swept around the principal town of the Laigin kingdom, around the place of the great alder trees, Fearna.

Standing in front of the monks were the two young girls, Muirecht and Conna. They were shivering in the frigid early morning air in spite of the woollen cloaks given them by the kindly Brother Martan. They were bewildered and scared by the developments. Brother Martan looked on unhappily as he viewed the unfolding scene from beneath his cowl.

One of Fianamail's warriors was standing with the horses of the company, holding them with the reins drawn loosely into one hand. Abbot Noé stood slightly to one side of Brother Martan's group, seemingly disinterested by the proceedings. Only the young King Fianamail, already seated on horseback, appeared impatient.

Outside the gate were several trees but one tree caught the attention immediately; a twisted black oak that seemed as old as Time itself. From a low branch, the burly Brother Cett had secured a hemp rope which he had expertly fashioned into a noose. He had placed a three-legged stool, borrowed from the community, underneath it. Now he looked questioningly towards Fianamail, indicating that he was ready.

Fianamail glanced up at the bright sky and smiled, a thin-lipped smile of satisfaction.

'Let's get on with it,' he called harshly.

Three of his warriors emerged from the gates, propelling Eadulf before them.

Eadulf was no longer frightened of death. He would have admitted that he was fearful of being hurt, but not of death itself. He walked with a firm step. He felt sad at the unjust manner of his death as it seemed to him to serve no useful purpose. But he was resigned to it and the quicker it was over the sooner his fear of pain would be gone. He even stepped up on the stool without being asked. He found his thoughts were filled by images of Fidelma. He tried to keep her face before him as he felt the noose being secured around his neck by Brother Cett.

'Well, Saxon, do you confess your sins?' cried Fianamail. Eadulf did not bother to answer him and the young King turned impatiently to Abbot Noé. 'You are his religious superior, Noé. It is your task to take his confession.'

Abbot Noé smiled thinly. 'Perhaps he does not believe in the Roman form of public confession and would prefer to whisper his sins into the ears of a soul friend in the manner of our church?'

'You will not be interested in my confession for I am innocent of the crimes laid against me,' Eadulf replied, irritated by their delay. 'Get on with this murderous business.'

Yet Fianamail appeared conscious that the law should be assuaged by a confession.

'Do you refuse to admit your guilt even at this moment? You are about to come face to face with the Almighty God to answer for that guilt.'

Eadulf found himself smiling in spite of the imminence of death. It was an automatic reaction.

'Then He will know that I am not guilty. Remember, Fianamail, King of Laigin, that Morann, a Brehon and philosopher of your country, said that death cancels everything – except the truth.'

He heard Fianamail's exasperated sigh and then he felt the noose tighten as the stool was kicked from under him.

Bishop Forbassach and his prisoners had arrived back at Fearna. They were led directly into the abbey courtyard, ordered to dismount and ushered into the chapel of the abbey under guard. Sister Étromma had greeted the appearance of Fial with some degree of astonishment. The abbess took personal charge of the young girl and led her away, presumably to be cared for.

Fidelma, Coba, Dego and Enda were left facing Bishop Forbassach, who examined them truculently.

'Well, Forbassach?' Fidelma asked. 'Will you hear me out? Will you allow me to continue the arguments that I was making in the hall of Coba?'

A look of satisfaction spread over his features.

'You are as wily as a fox, Fidelma of Cashel,' he said. 'No, I will not let you spread your lies any further. Abbess Fainder explained to me on the journey what you are trying to do. You are trying to defame this abbey, the abbess, the religious and law of Laigin. It will not work.'

'You are either foolish or culpable of these crimes, Forbassach,' Fidelma replied in an even tone. 'You are either compounding them after the event or are guilty of involvement in them. There is no other explanation for your stupidity.'

The bishop's eyes narrowed belligerently.

'I am minded to bring charges against you and your companions, Fidelma. I know well enough that you are sister to the King of Cashel but even the threat of incurring his displeasure does not make me flinch now. You have gone too far. Your brother's influence will no longer safeguard you. I will discuss this matter with Fianamail before I reach a decision and, in the meantime, you will be imprisoned with your companions here in the abbey.'

Dego stepped forward.

'You will regret this, Bishop,' he said quietly. 'Lay hands on Fidelma and you will find the army of Muman marching on your borders. You are twice condemned by threatening my lady. You are condemned that you dare threaten a *dálaigh* of the courts and you are condemned because you dare threaten the sister of our King.'

Bishop Forbassach appeared unimpressed by the young warrior's bombast.

'*Your* King, not *my* King, young man. And your threat to me has also been noted. You will have plenty of time to contemplate that threat and how such a threat is punished in this land.'

Dego was about to make a move when Fidelma laid a hand on his arm. She had seen Forbassach's warriors ready with their swords.

'*Aequam memento rebus in arduis servare mentem,*' she muttered quoting one of Horace's Odes, to remind Dego to maintain a clear head when attempting difficult tasks.

'Wise advice, if you want to live,' smirked the bishop. Then turning to his warriors: 'Take them away!'

'One moment,' Fidelma commanded, her forceful tone causing them to hesitate. 'What do you plan to do with Coba?'

Bishop Forbassach glanced towards the *bó-aire* of Cam Eolaing. Then he turned back to Fidelma with a malicious grin.

'What would your brother do to a traitor who has gone against the law and rebelled against his authority? He will die.'

Brother Eadulf heard the sound of the shout and he closed his eyes. Then he experienced the sensation of falling and felt a hard thump as his body hit the ground. He lay for a moment, gasping for breath and puzzled until he realised that he had, indeed, fallen on the ground. The rope must have broken as the stool was kicked from under him. His immediate thought was the anguished one that he would have to go through the process all over again. He opened his eyes and peered up.

His first sight was of Brother Cett, standing with an expression of amazement on his features; his arms were spread, almost in a position of surrender. Then he was aware of more shouting. Another figure was bending forward and hauling him to his feet. He saw a young, vaguely familiar face whose features wore a grin.

'Brother Eadulf! Are you all right?'

He looked blankly at the young man, trying to recognise him.

'It is I, Aidan, a warrior of the bodyguard of King Colgú of Cashel.'

Eadulf blinked in confusion as he found the young warrior cutting his bonds. He could not speak for the soreness of his throat.

He was aware of several mounted warriors, richly dressed and armed, and a great blue silken banner being carried by one of them. Fianamail and his companions had frozen in shocked surprise at their appearance.

Among the newly arrived horsemen, seated on a powerful roan mare, was a man of indiscernible age clad in robes that denoted some high rank or office. He had a prominent nose, and his eyes were bright, unblinking; and he bore a stern, thin-lipped expression.

Fianamail began shaking with rage. His face was red as blood coursed through his cheeks.

'Outrageous!' His voice came almost as a gurgle. 'This is outrageous. You shall pay for this! Do you know who I am? I am the King. You shall die for this insolence!'

'Fianamail!' cried the brittle voice of the man on horseback as he edged forward to where the King sat. 'Look upon me!' His tone was not loud but it demanded attention.

The King blinked at him, trying to control his passion.

'Look upon me and know me. I am Barrán, Chief Brehon of all the five kingdoms of Éireann. These are the Fianna of the High King. And here is my authority which you must now obey.'

He thrust out an ornate wand of office, beautifully bejewelled and scrolled in gold and silver.

Fianamail's face went from red to white. After some hesitation he muttered in a more controlled voice, 'What does this mean, Barrán? you have interrupted a legitimate execution. That man is a Saxon who was found guilty of raping and murdering a young novitiate. He is a dangerous man. He has had a fair trail and a fair appeal was heard by my Brehon, Bishop Forbassach, and myself. The execution of this sentence is legal and . . .'

Barrán raised a hand and Fianamail fell silent.

'If it is as you say, then you will receive an apology from no less a person than the Chief Brehon. But many things trouble me as they have troubled the High King. It is better to examine matters and rectify the mistakes while the man is alive than attempt to rectify them after he is dead.'

'There *is* no mistake.'

'We will discuss this matter further when we reach your fortress, Fianamail,' Barrán's voice was soft yet its quiet tones commanded obedience even from kings and Fianamail was still young and immature. 'The High King also finds it a matter of great concern that word comes to his court at Tara that our native law system is no longer considered worthy in this kingdom. It is said that you have proclaimed the Penitentials as legitimate law above the Law of the Fénechus proclaimed by the brehons. Can this be true?'

He glanced to where Abbot Noé was standing.

'Is it also true that you have advised this young King on this matter, Noé?'

Barrán had already clashed with the abbot at Ros Alithir. They were not friends.

'There are good arguments for adopting the Penitentials, Barrán,' Abbot Noé replied stiffly.

'Doubtless we shall hear them,' replied Barrán dryly. 'It is strange, however, that the Brehon of Laigin, the spiritual adviser to the King, even the King himself, had not thought to come to Tara and discuss this matter with the other brehons and bishops of the five kingdoms. For the moment, it is the Law of the Fénechus that runs through this land and that is the only law to which its people are answerable. I know of no other law. It would pain the High King and his court if further violations of our laws have been made without our knowledge.'

Eadulf was still standing rubbing his wrists in bewilderment; his throat was paining him from the rope burn.

'What is happening?' he whispered to Aidan.

'The lady Fidelma sent me to Tara to bring the Chief Brehon here with all speed. I thought we would arrive too late. We almost did.'

'But how did you know where I was? She does not.'

'We didn't know, either. We haven't seen Sister Fidelma yet. We have ridden through the night and an hour ago we were crossing the mountain road below as a short cut to Fearna. The road led past Fianamail's hunting lodge and we saw some activity there. Barrán had one of his men enquire if Fianamail was present. We were told that he and Abbot Noé had ridden for this place to hang a Saxon outlaw. I thought that it could only be you. We came up with all speed.'

Eadulf felt weak as he began to gather his wits.

'You mean that it was purely luck that I did not . . .?' He shuddered violently at the realisation.

'We arrived just as the big fellow there,' he pointed to Brother Cett, 'kicked the stool out from under you. It was providential that my sword was sharp.'

'You cut the rope even as I fell?' asked Eadulf incredulously.

'I cut the rope and not a split second too late, thanks be to God.'

The Chief Brehon had turned his horse, approaching the spot where Eadulf stood.

'Are you the one who is called Brother Eadulf of Seaxmund's Ham?'

Eadulf gazed up into the bright eyes of Barrán. He felt the personality and inner strength of this man who was probably more powerful than even the High King for he stood at the head of the law system in all the five kingdoms of Éireann.

'I am he,' he acknowledged quietly.

'I have heard of you, Saxon.' Barrán's smile was gentle. 'I have heard of you as the friend of Fidelma of Cashel. She has sent for me to be judge over you.'

'I am grateful, my lord. I stand before you innocent of all that I am accused of.'

'That we shall see in due course. Are you well enough to travel directly to Fearna?'

'I am.'

Here the young warrior, Aidan, intervened.

'It might be better to allow a moment's rest so that we can attend to the burn mark on Brother Eadulf's neck. He had a narrow escape.'

Barrán peered forward at the mark on Eadulf's neck and then inclined his head in silent agreement.

Brother Martan had come hurrying forward with a jug of mead.

'I have some knowledge of these things, Lord Brehon. Mead for the stomach and a salve for the burn.'

The stool which would have been an instrument of his death a moment before was now placed upright so that Eadulf could sit on it. Brother Martan bent over him, tutting and making sympathetic noises. He took out a small jar of ointment from the leather satchel at his waist and began to gently massage some of the salve onto the mark made by the rough rope. It stung so much at first that Eadulf winced.

'It is a salve made of sage and comfrey, Brother,' explained the old monk. 'It will sting at first but later you will feel comforted.'

'Thank you, Brother,' Eadulf tried to smile through the stinging sensation. 'I am sorry that I have brought such problems to your peaceful little community.'

Brother Martan's expression was one of amusement.

'The church is the harbour for problems, a place where exchanges should be made – problems for peace.'

Eadulf began to feel in better spirits for the first time in days.

'What I would not mind is an exchange of my problems for an apple. This hanging has made me feel hungry and while your mead is good it does not make my hunger less.'

Brother Martan turned and made the request to one of his brethren.

Fianamail was still in a controlled rage and his temper got the better of him when he saw mead and an apple being given to Eadulf.

'Is this murderer to be pampered while we stand about in the cold waiting for him?' he demanded of Barrán. 'What is the point of putting salve on his injury when I shall doubtless hang him later?'

'I will eat my apple on the journey,' Eadulf told Barrán as he stood up. 'I have no objection to speed, if speed will clear me and bring us closer to the truth of this matter. Yet I fear that Fianamail's speed is only the desire to speed my death.'

Aidan helped Eadulf clamber up behind him on his horse. Two of the warriors took the two young girls up behind them. Muirecht and Conna had remained mute and frightened throughout all these dramatic events. Then, with Barrán, Fianamail and Abbot Noé at their head, the column of riders set out down the slopes of the Yellow Mountain with the white frost now visibly disappearing in the growing warmth of the morning sun.

Chapter Twenty

The great hall of the King of Laigin was filled to capacity. Centre of attention was Barrán, seated in his rich robes of office and carrying his ornate wand which designated that he spoke with all the authority not only of the law but as the personal representative of the High King. By his side, on his seat of office, sprawled Fianamail, looking more like a sulky youth than King of Laigin. By comparison to Barrán he scarcely merited attention for it was Barrán who exuded all the command in the hall from his very poise and natural attitude.

Along the sides of the hall sat several scribes, intent over their clay tablets on which they would make their notes before they were transcribed to vellum as permanent records of the events. There were Brehons, trainees as well as those qualified, all determined to absorb the wisdom of the Chief Brehon. Once word had spread through the township that Barrán would judge the case, everyone who was able tried to squeeze into the King's hall to hear such important judgments.

On the right side of the hall sat Bishop Forbassach; next to him was Abbot Noé, Abbess Fainder, Sister Étromma, and several other prominent members of the community of the abbey, including Brother Cett and the physician, Brother Miach.

Opposite them, on the left-hand side, sat Sister Fidelma with Eadulf by her side. Behind her sat her faithful companions Dego, Enda and Aidan.

Mel and his warriors seemed to be in charge of the security of the King's hall, although Fidelma noticed that the Fianna warriors, who had accompanied Barrán from Tara, were positioned strategically throughout the assembly.

It was midday and much had happened that morning. Barrán had resided over several private hearings. Now it was time for matters to be brought into public scrutiny.

Barrán glanced towards his chief scribe and gave a gentle indication with his head. The man rose and banged his staff of office on the floor three times.

'This court is convened to hear the final submissions and judgment in matters relating to the death of one Gormgilla, of an unknown boatman, of Daig, a warrior of Laigin, of Brother Ibar, a religieux of Fearna and of Gabrán, a merchant of Cam Eolaing.'

Barrán began without further preamble.

'I have before me a submission from the *dálaigh*, Fidelma of Cashel, for the vindication of Brother Eadulf of Seaxmund's Ham, a Saxon ambassador in our land. She submits that his conviction by the courts of Laigin, his sentence, and any subsequent infractions of the laws of Laigin in attempting to prove his innocence, be quashed and removed from the record books of this kingdom. Her argument is that Eadulf was innocent of all charges and all else that followed was a pursuit of injustice. The said Eadulf then acted in defence of his life and was within the law in doing so.'

Barrán glanced towards Bishop Forbassach.

'What do you say in response to that appeal, Brehon of Laigin?'

Bishop Forbassach rose. He was slightly pale and his features mirrored his displeasure. He had already spent several hours in the company of Barrán and Fidelma that morning. He cleared his throat before saying, quietly: 'There is no objection to the appeal by the *dálaigh* of Cashel.'

There was an audible gasp of astonishment among those in the hall as they realised what had been said. Bishop Forbassach sat down abruptly.

Barrán's chief scribe banged his staff for silence. Barrán waited for the murmurs to die away before he spoke again.

'I now formerly declare as invalid and void that conviction and sentence against Brother Eadulf of Seaxmund's Ham. He leaves this court in innocence and with no stain upon his honour.'

On the benches, Fidelma reached impulsively over and caught Eadulf's hand and squeezed it while Dego, Enda and Aidan clapped the Saxon monk on the back.

'It is further declared,' went on the Chief Brehon, ignoring their demonstration, 'that the Brehon of Laigin must pay compensation to the said Eadulf in the term of an honour price fixed at eight cumals. The amount is fixed in law because Eadulf is an emissary between Theodore, Archbishop of Canterbury, and Colgú, King of Cashel. He carries the honour price equivalent to that of half the man he serves. Does the Brehon of Laigin raise any objection to this?'

'None.'

The reply was almost missed, being a quick and embarrassed response. Yet another gasp went round the hall as it was realised that Bishop Forbassach was agreeing to compensate Eadulf to the amount of the value of twenty-four cows. Even Eadulf looked bemused at the munificence of the sum.

'There is an end to Eadulf's guilt,' announced Barrán. 'But let it be recorded why this verdict and sentenced is revoked. I, and other witnesses, made a preliminary examination before entering this court. What we learnt there was a matter which horrified us and caused great sorrow.

'The river-boat captain, Gabrán, was engaged in a degenerate and perverse trade. He played on the suffering of needy families by persuading them to sell their young daughters to him. He took these frightened children, for none were of the age of choice, from places in the northern mountains of this kingdom and brought them down to the river. He placed them in his boat and transported them along the river to the sea port at Loch Garman. There he sold them to slave ships which transported them beyond the seas. Yes, he sold these young girls into slavery.'

There was an icy silence in the hall, a sense of shock and horror at what the Chief Brehon was telling the people.

'We heard from the witness Fial, one of the young girls who survived this ordeal, that Gabrán had sunk to the level of an animal and actually used his captives for his own sexual appetite. This he did, even though they were not of age.

'We have heard that on the fateful trip, from which Eadulf became an innocent victim, Fial's companion, a girl called Gormgilla, was taken by the drunken Gabrán, while his boat was tied up at the quay of the abbey here. We may guess the details. Gabrán raped the girl and she fought back. In a drunken rage, he strangled her. It was decided to put the blame on Eadulf of Seaxmund's Ham. Those who thought up this evil scheme arrogantly presumed that he was merely a passing foreign pilgrim and that no one would notice if he were sacrificed to cover up the murder. They had been forced to find an explanation for the murder because of the arrival of the abbess and Mel before the body could be disposed of.

'It was a wicked scheme but one which nearly worked. Luckily, they had not realised that Eadulf of Seaxmund's Ham was not someone whose death could be so lightly passed over. Their haughty presumption was their undoing.'

Barrán looked towards Fidelma.

'I believe, Fidelma of Cashel, that you have some observations that you wish to make at this time?'

Fidelma rose in the expectant silence of the hall.

'Thank you, Barrán. I have much to say for this matter cannot simply rest with the exoneration of Brother Eadulf of Seaxmund's Ham.'

'Why not?' snapped Bishop Forbassach from across the hall. 'That's what you wanted, isn't it? He has been compensated.'

Fidelma turned a glinting eye on him.

'What I wanted from the outset was for the truth to be made known. *Veritas vos liberabit* is the basis of our law. The truth shall make you free – and until we know the entire truth of this business then this kingdom dwells in darkness and suspicion.'

'Do you now seek vengeance on our mistakes?' demanded Forbassach. 'Gabrán, the slave trader, is dead. That is surely vengeance enough?'

'It is not that easy,' replied Fidelma. 'And while we have heard of Eadulf's innocence, what of the innocence of Brother Ibar? What of the death of Daig? What of the innocence of Gormgilla and countless young girls whose lives are now beyond recovering? It is not vengeance that is needed to explain these tragedies but the truth.'

'Are you saying that the death of Gabrán, the man who engineered this evil trade, does not satisfy you, Sister Fidelma?' It was Abbot Noé who spoke. His tone was measured and it was clear that he shared Bishop Forbassach's unhappiness with the developing situation.

'I will be satisfied with the truth,' she repeated. 'Have you forgotten the testimony of the young girl Fial? It was not Gabrán who asked her to give the false testimony against Eadulf. He was drunk or knocked unconscious. Nor was it the boatman who was subsequently murdered on the following day. You will remember how Fial described what happened?'

There came a sigh of exasperation from Bishop Forbassach.

'We do not have to rely on the word of a young murderess.'

Fidelma raised an eyebrow in quickening anger.

Abbot Noé spoke before she could. 'The girl, Fial, obviously killed Gabrán and it is clear that she did so in a state of great emotional stress.

We understand that and no blame is placed on her for it. My friend, Forbassach, does not mean to condemn her; nevertheless, it is the truth. Be content with that, Fidelma.'

'This morning, before the Chief Brehon, we went through all the testimony that was heard in Coba's hall,' Fidelma returned. 'I thought it was clear then that Fial had *not* killed Gabrán.'

Bishop Forbassach almost exploded with anger.

'Another innocent for you to defend?' he sneered.

Barrán leaned forward in his direction. His voice was flat and assertive.

'I would advise you to be more considerate with your words and manner of using them, Brehon of Laigin. I remind you that this is my court and the rules of courtesy between those who plead before me apply.'

Fidelma glanced with gratitude towards Barrán.

'I am willing to answer Forbassach. Indeed, Fial *is* another innocent – and I am ready to defend all who are innocent of crimes against which they are unjustly accused.'

'If you are willing to state the truth, you will acknowledge that you only wish to defend Fial because you want to lay the blame on Abbess Fainder for the murder of Gabrán!' Forbassach had risen angrily to his feet, his face flushed. The abbess, pale, tried to grab at his arm to pull him back to his seat.

'Bishop Forbassach!' Barrán's voice cracked like a whip. 'I have warned you once before. I shall not warn you again to moderate your behaviour towards a respected *dálaigh* of the courts.'

'As a matter of fact,' intervened Fidelma mildly, 'I have no wish to accuse the abbess of Gabrán's murder. It is obvious that she did not carry out that killing. You seem determined to cloud the real issues here, Forbassach.'

Bishop Forbassach dropped back to his seat deflated and abashed. Fidelma continued: 'The person who killed Gabrán was part of the slave-trade conspiracy and was ordered to do so because Gabrán had become a liability to that conspiracy. His increasingly corrupt behaviour was endangering the whole enterprise. Too many deaths were occurring around Gabrán and bringing unwelcome attention.

'The rape and murder of a young girl on the abbey quay by Gabrán and the stupid attempt to shift the blame on an innocent passer-by was what led to the subsequent mayhem. The person for whom Gabrán worked, the real power behind this evil enterprise, finally came to realise that it was time to dispense with Gabrán's services – and in a permanent fashion.'

The silence in the hall was absolute. It was some moments before Abbot Noé decided to intervene.

'Are you claiming that all the deaths are connected?'

'The murder of the crewman followed in the wake of Gormgilla's death. Now, what was Fial's evidence which we listened to again this morning?'

Barrán turned to his scribe.

'Correct me if the record speaks against me,' he instructed. 'As I recall, when she was taken from her confinement by one of the crewmen, in the next cabin she saw Gabrán unconscious either in a state of intoxication or having been rendered unconscious. There was a hooded figure in that ill-lit cabin dressed in the robes of the religious. This was the person who instructed her to identify the Saxon as the same who killed Gormgilla. Do I have it correctly?'

The scribe, who had been referring to some notes before him, muttered, '*Verbatim et litteratim et punctatim,*' to confirm that it had been accurately rendered.

Fidelma thanked Barrán for reminding them of the record.

'The crewman who released Fial was actually the same man who was murdered the next day. I must make some conjectures now but they are threaded together by facts – information that Daig passed on to his wife. I acknowledge that no surviving witnesses can confirm each detail independently. May I do so?'

'Providing it elucidates the mystery,' Barrán said, 'but I will not take conjecture alone as evidence towards convicting any individual.'

'You do not have to. I would imagine that the crewman, who was, of course, of the same low morals as Gabrán, saw his involvement in the covering up of his captain's crime as a great chance to make some extra money by blackmailing Gabrán. They had a row in the local inn – the Inn of the Yellow Mountain. The row was witnessed by Lassar, the innkeeper. She also saw Gabrán giving the crewman some money to keep him silent. Gabrán later explained this sum by claiming it was the man's wages. The sum that was passed was a large one, however – too large for the wages of a boatman.

'The boatman went off happy with his spoils but he did not realise that Gabrán was no easy target. Gabrán followed the man from the inn, caught up with him down by the quay and killed him. It would have been simple had not Daig been passing in the vicinity at the time. Gabrán had only time to run off and hide before Daig arrived. Daig actually heard his steps receding but chased him in the wrong direction. Daig's other mistake was not checking the body thoroughly first.

'When Daig went off chasing shadows, Gabrán returned to the body of his comrade and retrieved his money. He removed the distinctive gold chain that the crewman wore around his neck and returned to the inn where Daig later came to speak with him. I think Daig's questions may have panicked him. He sought protection for his deed and went off to the abbey to see his employer. He demanded help or threatened to confess everything.

'I can imagine that this person was not happy with developments. Perhaps the decision for the eventual removal of Gabrán was even made there and then. After all, the whole enterprise was being put in jeopardy by this evil little man.

'But there was another problem and one which this terrible deed might help to solve. Brother Ibar was also a weak link in the chain. Oh yes,' she said as a murmur arose, 'Brother Ibar was part of this trade, but I believe that he was a wholly innocent part of it. He had been ordered to make manacles. He thought that they were shackles for animals. He told Eadulf as much, but he was growing suspicious as to their real purpose. And, of course, Ibar could identify the person who had ordered him to make those manacles. That same person now took the neck chain and money from Gabrán, assuring him of their return if he complied with the scheme.

'The scheme was simple: they planted these items in Brother Ibar's cell. The rest was up to Gabrán. He was instructed to tell Daig that Brother Ibar had tried to sell him the gold chain in the market and he had recognised it as the one worn by his crewman. A search was made of Brother Ibar's cell and the planted evidence was found. That dealt with Brother Ibar.'

She paused, realising that she held all present spellbound by her story. She saw the scribes looking at her wide-eyed.

'*Verba volant, scripta manent*,' she admonished sharply. 'Spoken words fly away, written words remain.' She wanted all this down in writing. It was a complicated tale and she did not want to repeat herself further. The scribes bent industriously to their tasks.

'We have the saying that one should not count the eggs until one has purchased the chicken. Perhaps it was something Gabrán said or that Ibar had told him, but Daig became suspicious that he had arrested the wrong man. Unthinking, Daig probably mentioned as much to Gabrán for, shortly afterwards, on a dark night on the same quay, Daig met his own death.'

'Are you saying that Daig was murdered?' protested Bishop Forbassach. 'It is well-known that it was an accident. He fell, hit his head and drowned.'

'I would argue that Daig was hit on the head, fell and drowned in that order, that is if he was not dead before he hit the water. The motive was to prevent him proceeding further with his suspicions.'

There was a pause while the resultant hubbub of sound rose and was then allowed to die away. The assembly turned almost as one towards Barrán. The chief scribe banged his staff for their attention.

'Continue with your presentation, Fidelma,' the Chief Brehon instructed. 'I remind you that this is still conjecture.'

'I am aware of it, Barrán, but I am sure that, at the end of my surmise, I shall bring forward those who will give testimony to the various foundations on which I make it. Thus I hope to confirm a picture that leaves no reasonable doubt in our minds.'

Barrán indicated that she should continue.

'My unexpected arrival put a halt to some of the plans. It was realised that Fial would not stand up to close questioning from a *dálaigh* who was looking for faults in her story and so she was replaced on Gabrán's boat. She had to be disposed of. However, Gabrán being the licentious man he was, decided to use the poor girl until he had grown tired of her. She was kept like an animal, manacled below deck.'

'Until Fial killed him?' interposed Abbot Noé quickly.

'I have already said that she did not kill him,' snapped Fidelma.

Barrán was irritated.

'You should listen carefully to the *dálaigh*'s arguments, Abbot. Fidelma of Cashel has already stated this clearly.' He turned to Fidelma. 'I have a question.'

Fidelma turned enquiringly.

'All the while Brother Eadulf and Brother Ibar were alive they were surely a danger because they might prove their innocence or let out some vital information which might lead a thinking person to investigate. Under our own laws, without a death penalty, it would be worthless to lay the guilt on another as there would always be a chance that they could demonstrate their innocence . . .'

'But who questions the innocence of a dead man?' queried Fidelma sharply.

'So, does the fact that Abbess Fainder insisted on punishment by the Penitentials, meaning execution, have anything to do with this matter? Does the fact that Bishop Forbassach, apparently forgetting his oath as a brehon, agreed with the abbess relate to this matter? If so, we must bring into account the fact that Abbot Noé influenced King Fianamail to accept the Penitentials in place of the Law of the Fénechus.'

Fidelma did not bother to look at the opposite benches.

'It has everything to do with it, Barrán. The plan to lay the blame on Eadulf and Ibar rested on the end result that they would be executed. *Mortui non mordent!*'

Barrán looked grim.

'Dead men don't bite,' he repeated, savouring the phrase.

Before the murmurs of surprise rose, Fidelma continued: 'The plan might have worked out, in spite of my appearance, had it not been for the *bó-aire* of Cam Eolaing.'

Coba glanced up in surprise. He had been sitting in an attitude of close attention.

'What had I to do with this?'

'You are against the use of the Penitentials. But neither Bishop Forbassach nor Abbess Fainder realised just how much against them you were nor how far you would be prepared to go in support of the legal system of this kingdom.'

Coba grimaced ruefully.

'I am too old to embrace new philosophies. What is it that the Brehons say? The soft twig is more durable than the stubborn tree.'

'Eadulf owes his life to your stubbornness, Coba. You did the one thing that no one was expecting by rescuing Eadulf and giving him sanctuary.'

'For which you will be accountable,' muttered Bishop Forbassach with a sideways glance of anger.

'Not so,' Barrán intervened sharply. 'Defence of the law is no crime.'

Bishop Forbassach glowered with hatred at the Chief Brehon but he wisely said nothing further.

'However,' Fidelma went on as if the interruption had not occurred, 'it made me suspicious of you for a while, Coba. You had given Eadulf sanctuary and then claimed that he had abused it and escaped. Thus he could be shot down at will. I knew that there was a good reason for Eadulf to leave the confines of the *maighin digona*. He understood the law well. I thought it might have been you who had tricked him into leaving the sanctuary. It was not until I spoke with Eadulf a short while ago that I realised you had no hand in the matter.'

Coba looked uncertain and then shrugged. 'For that, I am glad.'

'It was Gabrán again, but this time acting on the orders of his employers who had found out where Eadulf was. Gabrán went to Cam Eolaing. He knew a warrior there called Dau, who was in Coba's service. Dau could be bought and was. Gabrán killed the guard at the gate, hid the body behind it and then, pretending to be acting for you, Coba, he told Eadulf he was free to go. But things do not always proceed according to plan. When Gabrán and Dau tried to shoot Eadulf down, he eluded them and escaped into the hills. Now things began to get really complicated for the puppet-master.'

'Puppet-master?' The Chief Brehon was frowning at the unusual expression.

Fidelma smiled apologetically. 'You'll forgive me, Barrán. It refers to an entertainment I saw on pilgrimage to Rome. I mean one who manipulates others but is unseen. We have the old expression *seinm cruitte dara hamarc*.'

The ancient proverbial expression she used related to one playing a harp without being seen.

'How did this . . . er, puppet-master, know Eadulf had been given sanctuary in my fortress?' demanded Coba.

'You told them.'

'Told them? *Me?*'

'You are a careful and moral man, Coba. You obey the Law of the Fénechus. You told me that as soon as you took action and granted Eadulf sanctuary you had sent a messenger to the abbey.'

'That is correct. He was to tell the abbess that I had granted the Saxon sanctuary.'

'Lies!' shouted Abbess Fainder. 'I received no such message.'

Coba looked at her sorrowfully and shook his head.

'My messenger returned from the abbey and confirmed that the message had been delivered.'

Every eye in the assembly now turned towards the shaken abbess.

Chapter Twenty-One

'I knew it,' stormed Bishop Forbassach, rising in anger from his seat again. 'This is some plot to attack and slander Abbess Fainder. I will not tolerate it.'

'I have no plot to involve Abbess Fainder any more than she is involved,' replied Fidelma quietly. 'I did have suspicions, especially when I gathered that, since coming to the abbey, Fainder has acquired much wealth.'

'Barrán! I accuse this woman of persecution!' cried Abbot Noé, also rising from his seat. 'We cannot sit by while she criticises Abbess Fainder in this fashion.'

'I have said that—' began Fidelma.

'Deny it!' screamed the abbess, suddenly losing control of her temper. 'You are trying to trap me in your web of lies!' It was some time before she was persuaded to regain her composure. When calm was restored, Barrán addressed himself to Fidelma.

'It does sound as though you are leading up to an accusation of Abbess Fainder's guilt. You point out that it was essential that the punishment of death as prescribed by the Penitentials was enacted. You point out that Abbess Fainder insisted on that and for reasons best known to himself the Brehon Forbassach agreed and persuaded the King to give his approval. You keep mentioning this, this puppet-master – as you call him – as being a member of the abbey community. Who better to be at the centre of the terrible web which you describe than the abbess herself? And now you claim, as if with significance, that she has become wealthy since arriving at the abbey?'

'Lies! Lies! Lies!' cried the abbess, banging her fist on the wooden arm of her chair. She had to be calmed again by Bishop Forbassach.

'Abbess Fainder is indirectly responsible for much of what has happened here and we must now deal with that matter. But I have already shown that she did not kill Gabrán.'

A rumble of noise came from those present. Barrán called immediately for silence.

259

'In fact,' went on Fidelma, 'it could be said that Abbot Noé was more indirectly responsible than anyone else.'

The abbot shot up from his seat in a belligerent posture.

'Me? You dare accuse me of being involved in murder and this terrible trade in young girls?'

'I did not say that. I said you were *indirectly* responsible for what happened here. For some time now you have been converting to the philosophies of Rome. I realised that your conversion must have occurred when you first met with Fainder in Rome.'

'I'll not deny my conversion to the Penitentials,' muttered Noé, reseating himself but placing himself in a defensive posture.

'Do you deny that Fainder exercised a strong influence over you, persuaded you to bring her back to Laigin and appoint her abbess while you invited Fianamail to make you his spiritual adviser, thereby giving you a power throughout the whole kingdom?'

'That is your interpretation.'

'It is the facts of the matter. You went so far as to overrule the system of appointments in the abbey in order that Fainder could be made abbess. You claimed she was a distant cousin; she was not, but no one seemed to challenge the appointment, not even when they knew that Fainder bore no relationship to you. Once Fainder was abbess she ruled the community by the Penitentials. You were besotted by her. *You* started the process, Noé. The ground on which the laws were changed and these events were able to happen was sown by you through your infatuation with this woman.'

'How do you know that Fainder is not related to Noé?' asked Barrán quickly. 'And where does this question of her new wealth come into the story?'

'Her sister is Deog, widow of the watchman Daig,' explained Fidelma. 'Deog told me about her sister's new-found wealth. Fainder frequently visited Deog but, alas, it was no sisterly love that caused the abbess to ride to her sister's cabin so regularly, was it, Forbassach?'

Bishop Forbassach's face crimsoned under her gaze.

'You also became a very recent convert to the use of the Penitentials, didn't you?' queried Fidelma. 'Do you want to tell us why?'

For the first time in the proceedings, the Brehon of Laigin was silent before her question.

It was Abbess Fainder who answered. She was broken and trying to suppress her sobs.

'Forbassach's love for me had nothing to do with his embracing true Christian law,' she cried defensively. 'He became an advocate for the Penitentials based on logic, not on our love for one another.'

A cry of outrage rang out and a woman was led outside from the back of the hall by two other women. Forbassach half-rose but Fidelma gestured for him to reseat himself.

'That is something you will have to sort out with your wife later, Forbassach,' she said. Fainder's eyes were fixed with malignance on her but she met their gaze without rancour.

'The new wealth was merely an over-abundance of gifts from both Forbassach and Noé, isn't that so? They were showering you with presents in an effort to court you. *Amantes sunt amentes*. Lovers are lunatics.'

The look on the face of the abbess was enough to frighten a lesser person. Forbassach was clearly embarrassed by the revelations but was not demonstrating guilt. Abbot Noé sat in silence, completely stunned by these revelations. Even Fidelma felt a pang of remorse that she had revealed Fainder's duplicity to him. He was obviously so intoxicated by the abbess that the idea that Forbassach was also her lover was like a knife-wound.

'At least my deduction that you were not guilty, Fainder, was confirmed when you fainted at Cam Eolaing when I pointed out that the person behind this evil was someone with a high rank at the abbey. You fainted because you thought that I was referring to one of your lovers. *But which?*'

Abbess Fainder's face was red with mortification.

'If I follow your reasoning, Fidelma,' interrupted Barrán, 'you are saying that Abbess Fainder did not kill Gabrán. Yet you also say that Fial did not kill Gabrán. Who did, then – and was it by Abbess Fainder's orders?'

'Let me lead to it in my own way,' Fidelma pleaded, 'for I have never come across such a complicated conspiracy. Our puppet-master was beginning to panic at the increasing number of deaths that were occurring following in the wake of Gabrán's first crime. Things were not working out as expected. Each attempt to cover up the guilty led to an even worse disaster. As I said, it was decided that Gabrán had to be silenced and the trade ended – for a while at least. The person designated to kill Gabrán was due to leave the abbey to visit a relative who lived nearby where Gabrán's boat had been moored. Gabrán was waiting for his new cargo. Two girls were to be picked up that morning. The killer set off to find Gabrán's boat not realising, perhaps, that Abbess Fainder was a short distance behind him.

'He arrived at the boat and found Gabrán having sent one of his men into the hills to collect his merchandise. The arrival of the girls on the boat always took place in a secluded spot. Most of Gabrán's crew were given money and told to take the asses, which drew the boat along the river to this point, and not return until the next day. While they were away, the girls would arrive and only one or two of the crew would know of their existence.

'Our killer found Gabrán apparently alone. He killed him with the powerful stroke of a sword on his neck. The killer then had to wait, presumably to kill the other man when he arrived with the young girls. He would probably have killed them as well so that all the mouths were shut. However, the killer then saw the abbess approaching along the bank. There was no alternative but to leave hurriedly. He went into the hills. Perhaps he thought that Gabrán's man and the girls might be encountered on the road and the murders completed. When he could not find the man and the girls, the killer continued on to the relative that they had promised to visit.

'Back on Gabrán's boat, unbeknown to anyone, in the tiny cabin where she had been a prisoner for several days, poor little Fial had freed herself from her foot constraints. Not knowing what had happened, she climbed up into Gabrán's cabin and saw him lying dead on the floor. Her first thought was to break for freedom and she grabbed the key that she knew opened her wrist manacles.

'Then she paused as a great rage welled up in her. She seized a knife and dragged Gabrán's head up by the hair and plunged the little knife into his chest and arms in a frenzy of anger. He was already dead and no mortal wounds were struck. It was an expression of rage only for all the harm and hurt he had done to her. Then there came a knock at the cabin door. The abbess had by this time come aboard. Startled, Fial dropped both Gabrán and the knife, and fled back into her hole, grabbing a handful of keys as she did so. The abbess entered.

'Fial eventually found the right key among the four she had taken, escaped through the length of the ship into the hold, climbed up onto the deck and jumped into the water. She was swept away downriver until she was able to climb out, but then found herself pursued by Forbassach and Mel.'

'It is a good reconstruction, Fidelma,' observed Barrán. 'Do we come near to proving any of it? Some of it I can see has the weight of evidence from Fial and the abbess, but what of this mysterious killer? And how do you know about the relative in the hills?'

'It is not so mysterious. Thanks to what Brother Eadulf has told me of his adventures, we can identify this man.'

'The Saxon? How can he identify the killer? He was already a fugitive,' asked Barrán.

'Brother Eadulf found hospitality with a blind recluse named Dalbach.'

Fianamail stirred for the first time since the proceedings began. He sat up suddenly.

'Dalbach? But he is a cousin of mine! He is my relative!'

Barrán smiled thinly at him before turning to Fidelma.

'Are you saying that it was the King of Laigin himself who was visiting his cousin that day?'

Fidelma sighed impatiently.

'Dalbach told Eadulf that his relative was one of the religious at the abbey of Fearna. The identity was obvious.'

When no one responded and made what seemed to Fidelma the obvious identification she continued testily.

'Very well, let me lead you further. Dalbach obviously made the mistake of confiding to his cousin that he had given Eadulf hospitality. Willingly or unwillingly, he told that cousin that he had recommended that Eadulf should seek sanctuary that night on the Yellow Mountain. This relative of Dalbach's, realising that Eadulf's death was vital to the plan to hide the traces of this conspiracy, rode for the Yellow Mountain.' She paused and looked at Fianamail. 'You were at your hunting lodge which was close by the community of the Blessed Brigid, where Eadulf had taken the two girls. In the middle of the night, someone arrived to inform you where Eadulf might be.'

Many eyes had fallen on Abbot Noé but Fianamail was looking askance.

'It was my cousin, my cousin . . .'

Brother Cett had made a curious animal cry and was trying to fight his way out of the hall. It took four of Barrán's guards to restrain the big, powerful man.

Fidelma spread her hands.

'*Quod erat demonstrandum.* It was Brother Cett. I knew he was your cousin, Fianamail, and when Eadulf told me only Dalbach had known where he was hiding last night and that Dalbach was also related to the royal family of the Uí Cheinnselaig and further, has a cousin who was a religieux at Fearna, I simply put two and two together. For further proof, if you examine Brother Cett's robe, you will probably find that it has a tear and is frayed at a point about fifty centimeters from the hem.'

A warrior bent to examine the area and sprang up to give confirmation to Barrán.

Fidelma took out some frayed strands of wool from her *marsupium*. 'I think these will match his garment. Cett caught his robe on a nail in Gabrán's cabin.'

It was confirmed in a few moments.

'Only a strong man like Cett could deliver that upward blow that killed Gabrán, not a weak girl like Fial nor even the abbess.'

There was a murmur of applause among those in the hall. It was interrupted by Bishop Forbassach's cynical tones. He had recovered something of his old aplomb and he was looking for revenge. He was actually chuckling.

'You are doubtless very clever, Fidelma, but not that clever. The religious who was aboard the boat when Fial was instructed to lie was not Brother Cett, otherwise the girl would have remarked on the burly build of the man. In fact, she denied it was the same person.'

There was a moment of silent anticipation while everyone looked towards Fidelma.

'Let me congratulate you on your perception, Forbassach,' she acknowledged. 'It is a shame that such close scrutiny of evidence was singularly lacking when you made your examinations of Eadulf and Ibar before you sentenced them to death.'

Bishop Forbassach let out a bark of angry laughter.

'Insult does not disguise the fact that your story does not scan. Fianamail will forgive me when I observe that Cett is not the brightest member of his family. Apart from the difference in description, the very idea of Cett being able to be the ... what did you call it? ... the puppet-master – that is blatant nonsense!' And Forbassach sat back with a satisfied smirk.

'If I recall, in the discussion of this matter at Coba's fortress – and I am sure that Coba will confirm what I say – I also said the puppet-master was someone with a position of power in the abbey.'

Coba nodded eagerly. 'You did, indeed, but Forbassach is correct.

Fial's description hardly fits Cett. Nor does Cett have a position of power in the abbey.'

'I agree,' Fidelma said. 'The person who thought up this sordid means of making money and who persuaded Cett and Gabrán to support them was Cett's sister; his real sister, Sister Étromma, the *rechtaire* of the abbey.'

Sister Étromma had been sitting stony-faced with folded arms from the moment Cett had been denounced. She did not change her attitude now even when two of Barrán's warriors approached and stood on either side of her.

'Do you deny this, Sister Étromma?' demanded Barrán.

Sister Étromma raised her head and stared at the Chief Brehon. Her features were without emotion.

'A silent mouth is melodious,' she replied quietly, quoting an old proverb.

'It is wise to make a statement,' urged Barrán. 'Guilt can be interpreted from silence.'

'A wise head makes a closed mouth,' the stewardess responded firmly.

Barrán shrugged and signalled to the warriors to remove her from the hall along with her now subdued brother, Cett.

'I think that a search of Étromma's personal possessions might reveal where she has been hoarding money,' offered Fidelma. 'I recall that she once said to me that she hoped one day to settle on the island of Mannanán Mac Lir. I had assumed that she was going to join the Abbey of Maughold. Now I think she meant to go to the island with her brother, simply to live in comfort on the money she had made from her evil enterprise.'

Coba stood up.

'Chief Brehon, I have just spoken to the messenger that I sent to the abbey. He confirms that when he went there on my instruction to tell the abbess that I had granted the Saxon sanctuary, Fainder was not available. He gave that message to the *rechtaire*. Étromma knew where Brother Eadulf was on the evening before Gabrán came to my fortress and attempted to kill him.'

'I have been suspicious of Étromma for some time,' Fidelma told them all, 'but I could not work out why. It was only when I realised that Fial had been taken from the abbey and placed on Gabrán's boat that I was certain she was at the centre of this enterprise.'

'Why?' Barrán wanted to know.

'I had asked to see Fial. Étromma left me with the physician Miach while she went in search of her. Instead of waiting for her at the apothecary I went back to see Eadulf again. When I arrived, Brother Cett, who had been his jailer, had disappeared. The new man told me that he and Étromma had gone down to the quay. The reason why, I later deduced, was so they could get Fial out of the abbey and onto Gabrán's boat before I could speak with her. Étromma then returned to tell me Fial was missing. Very convenient! A short while later, I learnt that Gabrán's boat had left the abbey quay.'

'I think the path has now been made clear, Fidelma,' Barrán thanked her. 'However, can you shed some light on why this woman could bring herself to engage in such wicked work?'

'I think the immediate motive was acquisition of sufficient wealth to live in some degree of comfort and independence. What is it that Timothy tells us in his Epistle? *Radix omnium malorum est cupiditas.* The love of money is the root of all evil. Étromma is an unfortunate woman: many people know that. She is of the royal family, but a poor relation. She and her brother were taken as hostages when they were children, and not one of the branches of the royal family offered to pay the honour price for their release.'

Fianamail stirred uncomfortably but said nothing in defence of his family.

'Étromma and Cett effected their own escape and, being still children, entered the service of the abbey. Cett was, through no fault of his own, simple and mainly dominated by his sister. Étromma was not outstanding enough to rise beyond the office of *rechtaire*. She was bitter because of that, although it was an influential enough position. She had been *rechtaire*, running the day-to-day business of the abbey for ten years, when Fainder was brought in over her head and made abbess. It was a considerable blow to her. Perhaps it was then that her thoughts turned to acquiring enough wealth to be able to leave the abbey and become independent. She worked out the plan and her brother Cett and the boatman Gabrán became her willing accomplices.'

'It seems clear enough now,' muttered Forbassach begrudgingly.

Fidelma smiled but without humour.

'As my mentor Brehon Morann would have said, it is afterwards that events are always understood.'

While Barrán was instructing the scribes and explaining the law to the Brehons, Eadulf turned to Fidelma and spoke for the first time since the hearing got underway.

'When did you start to suspect Sister Étromma?' he asked. 'You said that you had had your eye on her for some time, but only confirmed your suspicions when you realised Fial had been on Gabrán's boat.'

Fidelma sat back and gave the question some thought before answering.

'I suspected her when she was showing me the quay on the very first day that I arrived.'

Eadulf was astounded. 'The first day? How can that be?'

'I had, as I said, learned that she and Cett had gone to the quay when she was supposed to be looking for Fial. She had come back to tell me that Fial was missing. Then we went to the quay. A religieux interrupted us to say a river boat had sunk and it was thought to be Gabrán's. Étromma seemed unduly concerned, although she did her best to disguise it. She went off immediately to investigate. Had it been Gabrán's vessel, Fial might have been rescued or the wreck searched, in which case the terrible trade in young girls might have been revealed.'

She paused for a moment.

'That was one thing. Then, of course, she lied about having witnessed me finding the wand of office and letter to Theodore in the mattress where you had placed it. She had seen me find them: I knew it. I thought at first she might simply have been in awe of Forbassach and the abbess, but the real reason was that she wanted my enquiries to end with your execution . . .'

Several days later, Eadulf and Fidelma stood together on the quay by the side of Loch Garman. It was not technically a loch or lake at all but a big opening to the sea, a main port for ships from Gaul, Iberia, from the lands of the Franks and Saxons and many other countries as well. Loch Garman was the busiest port in the five kingdoms, standing at the south-eastern tip of the island and thus being the most easily accessible stopping off point; a fact which benefited Laigin by a rich trade as well as bringing a curse by attracting frequent raids from buccaneers.

Fidelma and Eadulf stood facing one another with the wind gently ruffling their hair and tugging at their clothes.

'So,' Fidelma sighed, 'that is that. Young Fianamail has been summoned to Tara to be admonished by the High King. Forbassach has been stripped of rank and can no longer practise in law. He has been sent to some obscure community and his wife is divorcing him. Abbess Fainder has already gone abroad again, presumably to Rome, and Abbot Noé . . . well, I think he too will be heading to Rome now that he is no longer spiritual adviser to Fianamail.'

'Fainder is a curious woman,' Eadulf reflected. 'On the one hand she is a fanatic about the Penitentials and the Rule of Rome. On the other, she had no compunction about using her sexuality to claw her way up to the position of abbess. How she could dominate both Abbot Noé and Bishop Forbassach, I cannot understand. I did not even think she was attractive.'

Fidelma threw back her head and chuckled. '*De gustibus non est disputandum.*'

Eadulf grimaced wryly. 'I suppose it is so: that what I find abhorrent others may find attractive.' He pursed his lips reflectively. 'So, as you say, that is that. I presume that Laigin will now return to the rule of the Fénechus Law?'

Fidelma smiled confidently. 'It will be a while before the cruel punishments of the Penitentials are tried again. I hope that may be never.'

There was an awkward pause between them before Fidelma raised her eyes to his.

'Are you determined on this course?' she asked abruptly.

Eadulf seemed sad but resolute.

'I am. I have duties both to Theodore, Archbishop of Canterbury, as well as to your brother, for whom I undertook to take these messages.'

Fidelma had been confused these last few days at Eadulf's quiet determination to continue his journey back to the lands of the Saxons. She had made it as clear as she felt possible that she would welcome him returning with her to Cashel. She had never seen Eadulf so stubborn before. Her pride had not permitted her to unbend further to him. He must surely know how she felt and yet . . . yet he would not return with her. He had insisted on travelling to the seaport to seek a ship and she had accompanied him, thinking to change his mind and persuade him to return with her. Brehon Morann had once told her that pride was merely a mask for one's own faults. Was she at fault? What else could she say or do? Fidelma was hesitant, as if finding it difficult to express herself clearly.

'Are you sure that I cannot persuade you to return with us to Cashel? You know that you will be most welcome at my brother's court.'

'I have my duty,' replied Eadulf solemnly.

'When duty becomes a creed then we may as well say goodbye to happiness,' she ventured, remembering her own excuses about duty which had previously caused her to deny her feelings towards him.

Eadulf reached out to take her hands in his.

'You are fond of quoting the sages, Fidelma. Wasn't it Plautus who wrote that to an honest man, it is an honour to have remembered his duty?'

'The Law of the Fénechus says that God does not demand that a man give more than his ability allows,' she countered hotly, thinking that he was teasing her about her previous opinions.

There was a shout across the water and a small skiff was pulling away from one of the large sea-going ships which lay at anchor in the inlet. The rowers were pulling rapidly towards the quay and several people, carrying baggage, were gathering to await its arrival.

'The tide is on the turn.' Eadulf raised his head and felt the change of wind on his cheek. 'The ship's captain will want to get away. I must go on board now. It seems, then, that we are always parting. I remember the last time we parted at Cashel. You determined then that your duty lay in going on a pilgrimage to the Tomb of St James in Iberia.'

'But I came back,' Fidelma pointed out reproachfully.

'True,' he agreed with a quick smile. 'Thank God that you did or I should not be here now. Yet you told me then that I had a duty towards Theodore of Canterbury. I recall your very words: "There is always a time to depart from a place even if one is unsure where one is going".'

She bowed her head contritely. 'I recall those words. Perhaps I was wrong.'

'And do you recall me replying that I felt at home in Cashel and could find a means to stay in spite of the demands of Canterbury?'

She remembered his words very clearly and she also remembered how she had answered him.

'Heraclitus said that you cannot step twice into the same river for other waters are continually flowing into it. That is what I answered. I remember.'

'I cannot return to Cashel now, for honour's sake. I have promises to keep at Canterbury.'

He made to turn away and then swung back, seizing her hands again. His eyes were moist. He was on the verge of telling her that he would return to Cashel but he knew that he had to be strong if they had any future together.

'I do not want to be parted from you again so soon, Fidelma. One of your ancient triads asks – what are the three diseases that you may suffer without shame?'

She reddened a little and replied softly, 'An itch, a thirst and love.'

'Will you come with me?' Eadulf asked with rough enthusiasm. 'Come with me to Canterbury? There would be no shame in that.'

'Would that be a wise decision for me to make?' Fidelma asked with a ghost of a smile trembling on her lips. Her emotions wanted her to say yes, but logic held her back.

'I am not sure wisdom enters into such matters,' Eadulf said. 'All I know is that no wind will serve the sails on your ship of life unless you steer for a particular port.'

Fidelma glanced behind her.

Along the quay Dego, Enda and Aidan were standing, waiting patiently while Fidelma and Eadulf said their farewells. They were holding the horses ready to commence the journey back to Cashel. She thought for a moment. No decision would come immediately. Perhaps being unable to make a decision, *was* a decision in itself? She did not know how to respond. Her thoughts were too confused. Eadulf seemed attuned to her doubts.

'If you need to stay, stay; I will understand,' he told her, his voice soft in resignation.

Fidelma met his warm brown eyes with her fiery green ones for several long seconds before she squeezed his hand, smiled quickly, let it fall, turned and walked silently away.

Eadulf made no attempt to say anything else. He watched her walking with a firm step back towards her mare. Aidan and Enda mounted their horses in readiness and Dego moved forward, leading her mount. Eadulf waited, his mind in conflict, torn between uncertainty and anticipation. He watched as she spoke a few words to Dego. Then she took her saddle bag from her horse. When she returned to Eadulf her face was flushed but she was smiling confidently.

'Brehon Morann said that if reason cannot be satisfied, then follow the impulse. Let's go aboard the ship before the captain sails without us.'

Come explore the world of Sister Fidelma.

The International Sister Fidelma Society is an organization devoted to the readers of Peter Tremayne's Sister Fidelma Mysteries. Members receive three copies per year of its official publication, *The Brehon*. The magazine is primarily a forum for the fans of the series, containing articles, competitions, readers' letters, and photographs—including special contents such as the first-ever publication of a Fidelma short story, "The Blemish," (September 2002), among others.

Come visit the Society's Web site at www.sisterfidelma.com for further details, news, merchandise, and updates.

Annual subscription for members is $29.95
(U.S. funds drawn on a U.S. bank).
Checks to be made out to:

David Robert Wooten, director & editor
The International Sister Fidelma Society
PO Box 1899
Little Rock, Arkansas 72203-1899
U.S.A.
david@sisterfidelma.com